THE GENERAL

Natalie Edwards

LifeRich
PUBLISHING®

LifeRich Publishing is a registered trademark of The Reader's Digest Association, Inc.

LifeRich Publishing books may be ordered through booksellers or by contacting:

LifeRich Publishing
1663 Liberty Drive
Bloomington, IN 47403
www.liferichpublishing.com
844-686-9607

Because of the dynamic nature of the Internet, any web addresses or links contained in this book may have changed since publication and may no longer be valid. The views expressed in this work are solely those of the author and do not necessarily reflect the views of the publisher, and the publisher hereby disclaims any responsibility for them.

Any people depicted in stock imagery provided by Getty Images are models, and such images are being used for illustrative purposes only. Certain stock imagery © Getty Images.

Cover Image Credit: Natalie Edwards

ISBN: 978-1-4897-5106-5 (sc)
ISBN: 978-1-4897-5114-0 (hc)
ISBN: 978-1-4897-5105-8 (e)

Library of Congress Control Number: 2024917731

Print information available on the last page.

LifeRich Publishing rev. date: 10/02/2024

1

Leafe

Lilly's engagement was announced today in Zion. I have yet to see the royal couple, but they will arrive shortly with wedding plans to ensue. The royal palace has already begun prepping for the extravagance. Zion's Angels are anticipating the big day.

Why does it make me anxious? Angels don't feel anxiety, do they? Yet, I have fireflies racing through me, the speed of lightning, at the thought of seeing Lilly again.

In all my eternities, I have never glimpsed one more beautiful. Her green eyes matched mine. I remember them like I remember the setting of the sun and the dawning of the north star upon the earth's night sky.

Skye will want me to be the best man.

I swallow as I breathe in the weight of that responsibility.

My wings have flown in every galaxy of King Worthy's universe, but the idea of standing near Lilly on that stage feels too big a task. Obviously, I will be standing near Skye mostly. But I know Lilly is all I will be able to see.

White lace and diamonds will cover her like a queen. Skye will loop the ring on her finger. That is, if I give it to him.

Should I hold back the ring and say it must have been lost? Should I toss it into the River of Life to be buried in its depths?

I know my place.

I will give Skye the ring. The King will say, "kiss the bride." Lilly will be Skye's forever.

Inhale, Leafe. Exhale.

You know Lilly belongs to Skye. Skye saved her just like King Worthy orchestrated. The King wrote their love story. You must not interfere with destiny, I tell myself.

But lately, I've felt a change in the wind. Perhaps destiny is still yet to be written.

"Captain Leafe!" Purity, the holy dove, soars up to my left side where I hover in the Milky Way galaxy. King Worthy said hinlors were out lurking. Winged, brooding villains of vicious intent. I personally find The Raven more problematic than hinlors. It only takes one detonation of my eyes to disintegrate them. Like ash, they fall into the vacuum of outer space. The Raven, however, still waits for his final death in The Black Hole.

"Purity, I have everything under control."

"I have no doubt, Captain Leafe," she assures me with a soprano voice. Gold dust sparkles around her as she hovers on my shoulder. She is King Worthy's spirit of truth. If she has come to find me, there must be a reason.

"What message do you have for me, Purity?"

"Prepare for Armageddon. It is coming sooner than anticipated. Word has gotten out that Lilly is coming to Zion. Hinlors will be watching for her. We need you on high alert, ridding out the threat."

"Understood," I answer unphased and ready.

I knew Armageddon would be coming soon. Hinlors have been out here more than usual, and I am not surprised Lilly is their object of desire. Human life rarely breaches the earth's atmosphere. Her presence will be craved once she crosses into celestial territory.

"I will alert you when the time comes."

I nod and look out into the navy-blue, velvet cosmos. Stars twinkle and planets orbit in rhythmic fashion. Flashing lights burst in every direction, some near and some lightmiles away.

"I never get over the beauty of this universe," I tell Purity as she rests on my shoulder. "I can only imagine what New Zion will be like."

"Unimaginably wonderful," she replies with vibrant delight.

"Yes." I reply.

"Your efforts will be rewarded, Captain Leafe. Be sure of that." Her wings lift off and she flutters around to meet my gaze with golden eyes. "Remember The King's strength is always with you."

I nod graciously as we hover in space. "I'll see you back in Zion."

With a flap of her wings and a glittering wink, Purity soars away and leaves a trail of glitter in the wake.

Boom!

More light shines in the distance. Hinlors are close. With every flash, I begin to see flashbacks of battles past...

❧

"Leafe! The King is dying! His crown is in flames!"

I stare into the expanse of smoking devastation and see a thin film appear over the palace with fire blazing. Something doesn't feel right. Angelic voices grow faint and ominous spirits lurk in the air. It's eerie out here.

King Worthy sent me to keep watch here at the waterfalls' edge. He said He'd be protected and not to worry.

If the King were truly in danger, where are all the seraphim? They would be circling above the palace where His Throne resides, attacking the threat. Blare horns would be sounding off.

"It's an illusion!" I affirm calmly, as I scan my surroundings. I shout louder to ensure Jasper hears me over the ruckus of flying objects. "The Raven is showing you a deception!"

"How can you leave The King alone like that?"

"I'm not leaving The King to fend for Himself! He told me He would be protected," I shout. "It's a trap!"

"I don't believe that!" Jasper argues. "Besides, the darkness looks so enticing, doesn't it!? I want to feel what it's like to fly in it."

Jasper's eyes turn yellow and greedy.

"Too many angels have succumbed to The Raven's deceptive devices. Trust me!" I tell Jasper plainly. "Don't go!"

Jasper shakes his head and laughs wickedly. "Come with me!"

"I will stay committed to my King by following His advice. He said not to worry!" I resolve with anchored feet and ready wings.

"Suit yourself. I'm out of here!" Jasper flies off the waterfall's edge towards the smoke.

Blast!

"No!" I scream in horror. Poisonous fire injects into Jasper's heart. Black soot covers his wings, as The Raven rises with Jasper in his grasp, singing an eerie tune. "Raven, let him go!" I command.

"You're smart, Leafe. I'll give you that. I set off all the tricks in the book and you still wouldn't budge," The Raven snickers creepily. "Jasper just couldn't help himself but give in to the dark side."

"You disgust me, you evil traitor!" I yell with force.

"At least you have some emotion towards me!" He smiles with an evil smile that wreaks of psychopathic disturbia. Then he backs into the mist with Jasper in his clutch.

My wings rise in flight to reach for Jasper.

I can't let The Raven have him. I will pull him back and he will see this was all a mistake. He does not have to follow The Raven.

I lunge forward. "Jasper, come with me!" I say urgently.

Jasper's face turns yellow with pale dark purple rushing over his countenance. "I don't want to live for Zion!" Jasper yells. "Long live The Raven!"

"Jasper, what are you saying!?" I shout to bring him back to the light. "The Raven is a monster! Look what he has done to you!"

"Ahhh!" Jasper screeches again, this time with sharp teeth and black talons protruding from his wings.

"The King can change you back!" I assure him, cringing.

"I don't want The King to change me!" Jasper retaliates. The Jasper I once knew is gone.

The Raven grins and snickers again with the eerie voice. "Not all angels stay in Heaven."

Poof!

They're gone.

A mass of dark smoke combusts. No sign of Jasper. I wave my hands to clear away the smoke as it smells like the stench of death. Why did Jasper give in to his madness? Does he not see the deception?

That makes the twenty-second angel who has abandoned Zion to join The Raven.

But I will not be one of them.

I will not give in. King Worthy is my King. And my loyalty will remain steadfast to the crown of Zion.

"There you are, Leafe!" An evil voice howls.

I turn my head.

"You thought you could escape The Raven, couldn't you?" A hinlor hovers in the air with red eyes.

"The Raven has no power here! And I will not succumb to you either!" I assert boldly. "This is King Worthy's kingdom!" I keep my wings steady with a keen eye targeted on the intruder.

Screech!

It darts towards me with jagged wings of decay.

Blast! I detonate my eyes of emerald light.

Disintegrate.

"Don't ever threaten me again." The hinlor falls to the ground in ashy speckles and washes down the river and over the waterfall's edge.

∽

Boom!

My eyes refocus and I come out of the flashback. It happens, every so often, being out here alone.

Boom!

Explosions go off again.

A supernova bursts in front of my eyes like neon mosaics of bright light. I breathe in and out. Its signal alerts me to prepare for battle.

The King always sets off supernovas to lure in the hinlors. When He does, I approach unseen, detonate light, and they disintegrate like ash. Too easy, one might say. Yet, The King only entrusts these battles to me.

2

Skye

"Worthy!"

My head flanks back. My blue eyes scan the perimeter. Fire rages in every direction and illuminates the devastation of the beachfront. Smoke thickens.

"Worthy, your reign is over!" The screeching voice howls again.

"Who are you!?" I reply with sharp eyes.

My impulse remains intent on locating the source of the agitation, but I have a feeling I know what it is. The taunting voice carries a tone unlike the angels of Zion. The pitch rings scratchy and its spirit echoes with darkness like red eyes lurking in the shadows.

"Show yourself!" I retort. "Come out of hiding and show yourself!"

Ash billows from the fire like gray, thunderous clouds rolling in. The seas of Ala Moana Beach rage with flames like a forest fire, but the trees are missing out in the ocean expanse. Fire burns without reason. Water erupts like molten lava under the earth's surface. Stars spin in the earth's navy-blue sky.

Is it Armageddon?

My father said it was coming. Soon.

He said He would tell me the day and hour it would unfold when He sends my angel armies into battle. Then the earth will shake in the uproar of New Zion's unfolding.

"Surrender the time to Me, son," He once told me. "The weight of the end is not yours to anticipate," He said with His echoing resonance.

My father's vision for New Zion stands to bring healing and eternal life to everyone who wants His love and His Throne to endure. How could anyone be against it?

The Raven stood against it. At every turn, his eyes were on anything but my father. He wanted more glory, more power, and never advocated for the light to keep shining. His vision was death.

"I'm ready, Father," I told Him as He foreshadowed the end. "I'm ready to war for New Zion. To unfurl the end of days for our people's peace."

"You will, in time," He said with His regal tone of glory. "Wait on Me."

Peace finds me every time He speaks to me. I never found a reason to fight Him on it. My only battles are to war against anything and everything my father instructs me to defeat. For the good of Zion. For the glory of the crown.

Blast! In the distance, flames explode and the ocean water beneath shines like blood orange liquid in a fiery furnace. Smoke and smog puff out from the radiation. Something emerges from the fire.

"Your crown is mine, Worthy!" the evil voice screams. "Now is your time to die!!!"

"Never!!!" I lunge forward with sapphire eyes blazing. "You will never take my father's crown!"

⌒⌿⌒

Boom!

Eyes open.

Daylight pours into my senses.

It was just a dream. I rise quickly and look for Lilly as I am not supposed to be sleeping, especially with her in my care. But I had been pacing back and forth during the night while Lilly slept. I get anxious thinking about Zion's Angels and warfare without me.

Angels are supposed to stay awake forever. My father will want me to keep my eyes on her at all times. I should have stayed next to her. Then she wouldn't have gotten lost.

Lilly, where are you?

Now, my only vision impairment remains the absence of my Lilly flower.

Meanwhile, an oblong ball with white laces and brown leathers ricochets off the palm tree beside me. I rise and stand over the sand involuntarily.

A mass crowd of humans runs towards me as I look about my surroundings for my Lilly flower. Lilly, where are you?

The serene presence of my fiancé was just here beside me as the moon serenaded the stars. Now the fiery beach of my dream is a peaceful turquoise impression of a painting I will want to keep forever to remember the first morning of waking up next to Lilly as my fiancé. Where is she?

My eyes dart back and forth. My feet hover over the ground with wings erect.

"Whoa! Dude's got hops!" sounds the voice of a youngster now staring at me like a fish out of water.

More footsteps encroach as I hover over the sand.

I rise higher and erect my wings to soar over the beach in search of her missing body. My heart palpitates at the thought of her absence.

"Can I have my football back?" asks the young boy blue checkered swim trunks.

My attention diverts to the object in question. I reach for the football lying by the tropical palm tree trunk and coconut husks.

"This?" I reply.

I hold out the football as I hover over the sand. His eyes grow bigger as he looks at my stance above ground.

"What are you, an angel or something?" he responds in amazement.

It is not my goal to terrify the boy nor bring attention to my wingspan but the cat is already out of the bag now. I figured onlookers may see me here at a public beach such as Ala Moana but this was Lilly's request. To watch the sunset at this spot.

"Quite right, I'm afraid," I reply as he stands intrigued. "What's your name?"

"Sam Kanapali," he says assertively.

I smile and nod my head. "Nice to meet you, Sam. I'm Skye."

"My Grandma told me about angels," he says. "She said they're a lot fiercer in person than in the storybooks."

"Your grandma knows a thing or two about the supernatural," I give him a wink. "Here." I raise my arm with the pigskin in hand and let it fly. "Go long!"

Sam runs ahead as the impromptu Hail Mary weaves in and out of the Honolulu clouds. He cuts left as the ball narrows in on his position.

Catch! He waves his hands in victory. "Yeah! Nice throw, mister!"

"It's Skye," I say.

Cheers burst as the boy snags the football yards away. I look over at the scene of victory and smile at the innocence of humanity reveling in celebration. What a celebration it will be when I make Lilly my wife. All of Zion could not contain the revelry of my heart for her.

"Do it again!" The boy yells with bright eyes and determination.

My heart races in a panic. I need to find Lilly. I hesitate receiving the ball as my eye-focus remains on the beachfront weaving in and out of clusters of humans under beach umbrellas and peering into the ocean for her ballerina frame.

Lilly, I know you hear my thoughts for you… Tell me where you are, my love…

"What, are your scared!?" The boy hazes again.

He lifts his arms and waves them in the air.

"Scared!" I answer a little jarred. "I am an angel, after all!" I answer back.

Then, I raise my right hand and motion for the ball. He tosses the ball back to me and I strategize how I want to throw it. My right arm rotates back.

"Watch this," I say ready to show how angels play ball. I know just the trick.

Swoosh! The football darts through the air and over the volleyball nets 50 yards away. I lift off the ground and send a wave of blue radiation from my eyes to propel the ball back in my direction. It halts in its course and zooms back.

"Whoa, how did you do that?" Sam replies.

Catch!

My hands grab the ball and I look at Sam in the eyes. "Let's just say it's supernatural." I give him a wink.

"You know how to sling it, don't you!?" says a voice from behind. I turn around and see a man in a baseball cap with a stunned grin. "We could use a quarterback down at the U of H Manoa!" he exclaims eagerly with a collegiate track jacket that says *Coach Militualoa*.

"I'm not in the age range for college, Coach Militualoa," I reply firmly, hoping that will satisfy his curiosity.

The coach looks at me with a twinkle in his eye, like he knows a thing or two about bending the rules. "We can accommodate that."

"I am well past the age of 22. Past the age of 30."

Zion's Angels have no ages nor do we keep track of time as Earth does.

"We do whatever it takes to put our program on the map!" he exclaims proudly with a pat on the wing. "Plus, I know a guy who can help out with the winged extremities."

"Winged extremities?" I ask, knowing where this is going.

"It's no secret you have some paranormal activity going on there, but I am not one to discriminate!" He smiles and smacks his peppermint gum.

"Father," I echo into Zion. *"Would you strike down your lightning from Heaven and blast this man into oblivion!"*

Skye, my love… there is no need for violence… the thoughts of Lilly infiltrate my mind and inhibit me.

"Lilly?"

I turn around to her lovely face looking back at me.

She smiles with bright eyes and sun-kissed skin. "You thought I left you forever, didn't you?" she says playfully.

"I've been looking for you for what seemed like an eternity," I reply with angst. "Don't leave me like that." I pull her close and lift her up to swaddle her in my arms. If only the football distractions had not gotten in the way I would have found her sooner.

"I wanted to gather hibiscus flowers for you!" Lilly giggles with excitement. "Here, smell!" She lifts them up to my nose and smiles at me lovingly. Then, she leans in to kiss my lips. "I could never leave you, my blue angel."

I take a deep breath. "Lilly, I had a dream."

My eyes gaze into her intently. Now that she will be my wife forever, I want to share everything with her. The foreshadowing of what is to come will soon be here. I need her to know. With the weight of Zion's future at hand, I need her calming aura to soothe me like only she can.

"Was it The Raven again?" Lilly inquires with concern. She touches my cheek softly. Her voice alone is enough to put me at ease when I know the future looms ahead with war.

"I have a feeling there will be others who defy Zion," I say with apprehension. "Lilly, I need you by my side no matter what–"

Lilly interjects peacefully and presses her finger over my lips. "You know I'm yours forever, Skye." She assures me. "You can tell me anything."

"I can't live without you, my Lilly flower," I reply with the urgent need to taste her again.

I press my lips against hers and continue my self-discovery of her morning flavor. Sweet pea and mangoes are the aroma of her essence. I trail my hands over her cheek, neck and chest. The diamond key necklace I gave her before we were engaged still adorns her neck like a jewel.

"Well! It seems like you two love birds have some lovemaking to do and I'll leave you to it!" Says Coach Militualoa with finality. Has he been listening the whole time?

I pause and look over at the championship-focused football fanatic. "Sir, this is a public beach and I assure you I abide by its decorum," I answer respectfully.

The coach grins. "Life is too short for decorum, angel!"

I rise above the ground with blue eyes aflame. "I command you leave us at once!" I resound.

"Skye!" Lilly shouts at me with that look she gives me every time she wants me to calm down.

"I'm sorry, Lilly, but he's pressing my buttons!" I say as my eyes heat up with blue intensity of sapphire light and rage to demolish everything that defies the virtues of Zion.

"You are the Commander of the angel armies. Nobody presses your buttons," she exclaims with a reassuring eye and peaceful tone.

Her words penetrate me as I hover 4 feet off the ground. Here I think more clearly. Here I see more clearly, as everything rests below me. I'm above it all. I don't have to be shaken by anything.

"That's right, blue angel. You don't have to be shaken by anything," she tells me with telekinesis. *"Come back down to the ground."*

She eyes me sweetly. My heart gives in to her wisdom, knowing it is exactly what my father would tell me.

"I love how you help me see clearer, my Lilly flower. My warrior love," I tell her with my thoughts.

My feet land on the beach and I reach out to grab Lilly in my arms. The palm trees sway peacefully, making Lilly's brunette hair flutter in the breeze. I tuck a strand behind her ear as the ocean tide rolls in like a lullaby.

"Come with me," I tell her and she wraps her hands around me ready to fly. "I want to show you the ocean from up high!"

Lift!

My wings outstretch and slowly fly over the shoreline and into the sea's airspace. The teal ocean shines like sequin-sparkling waters. Salt shimmers underneath. The passers-by on the beachfront linger in the distance where rainbow umbrellas paint the beach like a fresco. Below our feet, fishing vessels and cruise ships valiantly make their way into the deep. Holding Lilly from this vantage point feels right.

My heart dives deeper in love with Lilly every second I hold her in my arms.

"Kiss me, Colonel," she whispers softly in my ear. "Kiss me like you did when you brought me here on the eve of our engagement," she whispers again.

Choo! Choo!

Cargo ships blast off, carrying dragon fruit and mangos galore. To kiss Lilly like I want to kiss her… that is a sweet taste of nectarine goodness I still have not discovered. Not because I don't want to, but because I do want to.

I know what my adrenaline would lead me into if I were to kiss Lilly the way I want to. My body spikes in dopamine for her. Just a small taste of her love sends me into the highest ecstasy.

The way I kissed her on the eve of our engagement remains a secret only her and I can divulge. The fullness of our love is still yet to be shared, as I vowed to Lilly, I will not make love to her like a husband does to a wife until the night of our wedding when it is proper for me to love her without inhibitions.

My body can scarcely restrain the feelings of passion for her now.

"Just wait until I love you like I want to love you, my Bride," I tell her with unrestrained thoughts.

"I need to feel all of you, my eagle," she tells me with love and squeezes my chest.

"I love you Lilly," I exclaim as I hold her in my arms. "I have some news," I tell her as I kiss her ear. "Virtue wants to have a bridal shower for you. For *us.*"

"Virtue?"

"She's one of Zion's angels," I say. "My father will also want to see you first thing when we arrive."

I smile at the thought of my father meeting the love of my life. He orchestrated our divine meeting, and I cannot help but relish the delight in His eyes the moment He sees her beside me, where she is meant to be.

"I can't wait to meet Him," she replies enthusiastically.

"He is going to love you," I gaze into her eyes with sapphire blue light that still rages with passion for her like the first day I rescued her from Waimea Bay.

Lilly bats her eyelashes with a grin and my heart beats faster. "Of course, He will!" Lilly replies with sass and sophistication. "He chose me to love you, after all," she states most confidently.

She's right. He did choose her, and she knows it. I want her to know it. I want her to stand with confidence for the rest of her existence that she and I were destined to belong to one another. No one will tear us apart and nothing will take her place in my heart. She will always be my soul's divine love.

"Divine collision, remember?" Lilly tells me with her thoughts as she stares back into my eyes.

"We were destined for a divine collision," I reply with telekinesis.

I still remember the moment I found her precious body floating in the deep like a ballerina with eyes open, waiting for the light.

"Blue eyes find me in the deep," she thinks as she leans in to feel my lips on hers again. *"Kiss me, Skye."*

I will forever worship my father for creating that blessed moment under the raging seas of Waimea Bay.

We spin and descend onto the beach below us where green palm trees line the walkway.

"Skye!" My father's echo fills my ears. "I need you in Zion, My son."

"Father… what is it?"

"It's urgent, Skye."

Blast!

Lightning strikes in the sky over Ala Moana. Thunder clouds roll and dark clouds rise. Something stirs in the cosmos.

"We need to go now," I say.

Lilly sighs. "But we just got here last night. What about the fireworks by the marina and the–"

"Now, Lilly," I say rapidly. I lift her chin with my right and look into her eyes with affection. "Trust me. I promise, we'll come back."

She nods in agreement.

"I still have more sunsets to spend with you, my love," I assure her as I kiss her cheek.

My wings spread out with white feathers over the sandy beach. Light beams from the glow of its golden lining. Eyeballs peer up at us from the shore.

"Where are we going?" Lilly asks eagerly.

My blue eyes flame into her eyes like fiery hearts.

"It's time for you to meet The King."

3

Lilly

Whoosh!

Skye lifts off into the aquamarine skies with me in his arms. I feel his wings' circumference embracing me like a blanket of down feathers. Every one of them is lined with gold. Regal and majestic. Soft and snug.

Hold me forever, Skye.

On the shore below, palm trees grow smaller by the second. Ala Moana Beach sparkles like sequins under the morning sun. Beach towels and umbrellas array the sandy inlet where fireworks will set off tonight at 9:00pm by the harbor.

I hoped to watch the fireworks with Skye there after an adventurous day exploring our favorite spots from Waimanalo Beach to Yokohama Bay.

I wonder if there are fireworks in Zion.

"There will be tonight, my love," Skye tells me with his thoughts as we soar over the ocean. He loves how I read his thoughts now. *"Zion's lights are a sight to see."*

I can't believe I'm going to see Zion! What if I'm not ready? Do I need to change my clothes and prepare for a grand entrance? Are all the angels expecting more from me than I can give?

"You are the gift, Lilly," he tells me through his thoughts. A kiss ignites my cheek as we fly upwards through the clouds. *"Don't worry."*

"Promise not to drop my over the Pacific, my blue angel," I reply whimsically.

Skye tightens his grip on my embrace. "Never in a billion eternities would I drop such precious cargo," he assures me.

My face points towards the ocean and he soon rotates me around to face him like he always does.

I like looking at his face. As we soar over the ocean blue, he looks ahead, steady and focused. His eyes scan the horizon. His wings flap slightly with peaceful tranquility and effortless flight. Then he looks at me.

Blue eyes find me in the heights.

Heights of ecstasy.

Heights of dreams.

Heights of love.

It never gets old, looking into his eyes of sapphire light. At 20,000 feet above ground and counting, he still captivates me dreamily, like life couldn't get better than this.

"Your eyes are like the brightest stars, Skye," I whisper entranced.

"Brighter than the North Star?" he replies with a grin.

"Brighter than the sun itself," I assure him with a smile.

Skye embraces me tighter and twirls me around.

"Skye!" I shriek with a giggle. "You know how I get antsy when you do that!" I giggle more and more as I hold onto his chest. He spins me again and then comes to a halt. Then, he continues soaring straight into the galaxies. I look up. Stars twinkle all around us. A white sphere looms ahead.

"I wanted to twirl you over the moon," he says with blue eyes shining. "You are my moon, my Lilly flower."

"And you are my sky," I tell him as my heart meets his above the clouds. "I always want to soar in the heights of your love."

Skye looks at me intently, with a deep desire to know all of me and keep knowing me, like a discovery that goes on into eternity. The blue sapphires of his eyes nourish my every desire to see Heaven and feel it too. Twirling with him feels like walking on water with rose petals floating all around.

Whoosh!

Skye shoots up farther into the sky as the earth below shrinks to the size of a dime. Wind blows through his wings. Light reflects off the golden lining.

Skye leans in close to me. "You are my favorite flying partner, I must say," Skye exclaims with a passionate whisper.

"And you are mine," I say amorously.

Skye's arms embrace me like a velvet blanket. His wings cuddle me strongly as the coolness of the stratosphere increases. I breathe in and out. My chest tightens. All of the sudden, the flow of oxygen ceases to flow inside my lungs.

I try to breathe again.

Still no oxygen.

Oxygen! I need oxygen! The air is too thin at this altitude and the pressure weighs over my chest.

"Skye! I can't br–" I shout.

Before I can say "breathe," Skye presses his lips to mine with mouth open and puffs air into my mouth. I inhale quickly. My lungs compress. I breathe out through my nose as his mouth remains glued to mine.

"*I got you, Lilly,*" he thinks.

I can read his thought clearly now as oxygen renews my senses. He releases his mouth and his wings close in around me like a cocoon. He breathes out. The air surrounding me fills with oxygen. I breathe in and out. He keeps flying while filling my airspace with oxygen.

Thank goodness I can breathe. Never did I ever expect to be hundreds of thousands of miles up in the galaxies, but here I am.

"*How did you do that!?*" I think to him.

"The elements of the universe are in my father's hands, which means they are in my hands too. I can breathe out oxygen just as I inhale oxygen," he says confidently with timeless finesse. "This I inherited from my father, The King."

"And you can destroy forces of darkness, my regal Colonel!" I say now that the flow of oxygen helps me speak freely. He chuckles and smiles.

"Until New Zion is unleashed," he decrees. "I war for all people to believe in my father's love." He keeps flying. Then he looks at me with serious eyes. "The Raven is defeated. But there is still another battle yet to be fought. Armageddon. The war to end all wars. I will lead my angel armies into battle to destroy all that plagues the earth you call home. And I will end the curse that The Raven brought into Zion."

"You are chosen for such a war, Skye. Your father believes in you," I assure him with resolve. I lift my hand to touch his face and smile into his eyes.

"Yes," he says and nods. He looks away and then back at me. "You need to know, Lilly… not all angels follow my father. Some left with The Raven. Some chose to side with the darkness, and evil spread into their veins like wildfire. But the ones who remain loyal… they remain untouched by the evil one. Their hearts are pure. Their souls are devoted to Zion with fearless courage," he says with certainty. "It's my honor to lead them. I'll always be loyal to them just like I'll always be loyal to you."

Blast!

My body jolts.

Skye rotates around in the air like a spinning wheel. My heart pounds from the sudden impact and I cannot lift my head outside of the cocoon I am breathing in to see what the ruckus is. Are we in danger? What was that sound?

"It's an asteroid, my love. Don't worry. Just hold on tight," he says.

He grips me tighter and his feathers shake with increased speed. He swerves to the right, to the left. We spin again. His wings soar strong like indestructible gold flying through the universe.

I feel like a passenger in a roller coaster at Disney World's Space Mountain, only this roller coaster is really in outer space.

Then I remember, I don't like roller coasters! The speedy turns and jilts leave me nauseous. But Skye flies with me so gently, even at high speed. I don't feel afraid. I know he would save me if something went wrong. Either him or the stars. If only I could see the starry lights beyond his wings, speckling the galactic sky like confetti.

"Your wish is my command," he thinks to me with telekinesis. *"Let me show you the universe, my Lilly flower."*

Skye's snowy white feathers begin to transform into translucent feathers. The solid color becomes transparent, and I can see through them like glasses. Beyond the clear circumference of his feathers, clusters of stars shine with bright lights against the backdrop of the Milky Way.

Outer space looks like diamonds and rubies and emeralds on black velvet. The radiation of their light flames so much stronger from this altitude. Where stars shine the size of a sand grain on Earth, they shine like the size of a watermelon here.

Whoosh!

A bright strand of light shoots past us in full view like a golden ribbon on fire. It arcs over like a rainbow with a tail of fairy dust sprinkling in space as it descends.

"Skye!" I shout with awe. "I see a shooting star!"

I breathe in and out. Excitement flows through me at the miraculous sighting.

"I made it for you," he says with a wink. "You are my bright light."

And you are my shining star, my Colonel Worthy.

Whoosh! Whoosh!

Another flaming star shoots past us. Then another. Oh, my goodness! More stars! I giggle as the shooting star display continues with star after star glittering in the cosmos. His skills enthrall my enchantment. My love for him only amplifies as I see him rule the universe. Skye, you are so beautiful.

I smile at him and look back at the stars through his transparent wings. I hum to the melody of "Twinkle Twinkle Little Star" as the stars whizz past us like fireworks on the Fourth of July.

My heart steadies. I keep breathing in as Skye provides oxygen to my lungs. His oxygenated air breathes pure, like crisp mountain air in the peak of Winter. Here in his embrace, I feel I have already ascended Heaven.

Thank goodness for The King. He gave my blue angel such extravagant, supernatural qualities. I guess that is why He rules the universe.

Skye laughs with delight as he sends star after star into the galaxies surrounding us.

"You've only seen the beginning, my Lilly flower," Skye tells me as he holds me tightly in the wings of his feathery fortress. "We are almost to Zion's gates."

Almost there! My stomach twists inside of me. The One who reigns over Heaven and Earth is going to be standing in front of me.

I hope He likes me. What if He doesn't like me? After all this cosmic flying, there is no telling how my body smells or what my hair will look like once we land. I can't go into the presence of the King looking like this! I should have asked Skye to stop at the local ABC store at Ala Moana to grab some freshening up tools. A comb, a toothbrush, a bow for my hair, anything…

"You look perfect, my angel," says Skye with serenity.

My angel. The words echo like a canyon. He's never called me angel before. Do I look like an angel? In my lover's eyes, I feel like I could be. I also feel like a hot mess shivering from the arctic-like swirl of galactic air up here. I want to look my best when I meet the One who sees everything. There isn't time. This is all happening so fast.

"Lilly," he says peacefully. "You look perfect, and you are perfectly loved. Just like every angel in Zion." He breathes again with blue eyes shining.

When he looks at me this way, I believe him. The need to feel fancy and elaborate disappears. His eyes tell me I am enough and my hearts soars above the fears, weightless and whole. Gravity ceases to exist in this part of the universe where everything floats in motion because of The King's power upholding the cosmos. He will uphold me like Skye does, and I don't have to be anyone but me. To be loved like this exceeds all other feelings of love I could have dreamt of.

Flash!

"We're here," says Skye serenely.

Skye spins me around as my face comes out of the cocoon where his oxygen breathed into me. Bright light and pearls dazzle before us as the golden gates open like a hidden door of a treasure chest. Angels hover around the gates with symphonic melodies echoing.

This must be Zion.

I am here…

Oh, my goodness, this is happening! I knew eventually I would meet his father and fly to Zion, but the reality of my arrival here is overwhelming me to say the least.

"You are ready, my love." Skye assures me. His tone carries confidence and comfort.

I hope so, I think to myself.

"You are more than ready," he thinks to me.

"Then why do I not feel ready?" I think to him.

"Because you never feel ready for the biggest moment of your life," he says to assure me. "You cannot prepare for it. You cannot foresee it. You simply greet it with courage and look destiny in the face knowing you are chosen for it," he says boldly. Then he looks into my eyes as we hover into the golden light. He spins me around and my body floats in a foxtrot of galactic dancing. "You were chosen for this, my love."

I take a deep breath and exhale with peace. "Then I give into Zion's divine orchestration, my Colonel."

Blast!

The golden gates open.

"I love My divine orchestrations." A deep voice echoes like rushing waterfalls through the airspace.

"Father!" Skye replies with eagerness, as his father's spirit sets in. "He knows we are here."

Skye soars to the gates speedily with me in his arms. Flaming eyes of purple amethyst greet us from the angel guarding the gates. His wings tower high like Skye's. Dark, hazelnut skin and blonde hair accents his appearance.

"You look strong, Zeal," Skye says with authority. Skye rests his right hand on Zeal's shoulder as he holds me close.

"As do you, Colonel Worthy." Zeal bows and rises. "We have been expecting you and our future queen! The King is waiting for you in the Throne Room."

"Future queen?" I reply.

"Yes, Lilly," Skye says boldly with gushing eyes of blue sapphire.

"Your destiny is a bright one, my lady," says Zeal with a smile of respect.

He already knows my name.

Something about the way he knows me makes me feel like Zion is already my home. I guess I don't look as terrible as I presume, after the galactic flight from earth to Zion.

"You are beautiful, my lady," says Zeal with a deep voice as he bows to kiss my hand. Then he rises to regain his stance in front of the gate.

"I told you they are all going to love you, my Lilly flower," Skye thinks to me with telekinesis.

"I can't wait to meet the rest," I think back to him.

Skye nods to Zeal and then looks at me. "Lilly, every angel in Zion is here to watch over you just like me. If you need anything at all, call them. They will come," Skye affirms.

"We are loyal to the crown of Zion, my Colonel!" Zeal shouts with hands clasped and bright wings standing tall. He bows again. Then rises.

Skye nods to Zeal and Zeal returns the gesture.

Standing here at the golden gates of Zion's entrance, its glow shines with luminescence more spectacular than any gold I have seen on earth. I wonder what it looks like inside.

Blast!

A horn detonates as Zeal blows an ivory trumpet made of elephant husk and tilts his head back.

"Here we go, Lilly. Off to see The King whose voice fills the Heavens," he tells me through telekinesis.

We move through the pearly, golden gates swiftly.

Skye flies over the ground where gold covers the streets like the walls of a royal palace. We soar over a courtyard of marble tile towards a garden with a gigantic tree. Green and cherry-red leaves cover the tree with fruits galore hanging from its limbs. Red pomegranates, mangoes, liches, tangerines, and all kinds of apples speckle the tree like glitter. Below, the green grass glows like lime green frosting. My eyes widen at the wonder of Zion's ethereal beauty.

River rapids slowly trickle in the distance as we zoom over the tree. Turquoise blue waters fill the river like blue raspberry lemonade on a hot summer's day. The translucence of the water is so clear, even clearer than the ocean at Lanikai Beach.

"What do you think?" says Skye.

"That's a trick question, isn't it?" I reply with delight.

"Yes," he embraces me tightly as we soar over the turquoise rivers.

"I always know what you're thinking... I can tell you are getting hungry by the way you are enjoying the scenery," he thinks.

"Blue raspberry lemonade, please!" I say emphatically.

Skye laughs and spins me around.

"I have something even better, my love."

Skye flies me higher into the sky. The view of the river morphs into a view of a tall palace decked in diamonds and gold, with waterfalls flowing just behind it.

Skye spins me around and makes a dart for the waterfall. We soar over the meadows where wildflowers paint the grass. As we inch closer to the waterfall, the sound of surging waters amplifies like a symphony orchestra. Mist splashes my face refreshingly. Skye pauses us in the air and slowly hovers us close to the headwaters of the waterfall's edge.

"Taste it," he says. "Go on, it's okay."

I lean into the waterfall, hesitatingly, and open my mouth to taste the liquid. To my surprise, it does not taste like river water at all.

I lick my lips with a smile. "Peppermint and dark chocolate, it seems."

I taste it again and the water changes colors from turquoise to burgundy red. Skye cups my hands with his and shows me how to scoop the water into mine.

"You can savor it this way," he says kindly.

We both take a drink from the waterfalls as he holds me in the air. This time it tastes like a rich and robust Pinot Noir, aged beyond my lifetime. Perfect and delectable.

"Does everything in Zion taste like Heaven?" I ask, satisfied, and delighted.

"With you, it does," he whispers.

Skye pulls me into his chest gently and spirals us in flight over the waterfall. Then he kisses me midair over the waterfall's pools. Grapefruit, plum and blackberry flavors mix in with the exchange.

"We must fly onward," he says as he pivots with me in his arms. "My father is waiting for us."

"I'm ready," I say with assurance.

Zion's beauty exists as a breathtaking work of art, created by the Creator of all. Now I will meet this Creator of all, knowing I am loved by His own son.

"Skye!" A thunderous roar shakes the waterfalls. Technicolor mist covers my face in the wake like kisses of a rainbow.

"My father's voice," Skye says as he does an aerial 360 with me in his wings.

A thunderous chuckle fills the airspace so that all of Zion is sure to hear the resonance.

"My Son, I can't wait to see you!" His voice is deep and strong like the sound of a hurricane but peaceful and steady like a river.

Skye swivels and soars as we fly through the meadows of Zion.

"He wants to see you, Lilly," says Skye. "That I am sure of."

"Why me?"

"He picked you," Skye says. "Because you asked to see the light. His light."

You are my light, Skye, I think to him through telekinesis.

"And you are mine, Lilly," he thinks to me.

Skye twirls me around in flight and we soar over the grassy courtyard in front of the golden palace. Ivory columns stand tall by an entryway where more angels hover nearby with striking wings and towering frames. We soar through the columns inside. I hold onto Skye like he is my lifeline. My heart beats faster at the realization The King is closer than ever. I need to keep calm and poised, so that I don't say the wrong…

"Thing?" The regal voice echoes inside the palace. Skye lands. His wings recline. My bare feet touch the floor. "You don't have to be afraid, dear one," says The King.

My nerves prevent me from looking up at Him. I look over at Skye and hope to find comfort from his blue sapphire eyes aflame. They always steady my heart.

Skye smiles at me lovingly and grabs my left hand with his right hand.

"Just so you know," Skye whispers in my ear, "He can read thoughts too." Skye gives me a wink.

"I heard that, My son," booms The King's voice with serenity.

"Affirmative," says Skye.

The King walks towards us as we stand in the Throne Room.

His feet shake the floor.

I look down at the glass below me. It's sapphire stone, and underneath, a garden grows like a hidden forest of floral wonder. Oak trees with ivy. Sunflowers with violets. Butterflies with orchids. Hummingbirds flutter over the treetops. Fascinating…

The King's feet stop in front of me and He bows low. I look up and find infinity in the retinas of His eyes.

"I have been waiting to meet you, Lilly," says The King with a regal voice.

He keeps looking at me. Smiling at me. Peering into me like He can see through my soul. My heart races knowing The King of Zion is right in front of me. The one who sent the angel to me.

I speak up. "Thank you for hearing Me," I say. "That day at Waimea. Thank you for sending the light. For sending my angel. I am forever grateful," I exclaim thankfully.

The King smiles at me with glowing eyes of sapphire light. "Anyone who invokes the light of Zion invokes Me. You are most welcome."

He rises to stand.

"Skye!" The King resounds again with echoes of thunder. He looks at Skye as angels circle around the Throne Room and seraphim fly overhead. "I am pleased with you, My son."

"It is my honor to make you proud, Father," Skye says humbly and bows his head.

"Today is a special day," says The King. He lifts his right arm to signal a cadence of organs. The symphony resounds. "Bring in the gifts!"

Angels pour into the Throne Room and encircle me and Skye. Fire blasts from the Throne.

"This is for you, lovely Lilly." A dove flutters by my shoulder with a gown of pink satin. My eyes grow big.

"Is this mine?" I gasp wide-eyed.

"The Colonel's fiancé needs a proper gown for the ceremony," she says and flutters away. My hands are left holding the gown. Angels swarm around me like a cyclone with the scent of fresh linen and lavender. I lift my hands and, voila, I am wearing the dress, like a magic trick. Only, it is better than magic, since Zion's ways are supernatural.

The holy dove returns with diamond earrings in her wings. She fastens them to my ear. "You shine like a diamond, my lady."

"I thought we were going to have a bridal shower first?" I ask with hesitation.

Are they doing the wedding ceremony now? But I'm not ready. My family is not here.

Skye intervenes. "Father, we hoped to plan the wedding together and invite Lilly's family to Zion for the occasion," says Skye as angels encircle him with a royal robe of sapphire blue and golden decor. One by one, angels fasten medals on the robe. Skye looks up at his father, giving into His process. "But at Your Word, my King, I will follow Your way."

His Father walks towards Him with a star medal in His hand made of pure gold.

"Trust Me, son," The King whispers tenderly. "You still have time to plan the wedding. Right now, I have a star to give you."

4

Skye

"Angels of Zion!" The King's voice booms. "Let it be known this day My son, Colonel Skye Worthy has defeated The Raven and won the battle at Hanauma Bay. He has brought us one step closer to New Zion!"

"Hooray!" Angels cheer in unison.

"All hail Zion! All hail The King!" they chant joyously.

Smoke blasts and organs sound, as they normally do when my father speaks. His glory is all-consuming and awe-inspiring. Lilly's presence here amplifies the moment even more. I want to spend the rest of my life sharing moments like this with her.

I reach for Lilly's hand, gaze at her with loving eyes, and then look at my father. I take a deep breath.

"Now..." The King's voice echoes as he gazes around the Throne Room. "Colonel Skye Worthy will wear a title that Commanders of the Angel Armies are to be given upon exemplary victories, of which My son is most deserving. I entrust this leadership to you today, My son, alongside your beautiful bride Lilly Rose, who is soon to be called Lilly Worthy," my father continues. "This title, I now grant to you today in the presence of all the angels in Zion..." His suspense lingers. "General Skye Worthy!"

Smoke blasts and fire flames from the Throne.

"General Worthy!" The angels chant.

"Hooray for General Worthy!"

"Skye, you're a General!" Lilly says with bright eyes and looks up at me.

General.

The title sinks in as I hear her say it. I don't take it lightly. I would have never asked for this myself, but I trust my father's decision. I am who He says I am.

I address the room. "Not that I would have claimed the title myself, but I relish in the honor my father has given. So, I receive this position of General with honor," I decree in the middle of the angel witnesses.

My father steps forward and motions for me to incline my wings. They rise and tower high. Then, He fastens the golden star to my wings.

"You were destined for this, My son," He says up close. "I love you. Never forget that."

"I love you too, Father."

General.

Again, the title sinks in.

That explains the pageantries. For a moment I thought my father was expediting our wedding after a quick engagement. Even then, I would have obliged. I'd marry Lilly right now if I could.

"You have something new on your left wing, my General," says Lilly as she eyes me with love, standing next to me.

I love how she stands by my side. Her eyes water as she watches my father fasten the gold star.

"I am so proud of you, Skye," she says lovingly.

"I love you, Lilly," I whisper to my beautiful flower. I kiss her hand and my father continues to fasten the star, with permanence.

As honorable as this star is to me, it cannot compare to the stars I see in Lilly's eyes because of my love for her.

"Keep that love forever," He thinks. *"You know the price of losing that love."*

The price of losing love. I breathe in and contemplate the gravity of such a loss. I hope I never lose Lilly's love for all eternity.

"I vow to love Lilly for eternity, my King," I think to Him.

"Show Me, My son," He thinks back to me. He expects perfect love because His Kingdom is founded upon this virtue. I intend to show Lilly this perfect love. I want my father to be proud.

He fastens the star and steps back with a smile on His face.

I gaze around the Throne Room. Seraphim circle the Throne of my father where they have dwelt in loyalty since the beginning. Angels hover in the presence of His holiness.

"Many wars we have fought together and many more are still to come, but I assure you, my angels, we will fight together to the end, for the dawning of New Zion!" I exclaim for all to hear.

"All hail Zion! All hail The King!" Angels shout in coral unison.

Flames blast.

Smoke rises.

My father echoes, "All hail Zion!"

The angels repeat the chant. "All hail Zion!"

I lift Lilly in the moment of joyous revelry and spin her around. I have been craving to hold her since the ceremony started. Her pink gown of satin and green eyes of perfection make my wings feel higher than the heights of Zion's cosmos. When she is in my arms, I feel invincible.

"General Worthy!" she exclaims. "You are my shining star."

I smile. "And you are my galaxy of shooting stars, my bride."

"Let's hear it for the happy couple!" echoes my father in the midst of the Throne Room. "To Lilly and Skye!"

"Hooray for Lilly and Skye!" The angels chant.

I break out in joy and laughter as the moment carries us away into celebration. It's one thing to enjoy Lilly all to myself but to dance with her in the midst of every angel I have flown next to in battle makes me feel like the most blessed angel in existence. I want everyone to see how much I love Lilly.

"I love how you hold my heart, Skye. You never let go of me. You love me everywhere you are," Lilly thinks.

"I love you so much, my Lilly flower," I think to her.

"Lilly!" My father echoes. "I have something for you."

I set her down on the sapphire glass as her feet touch the glossy stone. He walks towards us. Regally, His feet shake the floor.

"What could it be?" Lilly thinks.

My father halts as we stand facing Him. His blue eyes beam with love and joyful bliss.

"Zion has been waiting for you," He says fondly. "With this oil, I bless you in the sight of all Zion's Angels and anoint you for your wedding day. Soon, it will come."

In His hand, He holds a sapphire jar of oil, anointing oil. The kind of oil that marks the anointing of The King. Father, Your ways continue to inspire me.

My father pours the oil on her forehead and rubs it into her skin. She lifts her eyes and looks at Him to receive the anointing.

"Eternity is in His eyes," she thinks. *"Just like Skye's."*

Now Lilly knows where I get my eyes from.

"I am forever grateful, my King," Lilly says gratefully with shining eyes.

My father smiles with endless elation. "You are our joy, My dear."

Lilly blushes and looks at me. "I'm ready for our wedding!" she says excitedly. "It's time to get this show on the road if we're going to win Armageddon!"

I smirk with fascination at her boldness.

"I told her about Armageddon," I confess.

"I see that, son." My father laughs.

"You told her about Armageddon?" The angels stir and shriek at the epiphany of her insider knowledge.

I rise to quiet the ruckus. "Lilly will know every secret there is in Zion's keep. She is the future queen, after all. She is trustworthy," I decree, for all angels to hear. Then I turn to look at her with affirmation. "You will be queen one day, Lilly. Right beside me."

The King bows low to look at Lilly, eye level. "My dear, when do you envision the wedding taking place?" Tenderly and gently, he waits for her reply.

I stand back and let her do all the talking at the realization of her newfound courage to speak candidly to my father.

"I see it during the wintry snowfall with juniper and pine trees. I want poinsettias and azaleas and red roses draped from the ceiling of an outdoor wedding by the Heavens shining brightly," she says with wide eyes. "I see shooting stars in the sky's scenery with ballads of "Just Like

Heaven" and "I Wanna Know What Love Is" playing in the ceremony," she says with certainty. "And of course, for the reception we will start with a cocktail hour of the finest wine from Zion's waterfalls which Skye has already introduced me to. Then, we will lead into a dinner of exquisite detail with hors d'oeuvres, filet mignon, champagne…" She licks her lips. I can tell by her whimsical facial expression, these must be her favorites. "Of course, I am open to whatever my blue angel wants at the wedding. Just say the word, Skye." She bats her eyelashes to finish the wish list.

My father chimes in, intrigued by her courage to speak candidly to Him. "Looks like Lilly has it figured out, My son!" He grins.

I lean in to kiss her cheek. "Have it all, my Lilly flower," I say with delight. "You can have every extravagance in the universe as far as I am concerned."

"The sky's the limit?" she replies with bright eyes.

"Your Skye is limitless," I say in third person. My hand squeezes hers and I peer into her eyes with blue sapphire.

Blue eyes find me in Zion, she thinks.

"I adore you forever, my Lilly flower."

"I love you, General," she says.

Ring! Ring! Ring!

Alarms sound in the Throne Room.

Angels perk up in a war stance. Bright light detonates. My father lifts His right arm and closes His eyes to sense the intruder.

"Hinlors are coming," He echoes calmly. Nothing shakes my father. Not ever. Hinlors could invade like ants and He would stand in regal posture just the same.

Zoom!

An angel soars into the Throne Room and lands at my right side with glorious wings lined in emerald.

"General Worthy!" says Captain Leafe. "An attack near the North Gate!" His face reads with urgency but his heart beats steadily. That tells me he is aware of the worst yet prepared all the same.

I clutch Leafe's shoulder. "Do we know the threat?" I inquire, strategizing my next move.

"Hinlors," Leafe says plainly.

"Skye, ready the fliers," my father decrees. "Captain Leafe, I need you at the North Gate executing the threat until Zion's Armies arrive."

"Yes, my King!" Captain Leafe affirms.

Then, Leafe turns to alert me further. "Skye, we will need every flier. They intend to send the whole fleet."

I pause with fire in my eyes, ready to decimate the hinlors. "Angels, gather at The Eagle's Pad!" I command in one accord. "We are going to fly out undetected and attack from the right side in front of the North Gate! I need a squad of angels standing guard at the North Gate's entrance where Zeal stands guard. No one in and no one out! We don't want any rebels turning sides! We fight this battle in the battle-air! No hinlors are breaching the gates!" I say with adrenaline coursing through my wings.

"Yes sir, General Worthy!" Captain Leafe responds.

"Yes, General Worthy!" the angels affirm.

I nod to Captain Leafe and he nods back, and then looks at Lilly. "A pleasure to see you, Miss Rose. As always." He soars away to the North Gate.

I address my father, ready to fight. "Is it time for Armageddon, Father? We just defeated The Raven. How many more threats will we see until it's time for the reckoning?"

"You will know when it's time," He tells me without giving away any more information than that.

"*I still have more souls waiting to see the light on Earth,*" He thinks to me.

Only I can hear His thoughts, and I understand that my father has a unique reason for why He has not unleashed Armageddon yet. Humans will join us in New Zion and my father wants them all to have the chance to choose Zion.

"*I understand, my King,*" I think back to Him.

"*I Am a King of mercy, Am I not?*"

"*You are, my King,*" I think to Him.

"*The time will come. First, we fight this battle.*"

"*Yes, Father.*"

Lilly clutches my hand firmly. I need to protect her.

Don't worry, my precious flower. I will not let a hinlor touch even one hair on your head!

"Virtue!" I call into Zion.

Flash!

Virtue flies in with white wings lined in sparkling amethysts.

"Here at your service, General!" says Virtue resolutely.

"I need you to guard Lilly," I tell her clearly. "She is my priority. If she is harmed in any way, I would never forgive myself."

"Yes sir, General!" Virtue answers willingly. "I know just where to go."

Lilly interjects. "I can go with you, Skye!"

Her bravery endears me. I know she would fly into battle with me, entrusting herself into my care but I cannot give in to that yet. I need to know she is safe. I cannot bear the thought of her body in the line of fire.

You know I can fight," she thinks to me. *"I don't want to be apart from you. I've spent so long waiting for you. Don't make me wait again, Skye..."*

"You're too precious to me, Lilly," I tell her. I stroke her hair and look into her eyes with blue light flaming like her face is a memory I want to keep in my mind forever. "Please stay, Lilly. I need you to trust me."

"What if you don't come back?" she asks petrified.

"I always come back." I clasp her hands and kiss them. "I promise."

"It's time, Lilly. We must go!" says Virtue as she reaches for Lilly's hands.

Tears well up in Lilly's eyes. My heart shreds inside of me every time I tell her I'm leaving.

Crash!

Blast!

The hinlors are coming.

Alarms sound off again in the Throne Room, alerting us of the imminent threat to Zion's airspace. My wings prepare for flight.

I reach my hand through the glassy floor and it opens for me at my command. I retrieve a red rose from the Throne's garden. The glass reseals. "Keep this for me." I place the red rose in her soft hands. "Until I return. Keep your heart for me and only me."

"I will, Skye."

With one last glance into her longing green eyes, I kiss her and lift my wings for takeoff.

My wings soar through the ivory column and over the courtyard as I make my way towards The Eagle's Pad.

My eyes flame blue. Wings increase speed. "Activate perimeter vision," I echo out loud. Perimeter vision gives me eyes into the cosmos outside of Zion. I blink twice and see the hinlors flying approximately 2000 lightyears away. Within five minutes time, they will arrive at our doorstep. Maybe sooner, once my father sets off supernovas to lure them.

My wings soar with urgency, sending me lightning speed through Zion. I keep thinking of Lilly. She is in good hands with Virtue, I know. Still, I don't like being apart from her now that we just arrived in Zion. Everything is new to her and I wanted to be the first to show her everything Zion has to offer.

I sigh and keep flying.

Hold it together, Skye. As long as I command Zion's armies, she will have this life. War. Separation. Longing. Waiting.

"More attacks will come until the end is here," my father echoes as I fly. He always does that to remind me to trust Him.

"I am ready, Father. Strengthen our angels with your light." Every angel must fly with resilience in these days, and they can. Angels are equipped for this. No threats of darkness can overtake us.

I flap my wings, soar over the roses of pastel lavender and cherry red, and land on The Eagle's Pad. Angels are in formation as expected, aligned in a perfect V shape with glowing white light hovering over the grass. I fly to the head of the V and turn to face the angels. Fearless and arduous, they wait for my command.

"Zion's Angels!" I echo. "Hinlors are approaching! They fly towards the North Gate as we speak! Our strategy is to fly with invisibility to approach them undetected and attack from the right side. Remember, angels of Zion… The Raven is gone but his demonic following remains! We will wage war until every threat of darkness is eradicated!" I command as they stand ready. "Your wings are strong and resilient! Your light is bold! My father has given you all authority to defeat the hinlors waging war against Zion."

I rise over the ground with wings outstretched. Blue eyes flame, ready for light detonation and war.

"Activate invisibility!" I command the angels.

In a flash like lightning, they transform from solid white wings to translucent light. A wave of radiation ripples from their aura like a stone casting ripples into a still sea.

I continue. "Your fellow angels will be able to see you, as will I. Hinlors will not! Once we approach the spot of the enemy, I will give the signal to detonate Zion's light radiation and we will deactivate invisibility and assail the enemy. On my count! We fly!"

"Yes, General Worthy!" the angels reply in unison.

I prepare for take-off. "For Zion! 3–2–1–takeoff!"

My wings soar over the edge of The Eagle's Pad and into galactic air. The angel armies follow in tandem.

From The Eagle's Pad, it takes 90 seconds to reach the North Gate at leisure wing speed. We will make it in 30 seconds at this pace as I strategically fly to see the hinlors and detonate radiation.

I tilt my wings to pick up speed. We curve around the edge of Zion's gates. There they are. I see them. But they can't see us. Yet.

Squawk! Squawk!

A flock of grey birds approach the gate with sharp teeth like metal scraps. Their wings are small and agile, to match their body. Their eyes burn like The Raven's with red poison oozing from the soul. They ravage anything living and show no mercy to anything weak. From the crevices of hell, they emerged. Into ashy soot, they will fall.

"Hinlors up ahead!" I alert.

We arrive on Zion's north where The North Gate shines with pure gold. Angels stand guard at the gate alongside Zeal.

Captain Leafe waits, mid-air, just ahead of us. I wait for his signal.

He knows the right moment for detonation, having already been out here among the conditions. I halt and Zion's Angels halt behind me, waiting on my command to detonate light into the incoming fleet.

Captain Leafe signals his hand for readiness. I follow suit.

"Ready!" I command the angels.

The V formation rotates from horizontal flight mode to vertical levitation, with towering wings ready to detonate.

To the left, stars loom in the galaxies. I cannot help but notice the wonder every time I step into the cosmos. It is here that Lilly's eyes manifest in my vision once again.

Keep me strong, Lilly. Your eyes keep me flying high.

"At my word!" I shout. "Detonate radiation and deactivate invisibility!" My blue eyes flame to detonate Zion's light, the most powerful light in the universe. My angels follow in sync. Rays of light fill their eyes to target the hinlors due north of our position.

"Yes, General Worthy!" They shout in unison.

"Ready... execute!" I command.

Blast!

Bolts of energy blast into the enemy's territory like a fire hydrant of flaming liquid.

"Shriek!" cry the hinlors. A thousand angel eyes blast with heavenly light as the hinlors scowl and shrivel. Red eyes scatter about the starry sky outside the North Gate, combusting one by one into ashy crumbs.

Hinlors should have known better than to attack Zion's Kingdom. Our light is too bright.

Zion's light carries intense radiation, meant to uplift the heart of the good and eliminate the soul of the bad. The King's light either repels the soul or magnetizes the soul to Him. In this case, our light will decimate all hinlors opposing Zion.

"Charge ahead!" I shout.

Wings rotate for flight mode.

"Yes, General Worthy!" shout the angels. "For Zion!" they follow in tandem.

We soar straight into battle-air.

More red-eyed hinlors creep out of the darkness and soar towards us.

Blast!

Angels detonate light.

Blast!

Hinlors fall all around us like dust.

To my right and left, angels keep detonating light. Hinlors shriek. Hinlors fall.

Meanwhile, Zeal shields the North Gate with angels stationed beside him. From the northeast side, I notice a flock of hinlors encroaching. Then arrows start to fly.

"Captain Leafe!" I shout. "From the northeast!"

Hinlors fly fast and throw arrows, gunning towards the gate. A new tactic, it appears. I've never seen hinlors throw arrows before but there is a first for everything.

Blast!

I detonate light into their flock and soar fast towards the assault.

Leafe turns to meet me and surges into the battle-air towards the flock of hinlors encroaching. We both prepare for detonation.

"On my count!" I say. Leafe flies by my side. "3-2-1-detonate!"

Leafe's eyes beam with emerald light.

My eyes beam with sapphire light.

Blast!

We obliterate the threat.

Ash combusts in the wake as hinlors evaporate in cosmic air. Arrows fall in tandem with the disintegration.

In a moment, eternity flashes before my eyes. I remember the moment I saw Lilly under Waimea Bay. Light glimmered through the waters like a lightbulb encased in glass. I dove. I found her. I brought her up to the air again, unhidden, and fully illuminated. She didn't trust me at first. Most humans don't when angels touch down.

"I didn't see that coming!" Leafe shouts.

Leafe flies up to my position and I pat him on the back.

"That's why I'm here for," I reply and give an affirmative smile. "I cover your wings, you cover mine."

Leafe nods back.

I scan my periphery. Angels to my left and right circle the battle-air checking for remaining hinlors. Their wings flew well and their light was strong. My father will be proud.

I smile at the realization I can see Lilly's sweet face sooner than later. I need her calming aura to console me and ease me from the battle sounds.

"Well, the battle is won," says Captain Leafe firmly and puts his hand on my shoulder. "All will return home safely."

"Lilly will be glad to know we are safe," I reply. I wipe my brow. Inhale. Exhale.

Swoop!

"General Worthy!" Leafe exclaims.

I turn my head. An arrow darts my way, flaming with hinlor havoc.

Leafe grabs my wings, flies upward, and grips the arrow with his left hand. The arrow that was headed towards me. I exhale.

"Thank you, Captain."

"Don't mention it." He nods.

With green eyes lit with Zion's light, He looks around and I do the same. I wait, ensuring every remaining hinlor has been exterminated.

"All clear!" Leafe says.

"Yes, all clear." Captain Strength soars up to us and nods.

No more hinlors. No more arrows. Victory is won. Zion's Angels wait for my victory confirmation.

"Zion's angels!" Bright, white wings with Heaven's glow gather in battle-air. Perfect V formation. I rise, to relay the news. "Victory is ours! Hinlors are defeated! Zion's gates are upheld!" My wings flare out and radiate with light as the angels follow suit.

"All hail Zion!" they echo.

"All hail The King!" they sing in a chorus.

"Let it be known Zion reigns forever!" I resound. "The light of Zion will never be usurped!"

"Skye!" My father's voice echoes all the way from the Throne Room.

"What is it, Father?" I echo.

Boom!

A dark shape rises in the far end of the cosmos.

"The battle isn't over yet, My son."

5

Lilly

"*The battle isn't over, My son.*"

"What was that?"

My head swivels. The whole universe could have heard that echo. It lingers now in the space of Zion's peace where tranquil rivers flow into delightful waterfalls and back again. I look up and find technicolor light catching my gaze.

"I'm sure everything is okay, dear one," says Virtue serenely.

"I heard it, Virtue. A voice said, '*The battle isn't over.*' Did you hear it?"

"I only hear what I am given permission to hear."

She didn't hear it, but I did.

Am I supposed to be able to hear things the angels can't hear? I wonder if I am hearing Skye's thoughts, all this way apart from him. It could be an echo of his spirit. Or an echo of his father's spirit.

Whispers from Skye's heart to mine are what I expected to hear when he left to battle at the North Gate. But I haven't heard anything since he left. When he returns, I will have no more reason to wonder. He will be with me, and I won't have to imagine what he is thinking any longer.

"How long are we on lockdown?" I ask.

Virtue pours steamy liquid into an opal glass teacup. Flower petals in the shape of diamonds float near the rim, simmering. The teacup is hot with my hands clasped around it. I bring the cup to my nose and smell the sweet aroma. Jasmine and rose waft in from the scent. I take a sip.

"Thank you," I say politely.

I take another sip.

"You are most welcome, lovely Lilly," she replies tenderly and takes a seat across from me. "I'm sure Skye will be back soon."

How soon, I wonder? In Zion, time is nonexistent. There is no sun and moon to rise and set, for the King's light makes everything alive and awake. I smile thinking about the garden I saw under the Throne Room's sapphire floor. And the River of Life. And the Tree of Life. So many unimaginable, whimsical, beautiful sights to behold wait for my discovery. I cannot possibly stay cooped up inside waiting for him to return. I want to see the universe where supernovas erupt and planets spin.

"Please take me somewhere!" I say with bright eyes.

"My lady, we cannot risk it. It isn't safe."

"The battle is outside the walls!" I exclaim excitedly.

"Yes, but–"

"Then we are safe inside the realm of Zion with The King in control!" I surmise with enthusiasm.

"Lilly, the hinlors could breach the gate. I am on strict orders to protect you, dear one."

"As far as I can tell those gates are not opening to hinlors when my angel is out there. Don't you trust Skye?" I gasp excitedly.

I look at her with smiling eyes and twirl about the whimsical tree house tucked in the Tree of Life. This tree house is a safe place, Virtue said, when we first arrived. No one can enter with a spirit of war. I have no doubt we are completely safe but I long to see more. My head is still in the clouds now that I'm in Zion, and in the clouds is where I want to stay.

"I can see you love to dance, lovely Lilly." Her voice carries the tranquility of soothing rain. I like the way it sounds.

"Of course, I do," I say. "Dancing is one of Heaven's greatest gifts. I especially like when Skye dances with me," I say giddily. I wonder what

Virtue thinks when I talk about Skye. She has known him far longer than I have. I know he chose me, but the inability to read her thoughts leaves me wondering what Zion thinks of the new human in eternity's bliss. Do they like me?

"We owe you, Lilly," says Virtue.

"For what?" I look up at her.

"For loving General Worthy."

"Doesn't everyone love Him?"

Virtue pauses and flutters up to the ceiling, avoiding the question for the moment. The room stands 30 feet high, nestled in the oak of the tree trunk, with scents of fresh oak and floral gardens. She returns with a trinket, places it in my hand, and then folds her hand over mine.

"This used to belong to The Raven."

"What a stunning watch." I eye the golden jewelry set with diamonds. "The design is gorgeous."

"Yes," she replies. "Skye found it in the waterfalls after The Raven was removed from Zion. There's only two made. Skye has the other match."

I eye the watch with particular fascination. "It looks like it is not moving."

"Zion is not bound by time, my dear. It is a symbol of Zion's eternal continuum. When The Raven decided he no longer wanted to follow King Worthy, he left it behind. And with that decision, he relinquished his eternal destiny in Zion altogether."

Skye told me about the story of losing The Raven's friendship and loyalty. His best friend betrayed him, and I know it still haunts him. "Skye said they used to fly together."

"They were the fastest in the universe, my dear," she points out. "When The Raven turned against The King, he lost this in the middle of battle. Skye found it. And he has kept it here ever since." She pauses. "I think somewhere inside him, he thought The Raven would come to his senses and return to Zion. Pledge loyalty to The King. Then he could give it back to him. It really shook Skye that The Raven rebelled. But Skye remains resilient. He is the Commander, after all. Still, we could tell something was missing." She pauses.

"What could possibly be missing? He has everything here in Zion," I exclaim.

Virtue hovers close to me and rests her hand on my head ever so gently. "You, my dear."

"Me?"

Virtue nods with peace.

"But I'm only a–"

"Human?" She smiles at me with angelic eyes, leans in, and touches my face softly with angelic hands. "Yes. Human. He needed your love."

My heart melts at the revelation. Do all the angels see it this way? How could an angel so perfect, like Skye, need *me*? I look up at Virtue and smile without a word to say. There aren't any words to describe the way he makes me feel at dawn's sunrise and how he dances with me under the stars. I needed his love more than I could have ever known.

Lightning flashes in my memory as I recall the ocean's roar that night at Waimea Bay when Skye saved me.

Beep! Beep! Beep!

The alarm sounds.

"Come dear, we must ascend the Mount of Zion!" says Virtue with eagerness.

Virtue picks me up swiftly and soars out of the tree house. Outside the Tree of Life, golden leaves flutter in the air like confetti blowing in the wind. Her wings flap and golden leaves twirl as she soars over the green, velvet grass.

Beep! Beep! Beep!

There it is again.

More angels gather with urgency, leaving no time for hesitation. We soar fast around the Tree of Life, and up and over the river towards the heights of Zion. The tree becomes smaller as we ascend. I glimpse the waterfalls. Their waters gush over the edge like turquoise gemstones pouring out of a treasure chest.

I wonder what the water tastes like right now. Is it another glass of Merlot or another flavor yet to be discovered? Skye will take me when he returns. If I could choose any flavor, it would be blueberry jam, just like the spread he ordered for us when he got me breakfast at Lanikai Beach before we got engaged. I love his taste and his sense of humor. I need you to come back to me safe and sound, my blue angel.

"Are you okay, my lady?" asks Virtue.

"Yes," I say. "The view of Zion from up high is spectacular."

"The King make everything beautiful, doesn't He?" Her voice carries peace and calm, even in the midst of panic. Angelic, indeed. I can't help but wonder how Skye is feeling and what danger is before him since I cannot read his thoughts from this distance.

"Zion is the perfection of beauty," I exclaim.

My eyes scan the scenery in front of us. Mountains appear in the distance, shimmering with pink and silver sparkles of light. The surface appears like snow and sea simultaneously, with its velvet, fluffy texture, and glassy coating.

More angels glow beside us as we collectively fly towards the mountains. Their faces shine like diamonds. I can see their wings in flight from this point of view. Gigantic, regal feathers of power, they are. I can only imagine what it looks like when Skye flies with me. He always keeps me shielded from the elements and takes me places I could never go without him. Skye, I need you to hold me now. Where would you take me if you could take me anywhere?

"Hold on to me, dear," says Virtue as she soars alongside the shining angels. "We are making our way to Mount Zion to chant the angels' anthem. That is what the alarm was for. It only comes on when there is a high threat to the intrusion of Zion. Our song wards off the enemy."

"To save Skye?" I ask inquisitively.

It makes sense now. They are not fleeing terror. They are fighting terror. With angelic melodies.

"To save the universe, my darling," she says matter-of-factly. "Skye knows what he is doing, my lady. Don't worry," she assures me. "His command sends out the alarm."

"Oh, glory to The King!" Angels begin singing.

"Worthy is The King! Worthy is The King! Zion's King is worthy!" chant the angels. I can hear Virtue's voice caroling as we fly.

"General Worthy, I love you," I whisper.

"I love you, my Lilly flower," echoes Skye through the clouds.

"Skye!? Is that you?"

"I can hear you, my love," he says through telekinesis.

I can hear his thoughts again!

"Skye, I thought I had lost you. I couldn't hear your thoughts!" I echo back to him in telekinesis.

"I'm coming for you, Worthy!" shrieks a voice like horror.

"What was that, Skye?" I look around me. The angels keep singing, unaware of the noise as we fly to the tops of the pink, shimmering mountains.

"Don't worry, Lilly... We will not be defeated," Skye tells me through his thoughts.

"Worthy is The King!" The angels sing as we crest the peaks of Zion. "Hallelujah to the giver of life!"

"You are done for, Worthy! Surrender to me! Your crown is mine!" yells the gremlin-like monster again. I look around, unable to see the threat.

Blast!

A wave of light detonates in the sky above us like an atomic bomb. The air shakes. Wings flutter around me as all the angels land on Mount Zion's peak.

Slip!

My clutch on Virtue's wings loses grip at the shock of the ripple effect. I fall downward fast. Air rushes through my hair. I descend in a whirlwind.

"Skye!" I shout into the atmosphere.

If only he could rush back to save me like he always does.

"I got you, Lilly!" Virtue echoes through the sky.

I look up and see her purple eyes on me as I fall fast like a sky diver. She darts towards me.

Swoosh!

Virtue scoops me in her wings and ascends towards the mountain peak again. Breathe in. Breathe out. My body calms from the free fall.

"Thank you," I manage to articulate as I take a deep breath.

"Zion won't let you fall, my lady. Even when gravity is in place."

"Is there a time when it is not in place?"

"Of course, my lady. When The King freezes gravity, everything floats in space. But we don't always need it. Eternal living is much more enjoyable with the freedom to fly and soar against gravity's pull."

"If only I had wings to save myself, I wouldn't need anyone to save me," I exclaim dreamily.

"The King wants you to feel the embrace of love's rescue, my dear," adds Virtue with smiling eyes. "That's why He didn't halt gravity. If he knew you would have fallen just now without an angel to save you, I assure you, He would have halted gravity itself. Then the waterfalls of Zion would upturn and rise to the sky."

"He can do that?"

"Most certainly. He can do anything."

"What about making the planets shake? Can He do that?" I ask enthusiastically.

"Yes, my lady."

"And the stars explode? Can He do that?"

"Yes, my dear. But why do you–"

"Can He make the nations rage and the sun stand still?" I ask eagerly with wide eyes.

"I'm not sure where you're going with this, my dear."

"I read it in a book once."

Revelation is my favorite. Skye told me Armageddon would soon take place, and when it does, I want everyone to see the light and choose The King. I want every soul to dwell here in Zion, the most perfect place in the universe.

"All hail King Worthy!" chant the angels scattered across the mountain peak. "Long live The King!" they echo.

Skye talked about New Zion and the spectacle of its grandeur. Then everyone will be protected from every evil in the universe.

"Where is Skye?" I wonder.

I look around at the host of angels singing. The detonation must have meant they won the battle. They should be back by now. Where are you, my blue angel?

Virtue strokes my hair with ease and gentle eyes. "He will arrive in time, my–"

"Dear Lilly."

"Skye!" I shriek and turn around.

Blue eyes find me on the mountain top.

Skye's blue eyes still pierce me with captivation like the first time I saw him.

His smile bellows with laughter as he picks me up and twirls me. The softness of his hair grazes my forehead in the wake. Behind him Zion's Angels fly in from the north, gathering together.

"I told you I would return," he says and sets me down gently.

"I believed you," I reply.

"I love you, my Lilly flower. You're all I can think about when I'm in battle," he thinks to me as I read his thoughts.

"General Worthy!" An angel soars up to his right side, across from me, with towering wings. The angel's green eyes stare at me intently and study my frame. Is there something on my dress?

"You look perfect, my Lilly flower," Skye thinks to me. *"I can tell he notices it too, but I assure you every angel is under my authority."* Here, only I can read his thoughts. Our telekinesis comes in handy when he needs to say something to me without anyone else hearing.

"What is it, Captain Leafe?" Skye asks. He pulls my left hand towards his right hand and interlocks his fingers with mine. I like how it feels when he does that.

"I found this in the ash," says Captain Leafe, "lingering in the battle-air." He extends his hand that holds a red gemstone like a garnet, with swirling hues of burgundy.

Skye lifts his left hand to hold the gemstone. "It's still hot," he asserts.

"Majestic, isn't it?" Captain Leafe stares at the stones with eyes of hypnosis.

"It's not what it appears to be, Captain," says Skye.

"The King only makes pure and radiant gemstones," he thinks. *"Its aura is evil, deriving from the very monster who left it."*

Skye blazes his blue eyes of sapphire light onto the red gemstone. Smoke puffs out from its core.

"If it is authentic from Zion's waterfalls, it will withstand the heat of pure light," Skye says.

"And if it's not?" Leafe inquires.

The red stone rattles in Skye's hands as his blue light penetrates.

"Into ash, it will return," Skye exclaims as smoke rises.

"Skye," I shriek. "I think it's going to–"

Blast!

It disintegrates.

Lightning strikes in the distance, due north of the mountains.

"Are they still out there, Skye?" I ask. The hinlors must have left the red stone. I wonder what else lingers beyond Zion's perimeter.

"They're gone, my love." Skye whispers. He leans in to kiss my cheek. "Whatever looms in the cosmos cannot stand. My father is still in control."

"I heard his voice," I tell him. The echo I heard came from The King, I know it did.

"He gave you ears to hear, my Lilly flower," he exclaims and strokes my hair behind my ear. "He wants you to hear for a reason."

"Then I want to listen to every word," I reply whimsically.

Skye smiles at me endearingly, tilts his head to kiss me, and then notices the audience of angels looking in on our intimate moment. He clears his throat and lifts me in his arms in front of all the angels.

"Zion's angels! It's no secret my lovely Lilly has captured my heart like the stars capture the earth. I ask that you keep watch over her at all times, in the event of warfare ensuing!"

"Yes, General Worthy!" The angels chant.

"They love you already," says a white dove fluttering around us. "So do I, my lady."

"Purity, see to it that Lilly has every provision waiting for her in her villa," Skye instructs with eyes intently focused on me.

"Yes, Skye," Purity flutters away with a trail of glitter.

"I have a surprise for you!"

"Do you!?" I reply. I love surprises.

"I think it's time we shop for the big day," he replies with sapphire eyes. He pulls me in close and wraps his arms around me.

"What do you have in mind, my blue angel?" I ask with enchanted eyes.

Blue eyes find me in love.

"Your wedding dress," he says. "Silk or chiffon, my bride?"

6

Skye

White silk drapes Lilly's body like an angel covered in lace and pearls. The dress she wears now contains the finest thread counts of Zion's silk. I would choose nothing less for my flawless bride.

I say she looks like an angel because she is one to me. If only she knew the way my heart leaped out of my chest flying away from her to silence the threat of hinlors invading Zion. It stirs me now, every time I have to fight and leave her behind. Spending eternity with her fuels me in every way. She is my reason to soar invincibly.

"General Worthy! You're not supposed to see the bride before the wedding!" says Honor with a smile as she ruffles the train on Lilly's ball gown.

Honor is one of Zion's Angels and an exquisite seamstress. She made my father's royal robe and all the angels' timeless accessories. All ceremonies are styled and dressed by her, with a team of angels who my father anointed to create fashionable works of art.

I interject. "The General must sign off on everything!" I reply light-heartedly and soar up to Lilly. I land besides her and eye the gown with focus.

Deep down, I know this moment is anything but light-hearted. It's one of the most sentimental moments of my eternal life. Seeing Lilly in a wedding dress makes me want to kiss her right here and now, and send for my father to come and marry us quickly. Forget the elaborate ceremony, and the pomp and circumstance. I just want Lilly. All to myself.

"Do you like it, Skye?" Lilly asks shyly with bright eyes.

"You look like an angel, my love," I say. Her beauty almost leaves me speechless. But I know she can read my mind where my endless creativity of expressing my thoughts for her remains. Thank goodness Honor cannot hear me in that space, lest she faint from the fantasies playing out in my mind.

Lilly giggles as she reads me. *"I like that you're here with me,"* she tells me through her thoughts.

"I love every second of your presence close to me, my Lilly flower," I tell her through my thoughts.

Lilly turns around and dips like a ballerina with her stunning eyes as the train follows her movement on the marble-gold floor. The grandiose gown consumes her tiny frame with the elaborate ball gown skirt, but it fits her like a princess. I can tell she likes it. So do I.

I imagine dipping Lilly in my arms as I twirl her and kiss her during our first dance. Her dress will be bustled, of course, in the back to give her feet room to dance. Honor will know what to do with the design. I leave that much to her.

I turn to Lilly. "I wanted to see you in a dress before anyone else," I tell her lovingly and stroke her hair. "Don't worry, we will still have that perfect moment when I see you in your dress for the first time. This is just the prelude fitting. Honor is making you a custom design with this shape in mind. I can't wait to see it on you, my perfect love."

Honor chimes in with her tape measure in hand. "General Worthy is right. This won't be your final dress, dear. I am going to have you try on many dresses and then design you a one-of-a-kind dress with your favorite parts all in one. A custom gown for a worthy bride," she says with a wink. "You picked a good one Skye," she says serenely as she moves into the alteration room and then back again with more materials.

"A perfect one," I insist.

"And you are going to be so handsome, my General!" Lilly throws her arms around me. I pick her up and sling the entire train over my wings with one thrust.

"General!" Honors shrieks. "That is fine woven silk you're tossing!"

"My Lilly is the fine woven silk," I assert with authority and a commanding smile.

"Yes, General," says Honor.

Honor looks away peacefully and continues threading pearls onto a headband attached to a veil.

"I would shred a trillion ballgowns just to pick you up in my arms once more," I exclaim. Holding her, I feel her heartbeat close to mine. I hope you can feel mine too, Lilly.

"I can feel you," she whispers.

Soon the veil between me and Lilly will be no more, and we will be wed as one in love forever. Husband and wife. No more waiting. I can have her. All of her. And she can have me.

"I love you with the strongest love you could fathom, Lilly." I lean in to kiss her gently. The taste of her mouth reminds me of honey and rose petals.

"Is that my rose of Sharon!?"

I recognize the voice.

Lilly will too.

I pull away from her lips. This interruption is a surprise that Lilly is going to like.

"Jenna!?" Lilly turns to face her best friend who stands in the bridal halls of Zion. "Oh, my goodness! Jenna!"

"I heard there was a royal wedding happening in Zion and I couldn't miss it for the world," Jenna says with a wink and runs to Lilly with a hug. Lilly embraces her.

"How did you get here!?" Lilly asks.

"I had one of my trusted angels give her a lift," I reply and kiss her on the cheek. With my left hand I rub her back.

"I want you to have your best friend here while you are getting used to Zion. You need her. Just trust me," I tell Lilly with my thoughts to her.

"Thank you for always thinking of everything," she tells me with her thoughts.

"You're welcome, my love."

"Ladies, I haven't the slightest notion of what color to use for the bridesmaid dresses. Perhaps you can help me look over the technicolor swath?" Honor inquires eagerly.

"You got it, angelic fashionista!" exclaims Jenna. She hops over to Honor by the windows where a sewing machine stands and a geode crystal-laid table displays every color of the universe.

Now is my cue to let them do their thing and catch up. They will accomplish far more without me hovering over the dress choices.

"I'm going to let you and Jenna have some time to try on more dresses," I whisper tenderly. "The next time I see you wearing white will be when we say our eternal vows in the halls of Zion."

"Stay here with me!" Lilly says, and leaps involuntarily like she always does when she gets excited or anxious.

"I'll see you in a little while," I assure her with blue eyes aflame and touch her cheek.

"I know you will," she says.

"Blue eyes find me in my wedding dress," she thinks to me. Peacefully, she looks into my eyes, like a flower blooming in the sunlight.

"What about river diamonds?" Honor echoes from across the room. "Oh, wouldn't that look marvelous on the train!"

"Diamonds are a girl's best friend!" Jenna exclaims. "Do you want to pick out a color Lilly?"

"Coming!" Lilly says.

"I'll see you tonight, my love. I want to save the final reveal of the dress until the big day," I wink at her.

Lilly nods back.

With a kiss on her forehead, I soar away through the high doors.

⨎

I feel Lilly's heartbeat even as I fly yards away from her. My heart pulsates for her just the same as I enter the light of Zion where angels glide and make music day and night.

I need some alone time before going anywhere else.

After the battle with the hinlors and the beauty of Lilly in her wedding dress, my heart is full of a million thoughts. From war to purity, and from evil to innocence. But I was called to this position of commanding. Until the day breaks forth where New Zion is here and we defeat the evil of the universe forever, I will keep commanding Zion's angels.

My wings flap and I soar to my favorite spot in The Rose Garden where I can hear the melody of the breeze. My thoughts unfurl here.

Is Lilly in good hands without me? Of course she is. Honor understands the importance of fine clothing and extravagant gowns to meet the wishes of my beautiful bride. Jenna will understand what Lilly wants and needs, as one who has been her life now since she was nine years old. My father has beckoned Jenna many times unto the light. She does not often feel deserving of it nor focused on it. But my father does not give up on a soul. Lilly loves Jenna and so I will do everything I can to show her the heart of Zion... Love, kindness, and truth. Lilly would want that for Jenna.

I reach for a journal nestled in the row of flowers where I have a hidden compartment that only I can access. There are compartments all over Zion, much like this one, only I and my father can locate. Just like there are souls on earth only we can find, to bring them closer to us.

> *Dear Journal,*
>
> *Lilly tried on a wedding dress for the first time. I almost fainted because of how beautiful she looked. But angels don't faint, we save the faint. So, I kept my wings steady... but my heart kept beating a mile a minute. It still is. I wonder if I will always feel this way about Lilly, and how I can handle the magnitude of the love I have for her. Then I realize it's not a weight at all, it's energy, just like the sun shining over earth for its livelihood. I need Lilly forever. I love her like the waterfalls love Zion's serenity. I love her like the rainforest loves the rain to bloom and grow its most dazzling treasures. Endless diamonds could not compare to her priceless worth.*
>
> *Lilly Rose*
> *fairest rose*
> *your love is*
> *the light of hope*
> *your love is my life*

I set down my journal and lie back in the velvet green grass. Roses encompass me like a blanket here in the garden. I wonder what color roses Lilly will pick to accompany her bouquet. She loves roses. This I know for a fact, not only because her maiden name is Rose, but because she glows every time I talk of The Rose Garden. She smells like roses too. Lying here with the floral sweetness of the roses surrounding me, I feel her aura.

"Skye!" My father echoes.

My eyes open.

I can feel the ground quaking from His feet. I sit up and He moves towards me, with gigantic, steady strides that ripple into the radius of the roses encircling me. The grass shakes when He walks. Everything does. His power is all consuming.

"I was not expecting you," I tell Him.

"Lilly is going to make a beautiful bride," My father declares as He kneels next to me in the grass.

"Yes," I say. "She tried on her wedding dress today," I divulge with a smile.

I look down at the clovers woven in the grass like embroidered greenery. My hand investigates its softness and I understand why its foliage is akin to velvet. Everything in Zion is custom-made. My father would not have it any other way.

"A bride's wedding day is one of the most important days of her life," He declares with bright eyes. "Lilly is not just any bride. She is the General's Bride."

"Father, I want to give her the best wedding she could ever dream of."

"Then she picked the right angel, My son. Everything in Zion is at your disposal. The universe is the limit."

He lifts my face with His right hand peacefully and slowly. I am used to the gesture. He does it anytime I am overwhelmed.

Am I? Overwhelmed?

"I could feel your heartbeat all the way from Zion's mountains, My son," He speaks to me tenderly. Gently He lets go of my chin and waves His hands as a lily appears, with pink petals and white strands.

"It's not that I'm overwhelmed, Father." I explain. "I'm just–"

"Faint with love?" He affirms.

"So faint. I feel I could melt when I'm around her," I confess. "Sometimes I feel weakness in my wings, and then surges of adrenaline in other places. It's more than before. Now that I've seen her in white, I cannot look away from the image of her in my mind. It's there. Permanently. Like the feathers in my wings. Now I keep wondering if she will always love me the way I love her. What if she gets tired of me? What if the passion fades away? I'm terrified of losing her and I don't know what to do with all of these questions."

"I want you to look at My hands, Skye."

Eyes gaze at the flower in the hands that made that sun. It's perfect. Just like Lilly. Soft, strong, whimsical, beautiful.

"Did the lily paint its own petals with pink?" He asks.

I look at the lily's perfect design. Its petals are intricate and loved by My father, the one who created all of creation to speak of His glory. Nothing comes to life without His touch, and everything flourishes in His light. He is the one and only sustainer of life itself.

"No. You did, my King."

"That's right, My son. And did the lily create its own life?"

"No. You did, my King."

"That's right, My son. And did you find Lilly on your own?"

"You found her for me, my King."

"That's right, My son," He declares with a firm serenity that only my father can enunciate. "Skye," He whispers. "You must understand that only you can decide how you want to love her. Don't let her go, General. Lest someone else steal her away."

My eyes fill with tears. I breathe in and out. "Father," I cry out as He hugs me tightly in His nurturing arms.

Even the Commander of Zion's Angels needs his father to lean on. I will always need Him in these times, to be the strength that renews me and aligns me with how He sees. "I want to be Lilly's forever."

"Lilly belongs to you," He replies. "Remember that."

Blast!

Fireworks light up the technicolor sky of Zion. Blue, yellow, silver, red eruptions of fire cascade over us. Confetti pours out from the light.

Purity zooms in with speedy dove wings of fairy dust and circles my father and I, leaving trails of rose gold in the wake. Her soft yet powerful spirit lands on my shoulder in the shape of a dove.

"Someone said yes to the dress!" Purity says with a wink.

My father chuckles with His fatherly billow. "Lilly Worthy is going to make a worthy bride," He declares with joyful eyes of sapphire.

My lovely Lilly. The shape of her in the white ballgown fills my imagination. The day I see her walking down the aisle towards me will undoubtedly be the best day of my eternal life.

I can already see the crescendo of the ceremony playing out with the Hallelujah Chorus as the angels resound in unison. Lilly will be in my arms as I give her our first kiss as husband and wife. My blue eyes will glow into her green eyes, and she will think *Blue eyes find me married.* I love it when she thinks about my blue eyes. I always want her to be captivated by me and no one else.

"General Worthy!" Captain Leafe soars up to our side with white, emerald studded wings and strong stature. He lands on the grass and kneels before my father who stands regally in the glowing light of The Rose Garden. "My King," he says to address my father, "We have an intruder in Zion!"

"Pray tell, Captain," says my father with ease.

Leafe stands. "I don't know how she got here, but she's driving Virtue and Honor crazy. Apparently, she has a cellular device and has been sending illicit messages down to earth."

"I think you're talking about Jenna, Captain Leafe," my father confirms with authority. "She's Lilly's best friend."

"Oh," he replies with a puzzled look. "So, she didn't sneak in through a dark spell or something?"

"I would know if she did, wouldn't I?" My father answers brazenly.

"Of course, my King." Leafe bows in reverence. "My apologies, sir. I did not know." Leafe hesitates and then continues. "It's just... she wears red high heels and plays that horrid leopard stuff."

"Def Leppard?" I ask to confirm.

"That's the one!" Leafe exclaims.

"What's the problem?" My father inquires.

The King already knows everything, but He chooses to communicate with everyone personally. It's one of the humblest attributes of my father.

Leafe continues. "Apparently she wants us to pour some sugar on her," Leafe exclaims with a perplexed look. "I offered to take her to the waterfalls when it tastes like skittles."

"Great idea, Captain!" my father says intrigued. He laughs. "And her response?"

"She told me she'd rather not taste the rainbow with me. And then she flipped her hair with a sarcastic look in her eye."

My father lets out a chuckle as loud as a roaring lion.

"Did I say something wrong?" Leafe asks seriously and looks over at me.

"You just met a strong Texas woman is all," I assure him. "Did it scare you?"

"Scare me? Nothing scares me, General! Into the darkest crevices of the universe, I will fly!" Leafe replies unshaken. He nods his head.

"Then I have a job for you, Captain," says my father with power. The roses sway at the sound of His inflection as His tone intensifies.

Captain Leafe turns to The King. "Yes, my King," he replies.

"I need you to take Jenna and Lilly to their villas in the palace," He instructs. "Skye, you have a fitting for your wedding uniform and regalia," He tells me with His fatherly tone.

"Yes, Father," I agree. My stomach churns at the revelation it's my turn to get fitted for the wedding. It's all happening so fast. My excitement remains, nonetheless.

"Captain Leafe, I want you take this. Test drive it for me."

Vroom! Vroom!

A motorcycle engine amplifies. I turn my head as Zeal drives in on a 1940's Harley Davidson, in pristine condition I might add. No rust nor moths have taken to it.

"Don't tell me you stole it from Earth?" I ask Zeal as he hops off.

He grins and flaps his wings.

My father interjects. "I've been stowing this one away for ions," says my father. "It's a 1940's Liberator. Popular during earth's World War II. With My touch, its restored and ready for riding."

Zeal hands my father the keys and my father tosses the keys to Captain Leafe.

I puff my chest. "Wait a second. You're not going to let him put Lilly on that thing, are you?" I protest. I cannot remember the last time I took ground-transit anywhere, much less in my own space of Zion. I cannot possibly allow Leafe to transport her on that contraption.

"Trust Me, son," my father interrupts my thoughts.

Then, He gives me the *I-know-what-I-am-doing* look.

"If Lilly crashes, I'm blowing up the moon! I guarantee it!" My blue eyes flame with intensity as my heart rages from the idea of Lilly being on any kind of contraption with two wheels and a radiator.

The King walks towards me. "My eyes are on her. She will not fall," my father exclaims. "Remember we are in Zion, My son. She is safe here. Even if the wheels themselves were to upend into the atmosphere, I can halt gravity and catch her in a millisecond."

He's right. I know He's right. I just don't understand it. But I put my hands up and retire from contesting the decision.

My father turns around to face Captain Leafe who eyes the bike with fascination.

"You've met Lilly, haven't you Captain Leafe?" says The King.

I remember when I sent Captain Leafe to earth with a note for Lilly, to tell her of my affection. Who knew she would be here with me now in Zion's fortress. I have no desire to let her return to that place ever again. I want her to dwell with me in endless perfection forever.

"Yes, my King. Lilly is incredibly beautiful," Leafe affirms with honest eyes.

"Remember Lilly is the future queen of Zion. You are to guard her as such," commands The King.

"Understood, King Worthy." Captain Leafe nods his head.

My father steps closer to Leafe and speaks frankly. "Jenna has yet to give her heart to the light. Be patient with her," my father orders. "You are to pick up the two of them from Lilly's dress fitting and take them to the palace. Opal will take over from there."

Leafe hesitates. "My King, of all the missions, may I ask why you need me for this?"

"Is it your place to question The King's ways?" retorts my father.

"No, my King. Forgive me."

"Off you go!" sounds my father.

Captain Leafe jumps on the leather seat and grabs the handlebars.

Vroom! The engine starts. My wings perk up and I hover over to his side for one last reminder.

"I'm trusting you with the love of my life, Captain," I say and stare into his eyes sternly. "No funny business."

7

Lilly

"What is your favorite part about Zion?" Jenna asks, looking in the 4-dimensional mirrors.

She tosses her hair and squeezes her cheeks, then glosses her lips in bright red.

"Skye is my favorite," I reply with enchantment.

"Of course he is, my little rose." Jenna winks at me through the mirrors.

Honor flies in from the back room of the Bridal Hall. "Ladies, here it is! The final bouquet with white roses covered in diamonds and calla lilies to accent. What do you think?"

"Let me see!" Jenna shouts with enamored eyes.

Jenna studies the diamonds on the flowers with fascination and smells the blooms. "Diamonds truly are a girl's best friend," she exclaims impressed. "Superb arrangement, Honor!"

I cannot say I disagree.

The arrangement looks flawless and timeless. The diamonds give it a royal touch as do the calla lily accents. I love it. From the Throne Room of Zion to the gates of its entrance, I want these everywhere.

"Skye will love them," I say confidently.

I want him to love them. I want him to love everything about this wedding. His reaction to every choice of this wedding is all I can think about at the moment. It's hard to make any decision without him. I need him here with me to affirm every color and every hem of my dress, as if it were his own choosing. I want him to love every detail.

"He will love your choice, my dear. I promise you that." Honor says with smiling eyes of kindness.

"You look like a princess with that bouquet, my Rose of Sharon," says Jenna with her hand to her heart. She leans in to smell the fresh cut roses and cala lillies again, and her eyes close to inhale.

"Cali-fornia loveeeeeee!" rings Jenna's phone.

Her eyes open and she reaches for her phone with an eager smile. "Hello?" she answers. "You're never going to guess where I am, Hunter!" She steps away and walks towards the window looking out into celestial Zion.

"Is there cell service in Zion?" I ask Honor.

"There is everything in Zion," she replies with a wink. Honor continues arranging the flowers with slight adjustments as I hold them in my hands.

"I'm so proud of you! I told you could do it!" Jenna shouts from the windows, still on the phone.

"Does she have a boyfriend at home?" Honor asks, charmed by the intrusion.

"I'm not sure, to be honest. The last time I saw him Skye was liberating him. Literally."

"Sounds like it worked, my dear!" She smiles and lifts her hands with finality. "Now! That bouquet looks perfect. I will have this design saved and made fresh the day of the wedding." Honor bats her eyelashes with a look of achievement now that the bouquet is finished.

"Thank you, Honor," I say politely and let go of the bouquet.

Vroom!

An engine roars outside the window.

Jenna presses her eyes to the glass window and looks out.

"Are there motorcycles in Zion?" Jenna turns around and asks with an inquisitive face. Then she looks back out the window.

"There is everything in Zion," says Honor.

"Wow, would you look at the grease on that angel!" Jenna says loudly, forgetting her phone call conversation. "Yes, I'm still here Hunter!" She turns and walks to the corner, and then back to the window with lurking eyes.

"Looks like your friend has eyes for Captain Leafe," says Honor.

Knock! Knock!

An angel hovers in with towering wings covered in emerald gemstones on the edges.

"Hello Lilly," Captain Leafe walks in and introduces himself again. "I'm Captain Leafe."

"We have met," I say politely and turn around to fix my ponytail in the mirror across from me. I stare at the dress, still imagining the final design. I twirl and smile whimsically.

"Per The King's orders, I must take you and Jenna up to your villas at the palace so you can relax," Captain Leafe informs me. "Jenna will need to get settled and you must be exhausted, my lady," Leafe says and walks towards me. Then he pauses and eyes the dress like he is frozen in space.

"Where's Skye?" I ask.

Leafe doesn't move.

I clear my throat to get his attention.

Leafe looks up at me, with bronze glowing skin and green eyes. "You will see him soon, I assure you," says the captain, respectfully.

He keeps looking at me, like he did on Zion's mountains. I look away as the gaze infringes upon my comfortability. I only want Skye's eyes looking at me closely. His eyes are the eyes into my soul, and I cannot let another claim that place.

Skye, where are you, my love?

"He is getting his uniform fitted right now," Captain Leafe exclaims.

How did he know what I thought? Can he hear my thoughts too?

"Do you want me to take your measurements, angel hottie?" Jenna smirks with her sassy voice and walks up to Leafe seductively. "I didn't know angels drove motorcycles. Does that make you a dare devil?"

"Excuse me?" he inquires.

"A dare devil," she repeats herself with amusement.

"Dare devils do not exist in the bliss of Zion, only heavenly angels," Leafe says.

"I dare you to sing," she commands convincingly with her hands on her hips. "You know, like angels do."

Leafe coughs and clears his throat, and then looks away from Jenna and over to me. "Is she always this uncouth, my lady?"

"I'm afraid so," I confess.

Captain Leafe turns his eye back to Jenna and stands respectfully, albeit with feathers ruffled and a flush face. "What would you like to hear, Miss...?"

"Houston. Jenna Houston."

"Miss Houston," he confirms politely and bows his head. "What would like to me to sing?"

"Eye of The Tiger," she declares and smirks.

"Eye of The Tiger?"

"Yes."

"Is there a specific reason you want me to sing this particular song, Miss Houston?"

"You're going to need it when I get you on the back of that thing." She points outside to the motorcycle.

"Who says I'm on the back?" Captain Leafe retorts unamused.

"I do!" She snatches the keys from his hands and scurries out the door. "Let's go, Lilly! Off to see the royal palace!"

"Miss Houston! You don't know how to start the–"

Vroom! Vroom!

"Engine," Leafe says with a sigh.

"Sure, I do, cowboy!" she shouts triumphantly.

"Jenna's been riding since she was in diapers," I shout from the inside of the bridal hall, alerting them I can hear every word.

Leafe stands and observes with shock, as he studies the female anomaly called Jenna Houston. "Who knew a human could make me speechless," I hear him whisper.

Leafe picks up His feet, spreads his wings and hovers outside to assess Jenna by the motorcycle.

"Alright Jenna. Hand over the keys and I will ensure you and Lilly arrive safely at your villas."

"That's a deal I can't make, Captain," she says and revs up the engine. "Besides, off-roading is my specialty."

"And picking up lost objects is mine," he says clearly. "The King gave me direct orders to accompany you and the General's fiancé to your palace villas." He eyes her with a sharp glance.

"I can get there myself!" Jenna exclaims brazenly.

Leafe flies to Jenna's side and turns off the engine. "Miss Houston, I am not going to ask you again."

Jenna sighs and scrunches her hair. "What if you fly ahead of us and I ride the bike?" she argues, trying to convince him.

Leafe eyes her again, with emerald light intensifying.

"Okay, okay!" Jenna concedes and lifts her hands with feet planted on the ground, on either side of the bike, to keep it steady. "Jump on, Captain."

Leafe lifts her off the seat and sets her down farther back. Jenna's face flares red.

"The nerve of this angel!" she says to me as I walk through the doorway.

"I heard that," Leafe retorts. "Do you want to go back to the villa or not?"

Jenna sighs and gives in, resolving to follow his command.

I walk towards the motorcycle with a new lavender dress on, ready to go. I can tell Jenna is flustered. She does not like it when her control is overridden. Leafe will have to get used to that.

"You look beautiful, Lilly." Leafe keeps looking at me again.

I look away.

I hesitate before jumping on it. I've never ridden on a motorcycle before, but Zion keeps my fears at bay. I know The King wouldn't let me fall anyways. Too many angels are around for anything to go wrong. If The King sent Leafe, it must be his plan.

I step forward and prepare to sit behind Jenna.

"Lilly, I want you behind me." Captain Leafe reaches for my hand. I take it. His grip is strong. He picks me up with one heave and twirls me behind him. "Hold on tight."

I take a deep breath. Then, hesitantly, I wrap my hands around him and Jenna holds onto me.

"Lead the way, Captain!" Jenna exclaims.

Captain Leafe presses his foot to the pedal. Off we go!

⌒

The golden road winds through Zion effortlessly as Leafe drives us. Wind blows in my face as we speed through the sights of Zion. Technicolor lights beam all around, reflecting from the gold speckles in the air.

Vroom! Leafe speeds up and jumps the bike into the air as the pathway inclines. He lands and curves around the golden road by the meadows where the River of Life meanders.

"You okay, Lilly?" he asks.

"Yes!" I shout back through the wind.

I'm used to whimsical travels at this point. Everywhere Skye takes me, he defies gravity, bends time, and flies through dimensions of earth and space that humans could not ordinarily pass through. Here in Zion, I know I am safe. Besides, I have so many places still yet to see, and I want to see it all. Soon, I know Skye will take me. If only he were here right now with me.

Whoosh!

We lift off the ground again as Captain Leafe leads us over the River of Life.

"Whoooo!" Jenna yells as we fly. "This bike's got some torque!"

"Purest water in the universe resides in this river!" Captain Leafe echoes in the wind.

"Simply divine," I say as I look at the sparkling waters of turquoise.

"Up ahead is the palace!" Captain Leafe enlightens. "Almost there."

Leafe drives strong and steady. I am surprised Skye didn't show up. I expected him to meet us in the air but The King's orders were for Leafe to take us to the palace. I don't want to stand in the way of that. If He said it, then I have to know that is exactly what is supposed to happen. The King has never given me a reason to doubt His love and divine intervention. It is because of Him and His divine orchestrations that I have Skye in my life. He always knows how to give what we could never think to ask for.

The palace comes into focus as we drive forward.

I hold onto Leafe as Jenna holds onto me. We zoom around Tree of Life and into the city of Zion where pearl and ivory shines on the outer walls. Angelic voices and lilac linger in the air. Henna clusters scatter the grass surrounding the palace as we near the entrance. I breathe peacefully. We're here.

Leafe stops. Turns off the engine. I step off the bike and ruffle my dress, breathing in the sweet aroma of Zion's gardens. Angels move in close to us and smile captivated by the presence of another human.

"Lilly, are they going to touch me?" Jenna whispers and stands still as if a bumble bee is getting too close and she does not want to make a move. Not making a move is a rarity for Jenna. But ever since she first met Skye on the balcony of Waikiki, she has been terrified of angels and their regal ferocity.

"They are here to welcome you," Captain Leafe says. Then he rests his arm on her shoulder. "Don't be afraid," he says respectfully.

"I'm not afraid," Jenna whispers with a loud whisper and shews away his hand. "I'm just–"

"In over your head?" Leafe replies.

Jenna looks away and a restlessness starts to set in. She does not like it when she is out of control and she knows it.

"You have nothing to fear with us, Miss Houston."

Captain Leafe is patient with her. I'm in shock of his persistence.

Jenna clears her throat. "Can you please take me to my villa?" she asks abruptly. "I need to freshen up and wash my hair."

"Would you like me to pour some sugar on you?" Leafe stares at her plainly.

"Excuse me?" she asks with a look of bewilderment.

"Bath sugar. I can have it rain down on you if you'd like. It's no trouble at all."

"You think you're getting into the bath with me!? What kind of angel are you?"

"You said earlier you wanted some sugar."

"I know what I said," Jenna sasses back. "It's a song, Captain. I like to play music." She smiles at him and begins humming the tune.

"Yes, Miss Houston."

Jenna stops and looks at him, curiously.

"So, what kind of bath sugar is it anyway?" she says, now intrigued.

"Every flavor under the sun," Leafe says politely.

"It's okay, Jenna," I assure her. "He is just trying to help. He has no wrong intent." At least I hope not.

"Vanilla bean, please," she says firmly. "If… it's not too much trouble," she clarifies.

"Out of all the flavors under the sun, you want vanilla bean?" Captain Leafe inquires.

"Yes, that's right," she retorts and plays with her hair.

"Yes, Miss Houston," Leafe replies politely.

"Alright, it's up to our villas!" Jenna throws up her hands. "Lilly, are you ready my little rose?"

"I can feel you close to me, Lilly."

Skye!

His voice echoes in the fragrant air like poetry in the wind. I look around and find angels soaring through Zion with tranquility. But no Skye. Where are you?

"You look stunningly beautiful in lavender, my love." He sees me. Wherever he is, he is closer than I think.

"Where are you, my blue angel?" I say through telekinesis.

"Your bags are in your room," Captain Leafe says with a strong voice. "Opal will accompany you there. If you need anything at all, just send for me."

Jenna's theatrics did not dishearten him, it seems. That is the great difference between angels and humans, I am coming to realize. Angels possess the innate resilience to withstand human complexity.

"What's the code?" Jenna flashes him a wink.

"Prayer, my dear," says an angel with opal studded wings and beige skin. She reclines her wings and lands beside us. "My name is Opal."

Jenna turns around to greet her and her eyes enlarge.

"Oh, my goodness! You look like a goddess!" exclaims Jenna happily.

Jenna covers her mouth in shock and smiles at me with her eyes. Then she looks at Opal again. The first time Jenna ever saw Skye, she screamed at the top of her lungs and ran away. She had never seen an angel before. Of course, she warmed up to him when Skye proposed to me. By then, she knew he was safe, and would be a part of my life forever. Her reception of Opal is quite different. No fear or screaming this time. She is entranced by her light.

"Can I touch your wings?" Jenna asks.

"Yes, my dear," Opal obliges with a voice of serenity.

"Divinely beautiful," Jenna exclaims stunned. "Of course, Leafe's wings are stunning too, but I usually wait until the second meeting before I touch a guy's wings."

"I am an angel, Miss Houston." Leafe corrects her.

"Right. Angel."

Opal ignores Jenna's inference and smiles. "You're too kind, my dear. Let me show you up to the palace villas."

Jenna nods without the need to question her. "Thank you," she says, at ease.

Meanwhile, I walk across the road to the garden where I can see a glimpse of the Tree of Life reaching for the light.

"Skye," I whisper into Zion's aura.

The breeze caresses my face like angel wings caress the wind. Here the fragrance of fresh oak and peonies fill my senses like a garden blossoming in Heaven.

Gardens always bloom in Zion. There is no fear of winter to frost the blooms. No fear of harsh heat to dry up the sprouts. The temperature is perfect, and the light is constant. Angels soar to and fro without worry of war. And when there is war, my angel defeats the darkness. He sends every light to light my path.

"He will be back soon, Miss Rose."

A strong breeze flutters through my hair.

I turn around and find Captain Leafe looking back at me.

His green eyes glisten. White wings tower high and his stature looms above me. I don't quite know what to make of him yet. Today he kept staring at me as if there was more to the observation, and I don't want to flatter it. I look away and imagine Skye's eyes looking back at me, the only eyes I want.

"You don't have to always call me Miss Rose," I reply.

"I am an angel of decorum, Miss Rose."

He steps closer to me and touches my waist.

"Leafe, what are you doing?"

I sigh and step back.

Then, he steps forward again and touches my waist again.

"Your ribbon, Miss Rose."

I look down at the lavender ribbon. It must have come undone on the motorcycle ride. I didn't notice it, but now I notice the tension rising in the air and the swift movement of his hands. I don't like it. His wings are tall, and I cannot see Jenna and Opal behind me.

Jenna! Do you see?

"That's enough, Captain." I try to step back but his hands keep tying.

"There," he says. "The loose ends are all tied." He gazes at me intently.

"I am engaged, Captain Leafe. Do you really think you can touch me like that?"

Leafe steps back. "Forgive me, Miss Rose."

"Don't touch me ever again!"

I push by him and make haste for the entrance where Opal and Jenna stand.

"Lilly!" Jenna follows me urgently.

Tears flood my cheeks as I run through the golden halls of the palace. I feel violated and invaded in the place I should always feel safe. I look to my right and left. Which way is my room? I don't know. Opal was supposed to show us, but I was tied up with Leafe. Or rather, he was tied up with me. I know it was only a bow, but his hands got too close. He should have never touched me like that. Skye isn't going to like it.

"What did he do?" Jenna exclaims, worried.

"He…" I hesitate. "He tried to come on to me. He touched my waist and got too close. Closer than he should have. He sees the ring on my finger. He's Skye's best friend! I don't get what he was thinking," I wipe my nose as tears drip.

"Even angels can cross the line. I read it once," says Jenna.

"I don't want to be near him anymore."

Blast!

I look up and see Skye, my angel, landing on the turquoise engraved floors of the palace. His wings are open wide, hailing bright light as he descends. He caresses my face softly. I grab his hand on my cheek and look into his eyes.

"There you are, my blue angel," I whisper.

"What did he do, Lilly?" Skye's voice tremors like an angel with a vengeance.

Blue eyes flame with sapphire fire.

I look down. If Skye knows what happened, I fear Captain Leafe won't escape the wrath of his fury. Skye lifts my face.

Blue eyes find me in the palace.

"What happened, Lilly?" He whispers tenderly.

With his blue eyes on me, I give in. "He touched me," I say clearly. "I ran away!"

Skye rages with sapphire fire in his eyes, like he is preparing for war. I've seen that look.

"Leafe!" He shouts. He looks out beyond the palace gate, searching for Leafe. His wings rise, ready to soar away and find the one whose audacity brought him too close to his friend's fiancé.

"Don't kill him," I plead.

"I don't know if I can do that, Lilly."

"Please! Don't kill him."

8

Skye

"**Y**ou crossed the line, Leafe!"

Water gushes between my feet as I stand across from Captain Leafe, overlooking the cliff's edge. I figured I would find him here. The waterfalls are his oasis.

I stare at his emerald wings shining brightly like my father made them to. Light is supposed to be his mantra. An ever-present motivation for everything he does in the universe. He should have known better. Lilly is not an object to be played with nor a flower he can explore. She is off limits to every angel but me.

Confronting him now is the last thing I should have to address. He should be my right-hand angel. My confidant. But it seems Lilly's beauty is too much for him to withstand.

"Maybe you should keep your eyes on your girl," he says boldly.

"You forget whose kingdom you fly in, Captain!" My wings rise and I soar closer to him on the waterfalls' edge. He looks back at me with a solemn face, reluctant to divulge his intentions. "Last time I checked, you were under my Command!"

Leafe's eyes flare with emerald, green flames.

"Then why did you leave her!?" he asks concerned.

"Leave her? What precisely are you talking about!?" I shout with agitation.

"You brought Jenna here to be with Lilly because, deep down, you wonder if you are enough for her." Leafe spreads his wings. "Isn't that right, General!?"

Leafe jumps, soars towards me, and halts in front of my face.

Breathe in, Skye. Don't let him rattle you. You are the General of Zion's armies. You need not answer to anyone but The King.

"Leafe," I reply clearly. "You speak what you do not know. Lilly and I are fine."

Leafe shakes his head and eyes me. "You fear she will get tired of you."

"I command you to be silent!" Burning fire steams in my eyes, as sapphire light rouses from the accusation. What gives him such a notion? He has never given me a reason to doubt his loyalty, but it seems that all it takes to divide friends is the presence of a lovely flower. "Who are you to assess my relationship with my fiancé? I spend every waking moment with her and want nothing else but to be with her everywhere I go! I don't want her to ever leave my side!"

The truth comes out.

Did I just say that?

It is the truth.

Here at the waterfalls' edge, my love for Lilly's constant presence echoes in the surging water rolling over the cliff like a torpedo. Leafe pauses. Says nothing.

A sigh of relief overwhelms me at my own recognition of my need for her.

I don't like leaving Lilly even for a second. All I want is to keep her close to me. I never needed my own space from her at the dress fitting. I never needed alone time without her at The Rose Garden. I tell myself she needs her space. But when I hear her thoughts, I know it's true that she wants me present with her at all times too. She needs me and I need her like the sun needs the earth to shine on. I need her presence like the ocean tide needs the moon to dance under the starlight.

My eyes look about the waterfalls as I breathe in deeply of the revelation. Turquoise gems shine in the water rolling over the falls. Shimmering perfection resides here at the edge of danger's fall.

Father, Your creation is beautiful. So are Your ways.

I gazed at the phenomenon for so long, I almost forgot Leafe was standing there.

"General." Leafe begins to speak.

I look back at him hovering across from me. "Yes, Captain?"

Leafe pauses, as if he were looking for the right words to say. His eyes shift over the waterfalls into the sky above where wars are fought. The War of The Raven, The Second War of The Raven, The Battle of the Hinlors. In all ages past and present, Zion has been triumphant. We always will be. For there is not a greater force in all the universe than the light of Zion's glory.

Leafe looks back at me with green eyes glowing.

"If you love her, why don't you let her fight in battle?"

Take her into battle? My wings flare at the insolence. What an absurd proposition!

I open my mouth to respond but I pause to keep myself from tearing him apart. How can I put her at risk like that when there are zero reasons necessary to include her in that mess of venom and poisonous talons? She is my delicate flower of beauty! I will not let her be touched! I will not let her be violated! I will not allow anyone to have my future queen but me. Not my enemy and surely not my ally, which brings me to my original purpose for confronting Leafe in the first place.

I hover closer and land on the waterfall's edge. Splashes of teal water shoot up from the landing.

"Because Lilly is the future Queen of Zion! That's why!"

Jolt!

Leafe's hands thrust into my chest.

I fall backward over the edge. Mist barrels into my face from the surging falls. Leafe looks down at me from the top of the waterfall and soars downward. I spread my wings in the free-fall and soar up to meet him in the air.

Blast!

I send rays of sapphire light into his eyes. He grabs my shoulders and detonates his eyes of green light into mine. We spiral in the air and through the waterfall with light reflecting.

I don't understand Leafe's incessant hostility. Ever since Lilly got here, his eyes were on her, and I should have known this could flare up. But how can you anticipate your best angel hitting on your fiancé?

"What's gotten into you, Leafe!?" I yell, as our wings clash over the waterfalls' pools.

"You should have protected her!"

"Protected her!? I saved her!"

"You took her future from her! College, dreams, goals... she gave it all up for you to be with you in Zion! Now you're keeping her on the sidelines while we fight battles," he shouts with zealous eyes. "She deserves more!"

Blast!

Leafe's head barrels into my chest. I reach for his wings and spin him around. He flies towards me again with eyes of ferocity I have not seen on this side of Zion.

"Zion *is* more! What more could anyone want but to be in Zion, the highest bliss in the universe!?" I exclaim.

"She needs a reason to exist!"

"I *am* her reason to exist!"

Flash!

My blue light detonates into his eyes.

Leafe's eyes soften and he lets go of my shoulders. He hovers back, slightly, from his proximity to me and looks at me in the air as we hover here next to the waterfall flowing down, 30 feet above the pools.

"I have no doubt, General." He looks down and then up again. Meanwhile, the waterfalls roll on just as powerfully as it did before my right-hand angel decided to push me off it. "I just want her to be happy," he says diplomatically. "I see the way she looks at you. The way she pines for you when you're gone."

"You see it?"

"Yes," he says firmly. "I saw it the day I met her on earth when you sent me to give her the note. She walked around the lobby looking for you with the purest love in her eyes. I saw it again today on Zion's Mountain, the way she smiles when you are beside her," he says and wipes his brow.

"I'm always thinking about her," I confess, smiling at the reality of love.

Leafe takes a deep breath. "It's excruciating, General, because I can't stop thinking about her too."

My heart skips a beat. There it is. The truth.

Captain Leafe is in love with Lilly.

I should have seen it. I shouldn't have brushed it off when Leafe looked at her on Zion's mountains. Lilly saw it. I read her mind when she noticed him staring at her. I did not want to believe that another angel would encroach upon us, but what did I expect? For no one else to ever notice the beauty I, too, discovered in Lilly? I am smarter than that.

I admit I have not been in touch with my perceptions of others' interest in her. I guess I did not want to have to face the dilemma it would cause. I wanted to believe our love is immortal. Guarded forever from the intrusion of anyone else, angels included.

Now is not the time to punish him for loving Lilly. I have to handle this the way my father would want me to, gracefully.

I breathe in deeply and exhale. "I understand, Captain." I lean in.

He tilts his head and stares at me perplexed.

"You do?"

"I, too, am an angel in love with Lilly. Remember?"

Leafe nods and ponders silently, as the weight of his vulnerability is exposed.

The truth does that. It sinks in once it is said. Then the question remains, how will we be received when we speak the truth? I need Captain Leafe to know he can trust me if he will.

"What you're feeling is normal, Captain. And I don't punish you for that. But you're going to have to find a way to let go of loving her."

"I know," he says.

"You're smart, Leafe. It's why I picked you as my right-hand angel."

Leafe appears unemotional at the moment, as if releasing all his feelings emptied the tank. I think it is his way of handling what he cannot control. He suppresses what he feels, even after the release has given way to vulnerability.

"Then you'll listen to me when I give you advice?"

"Depends on the advice," I reply.

He narrows his eyes on me, like he does when he is giving me strategy. "Take Lilly with you to battle. Queens can fight too."

Whoosh!

"General Worthy!" Purity soars up to my shoulder. Glitter trails her wings as usual, although it is anything but ordinary. The Holy Spirit rests in her. Therefore, light always illuminates her.

Captain Leafe shifts his gaze onto the dove called Purity who hovers over my right shoulder.

"What is it, Purity?"

"A hinlor at the palace!"

"A hinlor? I thought we exterminated them at the north gate?" exclaims Captain Leafe with concern.

I flame my eyes with sapphire light. My wings stand ready to attack and dismantle. I look over at Captain Leafe as Purity waits.

"We destroyed them there. We will destroy them here. Nothing invades the palace with the intent to assail Zion!" I assert with assurance.

A trail of glitter looms in my vision. Purity flies in circular motions and makes an infinity loop. She does that when evil retreats and goodness wins. She pauses as the glitter trail sparkles, and shines her bright, golden eyes proudly.

"It's already dead, General," she says.

"Dead?" I ask. I halt in motion.

"Yes," she says peacefully.

"Who found it?" I inquire. "Hinlors are tricky creatures, knowing for hiding in the shadows of the universe where the light escapes and darkness lingers. Once they infiltrate a space, they have no intent to surface until the object of attack is in sight."

Oh no… object of attack. There could be only one object in the palace a hinlors would seek to attack. Lilly!

"Lilly did," says Purity. "Miss Rose knows a thing or two about eradicating darkness. It disintegrated on the spot!" Purity swirls around the infinity loop, with sparkling light and triumph at the announcement.

Captain Leafe smiles, covers his mouth, and then puts his hand down again, with an I-told-you-so look in his eye. *"Queens can fight too,"* he said. It's not that I doubted it. I just never wanted to make my Lilly flower susceptible to the darkness of the universe.

"Zion will fly peacefully now with no lapse in the hallelujah chorus," says Leafe with a grin of satisfaction.

My lovely Lilly defeated the hinlors. My heart skips a beat as the reality of her power resonates within me.

Purity answers Leafe. But it all goes mute.

I cannot hear a thing as I hover here over Zion's waterfalls.

All I can ponder is the reality of my Lilly flower's power rising like the eagle. I had no intent to put her in harm's way. Zion exists in pure goodness for a reason, just as my father breathed it into being. Yet, ever since The Raven's rebellion, angels have fallen from The King's grace and evil spirits brood in the universe. I wanted to protect her. But maybe she can protect herself more than I thought.

I break my silence. "Zion is still susceptible to attack, until New Zion is birthed," I exclaim. I breathe in and out. Purity knows this, and yet I find the moment right for reminding everyone, especially Captain Leafe. "Hinlors may invade, but only if The King allows it."

I contemplate the reason why my father would allow such an intrusion. Then it hits me. My father knew it would happen. He knew the hinlors would find Lilly. Who else would it go after in the shadows of the palace villa away from the Throne of my father?

They crave her but they won't have her. I will make sure of that. They will not put one grimy wing on my lovely Lilly flower before I can decimate the fleet of their species into extinction.

"General, your father rules the universe," Purity reminds me. "He would not let anything invade if he knew it would hurt Lilly."

I agree.

Breathe in, Skye.

Your Father knows what He is doing. Just as He knew how to flavor with waterfalls with endless decadence and saturate its floors with silver beads of crystal and turquoise. I tell myself everything happens for a reason. Everything funnels through the hands of The King, and nothing passes through Zion without His consent.

Still, it rattles me that Lilly had to look evil in the face and defy it at the same time. Did she feel fear and dread? Or bravery and courage? I don't want her to feel anything that might take away the innocence of her pure light.

I scan the waterfalls' pools. Turquoise water falls from the edge into the deep pools every millisecond and counting. It never runs out of water to supply its minerality. Surely, Lilly will never run out of light to supply her heart with goodness even in moments of war amidst a war-torn cosmic universe. My confidence in her capabilities increases at the revelation.

"Captain Leafe, I need you to survey the lands of Zion for any traces of hinlor activity or other egregious sprits. I must go to Lilly now. She will want to tell me what she saw. What she knows," I say.

"Yes, General," he responds willingly.

"Purity, what about Jenna?" I ask.

"Jenna is in a mess, I'm afraid. Unnerved and 'freaked out' as it were. Her words, General, not mine."

"Freaked out?" I ask.

"Yes."

"So, the girl who likes Def Leppard is freaked out by hinlor activity?" Captain Leafe asks with a grin.

"I think she does want the light," I say. "Humans who like the dark wouldn't be freaked out by it. They get acquainted with it."

Purity flutters with golden glitter, making another eternity loop. "There was no getting acquainted with the hinlor, for Jenna, I assure you," she declares. "Only screaming and swatting it away with one of those pointy-edged high heels."

"Never judge a shoe by its sole," I respond, amused.

"I'm just glad those high heels came in handy for something," Leafe exclaims. "Maybe you should get Lilly a pair."

"I prefer her barefoot, actually." Her quintessential feet are perfect for dancing on the waves. My goal is to dance with her for the rest of my eternal life.

"Ready your wings, angels! Infinity beckons us!" Purity circles around us in an infinity loop as she prepares to fly onward. "Remember eternity is at hand! Armageddon is soon to come."

Purity constantly thinks of New Zion. Infinity lingers in her every thought, impacting everything she does, both here and on the earth. Her spirit is an extension of my father's. An enigma of kindness permeating a world where darkness abounds. She sends the light to woo souls to The King. To Zion. To the light. Even now, I can feel her spirit invoking something greater.

"New Zion is closer than we think," she prophesies. "The darkness is weaker than we think. Don't fear what is to come. Welcome it. Then new birthing will come." Purity swivels in a spiral, leaving a trail of golden glitter in her trail. Then, she ascends the waterfalls and flies away.

"She's right, Captain. The King will order the Battle of Armageddon in time, and we must be ready," I assert strongly.

My wings remain ready for the battle to begin. Still, all I can think about is how this will affect Lilly. But I am starting to see she can handle it far better than I expected.

I knew Lilly was more than special the day I found her. Deep in the ocean of Waimea Bay, The King drew me to a heart of gold. Rose gold. My Lilly Rose. She was chosen for me and I won't forget it, even as the last strike chimes on the clock of earth's timeline. She was made for this, and I was meant to be hers forever.

Gong! Gong!

Organ notes resound from the Throne Room.

We can hear it all the way up to the waterfalls when the music plays in Zion. Sometimes I linger up top, at the waterfall's edge, to bask in the melody. It's peaceful there. But isn't all of Zion peaceful? I think of the wars we have fought since the rebellion of The Raven. He divided our ranks of angels into those who are loyal and those who are not. His evil heart stirred an uprising. Then we saw who was loyal to the light.

I know it was meant to unfold this way, because my father is dividing darkness from light, but the reality of The Raven's betrayal still stings.

"Skye!" My father's voice echoes. His Spirit resonates in mine anywhere I am, so we are in constant communication at any moment. "I need to see you in Throne Room."

"Yes, Father," I say.

My wings spread and prepare for its descent from the waterfalls.

I look over at Leafe to tie up the loose ends of our initial conversation before I go. Lilly will no longer be the subject of his gaze. He needs to know that.

"Captain Leafe, I hope to never have this talk with you again regarding Lilly," I state firmly. "Hands off. Do I make myself clear?"

"Yes, General," he concedes.

I nod and soar away.

He needs to understand Lilly belongs to me. I cannot have this repetitive dilemma hovering over us in the goodness of Zion. She isn't going anywhere. Neither is he, as far I can tell. The burden rests heavy on my shoulders as my wings stretch over the expanse of Zion.

More angels probably have their eyes on Lilly. Captain Leafe may not be the only one who has feelings for her. There may be others who have fallen or will fall in love with her. I should not be surprised if there are. Am I ready for that?

Remember who you are, Skye. The Commander of Zion's Angels is always ready.

I flap my wings harder to soar over the hills and over the rivers. The River of Life flows steadily onward below me, like the faithfulness of the sun to rise for the earth. Somewhere in between my ponderings and the meandering of the water, I resolve to say yes, I am ready. I love Lilly and I won't let anything tear us apart.

"Blow the trumpet in Zion; sound the alarm on my holy hill. Let all who live in the land tremble, for the day of the Lord is coming. It is close at hand," sounds an angel stationed at The Tree of Life reading Joel 2:1, a scripture of prophetic utterance. Angels echo the reality of what is to come, at all times, until New Zion is birthed. Angels circle the area around the tree with fidelity because they want to. They live to honor the virtues of our home and prophetic destiny.

"General Worthy!" Angel wings whiz by me. A bronze, glowing angel circles back to join me in flight over the Tree of Life towards the Throne Room. "I met your stunning bride, Lilly. Remarkably beautiful, she is."

"Thank you, Captain Strength," I reply. "Her aura fits in perfectly with Zion, doesn't it?"

"Yes, General," he answers with enchantment in his voice. "Perfect indeed."

"Don't get any ideas, now," I retort. Just as I feared, more angels want Lilly's beauty.

Captain Strength looks over at me in flight. I can tell what he is thinking, and it involves crossing lines akin to Leafe's audacity. By the story line playing out in his mind, it seems there is much more than waist-touching he seeks to explore with her. Clear it out of your mind, Strength. Your angelic powers give you the off switch.

"Forgive me, General," he clears his throat. "I recall you can see through every mind."

"Never forget it, Captain."

"I probably have much to confess if that is the case."

"I am not here to condemn you, Captain. I may see through you, but I also know what my father instilled in you, and that is virtue. Still, I am wise enough to know angels are susceptible to human beauty."

"Then you know I'm not the only angel who has eyes for Lilly."

"But you did not touch her," I declare with insight.

I can tell that much is true.

"How do you know?" he asks.

"I always know," I reply. "If you had touched her, you would not be soaring up to me en route to the Throne Room, comfortably."

Captain Strength was given the virtue of trust, as all angels receive, from my father, but each angel must still decide how they devote themselves to The King. He has always shown me where his loyalty lies, and that is with Zion. But I will have to be cautious with him going forward and keep my eyes on him.

"You're right, General. I have no intention of violating your relationship with Lilly."

"You need to remember something, Captain Strength. You are an angel of Zion's light. You were created to behold beauty and appreciate beauty. I am not angry at that. It would be unreasonable to expect every angel to ignore Lilly's beauty. I am angry at those who would act upon their admiration of Lilly and try to interfere with my place as her fiancé."

"It's Leafe, isn't it?"

"Yes."

"I could hear the scuffle by the waterfalls."

"Captain Leafe made a move on her and it upset her."

"Better than her giving into it."

I sigh at the revelation of what he is getting at. I should be thankful Lilly did not hide it from me nor play it off as a trivial matter. But it bothers me that other angels want her and I'm afraid they always will.

"Skye, if I may be so bold," he states. "From my first time I met Lilly, and from what I have observed from how she interacts with the other angels, she gave me no indication she was interested in anyone else's love but yours."

"How many?" I ask sternly, as my wings descend in front of the Throne Room by the ivory pillars. Other angels have seen her, he says, and if that is true, then I know there will be others who feel attracted to her. He glides in tandem with me and we land on Zion's ground by the tulips.

"Pardon?" he replies.

"How many others have eyes for Lilly?"

He breathes in and out. "As many have seen her, my General," he says. "I saw the way Zeal looked at her when he gave The King an update on the North Gate just before I found you. Lilly was there waiting to see Him. She had just killed a hinlor, I heard."

"She went to see my father?"

"Skye!" Lilly shouts as she runs through the ivory pillars.

Lilly's lavender dress matches the tulips. She runs towards me with slippers fit for the most elegant of ballet dancers. Delicate and perfect, her green eyes beam at me. "Guess what! The King gave me this!" Lilly holds up a key with delight.

"My father is full of surprises, isn't He?" I twirl her around as the glimmers of Zion shine on us from above.

"He says it unlocks something very special," she concurs excitedly.

I pick her up. Uncontrollable laughter lets loose as I smile at my bride. "I heard you defeated a hinlor also, my beautiful warrior."

"It flew towards me and I struck it hard, General!" she says. I like it when she calls me General, especially with her spunky excitement on the current topic of hinlor warfare.

"Where is Jenna?" I ask.

"Honor took her to relax, after the incident, with a massage and some angelic beauty treatments. She is okay. They asked me to join but I told her I needed to see The King," she leans against my chest and looks into my eyes with giddy excitement.

"Blue eyes find me in the palace," she thinks.

I whisper gently, "I love you my sweet Lilly."

Boom!

Footsteps shake the golden grounds and tall Japanese cherry blossom trees sway next to the tulips. My father appears.

"I have a gift for you, My son!" My father's voice booms as He steps through the ivory pillars from the Throne Room.

Captain Strength kneels in His presence by the tulips with wings glowing in reverence.

"You may rise, Captain," my father commands.

Captain Strength stands honorably at the permission granted.

"Father, You have already been so generous," I reply humbly.

"It's My pleasure to be generous, My son. Everything I have is yours." He smiles at me tenderly. Then He kneels down to look at me and Lilly, eye level, with blue eyes. "The key Lilly holds unlocks the doors to your new palace in Zion."

"He said it has its own waterfall and it tastes like any flavor I wish for!" Lilly's eyes tell me she can't wait to see it. Her happiness is my happiness.

"I can already foresee many pomegranate waterfalls, my love." Pomegranate is her favorite flavor. Since my love for her sends me to the stars and back, my only wish is for her to have exactly what she wants and more. I love to make her beam with elation like I am the only one who makes her feel that way.

"You are my favorite taste of pomegranate, my blue angel," she tells me passionately.

"You are my favorite floral flavor, my Lilly flower."

Ring! Ring!

Zion sounds an alarm.

Angels circle up ahead to gather.

"Hinlors are invading!" Purity flies in.

"Where?" I ask urgently and rise to stand. Lilly grasps my hand, and I look at my father. He will know. He knows everything.

"Brachian Galaxy," my father answers. "Bring The Luminary, Purity."

She flies into the Throne Room and returns with The Luminary in her wings. She sets it down for viewing.

"I see hinlor activity flocking towards Earth," Purity says. "But they are no match for us. Hinlors may be many, but they are weak. One detonation of light, and they are done for."

My wings flare at the threat. It may be a small one, but it's still a threat, nonetheless. Lilly's family still resides on earth, along with trillions of souls, whom The King loves.

"I must go," I say and prepare my wings for takeoff. "Captain Strength, ready the armies for formation at The Eagle's Pad!" I command.

"Yes, General," says Captain Strength. He prepares to fly away, and then pauses at my father's hand holding him back.

"Wait!" The King exclaims.

I halt in motion and look at The King, confused. Why does He want me to wait?

"I don't want you to go, Skye."

"But, Father, there are lives in danger!"

"I said I don't want you to go!" He declares again.

"Who will you send?" Purity asks.

My father's voice rises. "I want Leafe to take this battle."

"Father, Captain Leafe is not fit to lead! He touched Lilly!"

My father's eyes intensify. "I am aware of the goings-on of my Kingdom, Am I not, General?"

"Yes, my King."

"I want Captain Leafe to go. You stay with Lilly. You may be the commanding General of Zion's armies but you don't need to fight a battle such as this when your bride is here. Leafe knows what to do."

I don't disagree with Him. I just did not want to make a case for my absence from a battle I am called to lead when I am Commander. I am glad to lead and war for Zion.

"There will be other battles, My son," Father whispers to me. Then, He rises and calls to Purity. "Send for Captain Leafe at once!"

"Yes, King Worthy!" Purity answers and soars away.

"Skye," He commands. "Show Lilly your new house. Zion's lights await you."

I nod. There is no fighting with Him on this one. Once my father has made up His mind, it's unchangeable.

Captain Leafe soars into the Throne Room and stands at attention. "At your service, King Worthy." He eyes me plainly and looks back at my father, unscathed, as if our pow-wow meant little. Let's just hope my angels will be in good wings with him at the helm.

"I need you to command Zion's Angels in Skye's place," my father instructs. "I trust you can manage?"

"Absolutely, my King," Leafe answers confidently.

"Good," King Worthy answers. "Prepare for take-off!"

"Yes, sir!" Leafe nods and eyes me again before soaring away. He pauses. And eyes me up and down, with a stern face. "You know I can't control Lilly any more than you can," he whispers in my ear. "I will have her. Mark my words."

9

Leafe

"Protect your head, Captain Strength!" I alert as I lead Zion's angels.

Asteroids fly through cosmic airspace as we fly in formation. A large meteor appears and whizzes by my left side, where Captain Strength flies. He swerves and misses the collision.

"All clear!" he affirms.

"Welcome to the Brachian Galaxy," I reply, wide awake.

"It's not war until a piece of galactic-rock zooms by my face," he chimes in with a grin.

Out here in the cosmos of wide-open thrills, we fly keenly aware of our surroundings. Angels were made for the layout of King Worthy's universe. Danger exists, but we know our mission is to keep humans safe. So, we fly no matter the conditions. King Worthy sent me to command Zion's Angels in this battle. So far, they have proven their resilience and stamina soaring in hinlor territory. As always, I am confident we will return to Zion victorious.

Right now, Lilly keeps my mind set on her, even out here in the freedom of endless space. When I touched her, I could tell there was something in her eyes curious about me. The material of her dress felt like butter in my hands. Her waist, like Heaven. If only I could feel her body on mine.

"Captain!" Strength shouts at me. "Hinlors! 50 light-kilometers away!"

I look ahead and see their red-eyes and foreboding wings waiting in the distance.

"Prepare for light radiation!" I command from the front for all angels to hear.

Zion's Angels follow my lead and ready their eyes for light detonation.

Up ahead, the hinlors wait. Frozen in space. Unguarded.

I often wonder if the hinlors think they will actually win against our angels as we soar at them head-on. They do this every time we battle. They wait to attack without any protection or defense, not realizing our light has power to obliterate them instantaneously. But evil forces, such as hinlors, often reveal their naivety, especially in war. They lack tact. They lack strategy.

Good always prevails because good always has the best strategy.

That is why we win every time.

We fly with torque, unlike the hinlors. When hinlors fight in battle, they have proven a habit of lurking apathetically as if to make their prey come to them first. Big mistake. Our force is too strong for their patient defense. They disintegrate every time. Not to mention, we see them ahead. We amp up our speed just before releasing detonation. They don't have time to readjust once we approach them and detonate.

"360 swivels after radiation! Detonate until completed!" I command. This will ensure every angle of their location is covered with light radiation. No spot will be missed.

The only one I miss right now is Lilly. How I wish she was with me to fight in battle.

I prepare to detonate.

"1-2-3! Execute!" I command.

Blast!

Flash!

Zion's Angels blast light radiation, and hinlors fall by the millisecond. Ashy substance begins to gather in the galactic air, hovering like floating black confetti. Light circles around the host of hinlors and encloses them like a fence. More light radiations flash. Hinlors disintegrate. They lack the time to beg for mercy, but even if they had the opportunity, now is not the time for King Worthy to grant them that. He would have told us if any hinlors were on the brink of turning back to Him. Pure evil is eradicated, as usual, in order to sustain the goodness of the universe.

Lilly's kind would sustain the goodness of the universe, I have no doubt. I wonder what her parents are like. The ones who bore her. Had I the chance to meet them, I'd thank them for creating a queen.

"All hail Zion! Long live The King!" The angels chant in unison as they watch the impending victory.

More light detonates and more hinlors falls. I circle around the battle-air looking for straggling hinlors left to destroy.

King Worthy did not make us to be killers, but threats to safety require our skills for demolition. Hinlors should know better than to attack Zion.

Swoop!

My shoulder jolts backward.

Blood pours, then floats in the non-gravitational atmosphere of space. I check my surroundings.

"You've been hit!" Forte, the right flank flyer with red hair and silver eyes, zooms to my right and scans my condition.

"Nothing concerning!" I assure her and press my wings. Eternal wings, I remember. Nothing kills me. Zion's Angels are invincible. Infinite. We live forever.

Forte nods and a host of angels surround me quickly. We were trained to quickly heal from King Worthy's design. In no time, my feathers will reform at the incision. I flap my wings and regain strength.

My only worry is where the attack came from. There are no signs of hinlors. Only angels. Surely, an angel hasn't turned on me. I turn and look about. Who would have done it?

I compose myself. "Align in formation!" I command.

Forte joins my right and Captain Strength my left, as I lead the front. Angels form quickly, in perfect succinct alignment. But there is one missing.

It's Zeal.

"Forte, have you seen Zeal?" I ask as we hover ready for takeoff back to Zion.

Her silver eyes reply honestly. "No, I haven't. I can retrace the battle air if you wish."

"Zeal here!" He soars up to my right side and waits.

"I called for formation, Zeal. Where were you?"

"Finishing off some hinlors still lurking in the outer regions. Forgive me for venturing too far. I thought I should check just in case–"

"Remain in battle," I interject.

Something in his eyes is off.

"Yes, Captain," he affirms. "Remain in battle," he repeats in agreement. He looks away and appears unlike himself. Whatever is going on with him will need to be addressed eventually. First, we must return to Zion since the job is done.

"Find your place in formation," I command. He nods. Then I address Zion's Angels as a whole.

"Your wings flew valiantly, this battle! Every hinlor has been defeated! The victory is ours!"

"All hail Zion!" Angels cheer.

"Back to Zion!" I command.

"Yes, Captain Leafe!" The angels answer in unison.

Angels wait ready for take-off.

I soar onward.

They follow.

I hear the sound of many wings soaring behind me as the host of angels follows my path back to Zion. Radiant light encompasses our presence, deterring every dark threat that would stand to threaten us in these parts of the universe. Hinlors have been invading Zion with all its bright light and have been getting wiped out because of it. The light attracts the darkness because of the beauty. But darkness never wants to join the light. Darkness only opposes it.

Just like The Raven opposed King Worthy.

"You really should join me," The Raven once told me when he recruited followers in his rebellion. *"I'll make you my right hand."*

"I already have one," I said plainly and held up my right arm.

"Funny," The Raven answered with a grimacing grin. He patted me on the shoulder and for a moment I pitied him. He used to be an equal. But he made himself an enemy.

The Raven had no idea what he was doing to himself. He thought he could take over The King's Throne. But all he did was sabotage himself and brainwash a host of angels to follow the same treachery.

Now as I lead the V formation of Zion's Angels, I understand the power of influence. These angels follow my every move. One swerve into dangerous territory and they'd follow. One leap into cosmic light, they'd follow. To the light is where I aim.

To the light.

"Where do you think you're going alone?" The dark voice still haunts me when I think about it. The Raven's voice. I remember the moment The Raven tried to agitate me on my way to give Lilly the message from Skye. Did he succeed? Of course not. No one ruffles my feathers. But The Raven tried that moment he found me in the starry hosts.

"I got a message to give," I told him and sped up. *"And you're slowing me down."*

The Raven soared up beside me and glared with red eyes. *"Leafe is a courier now!? I thought I had seen everything but my mind keeps getting blown,"* he retorted.

"Allow me to blow it off for the last time," I said bluntly and detonated a bolt of emerald light radiation into his core.

How did he find me? I still don't know. King Worthy dismantled my wing trackers to eliminate the possibility of evil spirits knowing my whereabouts and passing it to The Raven.

The King said he wanted me to be incognito when I travelled out of Zion. Too many eyes on me. Too many eyes on our angels. The King did not want any more angels being attacked or coerced into the evil side.

The Raven fell away from that point on and I never saw him again.

Soon after, Skye said he'd been thrown into the black hole before the Battle at Hanauma Bay.

There was no way I was going to tell The Raven where I was really going. Lilly would never be spoken of in The Raven's presence lest he know anything about her or her family. I made sure I got rid of him before crossing into earth's airspace. Then I found Lilly in that Italian café with her family. I gave the message. Flew back to Zion.

Lilly was always on my mind from that point on.

When I flew, I'd see her eyes looking back at me.

She makes me go faster. My wings soar invincible with her beauty strengthening me.

Blast!

"Explosion up ahead!" Forte shouts just behind me to the right.

I keep flying.

Red fire explodes in my periphery. The Black Hole. Forte may be distressed but I need to lead us home. There is nothing we can do about his imprisonment in that dungeon of hell. Nor is it our battle to fight.

"Keep going!" I command. "If there was a battle to fight, we would wage it. But fiery remnants only prove The Raven is in there and he is not coming out. The battle is over, at least for now."

We keep flying back to Zion.

Captain Strength nods. "Yes, sir!"

"Yes, Captain Leafe!" Forte affirms.

Forte has been flying with me ever since The Raven revolted against King Worthy. She pledged her allegiance to Zion, even after being enticed to join The Raven. Many left. She stayed. Her wings are strong, and Captain Strength flies well with her at the right and him at the left. All the fliers fly strong. I'd say any one of them could lead this V formation with finesse.

I think about Lilly's aura and the light she emits. She could fly with us, easily. Hinlors are drawn to her radiance. She would defeat them instantly. Light either compels one to the light or compels one to evil. It all depends on the soul.

Hinlors have no soul.

Like moths to a flame, they gather around the light only to feast upon its strength and leave it empty. Little do they know, the light cannot be eradicated. Good always wins. Light always eradicates the darkness. Light will never be empty or void. King Worthy's light completes the universe.

Hinlors will keep showing up in Zion while Lilly is there. They want her. I can sense it.

Deep in my bones, I want her too. But for vastly different reasons. I don't want to feast upon her light to deplete her. I want to kiss her angelic skin just like she kissed my soul the first time I saw her to fill her and complete her. Something supernatural sparked inside me that day I first saw her.

Spark!

Shooting stars burst like fountains in front of us as I fly towards Zion's gates. Their golden arches and pearly substance glow in the distance. We will be home in no time.

I veer left to head for the entrance. Meteor showers sprinkle by us, and I serve around the trail. Turbulence picks up in its wake. I ascend upward into a higher threshold of airspace. The angels follow behind me succinctly and peacefully without a hiccup. Their appearance of serenity matches their depth of tranquility. They fly perfectly, just as The King designed.

"Zion's gates are ahead!" I shout at the front of the V.

Blissful auras infiltrate the airspace as we breach Zion's airspace. I breathe in and breathe out. Honeysuckle and myrrh coat the air.

We reach the golden gates and they open at my body recognition. The angels follow in tandem and we soar through the gates.

"All hail Zion!" The angels chant as we enter.

It's a tradition anytime we enter Zion's gates.

I lead them to The Eagle's Pad by The Rose Garden and let every angel file in to debrief. I circle formation and find every angel in place, even Zeal, the one still in question. I make my way back to the head.

"Well done, Zion's armies!" I extend my affirmation. "Mission executed! Earth will sleep soundly another night because of your valor. Hinlors may invade, but we will triumph every time!"

"Zion reigns!" The angels cheer.

"All hail Zion!" They echo again.

I dismiss the formation and angels soar off to their well-deserved leisure. But there is one more angel I need to see.

"Zeal!" I look towards the purple-eyed angel and he turns to meet me. "I need to talk to you."

He nods, with a sigh under his breath, soars up to me, and waits. "Yes, Captain?"

"You were unlike yourself today. For a moment, I thought you were missing," I say.

"Like I said, I found hinlors creeping about the outer proximity."

I don't believe him. My instincts tell me he is hiding something.

"And like *I* said, you always remain in battle. If there were hinlors outside our radius, don't you think I would have sensed it?"

He diverts my gaze. "Yes, sir."

Zeal knows I see through him. But if he were truly a rebel, he would not have flown back with us before making his attack. He has another motive. Until I know what it is, I don't want to jump to conclusions.

"I'm keeping my eye on you, Zeal."

"I'm loyal to King Worthy! You know I am," he says zealously. Behind his purple eyes, flames rise at the idea of me questioning his devotion. If loyalty is not the infraction, what is? Only time will tell.

I nod and concede from asking him anymore questions. "That is all," I finish.

Zeal soars away in a trail of light that I pray is pure.

Beneath me, the velvet grass and green clovers light up from Zion's radiance. I breathe in. Breathe out. Zion puts me at ease effortlessly. To say it is the most perfect place in the universe is an understatement. I never want to be anywhere else.

It is also the only place I have ever seen grass illuminated.

"Follow me," a voice whispers.

My wings flutter as a breeze from the westerly mountains sweeps through.

"Who was that?"

A white dove lands on my shoulder.

"Purity," the dove says. I look to my right and see the holy dove resting on my shoulder with beaming eyes and gold dust sparkling on her wings. "Come with me!" She flaps her wings and darts forward.

Her Spirit shows an extension of King Worthy's own Spirit. The Holy Spirit, as it were. And still is. I'd be a fool to reject the invitation. I follow her quickly and she leads me around the Tree of Life and up into Zion's mountains.

Her glowing light makes up for her tiny size, so I can keep track of her quick flight. We reach the peak of Zion's mountains and she lands at the edge, looking over the lay of the land.

"You're fast, little dove."

"Holy dove," she corrects me with joyful, pearly eyes.

"Forgive me," I say humbly. "The view from up high is mesmerizing. I haven't been to this peak in many earth rotations around the sun."

Purity flies up closer, with holy dust trailing from her wings. "But you have had time to make your rotation around Lilly," she asserts brazenly, still holding a smile.

I hesitate before speaking and wait to hear her out.

"You must understand that Lilly is not just any human. She is the one King Worthy chose. If you are going to enchant her, don't play with her, Leafe," she says with a tone of both sternness and gentleness.

Although her words hit a nerve, I appreciate her pinpointing the issue at hand. I have not been able to share all of my pent-up feelings yet. I could divulge it all, but putting her at ease will suffice for now. I will make this quick.

"I have no intention of playing with her, Your holiness."

"Good," she confirms. "Remember you represent the highest angels of Zion. Love is our mantra. Being one with humanity is our future."

Purity dazzles a bit of gold every time her mouth moves. I nod to let her know her words are received. Calmness sets in like tranquility of soft rain. Lilly does that to me, also, anytime I hear her speak. She carries the mark of purity.

"Something about Lilly draws me in like a magnet. I see her and I can't keep my hands off her."

"Is it only touch you want? Or is it more than that?"

"More. When I touched her, it was like my soul was reaching for her soul, deep within. It's more than skin. I feel her aura."

Purity flutters around and halts in front of my face. Her eyes look into me with kindness and ferocity simultaneously. I don't quite know how to take it. But I am not one to look away.

"Lilly deserves to be known in her soul. If Skye can give that to her, don't stand in his way." She winks. Before she soars away I need to know more. My love for Lilly is growing with every passing second and I have to know what I can do.

"Yes, I understand." I respond. "But what if I love her more?" I add. "More than Skye?"

"Remember King Worthy is in charge. The King has Lilly in His hands. If you want her, you will have to go through Him."

10

Lilly

"Hold on tight!" Skye tells me.

Skye's voice breathes tranquility, even in the midst of urgency. Ever since I met him, I noticed it. He reminds me how angelic he is by the way he carries peace even when bearing the weight of the world on his shoulders.

I wrap my hands around his waist tighter. His arms enfold me.

Skye reminds me, *"hold on tight,"* every time we fly and I never get tired of it. His chivalrous heart cares for me consistently with intentional awareness of my every need. He is my angel, after all. My heart rests at ease when he holds me in flight. Equilibrium stabilizes and I have no need for anything else other than his wings to keep me secure like a velvet blanket.

I love looking into his eyes. Alert and focused, they remain, as we glide over the meadows of Zion, glowing with floral radiance. Skye's eyes blaze with fire and power as he takes us towards our palace, given by The King.

Skye's focus tells me he always stays alert to the elements around us. He can detonate his blue eyes of blue light at any moment and invaders are gone. In Zion, there haven't been any threats, except for hinlors. I think that is why he maintains his blue light intensity.

"The Commander must always be alert, my love. I live to watch over Zion," he whispers and smiles at me steadily.

"I would not fly under anyone else's wings but yours, General," I assure him sweetly.

Here in Skye's arms, my face looks intently into the eyes of Skye's blue sapphire. I like to fly this way, face to face with him, where I can see his tall, strong wings flying regally. His blonde hair sweeps across his brow and flutters with the wind like the angel he is. Perfect and strong.

Blue eyes suddenly look at me with a fire growing bigger by the second. He leans in, grazes my face, and kisses me sweetly, with luscious lips of peaches. I return the kiss with delightful reciprocation.

"You're getting good at this, Lilly," he says.

"You mean flying?" I ask, tongue in cheek.

He laughs at my playfulness, and it makes me feel giddy when he does. I can be my true self around him.

"I meant kissing," he clarifies.

"I had a good teacher," I say with bold eyes. "Some might even call him an *angel*."

"Would they, now?" he smirks at me. His nose nuzzles mine and he kisses me again with repetitive kisses on my lips.

"You are so adorable, my Lilly flower," he thinks to me.

"And you are radiant, my Commander of Zion's armies," I think back to him through telekinesis.

Twirl!

Skye spins me around in his arms, 360 degrees.

The wind flutters through my hair. His wings stretch out to soar again as he brings us to a resting position. Around us, the light illuminates. I roll over to scan the horizon stretching afar. Dazzling.

The sky beyond us glows with golden hues and sparkling colors of orangish red that remain strong and bright with every passing moment. No matter how many times I look at it, the light remains. An eternal sunset, it is, with swirling glimmers of light that shift and change like a lava lamp. The view shines so much brighter than any horizon I have seen on earth.

"It's Zion's lights, my love. My father made the northern lights in the northern hemisphere of earth. These are even brighter."

"Zion is so much bigger than I thought!" I exclaim, awestruck.

"My father created this land and every wonder of the universe," he says triumphantly.

Skye loves talking about his father. He understands that The King upholds everything by His royal power and cares for him also, personally, and compassionately. I see it when they are together.

"The King loves you, Skye. I can tell," I say.

"He and I have ruled the universe ever since its inception," Skye replies as we soar. "He understands me."

"You both have the same blue light in your eyes," I say eagerly.

"I admit I was worried you might fall in love with Him for that."

I lean into him face to face.

"You're the only one I love, Skye."

See my love for you, my blue angel. You will always have my heart.

I want him to know it will always be me and him. No other lover could ever hold my heart. Captain Leafe thought he could interfere, but he can't. I don't have room for anyone else when Skye already occupies my heart. He is the moon to my midnight. The star in my sky.

Why does he capture me like he does? Because he is the one who saved me when no one else could. I will never forget the eyes that found me under the ocean that night at Waimea Bay. His soul felt me and I felt his. Our spirits are connected. Intertwined. They always will.

Captain Leafe's fate remains a mystery. Skye has not told me what transpired between them when he confronted him. His thoughts are not giving it away either. He must not be worried about it, or else he would tell me. I haven't the slightest idea why Leafe chose to touch me when he knew Skye would find out. Maybe he thought I wouldn't say anything. But that is quite a gamble to take. Can he not see Skye is my entire world?

"He can see how you love me, Lilly," Skye tells me with his thoughts. Finally, I can hear him.

"Then why did he do it?" I think back to him.

Hiding my frustration is not easy, but I'm trying to. I don't want to cause a fuss over it nor taint the mood of the moment with unnecessary worry. But it bothers me. The memory keeps resurfacing and I find myself wondering... does Leafe like me? Stop, Lilly. Don't go there. It does not matter if he does. You don't want him, I tell myself. It's the truth. I don't.

Skye breaks his silence. "Leafe had a lapse of judgment. I don't want it to upset you any more than it already has, my love. Trust me, I took care of it."

"You didn't kill him, did you?" I ask, concerned. An angel's death is not something I want to be responsible for.

"I promise I didn't kill him," he assures me softly. His arms snuggle me tighter at the question. I feel angst in his soul rising as we talk about it.

I sigh. "I remember when The Raven found us mid-air over the ocean and I know what you can do, Skye. You are meant to protect me. To protect the universe. I guess I was worried you would take him out and I cannot bear that devastation."

"Even if I did kill him, you would not be responsible. He chose to do what he did. It's not your fault," Skye assures me.

"What if it happens again?"

I keep thinking of how it felt when he felt my waist.

Stop, Lilly.

Don't think about it.

My love is for Skye and he is the only one I ever want to kiss. He is the first one who ever showed me what it felt like. Still, the image of Leafe coming closer to me pops up in my head. I keep trying to shake it off. Why does he keep surfacing in my mind?

"It won't," Skye says.

I just want her to choose me and only me, his thoughts say.

"I will always choose you," I reply confidently. "Look at me, Skye." Captain Leafe becomes foggy as I behold Skye's face. "You can count on that."

"And you will always be my one and only love," he affirms to me.

His forehead touches mine. Feathery wings wrap around me like a cocoon of soft white silk as the light surrounding us fades into the background. All I see is the blue light flooding from his eyes into mine like waterfalls gushing into the deep.

Blue eyes find me in love.

"Kiss me, General."

Skye's wings lower us to the ground, and I feel the wind beneath us graze through my hair. He leans in. His eyes come closer. Friction touches my lips as his lips caress mine. Meanwhile, the scent of roses eclipses my senses. We must be in a rose garden. Then I see ripe red grapes ready for harvesting. It must be a vineyard, then, with roses. I love the creativity of Zion's lands. The King fits the most glorious creations together.

Skye sets me down softly in the roses and continues to kiss me gently and investigate every coordinate of my mouth. I kiss him back willingly and grab the back of his head to pull him closer.

He swirls his tongue in mine. Kisses taste like peaches and grapes, and his body gives off the fragrance of mahogany and linen. He strokes my hair and works his way down my back as his mouth leaves no mystery of passion's definition. I love the way he kisses me and touches me simultaneously.

"How do you kiss me like this?" I tell him with telekinesis.

"You keep me focused, my love," he tells me with his thoughts. His lips pull away and he studies my face intently.

"You are so beautiful. A billion years could pass by and I'd never find another rose as beautiful as you."

"I want more of you, Skye."

"All I want is to make love to her right here among the tapestry of Zion's grapes. We've already waited so long," he thinks. *"To know my Lilly most intimately… not even the poetry of Solomon's finest song could encapsulate the moment of bliss."*

His hands slowly graze over my neck and down the middle of my chest. He kisses my neck with delicate ease. My hands run through his hair and I open my eyes to Zion's light glowing around us. The roses beside me glow like neon plum and red. The lights above glow and change like gold against a backdrop of black cherry and teal blue, like the northern lights. Ethereal are my eyes at the sight of the radiation. But my body is heating up at the feeling of his hands now navigating to my navel. That's where Captain Leafe touched me.

I tremble.

Skye looks up and touches my face.

"Forget about him, Lilly," he exclaims with blue eyes of sapphire. "Eternity belongs to you and me." He strokes my face and my hair lovingly. My hands touch his and he brings them up to my heart. "Do you feel this?" he asks me with a smile. "This is your heartbeat when you are with me."

My heartbeat hastens as his eyes soothe my fears with angelic peace. He does that often. And I am reminded that my angel saves me from death.

I breathe in and out. "I'll never forget the way it felt when you pulled that piece of coral reef out of my leg atop Jump Cliff," I say playfully. "I thought you were a monster! I couldn't break free fast enough!"

He laughs at the recollection and squeezes me tight with a quick kiss. "It's my job to protect you by any means necessary, Lilly. I am your angel, after all," he smirks. "Angels are fierce."

"I'm so glad you are, my handsome blue angel."

I stare into his eyes with longing. The eyes of my angel. The eyes of my lover. I cannot hold it back anymore. And I don't need to when he makes me feel safe and cared for. I dive into his mouth with eagerness to explore the coordinates of his mouth to repay the favor. He rubs my back and lets his hands travel down the backside of my body. Goosebumps cover me.

"Skye!" I shout.

"I'm sorry, Lilly." He stops the movement of his hands, looks down, and pulls away. "We're getting too hot. Maybe we should stop."

"No, General." I reply quickly. "I was going to tell you to untie my bow," I say shyly.

His blue eyes look up at me. "I can do that," he says and moves in closer. His hands touch me at the waist and instantly the memory of Leafe's intrusion is quelled by Skye's claim on me. He is the only one who has my heart. The only one who saved me. The only one whose eyes will captivate me with angelic bliss.

His hands meander along my body and up to the ribbon tied in a bow. He slowly pulls it loose. I sigh. It's happening, isn't it… I've never been unclothed with a man before, much less an angel. Jenna is the only one who has seen my bare body and that is because she is my best friend, and we are only girls. I never once felt any kind of rush like I feel now when I am with Skye. I thought we might wait until our wedding night. But here we are, and I don't know how to stop myself from giving into the momentum.

"Tell me what you want, Lilly."

I pause and think about it. What do I want? "I want you to take the lead," I exclaim rapidly. It's true. I want him to have me now.

"I don't want you to hate me for going too far," he thinks to me with his thoughts.

"You can go as far as you want to, General," I think back to him. *"This rose is yours for the taking."*

He kisses my waist as my dress still rests over my skin. His hands move to my knees and work all the way up my thighs. My heartbeat increases. I breathe in and out. His hands find my backside and I tilt my head back as his touch rouses me.

The fragrance of grapes and roses intensifies with every touch, as if his hands have unlocked my senses to ascend new levels of encounter. My eyes are closed and, yet I see every color of the rainbow and taste it too.

His hands work their way up my chest and he slips my dress off of my neck. The lavender sundress nestles in with the roses as my body lies exposed before him. His hands sweep across the midsection of my stomach and down to the most sensitive area of my body.

"Skye!" I gasp. His mouth enters me below and my toes curl to dig into the fresh roses. Petals rub my feet, soft and delicate. "Skye, you're an angel!" My body ascends to euphoria from the artistry of his mouth's fusion. Deeper and deeper, he sends me up the artic trail to Zion. Like a volcano erupting, I can feel the magma rising.

"Relax, Lilly," he thinks to me.

I exhale and wait for my body to go to the heights of ecstasy. He really is an angel, isn't he... Every movement of his hands on my skin matches the dedication of his mouth to send me into clouds of bliss. I didn't know my body could feel this way. All I know is I don't want it to stop. I love the way you kiss me, Skye.

"I love kissing you, my Lilly flower," he thinks to me.

The magma of the feeling starts to burst from the volcanic edge as he massages my intimate region with his mouth. Sparks of fire shoot off in my mind, like I'm witnessing the wonder of the world glowing red hot.

Blast!

Eyes open. Fireworks shower us overhead with glowing lights on a red-orange sky. Skye rises to look at me face to face. "I want to wait," he says.

"But I need you to take me higher. My body is so turned on," I confess. Blue eyes find me in the vineyard.

"I love you, Lilly," he whispers angelically. "Let's wait until we go further."

I reach for his cheek, and he clutches my head. Short kisses paint my lips as he swaddles me. Then he lays beside me in the bed of roses that smell of luscious grapes and fresh ivy.

I breathe in and out to catch my breath. Meanwhile, my body is still pulsating from his touch and I don't know how to cure the rush. It still pangs with adrenaline.

My body feels miserable under the pressure of waiting for the feelings to subside that he left unfinished.

"Skye, I want it to be just you and I forever." Just like right now in the middle of the vineyards. There is nowhere else we need to be but here. No one else to see us.

Skye chuckles and kisses me with repetitive kisses. "You are more than enough for me for all of eternity, my love," he says joyfully. I love how sincerely his heart speaks to me. I always know he means every word of what he says.

"I only want her to love me. I need her to love me," he thinks to himself.

"I do love you, Skye."

I look into his eyes that shine blue like sapphire. Tasting him again becomes my highest priority. I dive into him. He kisses me passionately, like everything I have witnessed thus far was only a prelude to his torrential power to claim me. Maybe now my body will find a finale for the pleasure.

His lips ravish me like they never have before. His body moves to situate on top of me. I can feel his body heating as his wings perk up overhead, with golden light. I feel my body steaming again. Do it again, Skye…

He pulls away.

"Lilly Rose," he says with a smile and looks away. His eyes gaze at the roses in thoughtful pondering, and then he looks back at me tenderly. The look in his eyes tells me he is searching for the words to say. "In all my existence, I have never felt the way your love makes me feel. That's why I know I need to wait until…" he pauses. "Until I have you completely."

"Have me completely?" I ask.

"Yes. There is much more for us to discover, my love, in the realms of passion. I know I am your first love. When I make love to you, you will understand," he kisses me on the forehead and slips my dress back over my head and covers my body. "I want to wait until we go any further. Our wedding day is the day I will have you completely."

"I want you to be my angel forever." I smile, comforted, knowing I can entrust my choices to him. We are partners and that means he protects me and covers me. He knows how to be my angel and look out for both of us.

"And I want you to tell me what you want, forever, Lilly. It's you and I together. I don't ever want to assume I know what you want, even when I can read your thoughts. I want you to tell me. I want to know you, deep down."

"You can know all of me, General," I exclaim. "I will fly with you forever."

Whoosh!

A wind blows in from the west. Neon roses sway beside us with rose petals lifting into the breeze. Skye picks me up into his arms and stands up. I look at him and catch flickers of light brooding from his eyes.

"What is it, Skye?"

He lifts off the ground. "It's nothing," he says. I can tell there is more to what he hints. He notices everything surrounding him and something is stirring his focus.

"*I don't want her to worry,*" he thinks. "*The end of the universe is nearing, and I can feel it.*"

"I see the way your eyes flare with when you fight, Skye. You get fury in your eyes."

"I'm not good at hiding, am I?"

I shake my head. "Tell me what you see."

He takes a deep breath and looks at me with blue eyes flaming.

"The Raven is not dead."

11

Skye

"Not dead?" Lilly shrieks.

"No, not dead," I say.

Her countenances tenses. "How do you know?"

"I sense something dark in the galaxies. Different than hinlors, and more like The Raven."

Beyond the galactic space of Zion's threshold, evil approaches. My eyes can see its shroud transcending the cosmos in due time as Armageddon nears. I clutch Lilly tightly at the thought of it as her perfect frame rests delicately in my arms in lavender silk.

I pick her up and hover over the vineyard grapes by the blush roses and we land. Protecting her remains my highest priority. Not one vicious, toxic talon will come near her!

"You will defeat The Raven just like before," Lilly consoles me and massages my shoulders. Her lips graze my neck and my heart eases from the ardor of her confidence in me. I love her fervor. New power floods my spirit every time she rallies me to victory.

"I'm your loudest cheerleader, my blue angel," she thinks.

"And I'm your fiercest warrior, my love," I think back to her.

I love reading her thoughts. What a terrifying yet enthralling reality to know she can read mine. It keeps us in sync with each other.

Oneness with her feels right. Undeniably, she is a part of me. Heart and soul.

I breathe in and out. "I thought he was exterminated when I threw him in The Black Hole," I divulge to her. "He was. He should have been. But only my father knows."

She turns her head inquisitively. "Is it time for Armageddon?"

"Soon, it will be." I cannot give her any more information than that, since my father holds the key to this wrinkle in time, along with His holy dove, Purity.

"We can trust The King," Lilly smiles calmly.

I sigh with relief as her peace gives way to mine. "Yes, my Lilly flower," I gently kiss her shoulder and continue to stroke her brunette locks. Her hair smells of almond and orchid petals. I could stay tangled in them forever. "I am not worried over the timing of The Raven's release." My hands continue to stroke her hair. "Angels will fly when father says its time. Until then, I remain loyal to the Throne of Zion and The King who heralded me as Commander. If there is a battle to fight, I will know. Until then, I am going to show you the rest of Zion's beautiful scenery, my stunning fiancé," I declare delightfully. She lights up at the revelation.

I twirl her around, as her brunette hair flies in the wind. I gather her hair from her face and clutch her securely. I extend my wings to soar onward with the most beautiful woman in my arms.

"Lead the way, General!" she commands readily.

I love it when she tells me what to do. Her adorable tone reels me in. Hook, line, and sinker. The way she says it captures me because she never orders me around ruthlessly. She playfully charges me. She makes me feel invited into her space to be the one who takes charge, even when she makes a demand.

"*I can read your thoughts, my blue angel,*" she reminds me through telekinesis.

"I'm giving away all my secrets, aren't I?" I say aloud.

"Yes." She giggles. "I like it, though, when you think about me."

"You're always on my mind," I confess. Here I am, the Commander of Zion's armies, smitten and helplessly in love, and she knows it, too. To say I resent it is far from the truth. I love every bit of it. Feeling this way for Lilly makes me want to live for eternity. Fully known by her.

"Can I tell you something?" I ask.

"You know you can tell me anything," she replies tenderly.

My wings curl around her to swaddle her as we relax. I lean in and whisper where she can hear me intimately. "You are my only love."

She gazes up at me sweetly. "I know I am."

"You know?"

"You have never told me about anyone *else*," she bats her eyelashes.

"Detective Lilly nails it again," I exclaim, elated.

"Just like I nailed the hinlor today at the palace villas," she boasts triumphantly. "Though I really don't like killing things."

"You needed to," I affirm. "Hinlors are no object of sympathy. They aim to possess and kill."

Lilly's audacity still shocks me, but I am getting used to it, and loving it at the same time. Though I remain hesitant to let her fight, I know her power won't be held back for long. My father will know what she is capable of.

"It came at us fast. I thought Jenna was going to have a panic attack!" Lilly reveals candidly. "I couldn't let that flying object touch her."

My heart feels her heartbeat as I fly over the floral meadows. "You're a good friend, Lilly. An even better warrior in the face of darkness."

"Really?" She looks up at me with wide eyes. Childlike and captivated.

"Yes, really," I confess.

"Blue eyes find me in Zion," she thinks.

My hand strokes her hair as I fly onward with my treasure in my arms.

"I want Jenna to see the light," says Lilly. "She still wonders if all this is real."

"She will see, my love."

"How do you know?"

"She did not welcome the darkness. She rejected the hinlors. In time, The King will show her the light of Zion and she will want it forever."

Lilly squeezes me tightly. "I want her to see the light."

"I'm glad, little one," I say. "Look Lilly, I wanted Jenna here because I knew you needed your best friend. If I am honest, Captain Leafe said something to me and it got me thinking. I didn't know I would feel the way I do, but it is overwhelming me. I want to tell you."

"What is it?"

"He said–" I hesitate. Clear my throat. Breathe in and out, to regain my clarity. Vulnerability with Lilly is what I want and I need to tell her what I'm thinking. "He said I'm terrified you will get tired of me. At first, I thought it was ridiculous and insubordinate for him to impose such an idea on his Commander." I sigh.

"You don't have to listen to him, Skye. That's not what I think," Lilly insists honestly.

"I know, Lilly. But I think he's right about me." I look into her eyes, exposed. "I *am* afraid."

"Afraid? He's never been this vulnerable with me before," she thinks. *"I never knew angels could be afraid."*

I look away. Maybe this was not the right time to talk about this. "I'm sorry if I said too much."

"You didn't!"

"I'm sorry, Lilly. I shouldn't have told you those secrets. I should keep it to myself."

"No!" She protests. Her hands graze my face and I return my eyes to their faithful object of affection. "I want you to tell me everything, General," she smiles at me. "I would find out anyway if it were on your mind, wouldn't I? We read each other's thoughts," she concurs. "I want to know. Just like I want to be with you everywhere you are too," she confesses.

"You do?"

She nods her head with melting eyes.

"I love how you tell me your feelings. I am all ears, every second," she affirms with strong eyes.

I nod and grin with relief.

"So, we're both madly in love with quality time, it seems."

She twinkles her eyes at me. "Hopelessly in love, I'd say."

Blast!

Lilly turns her head towards the sound.

I circle around as golden flames flare in the distance. "The horns of Zion's palace."

"Did something happen? Why would it sound off like that?"

I hold her tightly. "Cosmic explosions, earth interventions, angelic appearances. My father has many reasons for what He does. The palace sounds the horn when something big is happening. Don't worry. If it were urgent for me to return, He would send for me."

Rip!

Lilly looks down at a strand of silk shriveling. "My dress!"

Below, a rose thorn snags her dress, causing it to tear. I avert our forward motion and make haste to land.

"I'll fix it, Lilly," I assure her calmly. I dip down to the ground with Lilly in my grasp. The thorn is buried in the hem of her dress. It must have caught while we were sitting, and latched hold as I flew upward. I grab the thorn from her hem, pull it out, and pick off the debris surrounding the site of the breach.

"Did it cut your skin, Lilly?"

"I don't think so. But it happened so fast, I can't see."

The lavender threads jumble around the hem and I clear it away to scan her knee and leg. "Let's rest here for a minute so I can make sure."

Meanwhile, Lilly pulls at her dress and quickly gathers the threads in her soft hands. "Oh no! It's going to be ruined!"

"I'll get you another one, my love. It's okay," I promise her.

She nods, and moves her hands frantically, still gathering the dress. "What am I going to do right now?"

I grab her hands. "Let go of the dress."

She looks up at me.

Her hands let go.

I look into her eyes.

"Blue eyes find me in the roses," she thinks.

"Yes, my Lilly flower. Blue eyes indeed."

I lean in to kiss her. Strawberry roses fill my taste buds at the thought of our collision. My heart palpitates as I get closer. All the sudden I feel a haze of grogginess setting in. My wings recline.

Then…

Thump.

My eyes go black.

12

Lilly

"Skye, wake up!" I shake his wings and attempt to wake him from his slumber but it's no use. "Are you okay?"

I look around the meadows of rose petals, feeling helplessly alone. Skye won't wake up, and I don't know what to do about it.

Flash!

I turn, startled.

"Hello, Miss Rose."

Emerald eyes flood into me like nirvana. It's Captain Leafe.

I look away.

I can't be looking at him like that. Nirvana? Pull yourself together, Lilly. Besides, he should know better than to show up to me after what happened back at the palace. He touched me, for crying out loud, knowing Skye was in the same vicinity.

I cover my legs with what is left of the ripped dress. "Where did you come from?"

"I live here, remember," Captain Leafe answers crisply.

Of course, he does. We are in Zion, where angels soar freely. And he will often. I am going to have to get used to him appearing unexpectedly in every part of Zion's wonders, from the merlot waterfalls to rose-filled vineyards.

Curiosity piques me now. I want to look at him. So, I give myself permission to look upon his bronze skin and emerald eyes again. His towering wings extend like peacock feathers, only white, with silver linings and emerald gems. Light radiates from his face like the noonday sun on a Texas summer day.

I can't look away.

He is an angel, after all.

And yes, his eyes are dreamy.

I tell myself I should not feel guilty for observing his angelic beauty, but something in his eyes tells me he is not just another angel. I still think about that moment he touched me. I don't know why. It didn't mean anything and I had no say in the matter. He came on to me without warning.

"You need new threads." He inches closer. He's always doing that. Getting too close.

I touch what's left of the hem that has ripped all the way up my thigh. "It ripped a moment ago. Before Skye…"

"Crashed?"

I narrow my eyes on him. "If you mean fell asleep, then *yes*. Right before that."

I shake Skye's wings, hoping he will awaken and keep me from Leafe's devices. He isn't budging. Is he alive?

"He's alive," Leafe exclaims. His voice is strong and direct, so I know he is not lying. For that much, I am grateful. Leafe bends down, touches Skye's forehead, and looks back at me. "He is only sleeping. Angels are not supposed to sleep, however. I don't know what caused him to doze off."

"What a relief!" I reply gladly. But I wish he were awake to kiss me in the grape-rose vineyards like he was going to, right before he fell asleep. The meadows were most surely waiting for our debut in this new arena, and my body is throbbing from the lack. My lips are in need.

Leafe stands. "How did he fall asleep?"

"We were about to–" I pause before telling my innermost secrets of our love-life, and then realize it's the only way to properly assess the situation. "Kiss," I divulge, "and then he passed out."

"Don't you need a lover who won't fall asleep on you?" He steps towards me with radiant wings towering over me. I look up at him without thinking and find his green eyes looking back at me with concern.

"It's not his fault," I assert. "He needs rest."

Leafe crosses his arms. "Humans need rest."

I break eye contact and start pilfering with my dress that has begun to shred even more with every moment passing.

"Then why don't you fly away or something to where you get your beauty rest, and I will wait here for The King to send someone for me," I respond.

"You're sassy." He smirks.

My cheeks blush raspberry red. I shouldn't have said that. He is one of the King's angels, after all. But he still touched me.

"I'm sorry. I just–"

"King Worthy sent me." He interrupts before I can finish.

"Not to offend, but why would He send you after what happened?"

King Worthy knows everything. He would have seen what Leafe did when he touched by outside the palace. Why He sent him doesn't make much sense, but The King's ways are often outside our comprehension.

"He always has a reason, doesn't He?" says Leafe confidently.

His eyes zero in on me and I cannot look away this time without searching for the light in his eyes.

Green eyes find me in the vineyards.

Light found.

His eyes dazzle beautifully.

Look away, Lilly.

Lift!

Before I can answer him, I feel his arms embrace me swiftly and pick me up. My feet float above the roses and grapes as Leafe carries me up and away, flying fast. Faster than I've flown before.

"What are you doing?" I ask confused. Skye still sleeps down by the roses and we cannot leave him there. He will wonder where I am when he wakes up and I need to be there with him.

"Taking you home."

"But Skye is still here!"

Leafe echoes in my ear. "He is fine on his own for now. Let him sleep."

To say his embrace is a discomfort would be a lie. Now he is getting his way, isn't he. First, he touched me and now he is flying with me tightly which renders me helpless at escaping his arms.

Lilly, admit you like how it feels.

I give in to his embrace and let him take me onward. Pastel pink and peach frame the colors of the sky as we fly over the vineyards. Golden sparkles still linger in the air, per usual of Zion's atmosphere. Evergreen trees situate the horizon up ahead, and I realize he is taking me farther away from the palace, not towards it.

I squirm in flight. "Where are you taking me? I thought you were taking me home?"

"Wait."

I don't want to fight him. The King sent him, so I should trust it. I breathe in and out as the smell of forest dew and sepia waft in from the ground beneath. I sigh and let him fly onward, resolving to give in to the assistance.

Leafe sets me down on the ground and spins me around facing him.

I gasp because his eyes shine intensely. Glowing, green, fiery eyes. They flame now, strongly, just like Skye's but green instead of blue. Hypnosis wants to pull me in, but I look away. The force of his light shines all around my periphery, wanting me to return to look upon those green eyes of fire. I look again and find myself on the borderline of captivation.

Green eyes find me in the forest.

Snap out of, Lilly. Don't let him lure you in.

I look away swiftly. My eyes find the trail of butterflies that dance around our feet as the earth lights up like stars nestled in its dirt. A fascinating wonder.

"Where are we?" I ask enthralled by the magic.

"Serenity Forest."

"I've never been here before. I've never seen stars in the earth, either."

"Zion lights up everything," he says warmly.

Leafe steps closer.

I sigh, as his nearness makes me breathe faster. "What are you doing? You already touched me once. Are you trying to do it again?"

Leafe reaches for my leg and touches my dress along the tear all the way up to its starting point. I sigh again from his touch. Make him stop, Lilly. I open my mouth to tell him I want him to stop, but words don't come out. He continues fingering the silky material and my heart surges.

He leans in. "Tell me to stop," he whispers in my ear.

I breathe out anxiously. Words still won't form, so I hold up my hands to signal my protest. He doesn't stop. And somewhere inside of me, I don't want him to.

Leafe grips my hands and lowers them down from my chest to my stomach and then lower. Lower. Lower.

"Feel it?" he whispers strongly. Then, he leans over my shoulder.

I sigh again as his chest presses up against me. "Feel what?" I whisper.

"Your body heating up for me."

I back away. "Stop!"

He stands there in front of me, confident and indomitable. Immovable. Emerald eyes flare with striking light, again, just like Skye's. Of all the angels, only Skye and Leafe's eyes shine at this decibel.

He says nothing. Just looks at me, unashamed, and waits for me to speak.

I open my mouth again and hesitate. Tell him to stop, Lilly! Tell him to take you home and leave you alone, Lilly! Is it wrong I love Skye but this angel, Leafe, makes me crave him in ways I didn't expect?

I need to deny whatever this is. I am engaged, and if I am going to live in Zion, then I cannot allow Leafe to come on to me anytime he wishes.

"You need to take me home, please."

His voice remains strong. "Okay, Miss Rose."

"This cannot happen again."

"If you say so." He grins, steps closer, and picks me up.

"Gently, please," I teach him.

He nods. Quickly, he lifts off the ground and soars away into the forest opening where the light bleeds in. He holds me gently, just as I asked. Not that I don't want him to pick me up rough. I just know what he is thinking and if he gets rough with me right now, we are both going to end up on this starry dirt for more than one touch.

"I can hear you, Miss Rose."

Did I say that out loud? I swallow and blush from the intrusion of the chance he may hear my thoughts. "I didn't say anything."

"I hear your thoughts," he says with a tone of pleasure.

"Can all angels hear my thoughts?"

"Only the ones King Worthy grants access to."

"So, you have access to me, then. To hear my thoughts and, also, to come and whisk me away from fiancé into the forest when he falls asleep."

"You got it."

"That wasn't a question, Captain." Why did I get feisty with him again? He is beginning to bring out a side of me that I didn't know was there. I just don't know why he is set on pursuing me when he knows I am taken.

He does not seem to mind, either, when I get feisty with him. There is something about it I like. Oh no, Lilly… This is dangerous territory and I need to be cautious with him.

"Miss Rose, there are some things about Zion you must trust and leave to the Great I Am."

"King Worthy has always given me a reason to believe," I smile at the reality of my entire world known by Him. My heart feels lighter. "I know the He will always protect me. He would never send someone to harm me."

King Worthy sent Skye to save me that day at Waimea Bay. Angels roam the earth with missions to save and protect. Sometimes we see them, sometimes we don't. I knew if I asked to see the angels, Heaven would show me, and it happened. The one who created the whole universe always watches over me.

"That's why He sent me." Leafe grins with a bright smile.

I gasp in the circumference of His ferocious wings. "You!"

"Yes."

I can tell he is smirking again.

I answer, "But you have, in a matter of minutes, taken me from Skye and showed me where to feel myself when my body is getting turned–"

"On?"

He finishes my sentences, too.

I take a deep breath as he flaps his wings to soar onward. My heart is at war inside, all in a matter of minutes. Before Skye, I had never fallen in love before. I had never kissed anyone before. All this is new to me. Delightfully new. Being in Zion makes me feel at home in its supernatural oasis. But now I have another angel wanting my heart when I just got here with Skye. His ring is on my finger. I eye the heart shaped diamond ring, glistening in the light. I won't give it up for Leafe. I love Skye. And Leafe will have to accept that.

We fly over Zion's waterfalls misting with guava juice. I open my mouth and taste its decadence. Scrumptious, this waterfall is. I love that every time I come here, it tastes different. A never-ending well of never-ending flavors.

"Has he never showed you how?" Leafe asks, still interested in the conversation.

I remain silent and blush. The only one who ever talked to me about touching my body like that was Jenna.

"You need to know what you like," she told me. *"...In the bedroom. Then, you can tell Skye."*

I never told Skye anything like that. We never got that far.

"How far do you want me to take you, Miss Rose?" Captain Leafe asks.

"Umm," I hesitate to answer. "What do you mean?"

If he thinks we are going to get sexual, I will have to let him down softly. I can't go there with him. I belong to Skye. I haven't even gone there with Skye yet.

Skye and I have never made love. Only kissed. And touched. A lot.

I admit, my fantasies drift into imaginations of what it would be like to make love to Skye because my body always gets turned on beyond what I can manage when we are together. His kisses heat me in between my legs and I'm always left throbbing and wanting more. Is that normal? I never feel fully satisfied. In fact, it feels miserable sometimes to have my body high in the clouds but never reaching the pinnacle. I find myself thinking about making love to him at night. Then I feel the urge to touch myself to heal the pain of my body's desire. If my body keeps feeling this way, I may need to tell him I want to go farther. I don't know how much longer I can last, always feeling aroused without being intimate with him.

"How far do you want me to take you on your property?" Leafe interjects. "I can drop you off at the front door or I can drop you off inside."

Oh. Somewhere in the middle of distraction and fantasy, I had not noticed the terrain change. In front of us, stands a tall house of pearl that shines translucent, with many windows reflecting technicolor lights of Zion. Floral gardens of pristine botanicals loop around the perimeter. Green grass spreads out in all directions around the house with the panorama of skies in the distant universe beckoning.

"Stunningly beautiful!" I gasp with wide eyes. "But I thought you were taking me to the villas?"

"King Worthy told me to take you home. This is yours."

"The front door, please," I reply kindly.

He sets my feet on the green, velvet grass with four-leaf clovers intermingling. I love four-leaf clovers, but never have I ever seen this many clustered together in such beauty. Only in Zion, I think to myself.

"Yes. Only in Zion." He looks at me with a smile, forthright and dutiful. Then, he walks me up the steps of glassy gold, inlaid with turquoise and onyx.

"Everything you need is inside. Skye should be home soon," he says with a tone of compassion. "Don't worry about him. He will be fine."

I nod and smile gracefully. "Thank you."

"Anytime," he says respectfully, with a smile.

I turn to walk inside, but I remember Jenna is still at the palace. She is going to be wondering where I am! "Jenna was waiting for me at the palace," I say eagerly.

"Jenna is here, Miss Rose. The King had Zeal fly her here while you wait for Skye to arrive."

"She is!?" I can't wait to tell her what happened with Leafe.

Jenna's fascination with the male species keeps her intrigue continually piqued. When she finds out an angel is getting naughty in Zion, she is going to have a heart attack, I guarantee it. It will only be a matter of time before she finds him and makes her moves, I am sure.

Then, I pause and think about it more.

Do I want her to? What if I want Leafe to myself? I turn to look at Leafe standing regally. What if I don't want him to touch Jenna the way he touches me?

Leafe blushes.

And I remember that my thoughts are not hidden when I am around this angel.

I compose my thoughts and clear my throat.

"Forgive me, Captain Leafe," I purse my lips, look away, and then back at him. "I forget how often my thoughts are under a microscope."

"You don't have to be shy around me." He smiles gracefully.

"And you don't always have to call me Miss Rose," I say, nodding back. He nods in return and waits for me to enter the house safely. I reach for the doorknob decked in canary diamonds with the inscription, "Friends welcome. Angels chosen."

Could Leafe be chosen for me also?

Before opening the door, I turn around to face him again. The bright light adorns his face like perfect stars in Heaven's constellations. Deep brown hair accents his handsome face with green eyes that peer into me like he knows me. When I look at him, it's as if I see parts of me. The green eyes. The brown hair. He makes me feel understood.

"Thank you for taking me home, Captain."

Leafe nods. "Anything for you, Lilly."

Finally, he called me Lilly.

Green eyes find me…

Look away, Lilly.

I look away.

I cannot let him captivate me, too. This is such a bad idea to think about him at all. To have him involved in my life at all. What was The King thinking?

Leafe steps forward and cups my cheeks. I try to back away, but it's too late.

Kiss!

Leafe's lips land on mine. Sweet lips. He tastes like caramel and spiced cinnamon. I gasp, my mouth opens in shock and his lips kiss me again. I sigh like I have been holding it in for centuries. My lips move in tandem with his.

Pull away, Lilly.

I pull away.

Smack!

My right hand meets the curvature of his perfect cheek bones.

"You shouldn't have done that," I say explicitly.

"You kissed me back." He eyes me boldly.

"I shouldn't have done that."

"Makes two of us, doesn't it?" Leafe grins.

"You and I are not–" I pause. Is he right? I think he is. It happened so fast, but I think I kissed him back. Yes, I most certainly kissed him back. In the merry-go-round of emotions racing in my heart, I resolve to hold my tongue and simply say, "Goodnight, Captain Leafe."

I run inside and lock the door. In front of me, Jenna stands in a pearly, bright hallway with curiosity doing cartwheels in her eyes.

Jenna walks towards me at the door and looks out the window. I hope Leafe is gone already. "I heard someone out there," she exclaims. "I could have sworn it was that angel, Leafe! I know his voice!"

I remain silent, soaking in the heat of his passionate kiss. Why did I kiss him back?

Jenna turns towards me. "Lilly! Why are you breathing so hard?" She checks my pulse. Then, she widens her eyes and grins. "Did you make love?"

"Not quite."

But his kiss felt like more than a kiss.

13

Leafe

Lilly's kiss felt like more than a kiss.

Sultry lips are hard to come by. Angelic lips, I have tasted before. Hers are angelic, undoubtedly, but much more passionate and sensual than any angel I have tasted in Zion. Pure innocence combined with the intoxication of Heaven. Gripping, to say the least.

I want to taste her again. Feel her again. I want to give her the love she needs. Skye has pursued her for this long, and still has not given her the pleasure she desires. She wants more.

Skye pushed me to this point, I could surmise. The King knows I never wanted to cross the line with his bride. But his bride likes the taste of me. I read her thoughts when I first entered her mouth. *Caramel and cinnamon,* she thought. Lilly's lips tasted like grapes and blackberry. She had spent time in the vineyards, which left her palate tasting like bliss.

"Captain Worthy!" The King's voice rattles in my direction.

Is He calling for me or someone else? I turn and realize He is calling for me.

It is not often that anyone calls me by my surname anymore. Most call me Leafe. *"Leaves are for the healing of the nations,"* The King told me when He named me. He looked at me like a treasure He had discovered. The name pleased Him. *Leafe.* It stuck.

"Yes, King Worthy," I answer. I bow in the reverence of royalty. The King, however, is not just royalty, He is the One Sure God. The Great I Am. I will bow to Him wherever He may be. "I am at your service, my King."

"I understand you found Lilly and Skye, is that correct?" His voice booms through the Throne Room as Zeal stands guard. Seraphim fly in reverence emitting light waves of pearl and fire.

"Yes, my King." I answer.

His blue eyes flame brighter as I rise to meet His gaze. "And what was Skye's condition?"

"Alive. Just as you said. Only asleep."

He rises at the confirmation. "Good job, Leafe."

"Yes, my King."

"I need my Commander awake at all times with Lilly or she will be taken."

"I understand, Your majesty."

King Worthy continues. "Hinlors. The Raven. Any and all forces of darkness. They're after her. She is not to be left alone without protection."

Word has been getting out that The Raven is not dead.

The Raven was exterminated by Skye after the Battle of Hanauma Bay and cast into The Black Hole. But his final fate awaits when King Worthy unleashes Armageddon and rids out all of The Raven's minions.

"I won't let anything hurt Lilly, my King." My heartbeat surges as I think about Lilly. Even here in the Throne Room, she is still intertwined with me. I am beginning to take her everywhere now. My mind cannot stop thinking about her.

"Tell me something, Leafe," The King's voice echoes loudly. My ear drums feel the vibration every time He speaks. "Are you in love with Lilly?"

"Since the first time I saw her, Your Majesty."

"I won't allow Lilly to be ignorant to the temptations of love," sounds The King. "If her and Skye are going to be married, she must know what to do when another angel intrudes. You see?"

"Yes, my King."

I understand what He is getting at. His ways are always pure and keen on love. He destined for Skye and Lilly to meet. I have heard the story over and over again, how He flew over Hawaiian seas to find her and rescue her. A divine collision, he calls it. I used to have no intent on interfering with The King's divine orchestrations. But then I saw her. I couldn't keep my hands to myself.

"And you know I have a propensity for training my angels and warriors for resilience."

I look up. "Sir?"

"I know what you are thinking, Leafe. Remember?" He bows low and meets my gaze. Blue sapphire flames flood into me fiercely.

"Yes. But you already destined Skye to meet Lilly."

"I'm doing something more, Leafe. And if you'll trust me, you'll see it works out to your advantage."

"I trust you, King Worthy. I always have and always will."

"Then you know I am the One who presides over love and the entity called 'the heart.'"

"Yes, my King." King Worthy understands the heart better than anyone in the universe. Every emotion, feeling, thought, passion and vibrancy flows from His own attributes of eternity. Without the heart, we can do nothing.

"I have a mission for you, Captain Leafe."

"Anything, my King."

"I need you to make love to Lilly."

I almost choke on my holy water. "You're giving me permission to make love to her?"

"If you love her."

King Worthy doesn't have to ask me twice. But I still have more questions. "Lilly loves Skye. Haven't they already–"

"They haven't made love. Lilly is dissatisfied. I need you to love her. I need her to have the choice: does she want to marry Skye or does she want to marry someone else."

"My King," I pause. "Lilly hates me. I kissed her. Undoubtedly, you see all, my King. She slapped me."

"Lilly is falling in love with you," King Worthy affirms with blazing blue eyes of Zion's fire. "I can see it clearly. And if it's you today, it could be another angel tomorrow. I need her to have experience in choosing who she loves. I care about Lilly's destiny."

Organs blare through the Throne Room and fire shoots up behind the King.

Lilly loves me?

I don't know what to say. The thought of her reciprocating my love makes my wings ready to soar through Zion's barriers into the galactic cosmos. My heart races. All I want is for her to give in to me.

"If she loves me, why does she push me away?" I press Him for more. And He is going to tell me. If He is the only one in the universe who can make sense of this love triangle, I need to know now.

"Because she has General Skye Worthy's ring on her finger. From My own treasury. She believes that Skye is her lover. She does not yet know she has a choice. And there will be others to tempt her." King Worthy looks me in the eyes. "I see all, Leafe. I am not shocked by the goings-on in My universe. Life is much more complex for humans than for angels here in Zion. The female heart is a garden of mysteries. She is just beginning to discover who she is."

"She loves me more than Skye?" I inquire again.

"Would you believe it if I told you?"

I swallow and take a deep breath. "Show me."

The King pauses. "You want to see the Luminary, I can tell."

"Yes, I do. Prove it."

"Purity, prepare The Luminary," commands The King.

The magic sphere appears, and my heart leaps at the thought of what I might see. Will Lilly be talking about me? Purity flies in circular motions and the image of Lilly comes into view. I lean in to glimpse every detail of her beautiful countenance.

"There she is!" Purity exclaims. "Oh, isn't she precious." Purity winks at me, flies over The Luminary, and lands on The King's shoulders.

I smile inwardly. Yes, she is. Precious as can be.

"He kissed you at the door!?" Lilly's friend Jenna covers her mouth, wide-eyed. I forgot Jenna was there. This ought to be dramatic.

Lilly's face blushes and she bites her lower lip. Her hair falls perfectly on her shoulders and she keeps grabbing it, playing with it. My wings perk up. Lilly, your face is beautiful.

"He kissed me, and then I kissed him back. I stopped, but it was too late. I already gave in," she continues and smiles. "Why did I slap him?"

Her disposition looks clearly bothered by the slap. I for one, knew it might happen. I kissed her, after all.

"Because you felt the tension of going behind Skye's back."

"But I didn't go behind Skye's back."

"You kinda did," Jenna says with a wink and takes a bite of a sandwich. "Look, don't worry, honey, you know I've done way worse."

"I didn't mean to," Lilly exclaims, trying to make sense of it all. "He found me and flew away with me into the forest… and before I knew it, he was…"

"What?"

Lilly shakes her head. "Nothing."

"Tell me!"

"He touched my leg in the forest."

"He did what!?" Jenna's eyes enlarge.

My heartbeat increases as Purity overhears. I look up at her, and she watches The Luminary still interested and intrigued.

Lilly continues. "My dress had ripped from the rose thorn at the hem, and he was touching the threads and then, my leg."

"Whoa, girl, he knows how to play." Jenna winks.

Lilly looks away and touches her cheek. "I don't know what to do now."

"Sure, you do. You forget about it. Marry Skye." Jenna takes another bite of the sandwich and then tightens her hair into a ponytail as she sits across from Lilly in the kitchen.

"I have to tell Skye."

"And put your engagement in jeopardy? No, you can't do that!"

"He will find out eventually! He reads my thoughts."

"You have a point there." Jenna walks to the fridge and pours some water for her and Lilly.

"I can't hide this, Jenna." Lilly dips her head onto the island and buries her face.

Jenna walks around to console her. "It's going to be okay," she offers her the water. "Just stay away from Captain Leafe for a little while."

Lilly drinks the water. "Yes, you're right," Lilly says.

"Temptation is there all the time, girl. You just have to decide who your one and only is."

"You're right," Lilly smiles and takes a deep breath like Jenna has just solved the world's greatest problem. "I will say no to Captain Leafe and remember that Skye is my one and only."

"I thought it was Skye. Now I'm not so sure," she thinks to herself. And I can hear it.

"Exactly! You will be over that kiss in no time!" Jenna replies, trying to be convincing.

"Skye is my fiancé, after all," Lilly exclaims.

"General Worthy!" Jenna nods and lifts her glass.

"I don't care about his title. I just want him to love me more. And talk to me how Leafe talks to me." Lilly thinks again. I hear her.

Lilly nods and remains silent.

"I can't wait to see you in that beautiful ball gown of yours, future Mrs. Worthy." Jenna winks and drinks her water.

Lilly's face looks distressed. She looks up and smiles. Then, drinks her water with panic in her eyes. All of the sudden, The Luminary changes its locale to the front door.

"What happening?" I interject.

The King answers. "Lilly is having a flashback. We are watching it play out in her mind."

The Luminary shows me now. There I am diving in to kiss her. Lilly definitely did kiss back. It's plain as day for all to see. I look up and Purity smiles at me. I can't help but blush.

Lilly's eyes brighten. *"Uh oh... I think I'm in love with Leafe."* Lilly's thoughts sound out for me to hear again.

Poof!

The Luminary shuts off to black.

King Worthy speaks up. "There you have it. Proof."

Lilly's thoughts tell no lies.

I stand unable to move.

"I told you she loved you, Leafe. I would not lead you into a losing war."

"You led Skye into a losing war. If Lilly chooses me, he loses."

"Lilly was his to lose." The King walks back to the Throne and anchors His staff in its place at His right side. He turns around to face me regally.

I nod, still surprised at the revelation Lilly loves me. "I want her."

"You see it in The Luminary, she wants you too. You have My permission to choose her just as long as you will not let go of loving her."

"What if she says no?"

"She will at first."

"And later?"

"She will love you forever for pursuing her and winning her heart. Don't give up."

I sigh. "But doesn't she want Skye? He's perfect."

"Lilly does not need the Commander to be happy. She needs true love. A love that brings out the best in her. A love that sees her and treasures her. Your voice wins her, Leafe. Don't doubt it."

"But my voice is invasive at times. When I say the truth, I fear I insult her and I do not want to."

The King steps off the Throne and walks towards me. The ground shakes as the sapphire glass vibrates. Seraphim glide overhead and fire flames from the hearth of Zion.

He stops in front of me with His massive stature. "Do you love her?"

"Dearly." I look up at Him and His stark royalty.

"That's the difference. You love her with every word you say. She knows it. She listens to you." King Worthy smiles. "You make her better. And she makes you better." His voice is fatherly in His tone. A voice I rarely hear except for in conversations like these. "I have given you access to read her thoughts and for her to read yours."

My wings outstretch at the thought of knowing Lilly more. "What do I do next?"

King Worthy's eyes flame. "Win her heart."

14

Lilly

In love with Leafe.

The thought lingers in my mind and seeps into my veins like an IV drip of morphine. The thought of breaking Skye's heart paralyzes me. But it's going to happen eventually. I can already see it coming. Skye will see through me and in that moment, my true feelings will be exposed.

Could it be The King allowed it? Why would He?

In love with Leafe.

I think more about the way he looks at me, and elation sets in like cosmic bliss. I imagine the emergence of fire in his eyes like Zion's flames–the ones that spark in the King's Throne Room. Leafe has a way of being blunt with me but kind at the same time. Skye never does that. Leafe tells me things I don't want to hear but need to hear. And in his voice, I feel the passion of his desire for me and the war inside him trying to hold it back.

Is it just lust? I have no need for lustful indulgence when Skye already captivates me. Is it flattery? But I have never given into another man's flattery before.

Leafe is not a man, though, I remember. He is an angel. Unlike every other man on Earth, just as Skye. Both intrigue me. But I'm in love with Skye, aren't I? How can I be in love with Leafe too?

I feel I haven't had enough experience in love to know what I want for myself. Still, I need to deny these feelings for Leafe and pretend my heart does not intensify with palpitations when he is around. Oh, but Skye will know! He always knows. And Leafe always gets closer.

As thoughts race, I twirl my hair around my finger and look for a safety pin to fix my dress. I would think that I'd find one in an elaborate mansion of this design. Kitchens usually have drawers filled with these kinds of things, don't they? Depends on the house, though. King Worthy built this house for Skye and me. He would think ahead to fill it with what we need.

I search around the kitchen. Cabinet drawers! Let's start there.

The King spared no expense in his design work. The cedar cabinets are covered in white and silver geode rock that shines like crystalline porcelain. What a fine invention. This is the kind of cabinet I would find in a whimsical house of heavenly bliss.

I pull out the cabinet drawer and it flings all the way out of its setting. Oh no! Did I break it? It hovers mid-air. Thank goodness, it's not broken. It's just… supernatural. Even better than a smart house. The drawer moves towards me like it has its own propellors and pauses in front of me. Is this for real? I reach inside the drawer and move about the contents. Safety pin found! Then the cabinet drawer rises and returns to its cabinet setting effortlessly.

I eye my lavender dress and ponder how I should fix the tear. The silk dangles off my left thigh and touches the floor with threads rippling. I quickly gather the fabric, close the gap, and pin it together.

"Why are you pinning an old dress in a new house?"

Poke!

I poke my leg as the voice alarms me.

I turn around. "Who was that?"

Footsteps sound across the glassy floor as the aroma of evergreen leaves and cedar waft in from outside. I breathe and smell the fresh scent, rejuvenating my senses.

"Me."

It's Leafe.

I know his voice.

I turn around from the cabinets, towards the grand room in front of the entrance, and Leafe stands, tall and regal, with wings extended and glistening. My heartbeat speeds up.

"Captain Leafe!" I gasp. "You're here again?"

"I'm here again."

Of course, he's here again. He's standing in front of me. Why did I say that? I make such a fool of myself when he shows up. I never know what to say.

I swallow and try not to blush. "Did you forget something?"

"Yes," he says very matter-of-factly. "You."

Me? What does he mean? I belong to Skye and he knows it. He saw me trying on my wedding dress earlier. Jenna is here to help with the planning, and I cannot think about what-ifs with Leafe right now. I am getting married for goodness' sake.

My wedding day is going to be the most spectacular day of my life. Skye says it will be the best day of our eternal lives. He reminds me all the time we were made to live forever, and we always will. I want to marry him. And I am going to.

"You shouldn't be here," I reply firmly. "You already kissed me once."

A kiss I haven't forgotten.

What a sultry kiss it was. But I am not going to tell Leafe that. As far as he is concerned, that kiss was a mistake and I won't repeating the infraction anytime soon. If he came back hoping he could claim my lips again, he will have to leave without the wish granted.

"We both know it was mutual," he states with a grin.

Leafe keeps staring at me. He always does that.

I look away. Then I look back at him and examine his face for clues to why he keeps coming back to me. Is it lust and fantasy? Does he want what he cannot have? Does he just want to touch me? His strong stance is not giving it away. His face is handsome, I must admit, even though I should not say it out loud. His short brown hair falls ever so ruggedly around his forehead and his green eyes sparkle angelically. That's because he's an angel. But I cannot let him be mine.

"No, it wasn't mutual!" I exclaim, trying to make myself believe it.

I cannot let him have me, even if his allure tempts me.

"Lilly," he says with a drawn-out tone of defiance. "I don't believe you."

"Well, you should believe me. I said, *no*, it wasn't mutual." I look away.

Who am I kidding? Of course it was mutual. I already told myself that. And I told Jenna about the kiss too. I know Leafe can read my thoughts. But I cannot allow him into my head any more than he already is. In fact, he needs to leave soon. His scent is starting to send my body into a place where passion rises.

I look up again. Big mistake. I should have protected my gaze from ever looking at him again. Now I can't look away.

Green eyes find me entranced.

Leafe's eyes burn intensely with bright green flames. Zion's hearth of volcanic magma could not put out the fire I see. Stunningly captivating, they are. I try to look away. But hypnosis grabs me and keeps me in its celestial clutch of ecstasy.

Lilly, you're falling into his spell again! Look away.

"You don't have to look away," he whispers gently and strokes my shoulder.

Even if I wanted to, I couldn't. He has me now.

Leafe blushes at the revelation my thoughts are giving away. "Did you miss me, Lilly?"

"It's only been a few hours, Leafe. Don't be silly." Finally, I break eye contact and look away. I push his hand off my shoulder and reach for my dress again. Why do I keep reaching for my dress? In the moment of angst, it is becoming a habit.

"I think you did," he states with audacity.

Keep your eyes off him, Lilly. Protect your heart or he will reel you in again and you don't want to be a blue fin tuna waiting to be devoured. I only want to be a princess waiting to be twirled.

"I'd like to devour you," Leafe adds. He read my thoughts again.

Leafe steps closer to me. He reaches for my left hand and presses it to his chest. "Do you feel *that*?" he whispers with the aroma of cinnamon and caramel filling my senses. I sigh.

His angelic hand on mine sends electric waves throughout my body. I can feel my pulse increasing and my body heating.

Hide it, Lilly. You cannot tell him how you feel.

"Feel what?" I ask, unwilling to give in.

Leafe's hand stops over his heart with mine interlocked. "Feel my heart beating fast for you."

I sigh, and butterflies enter my stomach like fluttering kites. I stop myself from looking at him again. I can't look at him. I shouldn't. Green eyes of hypnosis will captivate me deeper than before. Close your eyes, Lilly.

"Look at me," he continues.

It seems he is set on seducing me right here, right now. I open my eyes but remain unwilling to surrender. I keep my eyes low.

Fluorescent gemstones catch my attention as I investigate the mansion floors. Gold and silver filigrees interweave with more see-through glass-like geodes of purple and turquoise. The whole floor appears see-through with layers of geode stone and marble. Whimsically fitting for Zion.

"I want you to look at me, not the floor," He demands again.

Fighting back his seduction weakens and, in an instant, I give in. I look up. His green eyes flame for me like wildfire.

"There you are," he says, pleased.

His towering frame leans in and my eyes watch his lips making their way towards mine. I could slap him again. I could fight back and run away. I could scream at the top of my lungs until someone hears me. But as his lips inch closer to mine, my instincts don't react in time to push him away. And before I know it, his mouth is already one with mine like oxygen is one with hydrogen.

Kiss!

Leafe's lips collide with mine.

His kiss feels like an oasis of water flooding into me. Hydrating me. Rejuvenating me. Electricity courses through my mouth all the way to my shoulder blades. His hands clutch my cheeks and my mouth opens as his tongue enters me. Caramel and cinnamon are the flavors of his mouth, just as before. The second dose is just as satisfying. He grips my head and strokes my hair.

Then, he picks me up and wraps his arms around me in the doorway.

"I want you," Leafe whispers in between kisses.

I want you too, I think to myself.

No!

Stop, Lilly. You know you can't do this. I pull away and catch my breath.

I don't want you, Leafe. I can't want you.

"I think you *do*," Leafe persists and kisses me again.

His lips pour over my face and return to my mouth with his tongue waiting for mine. I open for him and he twirls his tongue inside every crevice of my mouth, like a swirling cyclone of pleasure. I kiss him back with the intent to savor every ounce of him.

Then he pulls away and looks me in the eyes.

I swallow. My eyes meander over the curvature of his bright wings and his dark bronze skin.

Leafe smiles with satisfaction and whispers, "I just wanted to tell you goodnight."

Slowly, he sets me down on the glassy floor, opens the door, and flies away.

"Goodnight," I whisper and watch his wings soar into the sky.

Breathe, Lilly.

I breathe in and out, regaining my composure. My hands touch my heart. I feel it racing more and more by the millisecond. My lips feel tingly and raw. I touch them and find glitter on my fingertips from the aftermath. I smile. His lips left glitter all over me. Is it angel dust?

Stop, Lilly. I shouldn't smile. What am I thinking to let him kiss me again? But he comes out of nowhere and I admit I like the way it feels when he comes on to me so strongly. It is like a rush of intoxication. It is a chemical reaction. Just like seismic activity.

"Were you talking to someone, Lilly?" Jenna enters the foyer by the front door where Leafe just kissed me.

I touch my cheek and ponder if I should tell her. "Leafe came back."

"What for?" she exclaims curiously. Her footsteps scurry over the floor in fluffy purple bedroom shoes.

"He said he wanted to tell me goodnight."

"Goodnight?" Jenna inquires and tightens her ponytail with a smirk on her face. "But there is no night in Zion. Surely, that's not all he came back for."

Nighttime may not exist, but we still sleep, even here, since we are human. Leafe knows that.

"I think he wanted to make a move," I say. This was his way of doing it. I like that he did. I've never had someone show up and kiss me like that before. The way he said "goodnight" felt intimate.

I lick my lips, still feeling the glitter. "Leafe came back to..." I pause before going any farther. Should I tell her? That he kissed me again?

Jenna approaches me before I can spill the secret. "Lilly, your lips are glittery!"

I blush. Then I realize I do not want to hold it in any longer. I want her to know Leafe kissed me. I want her to know I am feeling attracted to him. I need to talk about it, and there is no one else besides Jenna who could understand better.

"He kissed me again," I confess, still blushing. "I don't know what to do about this, Jenna. He just showed up so fast and before I knew it, his eyes were looking into me and I couldn't look away."

"Oh my gosh!" Jenna covers her mouth in shock... a rarity for this one, who has made her goal of feminine independence to seduce as many dashing men as she can. I don't judge her for it. I just never thought I'd be in any situation near what she has been in when it comes to men. Well, angels, that is. Skye and Leafe are angels. Yet, I didn't seduce Leafe. He seduced me. My heart flutters thinking about it.

"His eyes," I say in contemplative wonder. "Those green eyes. They're just as bright as Skye's, but different hues," I say recalling his handsomeness.

Jenna touches the glitter on my hands from where I touched my lips. "He sure left trail of pixy dust!"

I smile. "He is an angel, after all."

"Has Skye ever left glitter on your lips before?" Jenna widens her eyes at me with pursed lips.

"No."

"Sounds like someone's in love with Lilly and rivaling his Commander!" Jenna shoots straight and winks at me. "I've read about angels leaving glitter in their wake when they do a miracle."

"What would the miracle be?" I inquire. For someone who says she does not believe in all the wonder of Zion, she reads a lot about angels.

"You'll have to ask him that," she says with hands up. "All I know is Skye is going to be livid."

I inhale and exhale. "Yes, I have to tell him."

Jenna consoles me. "Honey, don't worry about it. Leafe came onto you, remember?"

"I kissed him back," I say honestly.

Trouble for Leafe is not my intent. Not now. I am too aware of my own choices in the matter. I definitely kissed him back, and I wanted him. Something about his aura commands me in a way I can't describe and can't push away. I need to let the chips fall where they may. Hiding this from Skye is not something I want to do.

Jenna touches my shoulders and looks at me with her maternal look. Oh no. Is she going to give me a sex talk?

"Look, my little rose," Jenna begins. "I know you. In the end, you will do what is right. You always have and you won't stop now."

I knew Jenna was my best friend for a reason. Her words resonate, and her faith in me renews my optimism that this will not break me and Skye. If anything, it will only make Skye and I stronger. Won't it?

I twirl my hair and keep pondering. "What about Skye?"

"Skye is a General, for goodness' sake. If he cannot handle, and subdue, a little drama in his own house, how can he command Zion?"

"Good point," I exclaim.

"And now, we must explore the rest of your house, my lady!" Jenna pulls my hand and starts down the long hallway. "Come with me!"

Lilly and Leafe. I like the sound of it already. The alliteration in our names matches. Maybe it was meant to be. Oh Lilly, stop it now! I'm letting my thoughts get the best of me. I am marrying Skye and that is the end of it. No more Leafe. I cannot do this. I was not made for two angels. Only one. I only want one.

"There's not just a his-and-her bathroom, but an entire suite for the bathroom! Seven sinks! You want to see?"

"Of course!" My eyes light up and we run down the fluorescent hallway. The walls are gold, lined with white crystals and more fluorescent gems. The pictures on the wall are memories of me and Skye together. Oh, I remember this one at the Eiffel Tower where Skye and I danced under the moonlight! And this one at Ka'a'awa Beach!

I turn to Jenna. "Who took these pictures?"

"The King can see everything, right?" Jenna replies.

He must have photographed them for us. Perhaps The Luminary came into play. "Zion thinks of everything, that's for sure."

Jenna glides down the hallways with lit eyes. She must have perused the house while me and Leafe were... well, together. "And before we get to the bathroom, check out this outdoor gazebo through the windows by the garden! Cumin, lavender, tulips, azaleas, orchids, and every kind of plant you could ever dream of. I already went outside and there is a Kindle set up for you Lilly with access to every book in human history."

"Even 'Sense and Sensibility?'" I gasp excitedly.

"Yes, my little rose. Even that God-awful tragedy of arranged marriage and classical Victorianism. I hope one day you will get past that."

"In due time, my lady." I say in jest.

"Mmm hmm." Jenna retorts. "This way!"

We run through the hallways of golden icy allure into a left hallway coated in tangerine bright colors. The wall stands see-through, revealing fruits behind the glass.

"This hallway is divine!" Jenna explodes. "Look at the fruits still perfectly ripe behind the glass! It's like it never spoils. Passionfruit, mangoes, kiwis, bananas, and fruits I've never seen before."

"It is Zion, after all," I exclaim, with intrigue and curiosity. Every part of the house is exceptionally reflective of Zion's bliss. I can't wait to see the pool and waterfalls. "Can you take me to the pool?"

"Pool?" Jenna asks.

"Yes," I say. "Surely in the General's mansion, there is a pool for good use and blissful swims." Diving into a fresh body of water is just what I need to refresh me after that unexpected, riveting encounter with Leafe.

Jenna pauses. "There is. I just didn't know you would want to go swimming after the–"

"Drowning?"

"Yes," she says softly. Jenna is still sensitive to the moment that almost claimed my life. I like to think of it as the moment that gave me life. Meeting Skye is a moment I would never wish away.

"I'm okay," I assure her.

"Really, Lilly? You haven't been swimming since then and I don't want you to drown," she states, revealing her maternal instincts.

"I promise!" I say readily. "Trust me, I want to feel the water again. I'm ready."

When Jenna's maternal instincts kick in, they kick in strong. Still, I'm grateful to have a best friend who senses how I feel.

"Okay, girl!" She backs off.

"Really, I'm fine. Besides, an angel always shows up to rescue me if I am ever in any danger," I proclaim with serendipity at the idea of it.

Jenna smiles and throws up her hand to signal the way. "To the pool, it is!"

Outside the giant windows, starry skies shine overhead. We run through the tall French doors painted in white sparkles and onto the checkered grass. A turquoise waterfall cascades from a hill into the pool where a river circles the body of water. Even under the moonlight, the water glistens like Swarovski crystals.

My eyes brighten and I do a little leap. "King Worthy told me there would be a waterfall!"

"Let's dive in!" Jenna removes her slippers and jumps in. The water churns and sways.

Waves rock and wiggle as I encroach upon the poolside entrance. The water settles at the edge and gets deeper with every footstep I take, just like at Waimea Bay.

My mind starts to shift in and out of consciousness. All of a sudden, I see waves sweep over my head. I wonder if I am hallucinating or if it is only my imagination. How do you know the difference?

I stop plunging into the water and stand up straight. "Jenna, I'm having flashbacks."

She halts in motion and looks back at me terrified. "Are you serious?"

Breathe in, Lilly!

Blast!

Tidal waves sweep over me and I am unable to breathe.

Plunge! I fall into the waters, on my back. The initial shock on impact renders my arms frozen. I cannot move.

Thunder rattles over me and water trickles into my ears. Waimea depths surround me. I dip into the icy sea and fall faster than a brick dropped from 20 feet above. Coral reef stabs my left leg again. My head whips from the impact.

"Lilly! Lilly, are you there!?"

I can't speak. Everything looks black.

"Lilly!"

My eyes shut.

Legs collapse.

Thump!

"Oh my gosh!" Jenna screams and her voice sounds muffled. "Lilly, you're bleeding!"

My body falls numb.

15

Leafe

"What happened!?" I ask Jenna hastily.

Jenna looks at me shocked and speechless, clearly rattled by Lilly's second near-death experience. The shock has her shook and unable to resuscitate Lilly. I step in and assess the situation.

I check Lilly's pulse. "Have you tried?"

Jenna eyes me. "Tried what?"

"CPR?"

"I…" she says frazzled, "I didn't know I was supposed to!" She throws up her hands and pulls her hair.

I nod and quickly position myself on top of Lilly by the secluded waterfall. "Move to the side, please."

Lilly's wet hair folds around her porcelain skin as her eyes lay shut. As much as I want to take advantage of the moment on top of Lilly's divine body, her safety is my number one concern.

Focus, Leafe. No time for toying around with her perfect lips and sultry tongue. She needs to breathe right now.

I press hard on her chest, and count, "1-2-3." Then I open her lips and breathe into her mouth. Again, I press hard on her chest, and count, "1-2-3." Then I breathe into her mouth. I taste glitter, just as I left her.

Cough! Cough!

Lilly spews up water rapidly.

"Oh my gosh, Lilly!" Jenna shrieks and smiles at her.

Lilly opens her eyes.

"Green eyes find me at the waterfall," she thinks.

I blush at the intrusion of reading her mind.

Lilly lifts her head and starts to speak. "What happened?"

Jenna gasps. "You said you were having flashbacks, then fell into the pool. Hit your head on the edge. I tried to save you, Lilly. You were falling under. Leafe heard it and dove in for you," Jenna affirms comfortingly. "You're okay now!"

"Is that true, Leafe? You saved me?" Her brown hair shines all wet. Green eyes glow. I love looking at her and I don't feel guilty about it at all.

I breathe in and out. "Yes."

Her eyes gaze at me still.

"Green eyes find me in the twilight."

I hear her thoughts again. Her porcelain skin glows in the starry sky and I remember my frame is straddling her. I quickly elevate and fly off her. I stand up and slick back my hair.

"I was doing CPR," I explain.

"I don't know how to thank you."

I smile. "You don't have to."

"Surely I do, Captain Leafe."

"We both know I wasn't going to be able to fly her up and out of the water fast enough!" Jenna interjects and tightens her ponytail. At least she is honest.

Lilly smiles and begins to laugh. I can tell Jenna lightens the mood for her. For that, I am grateful. But I want more alone time with Lilly.

"Have dinner with me."

"Dinner?"

"Yes," I say eagerly. "I have one of the most amazing chefs in all of Zion, next to the King. He tries new recipes frequently. I want to show you what you have never tasted before." So much more than food, that is.

Her lips look desirable and sensual under the moonlight. I do not doubt her innocence, but I like to imagine her wild side.

Be naughty with me, Lilly. Just for a twilight.

Get ahold of your thoughts, I tell myself. Just for a twilight? Lilly is anything but a one-twilight stand. She is an eternal stand of endless love and light. I don't want to make love to her just one time. I want it endlessly.

Lilly sits up and reaches for something. "Is there a towel?"

"Here, Lilly!" Jenna wraps a pink towel around her, and rubs her shoulders and arms.

"You haven't answered me, Lilly," I remind her.

"I'm thinking," she asserts and towels off her wet hair.

I wish she would have left it wet and dripping. Just how I like it.

I persist. "What is on your mind?"

She sighs and rises to her feet, regaining her beautiful smile with peachy lips. "Skye," she says.

I clear my throat and nod. "I know you love Skye. But I'd like to take you to dinner. Since I rescued you after all."

The nerve of this angel, she thinks.

I bite my lip at the thought of her considering it. I know she wants time with me just as badly as I do.

"I'll make you a cinnamon tea if it helps to persuade you. I know you like my caramel and cinnamon." I look at her directly, without breaking eye contact.

Lilly gasps, licks her lips, and turns her head, trying to hide her reddening cheeks.

"Am I missing something?" Jenna inquires.

Lilly finally answers. "Jenna and I were supposed to have dinner together to break in the new house." Lie. Lilly is searching for excuses.

"It's true!" Jenna responds. "We were going to make waffles and enjoy homemade syrup from the maple trees in that forest you took her to, Captain."

The gall of Jenna to assert her quick wit by me. "I'll have you know, I took her there for good reason."

I stop myself.

Inhale, Leafe. Exhale. Breathe.

Angels are protectors not instigators.

And Jenna is right. I did take her there. Whatever talk has transpired between the two of them about my advances on Lilly is a risk I knew

I was taking. I have to roll with the punches. Like it or not, Jenna will always be a part of Lilly's life. Skye found a way to include her. I must find a way not to expel her.

"What do you say, Lilly?" I ask again. She may turn me down out of loyalty to Skye but I am not one to back down easily.

Lilly looks at me again. Opens her mouth of succulent sweet lips. "Give me fifteen minutes."

I'll take that as a yes.

I'm in.

Yes, Leafe, you're in! I knew she would cave in to me. I only hope she won't let go of me. I am afraid I won't be able to dine with her just one time.

I nod and try to hide my grin. "I'll wait."

Hold back your racing heart, Leafe.

Lilly paces back to the glassy doors, with the pink towel wrapped around her. I watch her walk. Her feet are tiny and cute. Did I just think the word *cute*? I think I did. The word fits her well, and I like to think of her as such.

"So, tell me what your end game is here, big boy?" Jenna quickly digs in with crossed arms and glares at me.

Did she just call me "*big boy?*"

"Jenna, I'll have you know I am under the authority of The King of Zion to see to it that Lilly is cared for. My methods are not under your control nor your judgment."

She looks at me squarely. "No, I guess not. That's what The King does isn't it? Judge people."

"The King loves people."

"Then why are so many rotting in that God-awful place called Hell?"

My heart shivers at the questions, and I realize she doubts The King's love. That is her main reason for not trusting me, even more than the fact I am in love with her best friend.

"That is each person's own choice," I answer.

"Their own choice?" Her eyes widen.

"Yes."

Jenna looks down at the clover-filled grass and rubs her feet over its texture. "So, people willingly choose to go to hell instead of a beautiful place like this? That just makes so much sense." She rolls her eyes at me.

"Nobody would choose to deny a place like Zion, Jenna. It's that they deny The King. They deny their Maker."

The universe of endless stars in her Texas sky is the same universe she stands in right now, only the locales have changed. The King who reigns over it is the same. One day she will see it.

Jenna uncrosses her arms and looks about, unwilling to make eye contact with me. "So, if I deny The King I won't be welcome in Zion?" she asks.

"Looks like King Worthy already brought you here, didn't He?" I remind her.

"Well, I'm not dead though. I didn't pass into the afterlife."

I narrow my eyes on her. "But you accepted His invitation."

Jenna pauses and looks up at me fuming, like she has a vendetta to win this conversation. I just don't know if she will.

"I said yes to Lilly." Jenna clarifies.

"You knew who would be here, though, Jenna. This is The King's jurisdiction. This is Zion. And you still accepted His invite."

She pauses again and scratches her head. Looks away. Then, eyes me again.

"Yes, I can see your point," she sighs. "You'd make a good lawyer."

"I haven't the need for one. I am an angel, after all."

"Angel," she says in a drawn-out tone and smiles suspiciously. "How can I trust angels? I read once that the devil himself used to be bright angel." Jenna tilts her head and looks up into the starry skies.

"Trust me, you don't want to live outside of Zion's protection."

"What if I do?" she challenges me. "What if I want to leave and never come back?"

I look up at the stars and wonder what will become of all the angels who left Zion. "You know, angels have a choice also," I disclose. "We have a choice to let King Worthy be King or not. Your fate depends on this, Jenna."

"Why?"

"Because there is no one else out there to save you besides *Him*. Besides *us*," I affirm boldly. "You can choose your way. I choose King Worthy."

Jenna nods and bends down to play with the pool water, averting eye contact again.

I pause and let her think.

Her demeanor changes, she stands and looks at me anxiously. "You're not going to hurt Lilly, are you?"

"Hurt Lilly? No."

"I've dated guys like you," she says and turns to look at me again, like a bull ready to butt heads with a lion. "You come on to the innocent, pure girl and make her feel things she has never felt… and before you know it, she gives in to you."

"I wasn't the first one to domineer Lilly and you know that."

"No boundaries either! A real tough guy."

I step forward, with wings flaring and eyes fuming. "I am not a *guy*, Jenna."

Jenna eyes me, ready to spar.

"Oh, angel, sorry, I forgot," she says sarcastically.

"I'm ready!" Lilly announces.

My head turns as Lilly approaches us from the house in a teal sundress with her hair pulled back in a ponytail. I sigh with relief and satisfaction. Her entrance breaks up the tension between me and Jenna. I smile as I gaze at Lilly's beauty.

"You look beautiful, Miss Rose." My eyes, still flaming, look her over, and transform into loving fire.

"Green eyes find me in fire." I can hear her thoughts.

"You can call me Lilly, remember?" Lilly smiles at me and winks sweetly.

My serenity returns at her beautiful smile. I move closer to Lilly and lean in to kiss her, but Jenna is still there. I must hold back a kiss until I have Lilly alone. "Are you ready for dinner," I pause to say her first name, "Lilly?" I ask eagerly.

Lilly smiles. "Yes."

Lilly's eyes are gorgeously alluring. I swallow and spread my wings to prepare to fly away with her.

"Jenna, is everything okay?" Lilly asks. "I thought I heard you screaming at Leafe." Lilly is perceptive.

"We're good!" Jenna throws her hands up and backs away. "Don't worry about me, have a good time!" With a splash, Jenna dives into the pool and swims towards the waterfalls.

"Jenna!" Lilly exclaims and waves her hands at her to come back.

"Oh no, is Jenna mad at me? I should have turned down Leafe. What am I doing? Skye is not going to like this, and I have my wedding to think about." I hear Lilly's thoughts.

"Lilly, relax." I stroke her cheek. "She's mad at me, not you."

Lilly breathes out. "Why is she mad at you?"

"Because she is overprotective of her best friend who has a fiancé."

Lilly tilts her head in agreeance and smiles. "The irony of Jenna Houston. She sleeps with any man she wants but finds my dilemma with two angels upsetting."

"We are not a dilemma, Lilly," I say abruptly.

Lilly looks up. "What are we?"

"We are going to dinner. And I am taking care of the future queen while her angel is sleeping." I can't make any promises to her right now about what we are.

In time, our fates will align. If The King allows.

Looking up to the starry sky of Zion, I find my direction. Dancing under this light would be thrilling. I spin Lilly. Dip her backwards. Lift off the ground.

"Leafe, you go too fast!" She shrieks.

"You'll get used to it." I blush at her reaction. Deep down, she likes it. Even if she won't admit it just yet.

"My stomach just dropped as he took off, but I like the way it feels when he catches me off guard. I am not going to tell him that, though. I must keep my feelings to myself as much as possible without him reading me."

"I read you, Lilly," I remind her.

She clears her throat. "Don't drop me," she says sharply.

"Just hold on. Then, I won't drop you."

"You're rather blunt sometimes," she says.

"Safety demands it," I assure her. "Remember I can always tell what you're thinking."

"I know," she retorts.

"His wings embrace me differently than Skye's. Rougher and strong, with the smell of cedar and musk. He feels rugged and masculine. Brawny and dirty, even. He isn't dirty, though. He's perfectly clean and wistful, just as an angel should be. But his rugged smell makes me feel feminine, enclosed in his perfect, large wings."

I read her thoughts again.

Lilly's mind keeps racing. I know she cannot control it, but it intrigues me.

"Do you like it?" I ask.

"Lilly, he knows what you are thinking! Stop the fantasizing."

"Like it?" She asks as if I don't already know what she is thinking. "How dare you ask me such a question?"

"I hear you thinking about my wings, Lilly. And my scent."

She clears her throat again. "Forget what you heard."

"I'd like to remember, if it's all the same to you."

"The nerve of this angel! Keep your mind off him, Lilly. I stay quiet in the confines of his white wings. Heat entraps me. His feathery warmth holds me like a cashmere blanket glowing from the light of Zion's atmosphere. Emeralds gems line his wings like fireflies in an evergreen forest. His bronze skin accents his mahogany brown hair like potent chocolate. And here I am again thinking about him. Stop, Lilly."

I could stop her, but I don't want to. I want to hear what else she has to think about me.

"I love how he tightens his wings around me. He soars fast. Really fast. I feel like I'm holding on for dear life when he flies with me."

Her thoughts intrigue me.

I could slow it down for her, but I don't think she wants that. She wants who I am and I am different than Skye. And, truth be told, she soothes me more than she knows.

Rose petals waft in from the scent of her brown hair. I love the silky texture on my face as I hold her.

"Lilly, I see why Skye loves flying with you. You're the perfect flight partner," I confess.

She fits in my arms exactly right. I am excited for her to be inside my bungalow and eat beside me, just her and I.

"Does he mean it? Or is this just a dinner to satisfy his craving for me?"

I never stop wanting her, no matter how many times I try to stop.

"I can't let this go beyond tonight. We will have dinner of finest cuisine–that he professes to be undeniable–and then I will stop talking to him. Simple as that. He is just going to move on anyways. I have a fiancé. He will want his own. I will be left in tears."

Her thoughts crush me.

My feathers meld around her. "I would never drop you, Lilly."

Don't you see I love you, yet?

Of course, I haven't told her that I do. How could I? She has a fiancé and I am in the middle of this at The King's request, which, admittedly, is my wish also. I liked the idea of pursuing Lilly.

"How do I know you mean it?" she asks me.

She questions my motives and I will have to deal with that until she trusts me.

I tighten my grip on her. "Trust me."

She doesn't reply, but I can sense she wants to trust me. I hear her inhale and exhale. Her head rests on my shoulder. And I keep flying.

We fly over the River of Life meandering through the countryside of Zion's terrain. The starry light makes the water glisten like diamonds.

"I've never seen this part of the river before," Lilly gasps with excitement.

"We are miles away from Zion's city center."

"The river is beautiful from the vantage point." Joy is in her voice. Renewed joy. Nature brings that out of her. The awe-struck side. She loves what she sees in Zion. And I love what I see in her.

If I'm honest, I want to see more of her.

I remember the first time I saw her. She reeled me in right then and there, in that little Italian café, *Stromboli's*, with her family. She did not know it then. She still doesn't know it. I remember the night like it was yesterday…

⸎

"Congratulations to the happy couple!"

Onlookers raised their glasses.

A man proposed.

Lilly watched with sincere eyes, joining in the couple's celebration of engagement, even though she had no promise of her own. Little did she know, I had a letter from Skye professing his love. He sent me to find her.

"I need you to take this letter, Captain Leafe. It's high priority!" Skye assured me.

"Yes, sir," I answered.

I flew without question. That's my job. To do what is asked and serve my Commander. I didn't know Lilly yet, but I did know Skye and he only sends messages by couriers. I knew that if he was asking me to take this message to her personally, this girl must be special. He was right.

When I arrived, I quickly recoiled my wings, peered through the lobby, and made my rounds through the restaurant. I wanted to see this girl up close first, before giving her the letter.

She didn't know me at the time. So, I didn't have to worry about alarming her to my presence. I dimmed my angelic light not to alert the humans that something extraterrestrial was in the room.

Then I saw her.

I liked what I saw.

Peachy cheeks and lip gloss shown from her face. I saw bright eyes akin to the angels. My heart pulsed. The proposal ensued. Lilly beamed watching them. I knew I needed to leave the letter and get back to Zion before I began to fall more in love with her.

"I have a letter," I told the hostess dressed in black and white. "For the young lady at the Rose family table, please." I pointed at the table. "Her name is Lilly."

The hostess reached for a pen. "Thank you, and your name?"

"Leafe."

"No problem, I will let her know!" the hostess replied with ease.

I nodded and waited patiently.

The hostess meandered through the table aisles and alerted Lilly. Lilly smiled and looked around excitedly as if to look for the one who sent it. Quickly, she walked towards the lobby.

I told myself I needed to go. She's looking for Skye, I told myself. But I still needed to make sure the letter was received. So I decided to leave the letter on the hostess stand and watch to ensure she opened it. That was my job. I didn't need to cross the line.

I found a nook at the far end of the lobby to watch the scene play out.

The hostess gave her the letter.

My job was done.

Heartbeats rang loudly in my chest the whole way back to Zion. I couldn't stop thinking about her. Her purple dress with white at the *hem. Her peach cheeks and peaceful aura. Her voice. I would keep this to myself, however, and not alert Skye that he found the one. He'd see through me. He'd know I felt the same way. I had to keep my feelings to myself.*

"Leafe!"

I refocus and come out of the flashback.

Ahead of us, the edge of Zion nears where angels cross over into outer space. Only a few more galactic miles and we'd be in the cosmos headed towards Earth. Thinking about that memory made me get distracted.

"I got caught up." That's to say the least. "Hold on."

I veer my wings due west, towards my bungalow for dinner.

Lilly tightens her grip on me. "Where are we?"

"Still in Zion."

"Don't worry, Lilly. I am an angel, remember? I know every part of the universe like the back of my hand," I tell her through my thoughts.

"I'm trusting you, Leafe."

"Good," I say.

My wings pick up speed. I see the bungalow up ahead, nestled in the Swan Mountains. The King dusts the peaks with snow constantly, and the meadows at the foothills always have wildflowers. Lilly loves flowers, I can tell. After dinner, I will show her.

"What would you like for dinner?" I ask. "My chef can make anything."

"Surprise me."

I smile. "I thought you'd say that."

"But I didn't think it, yet. How'd you know?" she asks me intrigued.

"Just a hunch."

Smack!

My wings sting. "Lilly, why did you hit me?"

"That wasn't me!"

Zoom! Zoom!

Rapid wings speed by me in the air. Red eyes. Evil hinlors.

I surveyed the land earlier and found nothing. All the barriers of Zion were clear. Light rays were sent out for exterminating anything foul. They must have slipped in again because of Lilly's presence here. Her light keeps attracting attacks. But I will crush them into oblivion.

Screech! Its tone echoes dark and sullen. A familiar threat. This will be fast and painless. Hinlors should know better than to threaten Zion's angels. Their wings are no match for us.

"Let go of her now!" they scowl.

I shake my head and look them in the eye. "Not a chance."

Screech! Fire breathes from their mouth.

My wings absorb the fire and spit it back at them like a boomerang. It only feeds their fuel. I need to decimate them.

I pause mid-air. If I let them come to me, I can swerve to the left, to the right and up out of their grasp. Their reflexes are slow and, with the right maneuver, I can trick them into a crash. I've seen these come at me before.

I wait.

Then, I make my move.

Left, right, up. They clash beneath us and scowl at the collision. Ash falls like confetti.

Easy.

I cradle Lilly's head. "Lilly, are you okay?"

She takes deep breaths. "Yes."

"Don't worry," I say urgently. "I won't let go of you."

Dig!

Yikes, my back stings from an impact to my left wing. I turn around in flight. Red eyes peer back at me jaded. "Lilly is mine!"

King Worthy told me not to leave her out of my sight or they'd come after her. He was right. But these hinlors will not survive this encroachment.

"Lilly belongs to Zion," I state unphased. "And you owe The King an apology for trespassing on holy ground."

Scowl!

The last hinlor lunges at me mid-air. I slice it with the left wing. Front kick. Right jab. My studded emeralds break its jaw. "You're done for!" I decree. "No resident danger allowed in Zion."

One last flash should do it.

Flash!

My eyes send rays into its body and it disintegrates into pieces.

Lilly gasps and breathes heavily. "Oh, my goodness!"

We hover over the stench of dead hinlors. I move away from the site. By dawn, Zion's earth will absorb the dead ash and rejuvenate it with holy ointment. The King designed it that way. Death cannot stay. Life always births again.

I turn Lilly around to face me as I hold her in flight. "You alright?"

"I am, yes," she says a little frightened.

"You don't have to be afraid, Lilly. I promise you, hinlors can never take us out."

"I'm not afraid!" She snaps back at me. "Sorry," she pauses and sighs. "It's just... It's not that I'm scared. I want that to be made known."

"What is it then?"

"It's that they keep targeting me."

She's perceptive, alright. I knew that back at the house. Deep down, she knows. The dark spirits want her dead. And why would they want her dead? Because she is chosen. And she is destined to reign for eternity with us in Zion.

I soften my tone to ease her. "Consider it a compliment."

"I don't want compliments," she continues to overreact. "I want safety and sanity."

"There is no safety for the one The King chooses. Only courage," I spiral up into the fresh air, hold her tight, and prepare to fly onward. "You have a higher calling. Time to accept it."

16

Skye

"*Come, gather for the great feast of God!*"
Trumpets sound.

The angel who spoke stands in the sun on Zion's crest, where my father said the dawning of Armageddon would begin. Her face shines purely and regally, emitting the heavenly radiation of our Kingdom. Her arms extend outward to honor the King.

Zion's armies hover below her, in set formation, with wings outstretched and lit up brightly like The King's glory in highest resolution.

They wait for the signal.

When my father says go, Zion's armies attack. Zion will avenge Earth's people and destroy every work of darkness in the universe to inaugurate New Zion.

Swoop!

Birds fly overhead for the feast of all flesh that opposes my father. This is a prophecy foretold from long ago, where mutations of winged creatures eat the scraps of what's left of evil.

Flash!

Time shifts like a rolodex.

I see a vision of the lurking wings waiting.

Caw! Caw! They fly in circles, irked by the stench of death. Ready to consume.

"Let's get it over with!" the birds shout, ready for feasting.

"Not until I slay first!" The rider on the white horse appears. Crowned in glory.

His face, bloodied, shines like holy wildfire in the California redwoods of Earth. His eyes, afire, blaze like passion in a royal blue sky, ready to claim His Bride. The earth is His, and now we will have her people once again to be one with us.

A fierce warrior gallops through the cosmic air between Zion's outer edge and galactic airspace where Zion's Angels wait, peaceful and euphoric.

Angels perk up their wings at his entrance.

"Faithful and True" is written on His robe. "King of kings and Lord of lords" is written on His thigh, bloodied from battle.

"The war is yet won!" He shouts. "All the kings of the earth and spirits of the heavens against the light of our God have been brought low!"

He faces the front lines of Zion's armies on the white horse in galactic air.

Angels wait, resolute.

"Finish it!" He shouts.

"For Zion!" Angels chant in unison. "All hail King Worthy!"

He charges forward.

Angels follow.

Burst!

Bright, glowing light detonates from the host of angels carrying the goodness of Zion. Angels dawn upon the earth like a tidal wave surging into the shore and beyond. They overtake every spot of the earth's surface looking for souls who are waiting for The King's return. Eyes open all over the earth as souls lift to Zion.

Flash!

My vision turns black.

Flash!

The vision comes back.

Fire ravages the earth, and ashy soot paves its ground like dark cinders still hanging on to its last spark of fire.

The Rider on the white horse circles the aftermath. "Feast on the flesh, my birds of the air!" The Rider resounds.

Birds lunge towards the decaying flesh where flames brim and smoke rises.

"Tasty flesh!" They shriek. "Oh, the merriment of Armageddon's end!" Roar!

"Zion's Angels! Capture the beast!" The Rider announces as the angels storm towards the beast like a magnet on stainless steel. Only this beast is anything but stainless. It is grievous and despicable for luring souls away from The King. A spell, it will cast on the souls of Earth who succumb to its deception. Those who see through the deception will survive.

Flash!

The scene shifts like a rolodex.

"The earth is ripe for reaping!" The angel echoes in the sun, steadfast with enlarging eyes of Zion's intensity.

More of Zion's armies advance into every bit of Earth searching for souls to take up to Zion. The finale of Armageddon is here.

My eyes blink. Blinding light fills my vision. I can hardly make out my periphery.

"Skye." A voice whispers in the light.

I blink again.

"Hello, Skye," she whispers again.

A face comes close.

It's her.

The angel in the light.

✍

Eyes open.

Blink, blink.

Quiet meadows surround me in the same vineyard of rose and merlot. Skies paint the atmosphere with navy gloss and glittering champagne. I have always been one to indulge in the beauty of Zion's skies. Unlike Earth, it keeps its brightness regardless of day or night because time is nonexistent. Here in Zion, eternity is reality.

Night is never night here in Zion. It is merely a reminder that night exists on the earth. Light is still penetrating every picturesque view of our landscape, as the light of The King keeps it radiant for eternity. Just like my Lilly flower. Radiant and lovely for all eternity. Her aura reminds me of light's victory. Her voice sounds like tranquil waters in the teal green pools of Zion's waterfalls. I need to hear it again.

I look about and find Lilly missing.

My hands frolic over the fragrant roses and luscious grapes where Lilly's dress had gotten torn. It only seems like seconds ago.

"Lilly, where are you?" I sound out but I hear no answer.

How could she be missing? There is nowhere else for her to go without me. She can't fly without me.

I stand to my feet.

Crash!

My feet collapse from under me. That's never happened before. I look at my feet and check my body for injury. I must have been dreaming. If Lilly is gone, then something has transpired that I must discover at once.

Lift! I stretch my wings to fly. They stay stationary and my body is still stuck in the grapes of Zion's finest merlot.

"Skye," a voice calls out to me again. The same voice from the dream. The angel in the light.

"Go to sleep, Skye," the voice tells me.

A hand tenderly touches my eyes. The face, I cannot see, but for the light surrounding the aura of the presence.

But I don't need sleep… I need to find Lilly!

I doze off…

My eyes go black.

My head drifts back into dreaming.

⚮

"Blessed are those who are invited to the wedding feast of the Lamb!" An angel hovers over me with a fountain pen and white stationery. "Write it."

Write it? What for?

153

The angel draws in closer with peach plum eyes of fire. "To remember what is to come," he says.

"We are gathered here today to celebrate the wedding of the Worthy Son of Zion! And His exquisite Bride!"

It's my father's voice.

I look up and golden confetti floats in the air without falling to the ground, like a glittering canopy of open-air elegance. Beneath the confetti stand the groom and bride, facing one another.

"Who gives this woman away to be married?"

"I do." Grant Rose stands confidently, and my father nods in unison.

"Lilly!" I shout. "Lilly, is it you?!"

Whoosh!

Whirling winds rush into the vision. Golden confetti swirls like an ice cream maker churning sorbet.

Lilly's dress kicks up in the wind, making the train float in the air like a silk scarf tossed into the sky. Her veil flutters like butterfly wings. Her bouquet rustles. Rose petals emancipate themselves from the floral bouquet to join the wind.

"To Lilly, my perfect bride," begins the groom.

Flash!

My vision takes me to the altar and I see the face of Captain Leafe Worthy staring into my Lilly flower's eyes.

"No!" I beg and shout! "Lilly's mine!"

I lunge for Leafe, but my body does not land. I fly through him like a ghost, unscathed and unnoticed by him, Lilly, or anyone for that matter.

"Lilly, can you hear me!?" I persist. She doesn't see me.

"Your strength and beauty won me the moment I first saw you," Leafe recounts. "You are gentle, poised, fearless, and sassy. But I knew your sassy side would succumb to me," he says with a grin.

Lilly blushes.

I throw up my hands and rage. "Leafe! Leave my bride, at once!" I shout. I wave my hands in front of his face. "Hello!?" My attempts fall on deaf ears, as my presence in this dream is surely invisible. What kind of dream would make me invisible and Leafe wed to Lilly? Who is manipulating the story? Father! Surely You can hear me! Is this Your doing?

"I love you, General Leafe Worthy." Lilly recites back to him.

Leafe kisses her hands with slow kisses all the way up her arm.

"I love you, Lilly Rose," he responds with eyes that look at her hypnotically.

This has got to be some kind of joke, right? Is someone playing with me? Father, is the universe at war with the fate of Zion?

"Your audacity taught me how to fight. Your truth taught me how to love," Lilly recites as she holds his hands at the altar.

Didn't I teach you to love?

Breathe in, Skye. Breathe out.

I touch my chest and I feel it tightening. Fogginess sets in.

Flash!

My vision goes black.

Eyes open.

"Ahhh!" I let out a scream.

Inhale, Exhale. Repeat. Control yourself, General. You have an army to command. A Kingdom to oversee. A universe to protect. Get a hold of yourself. There must be a reason why the angels have shown you this dream.

Tears begin to flow, involuntarily.

I close my eyes.

Silence befalls me. My mind drifts into a state of dormancy. I don't want to think about the possibility of what I saw being real.

"Skye," a voice whispers.

I look around me and no one is in sight.

"What is it?" I answer, hoping to solve the mystery.

Wind picks up and flowers lift up into the air.

The voice speaks softly, "Lilly has been taken from you."

17

Lilly

Leafe's wings fold around me like satin palm branches. I like the way it feels in his wings. He didn't drop me when the hinlors fought him, either. He handled it without any pressure, like he had done it a million times. When the hinlors fired off at us with raging fire, my nerves relaxed in Leafe's wings. I didn't feel the need to panic. Leafe takes care of me.

I rest my head against his shoulder as we fly on. We follow the river meandering peacefully through the meadows. Memories of flying over Hawaii come to mind as I think of my only other flight partner, Skye. I remember how he flew me over the Ko'olau mountains in the moonlight. Then, to Paris on a starry night. But I never felt at ease the way Leafe makes me feel when we fly. I would never tell Skye that, though.

"You like how I fly?" Leafe asks.

Of course, he always knows what I am thinking. I don't know how I can ever be alone with myself ever again and feel the comfort of my own recollection.

"You already know it. You read my thoughts," I confess, mortified again.

Part of me wants to sigh with overwhelm at my personal feelings being known, and the other part of me says let him in. What if he ends up knowing me better than Skye? That's what I'm afraid of.

"Lilly," Leafe speaks. "The King would not grant me access to your thoughts if He did not want me to read you."

"Why would He want you to read me?" I ask confused.

The King led me to Skye. Now, He's involving Leafe. What good can possibly come from Leafe being involved when He knows Leafe is in love with me? The King can see everything.

"Bingo."

I speak up. "Is this just a game to you?"

"The King can see everything, Lilly. Let Him be King," Leafe exclaims.

Let Him be King, I think back to myself. I *am* letting Him be King.

"I know you are, Lilly. But He has a vision in mind. Let go of needing to know all the pieces right now."

I breathe in and breathe out.

Zion's skyline still shows the galactic space beyond the horizon as we fly. Navy blue skies speckled with stars and deep purple mosaics mixed with golden peaches paint the tapestry of the cosmos. It's bright out here. Brighter than any starry night in Texas. The light never ceases to dazzle with illustrious radiance and passionate hues of colors that make your jaw drop in every direction. Like endless sunsets and northern lights. Eternal bliss of limitless color palettes for the eye's pleasure. I could get used to this.

Watching the sunset was always my favorite pastime at home. That is, until I waited all night from sunset to dark for Skye to return from battle and he never came. I thought to myself, is this really the end of my poetic love for the sun? How can I look upon another sunset with him gone? But it wasn't another hour later and he was back. There. All along. Preparing our engagement and lighting fires in luminaries the shape of a heart.

Leafe squeezes me and kisses my forehead.

I gasp and feel the wind run through my hair. "Leafe!"

"My heart is on fire for you, Lilly," Leafe interjects.

My heart leaps at the sound of his emotions. It shouldn't leap like this. And it's no surprise to me, now. I can feel it from the way he holds me. He's been reading me and all my nostalgia of the engagement too.

I pause. I need to be better at hiding my thoughts. I close my eyes and wonder if going to dinner with him was such a good idea. This is only going to spark more fires and stir more flames.

"You need to contain the fire, Leafe. You know I'm engaged. I made a promise."

"And I promise I will keep the fire in my heart for you."

I bite my lip and cannot help but grin. I set that one up for him, didn't I... Clever angel. Smart, too. The way he flies and uses his wings to shift and dip under wind streams. The way he darted back and forth with the hinlors. The way he handles Jenna. His personality is attractive, I admit. But that doesn't mean I have to fall in love with him.

"Guard your heart from other lovers," my Mema used to say. *"When you find the one, keep him."*

Why would I ever want another lover?

I didn't know it could be possible to fall in love twice.

"Love only happens when your heart is open, Lilly. Why was your heart open?" Leafe inquires. Is he insinuating that I don't love Skye? I pause and think.

Was my heart open?

"I didn't know it was open until I met you," I say, processing the question out loud. "I had no intention of letting anyone in."

"I know you didn't."

"You know, I shouldn't have come. I made a mistake. Please turn around and take me back home! Jenna needs me, after all. She shouldn't be alone."

"I saved your life, Lilly. You promised me dinner in return."

"Well, I take it back! I want to go home please," I shout while trying to be as composed as I can. I can't make this any more of a mess than it is.

"This is not a mess, Lilly."

"We are not together, Leafe! Take me home!"

"What if I want you to be mine?"

"You know we can't do that!"

"Why not, Lilly?"

"Because I love Skye!"

"And you love me too. Are you going to live with me hosting these feelings for the rest of eternity?"

"I don't know what else to do!" I gasp with tears welling up, overwhelmed. I fight them back and demand him to land us at one. "Put me down. I will walk home if you don't put me down."

"You'd have to wiggle out of my grip first. I'm not letting you go." Leafe tightens his embrace.

"Don't hold me hostage!"

"You don't know the way home, Lilly. We are on the other side of Zion."

"I don't care! Someone will find me and it won't be you!"

Leafe turns me over in his arms to face him. "Lilly, I love you. And I'm not letting you go."

He leans in with emerald eyes smoldering from the flames of passion's intensity.

Green eyes find me in love.

Kiss!

Leafe's musky lips dive into mine. I pull back. "No! We can't," I say.

He pauses and stares at me with eyes still blazing deep green like the forests of Yosemite. I get caught up in looking at him. He begins to nuzzle my nose with his. He caresses my cheek with his angelic yet strong hands.

"I'll go slow," he whispers and kisses me again.

"But Leafe…" I try to protest.

My body sparks with heat at his touch. Glued to his mouth, I feel weak to pull back. Caramel and cinnamon are the flavors of his mouth, just like the last time. Pull back, Lilly. I try to pull back. But his kisses slowly trail over my cheeks, nose, and forehead. To my neck. I sigh.

My hands grab his hair and before I know it his lips are on mine again. I cannot hold back when he pulls me in like a magnet.

I kiss him back.

My mouth opens for him softly and his tongue enters me boldly. My body shutters.

We spiral in the air going downward and I hear the reverberation of his feet touching the ground. He swaddles me tightly and lays me down as my back feels the soft petals of flowers and the sounds of animals.

I look around and pandas feast on bamboo, furry and playful. Besides them are honey-gold speckled cheetahs cordially licking their fur. "Oh my gosh!" I yell and eye Leafe. "Why did you land us in the middle of danger?"

"They're not dangerous," he smiles and strokes my hair.

159

"Leafe!"

"Trust me," he says. "Zion's animals do not hunt. We are not their prey."

Kiss!

His kiss reminds me who the prey is, and it's me.

"I want you, Lilly. All of you."

Leafe's hands gently slip under my dress.

Rip!

He shreds it all the way up my thigh. He slips his hands under the fabric. Pulls the rest off of me quickly. I bite my tongue from telling him to stop. My body keeps heightening in elation and I don't want him to stop. I look at his green eyes flaming for me and feel mine miraculously heating along with his.

"Your eyes are on fire, Lilly. Tell me to stop and I will."

I sigh and breathe harder as his hands trace my stomach up to my breasts. "Don't stop," I say. I gasp as he slips his hands over my skin and massages my nipples. "I've never been touched there before."

His lips kiss me deeply again, and my legs throb from his presence on me. He kisses my neck and trails down to my navel and starts to remove my undergarments. I inhale, and then exhale. Am I ready to give him myself? I don't know if I am. I've never done this before. But it feels so satisfying and I don't want him to stop. Skye has never made love to me. He said he wanted us to wait and I agreed. But my body is pining every time he stops kissing me. I've always hoped he would do this… to just take me. Completely.

"I won't leave you pining, my queen."

Gasp! He dives into me with his wet tongue, angelic and satisfying.

"Leafe!" I sigh. My body shivers under him. A baby panda crawls over to me and licks my face.

"That's my jurisdiction, buddy," Leafe replies and rises from my wetness to position himself on top of me. With another kiss, he reclaims my rosy cheeks and dives into my mouth like a dolphin leaping under the Tuscan sun. "Tell me to stop, Lilly. And I will," he says.

I'm already in too deep… I cannot possibly say no to him when my body craves the culmination of ecstasy from his oneness. "I want you too," I tell him. "Don't stop."

He reaches down and presses his fingers inside me. My toes curl and I touch my head at the penetration. He takes his time. My body begins to rise higher and higher into euphoria. Then, he pulls out his fingers and readies himself to enter me fully.

"Are you ready, Lilly?" he asks me again.

I nod, wanting him more than words can say. I've waited for this moment so many times, and with him here to give me the pleasure Skye has yet to give me, I am not going to say no. I'm ready to make love with him.

"I'm ready," I say.

Leafe kisses me and then enters me slowly.

"Leafe!" I gasp.

"You feel so good, Lilly," he whispers softly and tenderly.

"Make love to me," I say.

His green eyes flare. Succulent lips meet mine and electric waves of light surge through my body.

"I want all of you," he says.

I pull him into me and let him have me. All of me.

Under the fragrant mist of Zion's rivers, ecstasy takes us all the way up.

❧

"You're so beautiful," Leafe says as I wake up in his arms.

"Have you been watching me sleep?" I ask playfully with a wink.

"Yes," he says unashamed. "Angels always stay awake, remember?" He kisses my forehead. "That's why Skye shouldn't have fallen asleep on you."

I rest against Leafe's chest as he holds me strongly. "Thank you," I say with bright eyes. "For loving me completely."

"It was a pleasure, Miss Rose," Leafe leans over to kiss me gently.

I look up at the enchanting skies. Zion's light peers over us, bright and golden, like mango gems frosted in glitter. That reminds me of the glitter he left on my lips when he dropped me off at my house. I wonder if the same phenomenon has repeated. I touch my lips and find the glitter on my hands again from the touch.

Leafe raises up and leans over me with arched brows and angelic poise. No glitter on his lips. Chocolate brown hair and bronze skin accents his masculine form and handsome face as his green eyes simmer. "I made the glitter for your lips," he expresses to me.

I touch my lips and feel the specks of glossy, fairy dust on my mouth. "How?"

"I'm an angel," he smiles. His eyes rouse with higher intensity. "I can do anything. I wanted to leave your lips glittering from me."

"It tastes like tangerines," I confirm delightfully. Licking my lips and rolling them together, I spread out the glitter across my lips.

"Has Skye ever told you your lips are gorgeous?"

I smile at his green eyes gazing into me intensely. He gazes back.

Green eyes find me in love.

Howl!

I turn around.

A furry grey wolf with sterling charcoal eyes lurks in from behind.

"Oh, no!" I shriek and press into Leafe's embrace.

Leafe reaches out and pets his head. "It's okay, Lilly." He gives it a paw shake. "All creatures dwell together here in Zion."

Its sterling eyes gaze at me with its tail wagging slowly. I guess it wouldn't hurt to pet him. I reach for its coat. The thick, velvety fur grazes through my fingers. "He's so gentle!" I say, shocked and enchanted. "I never thought in all my life I'd be able to touch a wolf without being eaten."

"Now you have," he turns to me and leans in to kiss me. My lips give in to the invasion of his caramel cinnamon lips that remind me of spiced apples and Christmas.

"Her lips taste like cherry blossoms in the garden of Zion. Every time I taste her, I want more." I hear his thoughts.

"I should get back to Skye now," I tell him.

"Skye is still asleep, Lilly."

"We should check anyways. He will be looking for me when he wakes up."

"He will find you when he is ready," Leafe says calmly.

Oh no. Skye is not going to like it that Leafe and I made love. I look at my left ring finger with the heart shaped diamond glistening and wish

I could take it off. I can't do this. But I have to do this. I'm supposed to get married. And I can't let Leafe interfere.

I cannot deny, though, that Leafe made me feel everything I've wished to feel.

Snap out of it, Lilly. You have to let go of Leafe. This cannot continue, you know it. You are going to marry Skye and that is the end of it.

I stand. "This should have never happened. I have to get married, Leafe."

"Wait, Lilly," Leafe rises and strokes my cheek.

There he goes again reeling me in.

"You know this will never work out between us."

Why won't he understand and give up pursuing me? I can't marry both him and Skye. I won't. There will be only one husband for me. I have to choose what I want. Why can't Leafe step aside and let me choose what I want?

"If I step aside, you never will."

"What is that supposed to mean?"

"You already made your mind up with Skye, so you think. But what if you and I are meant to be? If you don't let me show you who I am, you can't choose what you want. You can only choose what has been chosen for you."

"I want what has been chosen for me."

"Do you?"

"Yes!" I exclaim with assurance. How dare he question my choices!

"Then understand this, Lilly, The King chose to send me also."

I breathe out.

King Worthy sent Leafe?

King Worthy did send Leafe.

The King only sends angels to save, and He always does everything with a reason. Nothing is random in His universe. He would never let me fall, He said so Himself. But this feels a lot like falling. Or is it? If The King sent Leafe to me, did He also send Leafe to make love to me? What a shocking idea that would be… It couldn't be. Could it?

I sigh. If I'm honest, I do love Leafe.

How do I choose between Skye and Leafe? Did I just ask myself that question? It shouldn't be hard if I already knew, right? If I really loved

Skye, I wouldn't have allowed Leafe to have any space in my life at all. I would have turned Leafe away easily because I wouldn't have been attracted nor tempted. I never let anyone in before. But Leafe got in. Somehow, he got in.

I let Leafe into my heart the moment he came on to me by the villas. Stunned and insulted, I was, at the moment. Appalled by his audacity. I wouldn't have thought any more of it if I hadn't had the what-if's surfacing in the back of my mind. What if I saw him again? What if I liked it? What if he made me feel things Skye doesn't make me feel?

The King allowed Leafe to pursue me, knowing I was already engaged. What does He see in the great unknown that gave way to this rabbit trail?

"Lilly!" A bright angel with red curls and peach eyes appears.

"Hello, Captain Leafe!" Another angel with black hair, chocolate skin and navy eyes lands in the clover-filled grass.

"Hello, Goodness," Leafe nods and smiles, as he greets the angel with red flowing curls. "Hope," he nods again as he greets the other.

"We came to retrieve bamboo for the palace!" Goodness exclaims with starry light reflecting in her countenance.

"Leafe, would you like to give me a hand?" Hope asks, with a deep voice resonating.

"No problem!" Leafe says. "Lilly, I'll be right here if you need me. Just call for me." He kisses my forehead and soars through the bamboo fields at lightning speed, with their wings cutting bamboo in swaths.

"They won't take long, my love," Goodness soars up to me and rests her hand on my shoulder. "You look worried, my dear."

"I don't know where Skye is, and Leafe is here now..." I stop myself. Telling her about me and Leafe is not really appropriate yet.

"I can tell he has eyes for you, precious lady," she whispers serenely. "Skye will see eventually."

"How can you tell?"

"The angels already know," she says with a voice of tranquility, like she isn't bothered by the epiphany of his love for me.

"Know what?" I ask.

Goodness looks at me with rosy cheeks and peaceful eyes of fire. It puts me at ease. "That he's in love with you," she says smiling.

"Did you know bamboo leaf heals the nervous system?" Leafe returns and kisses me snugly. He glances at Goodness and nods, giving her bundles of bamboo to cradle in her arms.

"I learn something new every day in Zion," I say.

"You look beautiful in love, my future queen," Goodness says with her calming voice. "And your wings are glowing exceptionally bright, I must say, Captain Leafe," she adds, enchantingly.

"Always glowing," Leafe replies firmly.

"Not as much as they are right now, Captain," Goodness reiterates and lifts off the ground with slow poise and delicacy. "Until I see you again," she says as she departs.

Leafe waves and wraps his arms around me from the back. "You smell like rosy bamboo in a field of wonder."

"Maybe because I *am* in a bamboo field," I reply back to him playfully as he tightens his grip on me.

"I want you to have something, Lilly," Leafe whispers in my ear. He lets go of his embrace and circles around to face me. He loosens a necklace from his neck and places it in my hand. "It's an emerald heart."

My eyes light up. "It's beautiful!"

"I want you to have my heart with you at all times. I know you're engaged, but I'm not going to let you go that easily."

"Leafe, I don't know if I can accept this. I already have Skye's key necklace. You know I can't take it off." I press my hand to the rose gold around my neck and breathe out at the thought of its substance losing the sensation of my skin. I can't take it off.

"You don't have to say anything," he exclaims peacefully. "Just think about it. Hold on to it for me."

Leafe leans in again to kiss me. I lean into him with the innate desire to reciprocate his yearning for me. My stomach churns with butterflies from his touch.

Swoop!

Wings fly by and scoop the necklace from my hands.

Leafe turns his head and flares his green eyes to scan the air.

"The necklace!" I gasp.

"Let go of her, now!" A voice shouts. I grab onto Leafe at the sighting of white, glowing wings.

Then, I think to myself. I know that voice.

"Leafe, you crossed the line!" he says again, with a vehement tone.

Yes, I know the voice well.

It's Skye.

18

Leafe

"I told you what would happen if you left her alone!" I exclaim strongly.

I wrap my arms around Lilly to cover her body as her shredded dress lies on the baboo-covered ground. Holding her in my embrace, I want it to be known I claim her in Skye's presence. Her delicate frame fits perfectly in my arms as my wings tower over her. I won't be letting her go.

Skye's eyes rage with sapphire light, agitated by my advance. "I shouldn't have to worry about what happens when I'm away," Skye shutters and lifts off the ground. Flexes his wings.

Skye thinks he is indomitable, but his pride made him lazy when it comes to Lilly. She deserves me, an angel who will give her what she needs when she needs it. An angel who loves her like a lover. And gives her more.

I persist. "Didn't King Worthy tell you not to let her out of your sight?"

Skye zooms towards me and left hooks me in the face. I dodge the punch, pick up Lilly and fly around to his right. I cover her eyes.

"I never let her out of my sight," Skye protests with a right jab. I deflect with my left wing.

"You fell asleep, General!"

"How am I supposed to avoid that, Captain!"

"By taking care of yourself in the twilight!" I remind him. "What are you doing while Lilly is sleeping?"

He huffs and puffs. "Pacing."

"Why, General? You have an army at your disposal. Why would you be pacing when you could be resting your wings beside her, fully alert and at ease. She could get taken!"

"Because I have an army to command!" He yells with blue-blood-shot eyes.

There it is. The truth.

Skye still prioritizes the angel armies over Lilly.

"Why didn't you say so?" I exclaim, seeing through him. He knows it too. That I can see through him. Now I see why The King sent me. Lilly needs my love and I am not going to let go of her. I am not going to prioritize my missions over her. She is my priority.

Skye fell asleep because he won't admit he needs her more than he needs to command. And General Skye Worthy is too prudent to tell anyone the love of his life disturbs his peace of mind. He wants to hold all of Zion together himself and cannot juggle the power with the weight of love bearing down on him.

His own father sits on the Throne. He could have gone to Him and told Him he needed more help. But Skye never asks for help unless duty calls for it. Lilly has him entranced and I understand the feeling. But neglecting the love of his life is not the way.

"Skye!"

Lilly breaks free from my embrace and runs towards Skye. She picks up the dress, in shreds, and covers her porcelain body. His eyes look away from me. He lands on the ground and welcomes her embrace.

"Lilly!" He holds her and strokes her hair. "Your dress is in shreds!"

I sigh at the sight of them together. "The reunion ensues," I say to myself.

"The angels will make me another one," she exclaims whimsically. If only he knew the reason why her dress had managed to shred all the way up to the neckline, he would know who she really belongs to. Me. The one her eyes crave when he's gone.

"I shouldn't have let you out of my sight! I'm so sorry," Skye breathes heavily and kisses her head. "Did he hurt you?" He wraps his feathers around her.

"No," Lilly exclaims peacefully. She grabs his hands and massages them. "I'm okay," she says with ease.

"If he did, I will have him arrested!" Skye threatens and eyes me angrily.

"Angels are not arrested in Zion, General." He knows this. He just wants to puff his chest in front of Lilly and throw me under the bus.

"He didn't hurt me!" Lilly insists.

Lilly pauses and she turns to look at me with longing eyes. Before you know it, her thoughts are going to give it away. My eyes flame green and fiery as I sense the civil war between Skye and I brewing. He already knows it that we made love. I can feel it.

It's okay, Lilly. I will cover you. I hope she hears me as I think to her.

"I love you Leafe," I hear her thoughts in my head.

"You love him!?" Skye overhears, as his telekinesis with her interrupts ours. And now, all three of us are interlocked in both word and thought.

"I–" Lilly lets go of Skye's hands and looks away.

"Say it, Lilly. Tell him you love me." I urge her.

"How can you possibly love Leafe when he touched you and stole you away from me?" I can hear Skye's thoughts. So can Lilly.

"I… I don't love him!" Lilly announces out loud. *"Oh, of course I do! I do love him! But how can tell Skye that I love someone else too?"* she thinks to herself.

"Lilly!" I refocus her attention on me. "Say it out loud! Say you love me!"

"No!" Lilly protests. *"I'm not ready to say it,"* she thinks to herself. *"Am I?"*

"She's not ready, Leafe! Stop pressuring her!" Skye tells me through his thoughts.

I break the silence of telekinesis-talk and decide to announce it boldly. I want him to hear it.

"I'm in love with Lilly!" I profess. "And I'm not letting her go!"

Flash!

I love the way the wind blows through my wings when I get the truth off my chest. That is, until Skye pummels me below the waist. Within a millisecond, my wings shutter. I knew it was coming, though. There is no way Skye was going to let me profess my love for Lilly and stand resolute. But I had to say the truth.

"Traitor!" Skye knocks me to the ground in the middle of bamboo leaves and baby pandas. I roll over to the right to evade him and shoot into the air.

Blast!

A bolt of light radiation surges through my body from Skye's detonation. I send it back with boomerang ricochets.

"You can't kill me with light, Skye!" Angels absorb light from other angels. It only makes us brighter. He knows this, and I can already tell he is off his game by the way he's fighting. He is smarter than this. I'm getting to his head. Skewing his tactics.

Skye should remember how to fight. We both trained together on my first mission, when I was confirmed by King Worthy. We practiced light radiation and every tactic of Zion's warfare.

The memory feels like it was yesterday…

◈

"You have a gift, Leafe," Skye told me as the granite rocks combusted. "Fastest time of all cadets!"

"You trained me well, Major Worthy," I replied. "I detonated two clicks early. Aimed to kill. Blurred out distractions."

Skye rested his hand on my shoulder. "When the enemy appears unexpectedly, you'll need those two extra clicks."

Skye was a Major then. Same blue eyes. Fast wing-speed. Always loyal to a fault.

"I want Leafe briefed in all battle missions, Skye," The King said as He walked the training fields under the Zion sun. He always made a point to find me and talk to me, like I was one of His own.

"Your name is the same as Mine, young Leafe. Did you know that?" King Worthy told me one day, preparing for flight pattern methods. "Leafe Worthy. That is your name."

"Whoa! Leafe nails it again! Sharp eyes, my angel!" Captain Winter said.

"What accurate eyes!" added Major Sterling. "We will need you on the front lines of Zion's V one day."

The King moved me up to the front right flank by Skye when he promoted me to Captain. Winning The Battle of Hanauma Bay was one of the greatest feats yet to date. He's always been a brother to me. Never an enemy. Never a rival. Now, love has made us enemies.

"Patience has her eyes on you, Leafe," Sterling told me one day at Zion's Waterfalls, when we were recuperating from training.

"I'm not interested in love, fellas. I have too much practice to perfect if I'm going to make it to the front of the V."

"If you really want to make it to the front of a V, you will talk to Patience," Sterling winked at me as the other angels whistled. "Get inside her V!"

"As if she is going to give it up to the likes of you!" Favor flew in with chocolate hair and brown eyes of espresso. "Don't mind them," she comforted me. "They're harmless. But I did overhear them talking about Raven's latest ideas of rebellion."

"Rebellion?" I asked.

Favor leaned in to whisper. "There's been talk of Raven saying he wants to form a coup against The King. They want to take over Zion. At least, they think they can. I don't think it can be done, and I wouldn't want to join a coup against perfection. King Worthy is our great King. Anyone who comes against Him will fall."

She was right. It wasn't long after that, Raven surged against King Worthy. That was when we still called him Raven. After he rebelled, he became the enemy. Thus, The Raven was his identifier.

Sterling joined, along with many others. They thought they could usurp The King's reign. But they all fell away and were exiled from Zion to utter darkness.

Utter darkness. A place I never want to see the likes of for longer than I need to when war beckons. Peace and purity have long been our virtues. That won't stop now.

My eyes blink.

I snap out of the vision.

Skye still stands in front of me, with blue eyes raging.

"Settle down," I suggest. "Let's talk it out."

Maybe I can talk some sense into him and at least, let him know I'm not against him. I may love Lilly, but I am not his enemy. We already have enough of those, and I will always remain loyal to Zion.

Skye rebuttals with jealous fervor. "You will never be my ally after this, Leafe!"

My heart stings. I know what King Worthy asked me to do. *"Love Lilly,"* He said. *"She loves you,"* He affirmed. If I have The King's affirmation, then there is nothing Skye can do to interfere with His blueprint for her destiny and that of Zion. I am doing my duty.

Skye cannot see that right now.

All he can see is his fellow angel stealing his fiancé. One day he will know the truth. And Lilly must make a choice.

Does she love me or does she love Skye? The King told me she would be given this choice, and whatever I have to do to ensure she has that choice is my own fate. I already gave my word that I would love her. And I do love her. I am in this for her.

Skye right jabs and I dodge left. He swings his left wing and I flip over him and land behind him. He grabs my shoulders and we fly up over the bamboo.

"Skye, I am not against you! You're overreacting," I tell him.

"It's *General*, as far as you're concerned, Captain!" He retorts.

"Oh, excuse me General Worthy, I forgot the new title had replaced your sense of comradery between friends," I state sarcastically.

"Friends!?" He laughs. "We're no longer friends." His eyes burn with stormy grey cyclones in his sapphire ignited eyes. "I'm going to kill you!"

"We both know you can't kill me!" I really have gotten to his head if he has forgotten my identity and his. We're both immortal angels of Zion's heavenly oasis. There is nothing he can do to me.

"My father will once he finds out what you've done!" he exclaims and soars towards me with another assail. He grabs my shoulders and knees me in the chest.

"Your father already knows, General!" I divulge plainly.

Skye halts in the air. "What do you mean He knows?!"

I let out a breath. "Ask Him!"

Skye screams and charges at me, unwilling to accept the truth. I turn and fly upward. I'm not fighting him anymore nor will I flatter his madness.

"Stop!" Lilly shouts at Skye from the bamboo-layered ground.

"Lilly," Skye gasps and his eyes turn from grey cyclones to a purer color of blue.

I descend to the ground.

Lilly steps in front of me.

Skye gasps with shock at the sight of her stance in front of me. "What are you doing?"

"Leave him alone!" she commands with confidence. His wings descend and he lands in front of her, as she stands in front of me. I try to hold back a smile. She really does have him whipped. "I'm not going to let you hurt Leafe."

Skye sighs, looks down and then back up at her. "Lilly," he speaks to her gently, "he's trying to get in between us."

"I love him," she says boldly.

Skye pauses. Then, he breathes in for what seems like an eternity, refusing to say a word.

Then, he opens his mouth. "What did you say?"

"I said I love him, Skye. I love Captain Leafe."

I didn't expect her to confess, but now that she has relief sets in like a cosmic sunset. Lilly, you'll never know how much that meant to me. And now, I know Skye understands how much I mean to her.

Skye grunts and wipes his brow in distress. "Lilly, you don't know what you are saying. He seduced you," Skye exclaims with wings flaring.

"Yes, he did. And I wanted him to," she confesses shyly. "I wanted someone to love all of me."

"All of you?" Skye steps towards her with eyes raging again, with grey cyclones in his eyes. "What do you mean all of you?"

Oh no, he doesn't. He is not going to rage at her for this. I came on to her. I touched her. I made love to her. And I am going to tell him to his face.

I soar around Lilly and shield her. I face Skye, angel-to-angel.

"Skye," I say to his blue-grey eyes. "I made love to Lilly."

"Ahhh!" He screams and shoots rays of sapphire fire at me as if I were a gremlin to destroy or a hinlor to decimate. His wings flare. I reverse the light and it shocks him instantly. He falls to the ground and goes unconscious.

"Oh no!" Lilly rushes to his side and feels his head, with delicate hands. "Leafe, what did you do!?" Her eyes look of horror now, but he will wake up by morning. Skye should have known better than to keep charging at me with Zion's light.

"Leafe!" The King's voice rings through the atmosphere. I bow in reverence, at the presence of His greatness. He is still in the Throne Room, but His voice can reach us anywhere, anytime. Angelic communication puts us in sync with His voice when He calls.

"Yes, my King," I answer.

His voice booms again overhead. "I need to see you in the Throne Room."

"Yes, King Worthy," I echo back to Him.

"The King knows," she expresses frantically and covers her mouth in distress. If she only knew The King set it up. She would not worry for a moment.

My hands touch her alabaster cheek and her warmth returns as she looks in my eyes. "I promise you, Lilly, you have done nothing wrong," I affirm clearly and peacefully.

My eyes get caught up in gazing at her.

All I want to do is explore the curves of her breasts and the arc of her back once again. Looking into her eyes, I know one time making love to her will never be enough. I long to have her every moment, with endless passionate kisses and infinite reasons to make love to her.

"Green eyes find me in love." I hear her thoughts.

She loves me. Deep breaths course through me as I see the evidence. The King was right. She really does love me.

"We must go now," I say.

"But Skye! Is he dead?"

"He's not dead, Lilly," I assure her. "He will wake up soon."

He will wake up from more than simply being unconscious. He will wake up to the fact I am in love with Lilly, and she is in love with me.

King Worthy orchestrated this, and He will handle Skye. I leave that to The King.

"I can't leave him here," Lilly gasps, still shook.

"Trust me. When he wakes up, you don't know what he is capable of."

"He would never hurt me," Lilly insists. But she has never seen Skye when his favorite toy is taken away. I have. And I do not want her vulnerable to the antics of his retribution. King Worthy will not have her harmed.

"Retribution?" I hear her thoughts. *"You mean Skye would try to hurt me if he loses me? I've never seen him angry. All he has ever been is gentle towards me."*

"Lilly, come with me," I whisper and extend my hand to her.

She hesitates. Forlorn eyes switch back between him and me.

"Lilly!" I state firmly.

Her eyes land on me and she lets go of the shredded dress. "I'm ready."

I soar up to her. My hands greet her naked body, supple and ripe. I ease my lips over her lips and taste the fructose marinating in her tastebuds. The taste of strawberries and peaches linger deliciously.

I look into her eyes that shine the same color green as me. My soul finds her soul in the collision. "I want to make love to you again."

Her smile returns with rosy color cheeks. "Make love to me, Leafe," she replies readily.

Without hesitating I scoop her in my arms and lift off the ground to go to the Throne Room. But on our way, I am going to give Lilly more of the love she desires.

I let my wings do the navigating, while I let my mouth do the lovemaking. "Have you ever made love in the sky?" I ask her as I kiss her neck.

"Never," she sighs.

"Never say never with me," he replies.

My left hand cradles her body mid-flight as we soar over Zion's terrain under tranquil, golden light and pinkish sparkles. My right hand massages her breasts and makes its way down her body. I kiss her slowly, heating her up for my entrance. Lilly's lips feel angelic. They feel better than angelic. Her tongue kisses me like butter. My lips collide with her like a solar eclipse of blood orange passion. Lilly feels more a woman right now than I've ever felt her. Her beautiful body intoxicates my senses.

"I'm ready," she tells me.

My lips return to kiss her and I nod, "Okay, my queen." I position myself over her and enter her slowly, as my wings carry us over the rivers of Zion. She sighs. Again, I penetrate, and her warmth swells around me.

"Leafe!" she exclaims and tightens her grip on my back.

My wings electrify from her heat and I continue thrusting into her. "I love you, Lilly." She opens for me and sighs, as I feel her body intensifying. I speed up as we fly over the rivers and turn her over to be on top of me. I thrust again from the bottom and spin around to touch her from every angle. My lips glide over her mouth as she breathes heavily. I trail her neck as I keep heightening her pleasure down below with every stroke.

Then, I feel it. Her floral treasure tightens around me and she sighs deeply. My hands grip her breasts. I sigh with her. I let her feel every spasm and reach the pinnacle of bliss, and then, I release into her.

She inhales. Exhales. I kiss her forehead as she smiles into my eyes with delight.

My eyes return the pleasure. "That felt so good, Lilly."

"I've never felt more satisfied in my life," she tells me.

"Green eyes find me in ecstasy." I read her thoughts.

"I love you, Lilly. I want to spend the rest of eternity giving you what you need and more."

"If it were only that simple," she replies, and looks away to peer into the waters beneath.

"I still don't know who to choose. Skye or Leafe?" I hear her thoughts.

"Look at me, Lilly," I say lovingly. "Be true to your spirit. You will know."

Mist trickles into the airspace as we fly.

Zion's waterfalls pour over the edge with flavorful liquid. I taste the mist and Lilly does the same.

"Dark chocolate and blackberry!" she exclaims and sticks out her tongue to taste the mist again.

I fly us closer to the waterfalls. Dark purple liquid flows from the waterfall's edge and changes into the turquoise pools beneath. Only

The King could make the color change into mineral healing waters by the time the falls land in the pool. His inventions defy the impossible.

I reach out my right hand to feel the liquid on my skin as I hold Lilly with my left. "We need a shower." I soar rapidly down the waterfall's edge and into the pools with Lilly in my arms. The King will be waiting for us. A refreshing dip in the pools below is warranted.

"Leafe!" She shrieks.

I cover her face and nose gently. "Hold your breath."

Splash!

We come up to the surface and Lilly treads water smiling. "I didn't see that coming," she exclaims and splashes me, then dunks me under the water. I rise to the surface and pull her close.

"Now that you splashed me, I'm going to have to take you under," I say flirtatiously.

"You wouldn't dare," she exclaims with a sassy eye.

Dunk!

I pull her into my mouth and kiss her underwater, giving her oxygen from my breath. She kisses me back with circular motions of her tongue. Spiraling up, I pull her to the surface. She gasps for air.

Eye to eye, we tread water like two doves in a sea of bliss. Her naked body floats gracefully like Eve in the Garden of Eden. I look around ensuring no other angels are nearby to see her. All clear. Only I can see her naked from now on.

"Kiss me again," she eggs me on.

"You don't have to ask me twice," I whisper.

I pull her into my chest as we tread the teal blue mineral water and kiss her deeply, exploring every part of her succulent mouth. Sweet dark chocolate and blackberry linger on her tongue from the waterfalls.

She pulls away. "Skye will be there, won't he? When we go to the Throne Room?"

"Yes. I presume he will."

Lilly looks distressed. I know the weight of love's epiphany shocks Skye and she does not want to break her engagement.

"I feel like I am in a maze I cannot get out of."

"Telling the truth is the only way through, Lilly. Love is the truth. You don't have to be ashamed of that confession."

We float in the water eyeing each other for what seems like hours. Sounds of trickling water falling from her brow accompany the echoes of rushing waterfalls behind us. I like the sound of hers better. Everything about her makes me want more. I could float in these waters forever just to see another side of her, dripping wet from liquified H2O, doused in minerals.

"Leafe!" The King's voice echoes over the waters all the way from the Throne Room. "I'm waiting for you!"

"Yes, my King."

I hoist Lilly in the air and prepare to fly towards the Throne Room. "We must be going, Lilly. The King is expecting us."

"My dress is gone, though!" Lilly reminds me. "What do I wear?"

Lilly treads water, waiting on my answer. All I want to do is watch her wet body.

"I have an idea." I rise out of the water to pluck some of my feathers. With a quick wave of supernatural light, I spin the silk threads into a white dress perfect for Lilly. I want myself to be wrapped around her. "How about pure silk, Miss Rose?" I soar closer to her with the gown in hand.

Her eyes glisten. "A Leafe couture design, it is!"

19

Skye

Leafe made love to Lilly. My insides twist like a maze of corn in earth's farmlands. Heartbeats pulse through my chest slower and slower. My head becomes flush. My stomach churns like butter whipped from cow's milk as I think about the confession. My eyes faint as I imagine it. I close my eyes. I don't want to envision it. How could Lilly make love with Leafe?

Blink once. Blink twice.

Zion's surroundings are no longer clear. My feet stumble and I fall to the ground in the bamboo fields where pandas graze peacefully, as if they are immune to bad news. I reach out to touch the furry creature and find Lilly and Leafe are gone.

Horns blare in the distance. They must have escaped to the palace, and I am not going to let them get away. Leafe will pay for His insolence. Lilly is mine.

I rise and compose myself, stretch my wings and make haste for the palace.

The river meanders with light in its reflection, as usual. I wonder if my complexion will still be as bright with this new invasion of grief and anger. Angels were not made to live angry. My heart can hardly handle the pressure of grief. But handle this situation, I must. I won't lose Lilly.

Golden, ivory pillars surface ahead of me as I fly over The Tree of Life en route to the main doors of the Throne Room. I sweep through the tulips garden, soar through the doors and up to my father who sits regally with fiery eyes and hosts of seraphim.

"Where is she!?"

"Skye, slow down," says The King.

"I demand to know how and why you let him put his hands on her!" I zoom into the Throne Room rapidly. My eyes rage like molten sapphire.

"You weren't."

My mouth opens. Then closes.

Adjacent to my posture, Zeal stands guard with amethyst flames rousing from my disposition. I look down and back at my father, trying to compose myself in reverence.

"Was I supposed to?"

"You let your bride go without love. You withheld your touch. I sent in reinforcements," He echoes with a deep voice.

"Reinforcements!?"

"Do you dare question My ways! Forget not who you are talking to!" My father shouts.

Thunder roars. His blue eyes blaze with fiery hues and transform into turquoise flames and emeralds. My head bows.

"Lilly belongs to me," I protest inwardly and inhale a deep breath.

My father rises from the Throne and walks towards me. "Not anymore, General. My bride will not suffer the fate of your absent apathy. Do not arouse her and leave her to pine. Get the job done from now on."

Zeal hovers in and speaks with confidence. "King Worthy, Leafe is here to see you."

"Leafe!" I charge at him full force. Zeal steps in and blocks my arms from slamming into the heart of Leafe's immortality. "I will have your wings obliterated!"

He stands unshaken, strong face, and green eyes glowing. Without a hint of guilt. How can he stand there as if my eyes have not seen?

"You touched my fiancé!" I press against Zeal's shoulders as he stands between Leafe and me.

"The King gave me permission, General. Was I to deny His request?" Leafe answers.

"You could have, if you have any decency!" My feathers stand ruffled and outraged.

Leafe narrows his eyes on me, perplexed. "And be thrown out with the rebels?"

"That's enough!" My father interrupts me before I can head butt his halo into galaxies far away. "Listen, Skye Worthy. There is something you need to know."

"I hope you have an explanation for this, Father!"

"Remember who you talk to, General!" He continues and strikes the glassy floor with His scepter. Fire smokes in the back and I bow my head. "I Am King! I gave you that star and I have given you everything in the universe. Lilly is not a flower to be toyed with. She is a woman," my father blares like raging rivers.

Seraphim circle above His Throne unshaken by His tone. They keep flying to sing His praises because He is King. I kneel in reverence, knowing I will never be able to fight my way to win over my father. He will always be right, and that is just how it is. What I need to know is why He allowed this. Why would He give Lilly to Leafe?

"Then why did you let him make love to her?" I say from my knelt posture with eyes to the floor. Under the glassy, sapphire floor of the Throne Room are gardens of petunias and roses galore. I see a bee land hard on a fresh rose, pollinating its bud. The King always brings life to the living. So, the garden of Zion persists.

My father speaks. "Because she asked you and you denied her."

I look up and sigh, "Father, I wasn't ready."

"Yes, you were," He retorts. "So was she. You have been making her miserable by leading on her body to feel things you never finish. I had enough of it once I heard Lilly talking about it to Jenna."

She told Jenna? Her best friend knows all there is to know about sex. I can only imagine how that left Lilly feeling frustrated and more agitated with me for not satisfying her.

"Why didn't I see this before? I always read her thoughts." I say out loud.

"Lilly did not resent it in the moment," my father informs me. "She resented it when you were gone, and she was left alone with her body elevated to near-climax and no lover to mutually fulfill her."

"I was afraid, Father. She's still a virgin."

"Then you should have talked about it together, Skye. Instead, you chose for her and told her how you were going to be intimate." My father eyes me, unpleased.

I stand frozen, unable to respond.

"Look, My son. Love requires the same heart and same mind."

Meanwhile, Captain Leafe stands by with hands folded, hearing our every word. I can't blame him for that. He is a part of this conversation after all. I am not used to having my close angels involved in these matters. But he already is. And apparently, he has seen more of Lilly than I have.

My eyes rage at the thought of it.

"How can this possibly be good, Father?" I shout. "You are supposed to be a King of goodness and honor! This is grotesque!"

"The only grotesque action at the present time in my Kingdom was when you left the future queen of Zion to satisfy herself with her own hand," King Worthy echoes in return.

Breathe in, Skye.

Keep your mouth closed, Skye.

You cannot argue with King Worthy.

He always wins.

His way will always win.

The King walks towards me. I look over at Leafe who stares at me. I glare at him, wondering what will become of the V formation without him at the right flank. After this, I will remove him undoubtedly.

The King interjects as He reads my thoughts. "You have no jurisdiction over where I place my fliers, General," my father affirms. "If I want him at the front, what is that to you?"

I remain silent and grit my teeth.

Leafe responds. "Skye, for the record, I never meant to betray you."

I hold my tongue before saying something I will regret. Tears well up in my eyes. I try to conceal it before angels notice, but the liquification is too strong. Are Generals allowed to cry or am I supposed to be numb?

"Skye," my father walks towards me and the ground shakes. Leafe steps aside and waits patiently. My father stops in front of me and wipes the tear from my cheek. He looks at me tenderly. "This was not easy for me to ask of Leafe, but you left me no choice. Lilly is a human. She needs an angel who will meet every need and satisfy every longing. Can you do that?"

I raise my hands in frustration and let out a sigh. "I thought I could!" I say frustrated.

"This is no longer a matter of hypothesis. You need to know what kind of lover you want to be. And you need to know how to give the kind of love a woman needs."

In the corner of my eye, I see Leafe looking to his right repetitively. Someone is diverting his attention. I shift my attention back to father and contemplate the options. With Armageddon on the brink, I foresee war only coming between Lilly and me. How do I reconcile this mess when I will be away even more?

"What do I do now?" I gasp. "War is soon to be upon us and I can't live without Lilly!"

"Skye!" Lilly runs in and squeezes me tightly. I hug her back and feel the feathery silk of someone else's wing-threads covering her. Should I let go? Her frame fits me like I want it to. I ease my grip on her, knowing my hands may be holding her body but someone else is holding her heart.

Leafe shifts his gaze towards her. "Lilly, wait!"

"It's okay," my father interrupts with a warm smile despite his mood. "Hello, Lilly."

"Hello, King Worthy," Lilly answers kindly and looks back at Leafe who looks at her mesmerized.

"*I love you, Lilly,*" I can hear Leafe's thoughts for Lilly. "*Don't run back to him.*"

"*I love you, Leafe,*" her thoughts respond to his.

She looks up at me and lets me go. Backs away. Her eyes water as she studies my face as if to solve an ancient riddle still left unexplained. I try to read her thoughts but she speaks up before I can decipher them.

"Why didn't you love me more?" she asks plainly.

My heart sinks, and I look down at the glassy floor where the bumblebee once rested to pollinate the flower. It's gone now. Just like what's left of my dignity.

"I'm sorry, Lilly," I express.

Leafe rushes to her side and strokes her cheeks. "Let him be, Lilly."

"But I need to know," she tells him boldly.

Lilly's face smiles as Leafe hugs her, and she looks at me through the fold of his arms.

"Lilly, all I ever wanted was you," I confess with as much truth as I have ever told.

"All I wanted was you, Skye," she affirms. "I love you. But then… Leafe came to me and he loved me like you wouldn't. I feel things for him I can't explain. My heart is conflicted now."

"How can it be conflicted? I am your lover, Lilly!"

"I feel more myself than I ever have," Lilly expresses freely.

"Lilly, I know what you want! Our thoughts are intertwined… we *are* intertwined," I insist. Doesn't she see I was made for her?

"You say you can read me but you never did what it took to satisfy me," she says delicately. "Leafe did."

Leafe's wings light up at her revelatory confession. He remains silent, with a grin on his face.

I rub my brow and invite her response. "What do you want Lilly?"

She closes her eyes. Leafe rubs her shoulders and whispers in her ear. She smiles with blushing cheeks, perfectly rosy. All she can hear are the love-notes of Leafe's whispers. She ignores me.

My father eyes Lilly and Leafe lovingly and blue-emerald fire begins to burn in his eyes. His temperament changes from firmness to tenderness, all in a millisecond. He has always had a soft spot for Lilly. And there is only one plan of action when my father is in love: give the best. My father's best is always pure. Always selfless. Always right.

But how could Leafe be the best for Lilly? Is He taking her away from me?

Lilly opens her eyes in Leafe's embrace and makes eye contact with me. "I want the one who holds all of me."

King Worthy speaks to Skye. "Let her go, son. She belongs with Leafe."

20

Lilly

"Throne Room, halt!"

All angels in the Throne Room stand still, frozen in time, but seraphim keep circling me. Six white glowing wings in pairs of two cover their bodies with six eyes each. I feel vulnerable in their presence, like they can see through me but I don't feel afraid. I feel seen and cherished.

"Leafe, why are they circling me?" I look over at Leafe and he stands frozen, along with Skye and the rest of the angels in the Throne Room. It is as if the scene stopped and no one is moving but me, the seraphim, and The King.

What happened? Did I break the vitality of Zion?

"You are loved, dear Lilly." The King's voice booms.

I turn, and King Worthy walks closer to me. Footsteps rattle the ground. His voice echoes. My eyes light up from King Worthy's voice. His power brought me to Skye, and His light led me to Zion. Even if I can no longer choose Skye, I will forever be indebted to Him for all He has done for me.

"King Worthy," I say and bow to honor Him.

Then I rise to face His eyes shining with sapphire and emerald light. He looks at me with kindness, and I know He saw me with Captain Leafe. He knows. He sees everything. If anyone has wisdom to give me, it's Him. He knows Skye better than anyone ever could. He is His father. I don't want to put King Worthy in the middle of me and Skye's relationship but He already is. The whole universe revolves around Him as King. I think He can handle it.

"You're right, Lilly. I can handle it."

He must have read my thoughts.

Of course, He can. He always knows what everyone is thinking. Jenna usually talks to me about Skye and every ounce of womanhood I experience in my relationship with him. But I need more advice now. I cannot hold it in any longer.

I breathe in and exhale, ready to confess. "I'm falling in love with Captain Leafe, Your majesty."

He smiles and looks at me with fire in His eyes. "I know you are."

"I didn't mean to fall in love with someone else, but Leafe kept coming on to me. I've never felt this way before. I love Skye, but Leafe makes me feel–" I pause, reluctant to divulge.

"Passion," He answers for me.

"Yes."

"I knew you'd fall in love with Leafe. Nothing gets by Me."

Then why did He let Leafe get near me? Why would he put me and Skye's relationship in jeopardy?

"My Kingdom is good, Lilly. You do not have to fear what happens here. I have all power. You will always be held in the sovereignty of My love for you," He assures me with a voice that echoes like river rapids, and eyes that blaze with kindness.

"I don't understand."

"Skye had a choice. Love always has a choice."

"Does Skye not love me?"

"Skye loves you. But Leafe loves you more. He has more love to give you, and so I sent him to find you," His voice resonates like a god echoing in deep canyons. Only he isn't just a god. He is God.

"What about Skye? I can't just leave him. I was going to marry him."

I look up at the glowing seraphim circling with light illuminating the Throne Room. This altar is a place of loyalty and devotion, much like the word I have given Skye. I said "yes" when he asked me to marry him. It was my desire and nothing less than perfect to me. I have the dress. I have the arrangements made. The party is set. All of Zion is expecting Skye and I to say, "I do."

"Remember, Lilly. Love has a choice. You have a choice too." He rests His hand on my shoulder and I feel the serenity of a trillion butterflies fluttering peacefully. Skye is His son, and still, He fights for me as if my happiness is the priority.

"Why are you so kind to me?" I ask sincerely.

"I chose you," He says with a strong voice. "You will always be chosen. You will always be royalty. I made you to see the light, and the light is what you see. Zion waits for more humans like you." He lifts His hand with a golden scepter and begins to walk back to the Throne.

I respond. "Skye told me of Armageddon. Then, all the people of earth will dwell in Zion."

"All the earth will belong to Zion. Those that choose to, that is." He lifts His hands and sits on the Throne regally.

I ponder if I can say "I do" to Skye when I have another angel rivaling my heart. I need to be sure. My wedding day should not be a day of doubts and fears, but a day of endless bliss and confident assurance that my groom is the one. The only one. Two will never do for me. I need to figure out what I want, and until I have that assurance, I don't know if I can marry Skye.

I blurt out my hesitation boldly. "I don't know if I can marry Skye. I love him, but…" I pause.

"You love Captain Leafe too."

I look up with assurance. "I do."

The King looks at me compassionately. Blue and green swivel in the mosaic of His eyes. All the mysteries of the universe are contained in those eyes. I can tell by His look that there is more He is not saying. Does He judge me for falling in love with another angel? He said love has a choice, but I need to know He won't disapprove if I choose Leafe instead.

He turns to a sphere-shaped ball beside him. "You have brought more honor to the Kingdom than you could ever know, precious child."

I look at Him without fear. Something about His aura makes me feel known and confident to stand before Him. Still, I want to know what He thinks. "How?" I inquire. "If I may ask in your presence?" I add.

"By loving without pretense," He answers with assurance and resolve.

"I don't understand. I fell in love with another angel. I'm sure I have broken a code or violated a decree." And I am not afraid to admit it. He sees all of me anyways.

"You have not broken a thing," King Worthy exclaims. "You, my dear, have put things back together."

Swoosh! A satin cover pulls over the sphere and it lights up instantly.

"Skye!" There he is, in the sphere-shaped ball, soaring towards the earth among the stars. This vantage point shows everything in outer space, like speckled confetti in a purple-navy twilight. He flies onward and an angel finds him mid-air. She reaches for him, and then she pulls away. A dark red cloud grabs her and a dark figure swoops in.

"Ebony!" he yells. His hands extend and hers reach for him, but the darkness pulls her away hastily. It's too late. She's gone.

King Worthy interjects. "That was My son before he met you."

"Who is the angel?" I ask.

"Ebony. She was taken by The Raven."

"Was he in love with her?"

"Every angel loves."

"But he reached for her."

"Yes," He concurs. "That was the moment she was taken by The Raven."

"But only angels who choose to side with The Raven are vulnerable to his tactics," I say candidly. "That's what Skye told me." I look to The King's eyes for verification.

"You are perceptive, little one." King Worthy waves His hand over The Luminary and fire smokes in bursts of fire. Explosions detonate in the galaxies. Angels zoom up and down in bright light. War plays out as angels clash in the heavens. "War comes when trust fails," He adds with a solemn tone. Then He turns to look me in the eyes with burning blue and green light flaming in His eyes. "Angels who give their allegiance to any force other than Me are susceptible to deception."

"I vow my allegiance to you."

King Worthy's smile heightens. "I know you do. You loved Leafe without pretense. You did not consider him for his title nor did you remain devoted to Skye simply for his. I have tested the genuineness of your heart, Lilly, and I found you to be worthy."

"Worthy?" I echo to confirm his pronouncement. Worthy is who I would have been had I married Skye. My literal name change. My identity.

"Yes, my dear. Worthy." He smiles back at me with tender eyes and strength in His aura. His compassionate care puts me at ease. He says I am worthy, and I believe Him. I am who He says I am. Without hesitation, I run to Him, and He embraces me. Tears fall like raindrops as gratitude saturates my soul.

"Thank you, my King. I want to belong to Zion forever," I exclaim eagerly, as joyful tears run down my cheeks. "You are my King, and because you say I am worthy, I know I am."

His embrace feels like the pinnacle of immortality, where nothing can hurt me. The safety of a trillion angels resides in the strength of His arms. In His eyes, I am immortal, here in the Throne Room of Zion where angels and time stand still in His presence. Only Him and I can see. And I am fully seen for all I am.

He kisses my forehead. "Lilly, you need to tell me. Who do you love more? Skye or Leafe?"

"I love Captain Leafe."

"What do you love about him?"

"He challenges me," I giggle at the confession. "I've never had someone tell me the truth to my face and be right. Usually, I'm always right. When he comes close to me, my heart beats fast. I always want more of his presence, although it makes me feel guilty since I met Skye first. He makes me think about what I want and not what everyone else tells me I should want. He's mysteriously enthralling, and the way he talks to me pulls out parts of me I didn't know were there. I feel like I am a fuller expression of myself when I am with him."

"Lilly, I knew you would fall in love with Leafe."

"You did?"

"I am The King of Zion. Omniscience will always be my essence. I saw it coming before time began, my dear one. My fear is that the darkness would claim you. So, I chose you for myself and set you apart. I brought you here, so that no one on earth could claim you. And Leafe…

he will love you more than any man or angel ever could love you. My Kingdom will protect you if you give your loyalty to Zion."

"I will, King Worthy," I say. "There is no where I'd rather be than Zion's Heaven."

"I believe you, dear one," He responds comfortingly. "Now, you have a decision to make about the wedding," King Worthy advises me.

"Yes," I pause.

Oh, my beautiful dress! Jenna was so excited when she saw me dolled up in the boutique. Now, I can't wear it. How could I? My heart cannot walk down the aisle with two lovers on my mind. It would not be proper nor true to how I feel.

"I cannot go through with the wedding," I confess honestly.

The King nods. "Then it's time to tell Skye."

21

Leafe

I flex my wings and look to my left as Skye follows the sentiment. My feathers feel like they have been stuck in position for ages, but only minutes have passed since Lilly and I arrived. I flap my wings. The strength of their velocity returns. Thank goodness. I was beginning to worry if The King had presumed a curse.

King Worthy stands and every angel in the Throne Room faces Him in reverence.

He speaks. "Lilly has something she needs to say. And I adjure you to listen."

Lilly's eyes dart from The King to Skye to me. Her eyes soften as she lands on mine. Then, fierce light blazes from her. Her countenance shines like golden glitter in the heavens. Her smile invigorates my heart to beat for her rapidly.

Say what you need to say, Lilly. I'm listening.

"King Worthy changed my life the day he sent Skye to rescue me from the deep ends of the ocean," she turns to Skye. "I fell in love. But then I fell in love again." She turns back to me. "With Captain Leafe."

Angels shriek in the Throne Room and King Worthy hails His right hand to silence the commotion. He waits for her to continue, allowing her to finish before interjecting.

I prepare myself for the news I know is coming. Lilly has made her decision. Either she is going to break it to Skye and tell him she loves me or she is going to break it to both of us.

I inhale and exhale, looking around the Throne Room of King Worthy's greatness, the place I inherited because of His goodness towards me. I have every reason to be grateful, no matter what she decides. I just do not know how my heart will hold up if she lets go of me now. Love has consumed me, and I am sure I will never be able to let go of her. My eyes begin to burn at the intensity accruing as the milliseconds pass. Emerald fire channels from my heart and soul all the way to my retinas, and the sensation is increasing.

Lilly speaks. "Love is deeper than I knew it could be, and though I promised my heart to Skye in matrimony, I am sure I cannot go through with it."

Fire blasts from the Throne as smoke hails overhead where the seraphim circle about.

Can't go through with it? You mean, you're not marrying Skye?

"I'm not marrying Skye," she thinks as I hear her thoughts.

"Lilly!" Skye gasps and collapses on the floor.

My heart flips inside my chest like it does when I dart through the galaxies. Sensations arouse my wings to move. I reign them in. Is this really happening? Does she love me like I love her?

I look at her to find the truth. "Lilly, do you love me more?"

"I do," she answers.

Skye protests as rage envelops his posture on the floor. "Father, do something!"

King Worthy rises. "I cannot force her to marry you, Skye. Even if I wanted to. Lilly must decide."

Skye slams the ground and looks up. "Sure you can! You're The King for Zion's sake!"

"A woman has a choice in who she loves," King Worthy pronounces with a loud voice. "Love cannot be coerced. And love will not be tamed. My eyes see everything. When she says she loves General Leafe, her heart is true."

Did he let my title slip?

He never calls me *General.* It was His idea, after all, to keep my identity a secret. He did not want all the angels to know lest more of them revolt and give away strategies to The Raven.

"General Leafe?" Lilly inquires.

I nod. "Yes, Lilly."

Lilly looks at me stunned.

The King speaks. "Too many rebels started to follow Skye's every move, and angels were listening in on strategies, only to feed it to The Raven. I chose to keep General Leafe's status a secret. It diverted attention away from his secret missions and put them onto Skye. Then Skye and Zion's Angels could rid out threats while Leafe took care of urgent, secret operations. Every angel benefited. Zion benefited."

"That is, until Skye fell in love with Lilly," I add. "Then the hinlor threats on Skye doubled because they wanted to target her just as much as they wanted Skye. I had to start flying with Zion's Angels and going on secret missions. Doing both."

"Is this true, Skye?" Lilly asks with curiosity.

Tell her the truth, Skye. She deserves to know the truth.

"It is," Skye says. He slowly stands and sighs. "His title is General. Commanding General over Zion's Cosmos. We called him Captain Leafe to keep it a secret. As my father said, we needed to protect our strategies. Too many would have targeted Leafe if they knew where he was. We needed him to defend the cosmos unnoticed."

Skye takes a deep breath and then rages sapphire eyes in my direction.

"Leafe, you knew the code that you never fall in love with the object of your mission. You betrayed me! You betrayed my father!" Skye shouts visibly shook.

"Your father set us up!" I retort boldly. "Lilly was His idea and you know it's true. Besides, Lilly is not an object. She is a woman. Your father asked me to love her and that's why you're so angry. I know it's hard to hear, but you know I am in love with Lilly." My head turns in her direction. I have to tell her how I feel. "Lilly, I have been fighting for you since Skye met you. Literally speaking, keeping hinlors from finding you, both on earth and here in Zion. Zion needs you. More importantly,

I need you." I take a deep breath to divulge completely. "I am I love with you, Lilly Rose. And if your love for me is true, then I also have a choice to make. I choose to be your husband and make you Mrs. General Leafe Worthy forever."

Lilly gasps with surprise. "Leafe! I… don't know what to say!" she exclaims with smiling eyes.

"Say yes!" I encourage her.

She nods and responds, "Yes!"

Blast!

I turn and a door slams by the entrance.

"How can two lovers exist when rivals haunt in the background?" Zeal scowls as his voice looms from standing guard at the gold door. "Forgive me, King Worthy, but Zion will never be at peace with Lilly pulling at the heartstrings of our two strongest Generals!"

At the doorway, Zeal stands solemn and angered. Visibly disturbed. Uncharacteristic of his manner. I look closer, and his eyes flame in Lilly's direction with the kind of fire that only rouses from desire.

I narrow my eyes on him. "My guess is you are not as worried for our sake as you are for your own. Isn't that right, Zeal?"

"Ahhh!" Zeal shouts with a face of rage. "Lilly is mine!"

He soars towards me and before I can prepare for the onslaught, he right hooks me in the face.

"Leafe!" Lilly screams in terror.

I shake off the fresh jab and grab his shoulders with my forehead on his. I stare into his eyes with emerald fire to remind him who he answers to. "You think you can kill me, Zeal!? Remember your place!"

"My place is with The Raven!" Zeal shouts nastily.

"The Raven is in The Black hole! Is that where you want to be?" I shout back.

"Take your hands off him, Zeal!" Captain Strength shouts from the hosts of angels surrounding the scene of betrayal.

Captain Strength flies up to my position as Lilly stands beside me. Zeal circles us. I step in front of Lilly to shield her from Zeal and pick her up into my arms with my wings covering her.

Zeal scowls and aims for my face. He throws another left hook. I cover Lilly's head and dodge the punch, swerving to the right.

"King Worthy is not my King!" Zeal screams. "And I will have the girl for myself!"

Zeal lunges his body in my direction for another punch, but I soar upwards with Lilly. Zeal swoops around my left shoulder and jump-kicks Captain Strength as he tries to intervene. Zeal grabs Lilly with force.

"Keep your hands off of her!" Skye hoots and hollers. "She is the future queen of Zion!"

Captain Strength sends a blast of light radiation into Zeal and Lilly flies in the air.

"Lilly!" I shout.

I zoom towards Zeal's back and Skye zooms towards Zeal's front. We reach for Lilly.

Flash!

The King detonates holy light.

Zeal disintegrates into dust.

King Worthy stands with His golden staff in hand, outstretched to her, as Lilly radiates with Zion's glow.

"Zeal must be for My Kingdom, and My Kingdom alone. All other kingdoms will turn to dust," King Worthy decrees as Lilly hovers in the air, unharmed and sustained by the King. "Are you okay, dear Lilly?" The King calls out to her and walks towards her.

The surrounding angels stand at attention in dazzling white light as The King commands the floor. Peace and delight adorn their faces, exuding a pure angelic essence. Something in Zeal's face contradicted these virtues before his demise. I saw it when we were in the battle-air earlier. I would like to have known if he was contaminated by a hinlor. But The King knows. The King sees. I will let Him assess those possibilities later if He wishes.

"Yes," she replies. "I am okay."

He slowly moves His staff and Lilly descends to the floor and stands. I reach for her and embrace her feathery-covered frame in my arms. My feathers fit her perfectly.

"I'm so sorry, Lilly. I knew Zeal had eyes for you," I exclaim. I should have seen that coming. Didn't The King?

"I saw it coming," King Worthy makes clear. "The only way to bring a threat to an end is to let it play out. I was never going to allow Lilly to be harmed in my Throne Room. And neither were you," He pauses and eyes both Skye and me. "I saw you both reach for Lilly to save her. Your love is true. And as King, the truth of your love delights me more than you know."

Skye steps away and bends down to wipe his brow. "I can't do this," Skye says with angst. Heartbreak exudes from his eyes. I look away as the sound of tears fill my periphery. I should console him in moments like these. It's me who always flew by his side and ran to his rescue in crises and war. But I cannot console him on this. Lilly is between both of us now, and I fear she always will be.

Before Lilly can say, "Skye, wait!" he flies out of the Throne Room.

Lilly touches her cheek and closes her eyes, trying to release the pressure of his heartbreak.

"Lilly, can you handle the choice of choosing me over him?"

I need her to ponder it.

"Can I handle losing Skye? I have to be able to confront that reality if I am going to say yes to Leafe. I love Leafe. I need him in my life. Standing here before The King, my heart is wide open, and Leafe needs to know that I choose Him. Only Him." I hear her thoughts contemplating.

She opens her eyes and looks at me with strong resolve. Stronger than I've ever seen her. "Yes," she answers.

"Then, you must let go of him now."

"I know," she admits and exhales.

I nod and stroke her cheek, as a tear streams down her cheek in the wake of emotion. Many emotions have been shared in this Throne Room, but I have one more to provoke. I cannot let the moment slip away, and if I know anything to be sure, it is that I want Lilly to be mine forever.

I bend down on one knee to propose officially, now that I can secure the moment and place the ring on her finger. "Lilly Rose, I love you more than anything in this universe. And I would love nothing more than to call you Mrs. General Leafe Worthy forever. Will you marry me?"

Lilly smiles and presses her hand to her chest, as she laughs from the shock. "Yes!" she exclaims just as she did moments prior. Now it is official.

Angels roar with cheers. King Worthy chuckles at the witnessing of His mastermind plan coming to fruition. Her left hand still has Skye's engagement ring, and I will need to replace it with mine.

"Take off the other ring," I say. She eyes the ring for a second. That scares me. I know taking off Skye's ring is a big step. I don't want to rush her. I wait for her patiently. She looks up at me, and obliges, and slips it into her dress pocket.

I reach for my ring in my left wing that I have been carrying in case this moment arrived. It feels surreal that I am opening the box at all, to place it on the finger of my fiancé.

Fiancé. That word is going to take some getting used to. But soon enough, I will call her my wife. And forever she will have my name. *Worthy.*

"Lilly, this ring represents our love. Passionate. Daring. Destined." She eyes the ring with delight as I show her the delicate details of its craftsmanship. "The band is an infinity loop, which represents our love for eternity. The diamond is a rare red diamond from the sun's own furnace. I flew there and back to have it set in this band for you. It has this inscription engraved in it: '*Saved by the Skye. Won by the Leafe.*' I figured I would pay homage."

"I love it!" Her eyes beam and I place the ring on her left ring finger.

"Ooooh!" The angels sound as the ring lights up on Lilly's finger.

"This diamond has luminescent qualities. It lights up from love."

Lilly smiles at me with bright green eyes.

"Then it is destined to stay lit forever," she assures me.

"Kiss her already!" King Worthy encourages me.

I lean in to kiss the love of my eternal life, and her lips meet mine in the roar of angelic hosts cheering in the background. Organs blare. Smoke rises. Fire blazes as the Throne Room erupts in joyful celebration. On the inside, my heart sparks with fireworks in every color under Zion's stars.

"Now!" The King echoes loudly. "It's time for a wedding."

22

Lilly

"Leafe!" My fiancé picks me up and twirls me around in the Throne Room for all to see. "You're spinning me so fast!" I laugh and giggle with joy like a ballerina in pink slippers.

"I love how you love me, Lilly." Leafe kisses my face all over.

"Why wouldn't she love you?" Jenna replies as she finds us in the Throne Room. "I can see it all over her face." Jenna gives him a nod of approval. "You did good, Leafe."

Jenna always knows how to read me. She's been reading me since elementary school when we were 9 years old and boys were far from conversation. Then, it was all about Barbie dolls and manicures. She always gave the best manicures.

"Jenna! I'm so happy you're here," I hug her and she hugs me, and then looks at my engagement ring.

"I want everyone to see how much you love me, and how much I love you," Leafe says.

"Then they are sure to see it forever, my handsome fiancé." I kiss Leafe's glorious lips once again and taste my favorite flavors of caramel and cinnamon. "You know I love you," I say passionately. My whole being longs to make it known.

"I'm worried Skye will hover over us."

"If he does, you can remove him from our presence."

"Wow, so hostile!" Jenna says hysterically. "That's how you know she's in love. She doesn't want to have anything to do with any other guy."

"Angel," Leafe reminds her.

"Sorry, *angel!*" Jenna responds and throws up her hands with a clever smile. "By the way I was wondering where you two were. Lilly never came back after you flew her away to dinner."

"Let's just say we were busy," Leafe explains to her discreetly. "Look Jenna, I see how Lilly loves you and I'm glad you're here. I saw how it shook you when she almost drowned. You care about Lilly and that means the world to me."

"Is that a compliment?" Jenna asks entertained.

"Any friend of Lilly's is a friend of mine," Leafe exclaims.

"How did you get here from the house!?" I ask curiously. I know she might have not known the way, but Jenna is one independent woman. Maybe she found her way here. Or was it another angel who brought her?

"You'll never guess. That angel Zeal brought me. He was looking for Lilly."

"I knew Zeal was up to no good," Leafe interjects. "He's been acting funny ever since Lilly got here. I'm just glad he got you here safely. Go on."

Jenna continues. "He said he needed to bring me to the palace because something important was going to happen." Jenna points to the doorway. "Once we got here, he slammed the door and soared at Lilly. Then, everyone clearly saw what happened next. Poof!" Jenna tosses her hands up with wide eyes. "Poor guy."

"Angel," Leafe reminds her yet again, this time with a fascinated grin at her antics.

"Sorry, *angel!* I'm still getting used to all this!" Jenna plays with her hair and puts her hands on her hips.

Jenna's quirks lighten the mood. She brings joyful earth tones to Zion. I think that is why King Worthy wants humans here. Humans color the universe with enthusiasm and personality.

"Wedding bells are in order!" King Worthy announces loudly.

Wedding bells. I like the sound of that.

Before I met Skye, I never thought of the glamour of wedding dresses and the sound of wedding bells. But when the time came for me to say yes, I started to imagine the beauty of red roses against white silk, and the taste of a wedding cake made of blueberry cream cheese. Now that Leafe and I are engaged, I have so many more details to plan and ideas to talk about with him.

"Zion's angels, we have a ceremony to plan! Leafe and Lilly, I will leave the details to you." King Worthy's support keeps my hopes high that this will be the most beautiful wedding I have ever seen. I want Leafe to have everything he wants too.

"Yes, King Worthy!" Zion's Angels cheer and sing in response to the anticipated celebration. I look around the room, and angel eyes gaze at us dreamily with anticipation. It seems they are just as excited as we are.

Leafe squeezes my hand. "Let's go, my future bride. I still owe you that dinner."

"Please, I'm famished!" I reply readily. My stomach is ready for the finest of Zion's flavors after all the chaos of today.

"What flavor do you want?" Leafe wraps his arms around me and his wings coddle me in an angelic embrace.

"Flavor?" I ask.

"Yes. In the waterfalls when we fly over," he clarifies. "I want to make it taste like your favorite flavor."

"Raspberry lemonade," I say.

He nods with a smile and picks me up to exit the Throne Room. "Raspberry lemonade, it is!"

King Worthy doesn't step in to add more instructions about the wedding, and at that, I must assume there is no more to talk about at the present moment. Wedding bells will happen eventually. And I have a feeling it will be much faster than I think.

"What about Jenna!" I can't leave her alone again.

"I'm taking Jenna on a special tour of Zion," Virtue chimes in, angelically, soaring up to us. "Hello dear, what a beautiful human," Virtue says to Jenna.

"Your halo is gorgeous! Wow, I could shop in all of Nordstrom's and never find one that polished." Jenna touches the halo and Virtue flinches, while trying to maintain her calm demeanor. Virtue laughs to divert her hands away from the halo.

Zion's Angels have been graciously kind since I arrived, and also to Jenna since she arrived. My heart lightens knowing she will be in good hands. I want her to see all the beautiful sights Zion has to offer!

"Go have fun, you two! I have Heaven to explore," Jenna says excitedly. She gives me a kiss on the cheek.

"Let's go dear!" Virtue flies away with Jenna. I wave goodbye.

"Soon you will be my worthy bride, my future queen." Leafe kisses me tenderly. "Are you ready to taste the waterfalls?" Leafe looks at me lovingly and wipes a strand of hair from my forehead. Then he tucks it behind my ear.

"I'm ready," I say dreamily.

Whisk!

At once, we fly away through the ivory doors and over the courtyard of pastel-colored tulips. We pass the Tree of Life. Serenades of glorious hallelujahs sound out peaceful harmonies. Angelic symphonies put me at ease every time.

"I love the way the angels sing," I say entranced. "I guess that's because I'm in Zion."

"Yes, my love. Zion's Angels are pure bliss," Leafe assures me. His embrace tightens around me as we fly higher over Zion's Tree of Life and past the turquoise River of Life.

"Are they going to sing at our wedding?" I ask hopefully.

Leafe chuckles and kisses my ear. "That is a guarantee, my bride! Zion's Angels sing at every celebratory event in Zion."

Celebratory event. I like the sound of that. Me and Leafe getting married is a celebratory event, not just for us, but for the whole Kingdom of Zion. I'm still getting used to the change of Leafe being the angel I walk up to in my white wedding dress. But he is who I want.

"In time, I will be the only one you think about, my love," Leafe reminds me through his thoughts.

"I love you," I say back to Leafe through my thoughts. He knows I love him, but I will spend eternity reminding him.

"I know you do," he tells me through his thoughts.

Telekinesis keeps us in sync, like two dancers in a Viennese Waltz.

Whisp!

A sprinkle of raspberry lemonade liquid sprinkles my face and I open my eyes to the waterfalls.

"How does it taste?" Leafe asks.

"Decadent," I reply with a grin. I open my mouth to more showers of fruity liquid.

Leafe touches my cheek slowly and licks his fingers. "Nothing tastes better than you," he says. His eyes blaze with intense emerald green and my heart races at the sight of his eyes peering into mine.

Green eyes find me in love.

"Green eyes find me in love," he thinks.

Kiss!

With his passionate gaze, Leafe moves in closer to my mouth and I taste the intensity of his light. I kiss him back, fearlessly, tasting every drop of raspberry lemonade on his tongue. I caress his head and his wings flutter.

Our hands massage one another like we are making love in a bed of roses and our lips kiss deeply like we are in outer space. The air is our only foundation as we hover in Zion's airspace, beside the waterfalls, and everything is perfectly sound. Perfectly safe. It's like that with angels. Angel wings always hold me in perfect steadiness whether I'm in the air or on the ground.

"You were made for Zion's beauty, my perfect bride," Leafe whispers in my ear as we fly onward.

"I am going to love you forever," I say confidently. Then I gaze into his emerald, green eyes again and dive into his mouth as his tongue meets mine in blissful unison.

I believe it now. That he will love me forever. The way he holds me and kisses me tells me he is bound to me and I to him. No one has ever loved me the way he does. It's as if my body becomes one with his skin at the moment of contact.

"I need you, Lilly," he tells me voraciously.

His wings curl around me and swivel to a sturdy position and I can sense his body ready to make love to me by the way he is moving.

"I need you too, General Leafe." I smile into his eyes and his right hand makes its way to my intimate region. "Leafe!" I gasp.

"Let me love you," he says again.

"Okay, my angel." I lean in and kiss his lips once more, to give him the go-ahead. "Are you going to make love to me like last time?"

"Better than last time," he says. "I am going to be the best you have ever had, my ballerina bride."

At that, he turns 360 degrees in the air and dives into my mouth to claim my tongue as if it was up for grabs by anyone other than him. I clasp his head and stroke his hair as he massages my tongue with finesse and brings his core closer to my frame. His body presses on me and I can feel his heartbeat. I open for him, allowing him to do what he wants to. I feel his hand slip under my navel and his hands work downward.

"Leafe!" I sigh.

He kisses me intensely.

"Are you ready for me?" He asks with brawny strength on top of me, as the air holds us in its grip.

I breathe in and out. "Yes."

Thrust. "Leafe!"

He penetrates me with force, and my body catapults into the steep climb up Everest. Within seconds, he has me plateauing at the peak.

"Your body is heavenly," Leafe confesses. "I couldn't ask for a better lover. You're the pinnacle of perfection."

"Keep going," I say. "Take me to the stars."

His body makes love to me angelically, exactly as Zion would allow, and I find myself wanting more. I don't want him to stop. Not now. Not ever. Skye never loved me like this. That is why Leafe will always be the one I want.

My body ascends to elation and Leafe rises with me. Bliss finds us. He kisses me once again, as our souls collide in spiritual oneness.

"You are my star," he whispers in my ear. "My stunning, twinkling star."

We fly into the light of Zion's skies where pink and amber flecks of gold float in the air like confetti. My stomach growls.

"We're here," Leafe says. "No more stomach growling. I have the most amazing dinner in mind for you."

"General Leafe!" A bright, glowing angel with red, flowing hair and lavender eyes greets us at the entrance. "I was beginning to wonder if you got caught up in battle. I expected you and Lilly much earlier."

"You mean Captain Leafe?" Leafe tries to correct her kindly. He touches down on land, sets me down gently, and grabs my hand.

"You know the cat is out of the bag now, General," Serenity informs him with smiling eyes and intuitive awareness. Serenity reaches for my cheek and eyes me with a smile that matches her namesake. Behind her flowing locks, white wings flutter like diamond-studded rainbows. Every angel takes my breath away with their ornate beauty, altogether heavenly and strikingly unique. Not one looks the same as another. Each angel radiates with individual characteristics. The universe matches this sentiment. Everything has its own allure. "Word has already spread across Zion that King Worthy has been keeping your true title a secret. Truth be told, we all knew. You've been Captain far too long given the victories you've won."

"And we still have more to fight," Leafe says humbly.

"There will always be battles until New Zion is here, my good friend! But peace remains, nonetheless," Serenity expresses and flutters closer to me. As her wings move, an aura of calm steadies the atmosphere. I breathe in and out, like I'm standing on the shores of Lanikai Beach at sunrise.

"Her job is giving serenity to humans on earth," Leafe explains to me through his thoughts. *"That's why she carries an intense aura of calm."*

"I can feel it," I tell him through my thoughts.

"I want you to feel at peace with me all the time, my love. I will always be your serenity. Your passion. Your devoted lover," Leafe continues to talk to me through his thoughts. He looks at me with emerald fire blazing in his eyes. *"I will be all things to you."*

Green eyes find me in serenity.

"I believe it, Leafe. I love you so much," I tell him through my thoughts. *"You will always be more to me than anyone else could be."*

Leafe blushes and squeezes my hand.

"I love you, Lilly," he tells me through his thoughts.

"I love you," I tell him with mine.

"Serenity!" Leafe announces. "I have important news," he turns to me with beaming eyes. "Lilly and I are getting married!" He places his arms under me and whisks me in into the air like we are two dancers in a foxtrot. I feel like a ballerina when he spins me around, without a care of who's watching.

"I've never quite seen you this elated, Leafe!" Serenity laughs with an aura of peaceful pleasure.

Leafe spins me around once more and kisses my forehead as he comes to a stop. He holds me tightly and inhales Zion's air. I do the same. "I feel more in love than I ever have been," he says.

"I can see that," Serenity says joyfully. "You must be Lilly Rose." She draws in close again and reaches for my hand. Her eyes enlarge as she studies the rock on my ring finger glistening in the light.

"It's a once of a kind diamond," Leafe exclaims proudly.

"Exquisite," Serenity says.

Her head tilts ever so slightly as she beholds the ring, captivated by it. My hand starts to go numb in her grasp as she keeps eyeing it. In Zion, there is no timeclock to be kept. Zion paces to the will of eternity, where death and dying are never found and infinite pleasures are always at hand. In the present, moment, it seems she is spellbound by mine. My hand, that is.

"It's nice to meet you, Serenity," I exclaim happily.

"The pleasure is all mine, beautiful one," Serenity answers delicately. She lets go of my hand. "You must be hungry!"

"Is she your chef?" I ask Leafe quietly.

"Not a chef, although her creations are delicious. I decided I'm cooking for you tonight."

"You are?"

"Yes. I hope you love it, my bride."

"I will love anything you create."

We enter the bungalow, as Leafe likes to call it, with high, towering ceilings and a grand piano. Black and white gemstones are embedded in the floor with shiny gloss coating the surface. A circular staircase leads upstairs like a spiral. Gigantic paintings cover the walls with iconic wonders of the universe, only the pictures move with multidimensional layers, as if I could step in to its image and land on the other side.

Leafe moves towards the kitchen, but my eye is caught by the picture in the foyer. My feet stay still. It's as if I'm staring into the live picture, moving in and out of time.

"Are these videos?" I echo into the kitchen.

"They're portals," he echoes back.

I investigate the pearl-framed painting of a teal-blue midnight with shadowy lights dancing like ribbons. Fascinating.

"It's the northern lights of the Brachian Galaxy," Leafe kisses me on the forehead and hands me a glass of water. "The picture moves as if you were there looking at its lights in person."

"You said portals. Does that mean we can go there?"

"Yes," Leafe says. "Soon I will show you the rest of the universe... if you want me to." I smile like a butterfly in highest skies. He grabs my hand and leads me into the kitchen. Aromas fill the air. "Come with me. I want you to taste this!"

He feeds me a spoonful of berries, warm and sweet, with a hint of sugar.

"Mmm! That's delicious, Leafe!"

"They're caramelized starberries."

"Starberries?"

"Yes."

"The best berries I've tasted," I exclaim with a pleased mouth.

"They're for the tarts. I made it for dessert, but you can have as many tastes as you want my bride." He kisses me and licks the berry juice on my lips. I kiss him back gladly. "Starberries are only found in Zion. The stars pollinate their growth."

Who knew Leafe was such a Renaissance man. Or should I say Renaissance *angel*. He can do anything. "I love you," I say.

"I love you too, Lilly." He wipes the starberry dripping from my lips and smiles at me lovingly. "Can I pour you a glass of wine?"

"I've only tried Pinot Grigio with my family," I reply cautiously. "But I will try it!"

"This is Zion's finest Rosé. Fit for a rose," He gives me a wink, and pours a blush-pink liquid into a glass engraved with the name *Lilly*. He hands me the glass and my eyes enlarge as I notice the personalized detail.

"It says *Lilly* on it!" I turn the side of the glass to read the cursive letters. *Lilly and Leafe*, it says as I read the full inscription. "How did you do that?"

"I engraved it for you with my eyes." He smiles at me like his eyes could engrave love in the sky and write romance in the stars. I take a sip of the wine and he comes closer.

"I love it!" I kiss his lips endearingly and he kisses me back, tasting the wine.

"Nothing like Rosé on a rose," he says.

I take another sip of wine. "Mmm, its sweet," I say.

"My lips or the wine?" he asks with fond eyes.

"Both, I'd have to say," I say whimsically. I take another sip and my heart flutters as my head lifts into the clouds.

Leafe grins and lifts his glass for a sip. "You like it, don't you?"

"Yes, I'm surprised at how much I do," I concur, considering I never much thought I'd like wine. But the taste is thrilling and my mood lightened. I feel ready to dance a waltz across the extravagant foyer barefoot so I can feel the glossy floor caressing my feet.

"Let's make a toast then. Cheers to Zion!"

"Cheers to Zion!" I echo.

"I want to give you as many firsts as possible."

Leafe's eyes gaze into me like fire.

My heart quickens from the douse of wine and the ecstasy of his aura colliding with mine. I lean into him and I fall against his chest. He quickly takes the wine glass and sets it down. He holds my waist and wraps his arms around me.

"Have you ever been kissed... here?" He asks me tenderly, and then kisses me behind my ear.

I giggle from the sensation of his lips peppering down my neck.

"Or here?" He switches sides and sends shivers up my spine with more kisses.

"Not until now," I answer dreamily.

"What about here?" He aims for my chest with more kisses and trails down to my waist. "Lilly, I would make love to you right here, right now, but I want you to eat first. You need nourishment."

"What if I want *you* first?" I feel the wine setting in.

His eyes enflame with bright emerald fire and my body warms from the heat.

Green eyes find me intoxicated.

"Lilly, I think you have had too much wine."

"Not even a full glass!" I protest playfully and reach around his wings.

Leafe clasps my hands and brings them to his chest sweetly. "Lilly, I don't want to make love to you when you are even a little bit tipsy."

"But we've already made love." I bat my eyelashes and giggle, reaching for the wine glass.

Leafe grins. "Let's eat first. Then I will give you all the firsts you've yet to experience in my arms."

"I can't wait to try everything else you've prepared," I say eagerly. "Tell me what you made for dinner, my General. It smells like a garden of succulent flavors."

Leafe picks me up and carries me to the prepared dishes where the aroma of garlic and parmesan cream fill the air.

"We have asparagus risotto, spinach and lobster lasagna, and bruschetta with fresh basil, cherry tomatoes, Zion oil, and feta cheese. I knew you liked Italian," Leafe kisses my head and squeezes me tightly. "And salad of course, with all fresh ingredients from my garden."

"I love it!" My eyes twinkle at the sight of his skills.

"Don't get too used to it now, it's not often I cook," Leafe winks at me. "I also have a personal chef. But tonight is extra special."

"Thank you," I say happily.

He kisses my forehead and whispers gently. "For what?"

"For cooking for me. For loving me."

"No need to thank me. It's my pleasure, Lilly," he leans into kiss me and I taste the freshness of basil on his savory lips. "I pursued you for a reason. I knew what I was getting into. And I wanted you all along."

My cheeks blush and I feel a surge of desire coursing through me. I'd let him take me here and now, all over again, but dinner is ready and he put in so much effort. I look into the dining room where elaborate candles and a geode turquoise table center the room.

"Shall I set the table?" I ask.

"I have angels for that," he replies with a smile. "Angels were made to protect and bless humans. Now that you are here, I have endless angels asking to assist whenever you are around."

"You do?"

"Yes." His eyes peer into me like the sun at noonday.

"The table is ready, lovely Lilly," Serenity exclaims with beaming peach eyes. I turn to acknowledge.

"Thank you so much," I reply excitedly.

Leafe takes my hand. "Let's eat," he says, as we sit at the ornate turquoise, geode dining table with a shiny surface as if it had been placed inside a necklace on the queen of England. Leafe sits across from me and eyes me with green eyes of fiery passion. My whole body echoes his pleasure. With every bite I take, all I can think about is him touching me with those lips. Those hands.

"Would you like more wine, Miss Lilly?" Another angel with eyes like espresso holds a wine bottle at my side, ready to pour.

"I probably shouldn't!" I exclaim. "But let Leafe decide."

"It's okay, Cocoa," Leafe instructs. "Thank you. We will drink another glass after dinner."

"Yes, General," Cocoa replies with eager wings and flutters into the kitchen where laughter and angelic voices "ooh" and "aww". They watch us as we eat. I don't mind that they do. I love Leafe more than I thought I could love anyone, and at this point, I don't care who sees.

I take my last bite and set down my fork politely. The flavors satisfied my appetite like heavenly bliss. It is the best meal I have tasted.

"Dinner was delicious," I tell Leafe with a satisfied stomach. "Heavenly, in fact."

"You have something–" Leafe leans over from his chair and wipes my mouth with his finger, and I feel a smear of pasta sauce that had been streaming down my chin. "There. All better," he says with glowing eyes and a sliver of pasta sauce on his finger. He licks it.

Green eyes find me at dinner.

"I love staring into her eyes," his thoughts say.

"I love staring at all of you," I say with my thoughts.

He lifts his wine glass. "Now, it's time for dessert, my little rose."

"Starberry tarts with cosmic chocolate crust!" Serenity places the dessert in front me and follows with Leafe. I take a bite and my taste buds are invigorated.

"Mmm, so good!" I exclaim with a mouthful of starberry tart.

"It's been said that starberry cures bad memories of the past," Leafe divulges as he takes a bite of the decadent sweetness.

"What kind of memories?"

"Trauma. Stress. Abuse. You name it. Zion cultivates starberries because of the cosmic starlight fertilizing its roots. One day, when all humans come to Zion, they can taste this fruit, among others. The King seeks wholeness for everyone."

"Zion heals all things."

"Yes. Zion heals all things."

Any memory of Skye that may try to inhibit my love for Leafe will be forgotten in this bliss of Zion's paradise. Starberries will always rejuvenate my blissful awareness of my love for Leafe. He will always be the one.

"Lilly, you mentioned the portals earlier," Leafe reminds me. "I saw you enamored with them on the wall. You love art, I can tell."

"Yes." I take another bite of starberry tart. "Art expresses emotion and abstract ideals. I find it fascinating."

"I do too. These portals are more than art, they are like moving pictures," Leafe rises from his seat with the starberry tart in hand and comes closer to me to continue. "When battles strike, I step through the painting portal and I am in that locale immediately." He sits right next to me.

"Like time travel?" I ask curiously.

Leafe strokes my back casually, yet lovingly. I love when he sits close to me. I feel like he cares for my body at every moment, and never misses the cues for what I need.

"Only time does not exist. Distance does. These paintings are various locations around the universe that I can travel to instantaneously."

"The King thinks of everything, doesn't He?"

"Yes, He does, most assuredly. But this was my idea," Leafe tells me. He leans in and kisses my cheek. "When we started having more threats after The Raven rebelled, the universe was in disarray. Hinlors would invade and King Worthy wanted me clearing out the threats. This gave me a way to get there instantly before any more damage was done."

"That's why you were His General all along," I reply, as I connect the dots.

Leafe nods humbly. He takes another bite of starberry tart but doesn't say anything. He doesn't like to talk about being called *General*. I can tell. But he keeps flying and warring for Zion, with courage. All this time, he has been fighting battles nobody knew about. I respect him so much for that.

"Look Lilly, I don't do it because of the title. I do it because it's my job to watch over the universe. It's all our jobs. Zion's Angels keep the universe safe. I love what I do."

"I wish you could see how much I admire you, Leafe," I say dreamily. I do admire him. He is my quintessential angel.

"I know you do," Leafe confesses sweetly. "I feel your aura, Lilly. I always have, ever since the first time I saw in that Italian Café with your family."

"You saw me?"

"I sent the message," he says softly. "I saw you at the table after the couple's proposal."

I gasp as I recall the moment. How could I have forgotten? Me and my family were dining at Stromboli's, a family staple, and a man proposed to his fiancé. Then the hostess came by to tell me someone needed to see me. I looked around the room thinking it was Skye who came and left before I got to see him. All along, it was Leafe who came to me. "Have you loved me all this time?"

Leafe's eyes begin to water. "I feel like I have loved you for all eternity."

My heart skips a beat. He gently kisses my lips with the flavor of starberry tart.

"I love you, Leafe," I say. "I love how you love me."

Leafe looks over at the wall where the teal-blue lights dance and then smiles at me. "I know what you want. You want to see the universe and step into that painting," he says with angelic intuition.

I nod and laugh. He reads me well. "Yes, you caught me," I confess with a laugh. "We could be like the muses of Monet himself," I exclaim dreamily.

Leafe rests his hand on my cheek. "I want to give you everything you wish for."

"Will you take me there?"

"I thought you'd never ask."

23

Leafe

"Brachian Galaxy or Shooting Star Circle?" I ask Lilly.

With so many wonders in the universe, it is difficult to choose which one to show her first. All I want is to make her sparkle with awe. These two choices will surely get the job done.

"The one with the teal-blue lights!" Lilly responds with excitement.

"Your wish is my command." I kiss her forehead and take her hand. "Come with me."

With haste, I lead Lilly to the foyer where the painting portals drape the walls.

"We'll be back soon!" I echo into the kitchen where Serenity waits among other angels all too eager to glimpse me and Lilly's current relational state. Word has gotten out now that we are to be married soon.

"It's where you found my engagement ring, isn't it!?" Lilly recalls as we near the paintings where the Brachian Galaxy moves in three-dimensional live footage.

"Yes," I affirm. She remembered. The way she notices every detail means a lot to me. She never fails to appreciate what I give and how I love her. It only makes me want to give her more.

"I love your thoughtfulness in how you made the ring," she says heartfully and eyes the ring with satisfaction. "It's beautiful."

"You are my crown," I say blissfully. "I'd give anything to you, Lilly." I lean in to kiss her soft lips. Rosé and hints of pasta sauce still linger on her lips like savory potion. The intoxication of her kisses is the best dessert. Even better than starberry tart.

"And you are my true love," she says with eyes that bleed into me like shooting stars.

I know she loves me. Still, the scene with Skye in the Throne Room makes me wonder if she loves both of us. I only want her to love me. Is her heart divided?

I sigh and ask her what I need to know. "Do you love me, Lilly?"

"Of course, I love you, Leafe!" she responds surprised that I asked.

"I ask because you looked distressed when Skye left the Throne Room. I want to know your heart is mine," I say vulnerably. "Only mine."

Lilly looks at the engagement ring, and then back at me. "I love you, Leafe Worthy. And I am going to marry you." Her eyes gaze into me fiercely and confidently. I nod my head, finding the assurance in her eyes that I needed.

"I'll always be captivated by you," I confess with the pangs of love throbbing in my soul. "Just like the stars are captivated by the way the sun glows. Just like the bull is captivated by the open range. I'll be pursuing you forever."

Her green eyes melt into me. "For eternity?" She asks.

"For eternity." I kiss her hands delicately and grip her waist to carry her through the portal. "Are you ready?"

"Just promise me no meteor showers!" Lilly giggles.

"The only shower we will be taking is the one down the hall when we return," I grin and kiss her cheek.

Lilly laughs and wraps her arms around me in return. "I'm ready," she says bravely.

My wings prepare for flight as I step through the moving painting of teal, neon lights.

"Hold on!" I command and shield her face from the sheer force of the portal transition. "My air is your air," I tell her for last minute disclosures. Wherever I fly, I breathe naturally from my angelic design and Lilly will need me in order to breathe in outer space. "You can breathe oxygen when you are in my wings."

"I will stay in your wings, my love." Lilly smiles at me, at ease.

I hold her steady, we step through, and the painting closes behind us as we cross into the other side. Celestial lights burst in the distance, as I hold Lilly peacefully. I could soar towards it but I want to stay here for a second. In tranquil bliss. Hovering in the lights of neon pink, purple and turquoise.

"Oh, my goodness!" Lilly gasps as she takes in the panorama. "This view is gorgeous!"

"Not as beautiful as you, my eternal rose," I kiss her forehead again, as is becoming a habit. I can tell she likes it because she looks up at me with loving eyes every time.

"I love you, Leafe," I can hear her thoughts.

"I love you more," I tell her with my thoughts. *"No one has ever made me feel the way you make me feel. I feel at peace when I'm with you."*

I squeeze her tight and bask in the serenity of her presence with me. I like how it feels, to be here, alone, in the extra-terrestrial universe of the Brachian Galaxy with Lilly. No other angel can distract us. Rarely do angels fly in these parts unless King Worthy sends us. Humans do not reside here. But The King makes sure that every part of His universe glows with brilliant artistry.

Swoop!

"What was that!?" Lilly gasps.

My panoramic view swivels to locate the sound. I cradle Lilly's head and hold her hair, stroking it softly. "Don't worry, it's only a shooting star. There are usually more in the Shooting Star Circle, in the Milky Way Galaxy but we got lucky seeing that one."

More like divine intervention than luck. I have a feeling King Worthy sent that one. In the back of my mind, I know He sees us. He sees everything.

"Thank you for the star," I whisper under my breath. Somehow, I know He hears me. My wings enfold Lilly in my wings as I fly, reminding her my care is strong and steady. "No matter what soars by us, I got you," I remind her firmly. "Do you trust me?"

"Yes," she whispers.

Lilly's eyes enlarge as she focuses on me with the need to be protected. My eyes return the glance with affirmation and she looks out into the cosmic grandeur of outer space. I like how it feels when she trusts me to keep her safe.

Lilly beams with wonder as she continues to watch the neon lights swivel and glow before us. Humans rarely get the chance to see outer space from this viewpoint, especially the Brachian Galaxy. The magnitude of its beauty has her speechless. I want to take her somewhere she can bask in its beauty.

I fly leisurely through the starry airspace into the teal-blue lights that Lilly saw in the painting. Its luminosity peaks from the northern tip of the Brachian Galaxy and reflects from the moonlight. The Brachian moon, that is. Every galaxy has one. And there are trillions of galaxies in The King's universe. This one happens to be one of my favorites because of the raw beauty and stunning resources found here. Lilly's diamond ring being one of them.

Yet, I am reminded of the last occasion I flew through the Brachian Galaxy when asteroids were shooting straight at me and Captain Strength. Thankfully, the airspace is clean tonight. I know King Worthy will look favorably upon us and give us clean weather for the time being, until I return home with Lilly, safe and sound.

There is always a danger when encroaching upon outer space. But danger intensifies the discovery of what lies beyond the seen realm. Lilly first got the attention of Skye because she dared to see beyond the light and wait for the angels, that day at Waimea Bay. I will always feel comfortable taking her with me into the unknown.

I fly closer with her in quiet serenity.

Her presence washes over me with tranquility like Zion's Heavenly rain. So many thoughts fill her mind and I can read them all. Thoughts of awe and fascination. Thoughts of love and passion. Thoughts of how I hold her.

Reading her mind keeps me tethered to her beautifully. I know she has so many questions. And although I love her quiet presence, I also love when she opens up to me.

"How many galaxies have you been to?" Lilly asks me with curiosity.

"All of them," I reply honestly. "This is by far the best visit," I squeeze her tightly and soar closer to the teal-blue glows and turn 180 degrees around. "I have you with me now." I kiss her cheek. "Close your eyes. I want to surprise you."

Lilly obliges and closes her eyes, smiling. "Leafe! What is it?" she giggles with excitement.

"Only the best colors you've ever seen!" I exclaim with anticipation and kiss her eyes as I hold her in flight. Then I let my lips peruse her porcelain face like I'm searching for honey. I can't pull away when I get this close to her. Kissing Lilly beats any shooting star show I could see. She is my star. But I know she can't wait to see these lights. I stay focused on her for her reaction. "Okay," I pause and wait to tell her when it's okay to look. "Open!"

Her fluttering eyes open. "Oh!" Lilly gasps with bright eyes.

In front of us, teal-blue lights glow like lava lamps mixed with pastel lilac, orange, and gold strands of glittering light. The lights sparkle like embroidered rivers swiveling upward into the cosmos. King Worthy calls it a *galactic river.*

"Do you want to touch it?" I ask.

"Can I?"

I nod.

Her eyes brighten with enthusiasm. "Take me closer," she says eagerly.

"Hold on, my love." I clutch her tightly in my arms and soar closer. "Remember, you breathe my air. When we get close to the lights, moisture from the glow and turbulence from its momentum will be strong. Just stay in my wings."

My love, I just called her.

It dawns on me how much Lilly is softening me.

Calling her *my love* seems second nature now. I'm not one to use sentimental words, but with Lilly it feels perfect. Holding her tightly feels like all is right in the universe. Her aura makes me feel light as a feather. I want to spend eternity calling her the one I love.

"The lights are so bright!" Lilly exclaims with excitement.

"Yes, my love." I squeeze her tightly and soar through the navy velvet space into the teal-blue lights to take her closer. The lights amplify and Lilly's gasping continues to send shivers down my spine. My heart can no longer hold back. I lift her into the teal-blue galactic light and swivel her around like a ballerina. Then I dive into her lips ferociously, as if I haven't tasted them in 1000 years.

She clasps my head with her delicate hands. "Leafe!" she says in between kisses.

My eyes flare with emerald, green fire and I begin to laugh with sweet joy, like the stress of the universe doesn't hold me. Only Lilly holds me. My perfect Lilly.

"I don't know what's more beautiful," I whisper, "the lights or you." I stroke her hair and tuck a piece of her brunette locks behind her ear.

Lilly pulls in closer and dives in for a kiss. I give into the surprise with open wings and open heart. Her kisses are becoming more aggressive now. What a relief, given she had to break the news to Skye just earlier that she would be marrying me. Now I know she craves me like I crave her. I feel her adrenaline coursing from her body to mine when she kisses me.

I've kissed before, but not like this. Her kisses are the sweetest tastes of intoxication.

"Your lips are my salvation, Lilly."

Her cheeks blush. "Your touch is my deliverance."

"Finally, my body feels the relief of climax now that Leafe touches me how I want to be touched. Leafe always pleases me and leaves me wanting more after he takes me to highest heaven." I hear Lilly's thoughts. I blush in unison at the revelation.

"The feeling is mutual, my love," I tell her with my thoughts.

Splash!

Turquoise liquid spews in the air from the galactic river.

"Reach out your hands," I say. "You can touch the light like fountains." I show her first by outstretching my right hand to touch the light, while keeping her secure in my left hand. Turquoise light covers my hand with glitter from the touch.

Lilly gasps and eyes the glitter with fascination. Then she slowly reaches out her hand to touch the light. "Oh! It's so bright!" she exclaims captivated.

"Just like you, my shining star," I exclaim without the ability to keep my lips away from her. I kiss her again, as we spin in the light. Lilly giggles and kisses me back with succulent passion. I circle my tongue with hers as she strokes my hair.

I want to tell her I love her. But the words don't quite fit what I feel. My love is so much more for her than I can describe.

I whisper softly. "Lilly, you know I love you."

"Yes," she says.

"I've been in love before. And I know what it feels like to be so in love it consumes you. But what I feel for you is greater than that."

Lilly eyes me innocently. I stroke her hair and find my heart beating out of my chest.

"I love you, Lilly. More than you know."

"I love you too," she whispers tenderly.

I smile a trillion smiles, from my soul to my lips, at the reality of Lilly's love for me. Holding her in my arms with my ring on her finger is more than I thought could be real but it is real. Lilly is my one true love, and she is going to be my bride forever.

I look into her green eyes. "You are my perfect match. You bring out the tender side of me in a way no one else does."

"You make me feel whole in a way no one else does."

My heart leaps again. All I can think about is making love to Lilly for eternity. "You make me feel happier than I have ever felt in my immortal life. And this moment here is even more special because you're here with me. I wouldn't want anyone else by my side but you," I assure her from the depths of my soul.

Swoosh!

A gust of galactic wind barrels into my wings as I hold Lilly. I spin her around to shield her from the incoming gust.

"The wind is so strong!" Lilly gasps.

I curl my wings around her. "Don't worry, my love. Just currents from the south. It will dissipate soon."

"And the swirl behind us?" She looks at the light spinning like a funnel.

"It's a rip current from the galactic river. No need to worry. I'm here with you, so there is nowhere you could go outside my grasp."

"I believe you," she says with her arms wrapped around me.

I inhale and exhale. I love how she trusts me.

"Rip currents create stunning scenes in the Brachian Galaxy," I tell her from experience. "It creates a deep pool in the river, like an ocean in outer space."

Lilly's eyes widen. "I wonder what it would be like to swim in outer space!" she says curiously.

"Unlike anything you've seen on earth," I assure her. "The swells hang in the galaxy like a bubble with no shell. You can swim in one side and come out on the other side. No ocean floor here."

"Like a hovering bubble of water?" She looks up at me enchanted.

I smile. "Yes. A bubble of liquid light."

The way Lilly's eyes sparkle when she gazes at her surroundings makes me want to kiss her a trillion times. Her light shines brighter than the stars, and I want to show her every light in King Worthy's universe. My wings flutter as I contemplate my next move.

"I want to try something. Do you trust me?" I ask.

Lilly nods her head. "Yes," she exclaims. "I trust you."

"Hold on," I say and kiss her forehead.

Swoosh!

My wings wrap around Lilly like a cocoon as I dive into the galactic swell. That way she can breathe as we go through the galactic light. Shimmers of turquoise, teal, evergreen, lavender, and hot pink glow all around us. The viscosity of the light creates a feeling of swimming deep in the ocean. Synesthesia sets in. The light caresses my wings and body like salt water, only it's more akin to liquid glitter. Lilly can't see yet, and I realize my wings cover her vision.

"Wings, turn on transparent settings!" I command. My wings suddenly turn into see-through feathers, and Lilly's eyes widen as she watches the light from inside my grasp.

"Leafe! The light is like an ocean!"

"Yes, my love." My heart beats faster when I see her excited. The fact that I get to show her these wonders of the universe makes me feel on top of the sun.

I swim through the cosmic ocean swell and the neon lights move from the ripple effect. All around me, the light cushions like water and the bubble-like swell stirs with riptides. I use my hands to maneuver through it since my wings are wrapped around Lilly, and I kick my feet to propel us forward. I twist and turn to give her a view from every vantage point as I swim to the other side of the bubble-like sphere.

Swoosh!

A whirlpool spins above us. I look up and an object soars through the swell at high speed. I did not think anyone else was here but us.

"What was that!?" Lilly exclaims, worried.

I prepare my eyes for detonation and swim closer to determine the threat. "I'm going to find out," I assure her.

The light glows stronger and stronger as I move towards the invader. The being swims closer to us.

Flash!

Light rays beam around the invader as we almost collide.

"General Leafe!" Captain Strength halts in the cosmic ocean swell and lingers in the viscose light. He looks stunned to see us. "I didn't think anyone else was out here!"

"That makes two of us," I disclose. "Or should I say three!"

Captain Strength eyes Lilly and bows his head at the greeting.

"Hello, Lilly. You are getting quite the treat with Leafe bringing you out here! No other humans have seen it before. Too dangerous!"

"Dangerous?" Lilly inquires and looks at me.

"It's true," I reply quickly, and divert her attention away from fear. "You have an angel with you, so you are always protected," I say and kiss her cheek. I turn to Captain Strength and he grins with fascination. "You shouldn't be telling her that, Captain. Have you lost your faith in me to protect humans?"

"That's not the danger I meant, General!" Strength swims closer and spins in the light, treading the liquid freely. "I meant too dangerous for lovers."

"That's nonsense, Captain."

Captain Strength grins with playful intuition. "Lovers get swept up in the swells. You know that, Leafe."

"I do know that, but I've never wanted to bring a lover here except Lilly." It's true. Lilly will always be my one true love.

Captain Strength nods and smiles with a contagious chuckle, as he continues to enjoy the light. He spins again, swimming in circles. The light dazzles like fireworks bursting in the galactic river.

Lilly beams with excitement in the thrill of the wake. "Leafe, look at the light!"

"It's beautiful, isn't it, my love," I kiss her lips to claim her. She kisses me back with the intention to continue the ascension. In this moment, nothing will block me from loving her and taking her anywhere she wants to go.

"I'll leave you two lovers alone," Captain Strength says.

I keep my eyes focused on Lilly. "I'll see you in Zion!" I reply.

Captain Strength chuckles again, "Let's hope so, General Leafe! You lovers have fun!" Light moves as he starts to depart. "Don't stay too long, now! I want you to make it back home!" he adds.

The light ripples and bends into sparkling rays in the ocean swell as he swims away. The momentum of the swell carries us up into the currents where the surface looms just above. I could swim towards it or give Lilly more time. I want her to enjoy herself. Nothing will make me rush her or rush us.

"Lilly, are you okay?" I ask. The only one who can make me change course is Lilly. If she wants to go, I will.

"Yes, I'm okay. I'm not afraid." She looks at me childlike, as I hold her in my cocoon of safety.

"Good."

"I have you here. Why would I be afraid?"

My heart brightens at her disclosure. "I just wanted to check."

"I want to stay here with you," she says adamantly. "Until we're both ready to go home."

At that, I lean in to kiss her sweet lips as her chest rests heart to heart with me. "I like the sound of that, my love." I curl my wings around her and set them back into transparent mode.

Her kisses intensify as the light sparks around us in turquoise and plum swaths of illumination. The swell holds us in its oceanic sphere like a glove and I hold her like a cocoon, waiting to send off its butterfly. She is my butterfly. And I am her wings.

With every kiss, I feel her deeper and deeper, like we're funneling into a rabbit hole where Alice in Wonderland finds enchantment. Her mouth opens for me and my tongue swirls with hers like cinnamon roll bliss.

Swirl!

Our bodies begin to turn again, faster, and faster into a 360 spiral. The inertia of the light pulls us and I feel our bodies getting sucked into a riptide.

I pull away to assess the current, scanning the surroundings and our position in the swell.

"The light is funneling heavy!" I tell Lilly. "It's an undercurrent, but it will disappear. I got you."

I want her to know what is going on, especially since Captain Strength put doubt in her mind of what could happen in the Brachian Galaxy. I've swam through these waters before and I know how to maneuver it. It has no power over me.

"I trust you," Lilly looks at me with complete confidence.

"I know you do," I smile with assurance knowing she puts her life in my hands.

Crash!

I look up and the water crashes over us and spins us around. Lilly holds me tight. I keep my wings curled around her in my cocoon of safety. The force may intensify with the rip current but I won't let go of her.

The waters whirl faster. I swim towards the surface of the sphere kicking my legs with all my strength.

Another gust of water surges, but my wings keep steady. Then another gust. And another.

Flash!

"Leafe!" she screams.

Light surges all around us. Viscose liquid presses in like a pressure cooker. My wings flap stronger, shredding the force against our momentum. I keep swimming.

Flash!

We shoot up out of the light like lava erupting from a volcano. The sphere spits us out into a velvet dark cosmos.

"Where are we?" Lilly shrieks.

"Show her the stars." A voice echoes like a saxophone in a canyon.

I grin at the advice. "I think King Worthy has a plan up His sleeve."

24

Lilly

"I've never seen so many shooting stars!"

"I told you King Worthy had something up His sleeve," Leafe answers, pleased. "He drew us into a portal and it sent us here."

"He knows where we are?" I turn and look up at him shocked.

Leafe nods, with smiling eyes of euphoria. "He knows everything."

My cheeks grin at the epiphany. The King took us here. He never lets us miss a thing. I kiss Leafe on the cheek and giggle as I turn towards the panoramic view of endless stars pirouetting in the velvet navy sky.

"Are we in The Shooting Star Circle?" I inquire excitedly.

"How did you know?"

"Do you see how many stars there are!?"

Leafe grins at my enthusiasm. "Yes, my love. It's breathtaking."

"Now I have endless wishes to make!" I exclaim boldly. "Shooting stars were made for a wish."

Leafe whispers in my ear intimately. "What is your top wish?"

"To kiss you in my wedding dress," I confess. I turn and look up at him with fluttering eyelashes. His green eyes make my cheeks blush. My heart starts racing faster. His fiery retinas of passionate emerald fire blaze into me like supernovas.

Green eyes find me in the stars.

"There has to be more." Leafe leans in to kiss me gently and his lips remain on mine longer than normal. He slowly pulls his lips away and licks my mouth with his tongue, waiting for me to open for him. I open to let his sultry kisses in. He spins me around and his wings cause my hair to flutter. He tucks the locks behind my ear. "Tell me what else you want, my rose."

I reach into the depths of my desire and find the one thing missing. "The only thing I want more is to have a family with you."

Leafe's eyes begin to tear up but he holds back the tears. "My thoughts align completely."

"Really? You want to have a family with me?"

"Of course I do, my love," he assures me lovingly. "You will have your wish, my bride. *Our* wish."

"Our wish. I like the sound of that."

"If only she knew how I long to procreate with her. Then she would never doubt me." I can hear his thoughts. My heart rate increases as I hear his sentiments.

"I don't doubt you," I tell him through my thoughts. *"I love you with my whole heart."*

"And I love you with mine," he tells me with his thoughts. *"Lilly doesn't know it yet, but she was made to be a warrior."*

"You think I'm a warrior?" I ask him out loud.

"Yes, my love. Your instincts prove it."

"Take me with you! When Armageddon starts, take me with you!" Flash!

A shooting star whizzes by my head and I grab onto Leafe, covering his face with hands. I can't let him be harmed. I'd rather die.

"See." Leafe lifts my hands from his face and kisses my palms. "I told you your instincts were sharp."

"I didn't want you to get hit."

"Trust me, I can take care of myself. But I love that you want to make sure I'm protected. It proves your love to me. Lilly, I continue to be impressed with you. And the love I have for you grows every moment. It's your aura. You put me ease like no one else does."

"I love how you love me, Leafe. I needed your love," I tell him vulnerably. He cradles my head delicately, like I am his treasure and no one can touch me. "I loved Skye. But there's something about you that is deeper than I've ever felt."

"That makes two of us," Leafe replies dreamily. "I believe our love will last forever."

My eyes melt into him and all I can think about is meshing with his lips again and again. My body feels satisfied when he kisses me because I know he won't leave me hanging. He ensures I'm satisfied. I need that.

"Lilly smiles fiercely like she always does when she is ready to claim my mouth. I lean into her and kiss her luscious lips." I hear his thoughts. I love how he feels when I'm kissing him.

"I love how you taste," I say passionately.

"I love how you kiss me," Leafe replies fiercely with more kisses.

His lips mesh with me like we are puzzle pieces finding the perfect fit, trying again and again, and it always aligns. His lips remind me what it feels like to release my femininity and give way to pleasure.

"Lilly's kisses are Heaven. I love how she kisses my nose, my cheek, my ear and back to my mouth. Like a game of tik-tac-toe. She finds every part of me." I hear his thoughts as we kiss. His inner secrets pique my arousal.

Leafe chimes in before I can say more. "Tell me what you want, and I will always give in to you," he assures me.

"I know," I concur readily.

"You read my mind, Leafe. Everything you are makes me want you in every way," I think to him.

"No need to think twice about it. Anything she wants is hers." Again, I read his thoughts. His loyalty enchants me.

Bright stars fly by like rockets in mid-air. I watch, wide-eyed and captivated, as the lights blaze like fireworks of confetti. The tails of the stars glimmer as they fly over us, cautiously trailing outside of our position mid-air, as if they know how to avoid colliding with us. Something about the moment makes me feel safe, even in the frenzy of shooting stars soaring like wildfire.

Leafe turns to the starry cosmos. "Stars, burst with fire for my love!" he commands.

"I want the stars to shine brighter than they ever have for her," he thinks.

I didn't think the stars could shine any brighter than they are right now, but his command immediately multiplies their radiance.

Stars enlarge and light intensifies within seconds.

Flash! Spark!

"Oooh!" I gasp as another shooting star flames by us with glitz. "The stars are so bright!"

"Almost as bright as you."

"I love you so much," I say dreamily. "You are my shining star."

"And you are my perfect rose."

I turn to gaze at him and his eyes flame emerald fire with increasing intensity.

Green eyes find me in outer space.

"The fire in my eyes flame for her and I cannot hold it back. Lilly's eyes make me feel like she wants to leap across a mountain range and dance on the heights of Zion. I have so much more to show her. So much more to experience with her." I hear his thoughts again.

In the wide-open space of the Shooting Star Circle, it is just me and him. His thoughts are open for me. My heart feels connected to him deeper than ever.

"You truly are the brightest star I see," he thinks to me. *"Your eyes could shock me into hypnosis if I let them."*

He strokes my hair with his strong hands of protection.

"The brunette softness feels right in my hands. Every part of her humanity enthralls me and I want to discover more," he thinks.

Flash!

Another star shoots by us, closer than before and my hair flutters from the gust. I look to Leafe to make sure we are not in danger.

"Are we safe here with all the light blazing by us?" I ask worried.

Leafe smiles serenely, like he is not worried about a thing. "With me, you're always safe. I know how to protect you."

"I love that you do," I reply. "Thank you for holding me."

"Lilly looks up at me with elated eyes, and then turns back to gaze at the stars. My heart flutters, which is not normal for me. But with Lilly, it is becoming a habit.

I never knew my heart could feel the way it does now that I have Lilly in my arms. My heart races more than it ever has. Passion overcomes me every time she is with me." I hear his thoughts again, and my heart twirls like I'm on a roller coaster.

Keep telling me your thoughts, Leafe. I love to hear how you think of me. I touch his cheek gently.

"I tighten my embrace and feel her stroke my cheek softly. Her touch could provoke the battle of Armageddon to a truce, I am convinced. She would make the toughest angels like putty in her hands. I don't mind the melting that happens when she has me in her grasp. I want to melt from her love like a candle in metallic casing bleeding out into the universe." I hear his thoughts more and more, here in the open space of shooting stars. His heart is gushing now, like waterfalls of pent-up rivers. I love you, Leafe.

"Bleeding is what it feels like, loving Lilly. It's as if my internal lifeblood pours out of my veins with every passing second. My love grows deeper and deeper for her. I couldn't imagine giving her up." He thinks again.

"You don't have to give me up," I think back to him.

He tightens his wings around me.

"I want us to get married soon," Leafe expresses with certainty. "Really soon. I have waited for you."

"I'm ready to be yours forever," I agree.

"My eyes keep flaring for her with emerald fire. The heat is making me sweat. I can feel the effects of what she does to me sweeping over my body and into my extremities. My soul leaps a trillion leaps. Envisioning Lilly in a wedding dress is only making me weaker. In all my eternal life, I could never see another beauty as perfect as her." I hear his thoughts again.

"You have my heart, General Leafe," I tell him with my thoughts.

"Mrs. General Leafe Worthy," he announces, in our audience of stars. "I like the sound of it already."

"I love you, General Leafe Worthy."

Kiss!

"Lilly leans into my chest with green eyes of desire. I meet her with emerald eyes of passion. Our lips collide satisfyingly. My wings perk up and I swivel us in the air as the kisses send shivers up my spine." I love hearing your thoughts for me, Leafe.

His angelic lips collide again and again with mine. The sweet emotion of his craving for me makes me feel wanted in a trillion ways.

"I will always want you," he whispers. "I'll never let you go," he promises euphorically. I believe him.

Flash!

Stars combust like fireworks all around us in the navy-blue cosmos of the Shooting Star Circle. With every kiss, I feel the fire like lightning running through me. My lips tingle from his kisses, like electricity is flowing from his eyes all the way through his body to me.

Kissing Leafe is more than a kiss. It's touching every part of his soul. Every part of his heart. Every part of his angelic power. His touch leaves me feeling rejuvenated by his energy.

"Have all my energy, my love. Have all of me," he thinks to me.

Spin!

"Leafe!" I giggle as he twirls us around in flight.

"I want to show you something."

I gasp. "Leafe! The star is headed straight for us!"

"Do you trust me?"

"Yes," I give in. I do trust him. I remember it's his wings that hold me high above ground. It's his air that keeps me breathing safe and sound. I know he won't drop me.

"We're going to dance with the stars," he says with a wink.

25

Skye

Lilly is in love with Leafe.

Now she's gone.

How could my father let her be taken from me? He orchestrated our meeting after all! He is the one who led me to her in the depths of Waimea Bay, many leagues under the sea. I never would have met her if it was not for Him.

He said He brought Lilly here with Leafe in mind, and that He knew Leafe would fall in love with Lilly. Of course, He knew. He sees everything. Couldn't He keep Leafe away from her? I shouldn't have to worry about my fiancé being vulnerable to temptation in my own abode. I am the Commander of Zion's Angels for Worthy's sake!

"Do not take my name in vain!" The ground shakes. My father's voice echoes like organs shuttering in a canyon.

"I didn't think you were listening anymore!" I yell loudly.

I breathe in deeply. Then breathe out.

Silence.

That's unusual.

He always answers me, even when I overreact. He never leaves me and He always knows what to say.

Maybe I'm right. Maybe He isn't listening anymore. Of course, if that were the case, He wouldn't have shouted lightmiles away from the Throne Room to tell me to honor His name.

Worthy. What a weighty name. What a responsibility. He always told me I was worthy. It's who I am. It's who was made to be.

I bury my eyes in my hands and cry tears, knowing nobody is around to see. Lilly, I let you down! I was supposed to take care of you! I was supposed to look after you! I knew I shouldn't have fallen asleep on you. Angels never fall asleep. If you would just take me back, I promise I will never leave you in danger ever again...

Tears gush and gush.

I wipe my eyes.

I compose myself.

I grab a pen and my journal and begin to write.

Dear Lilly,

You deserve to be happy. Genuinely happy. Love begs that I die for it. Sacrifice for it. Give my life for it. I would give my immortality for you if I could, just to spare you from death. I loved you the first time I saw you under the sea at Waimea Bay, and I should have said it then. I let you wonder who I really was for too long. Long enough for you to think I was a monster. You knew soon enough, I was only trying to save you from the coral reef stuck in your leg. Oh, Lilly... Why do I hold back my feelings sometimes? All I want is for you to know how much I love you. But I feel as if every angel eye is on me. The pressure of war is on me. The fear of losing you is on me. And look where it led me... to losing you. The one I love most. Your heart belongs to you and you must decide whom you will give it to... I want you to know I will always love you.

Love,
Skye

I take a deep breath, and the pain starts to subside. I need it to subside. Feeling this angst is too much to bear. But writing always helps me express my thoughts. I still remember the first love letter I wrote for Lilly. How ironic it is that Leafe was the one I asked to take the message to her. I should have known he would fall in love with her. If only I could remove him from Zion.

Flash!

I turn my head.

My pens drops.

"Father!" I bow in reverence and breathe in the scent of red roses and juniper berries.

My father's footsteps shake the ground like an earthquake as He walks towards me. Only, the ground doesn't split when He walks. Not unless He wants it to.

"You need to trust Me, son!" His voice roars like a lion in the Sahara.

I look up at Him, trying to making sense of it all. "I don't understand what you are doing, but I'm trying to trust you. I needed to get away from the palace and think. I was writing in my journal. It helps me."

"It's amazing the things angels say when they think The King is not listening," He adds.

"You already know how I feel, Father. Is it any secret?" I express openly.

"You are going to have to make peace with Lilly's decision. Only she can decide whom she belongs to. I will not force her." My father's eyes are strong and unwavering. I peer into His face, wondering what He sees in the future that I don't see. Then I realize… the answer is everything. He sees everything.

"Love is one of the great virtues of life. Eternity depends on it, in fact." My father reaches into the rose bushes that line The Rose Garden. He hoists a red rose. "Love sustains the universe." He pauses. "Roses must be watered and nurtured here at The Rose Garden consistently for their petals to bloom most beautifully. It is like that with a woman. You can never neglect her. You must love her with every breath. Every touch. Every word. I want you to think about how you love a woman before I give you another."

"Another?"

"If love is what you desire," my father says firmly.

I sigh as the complexity of this situation overwhelms me. Yet, I breathe deeply knowing love is worth the risk. I twirl the rose in my hands. I don't know if I want another woman besides Lilly. She was the first woman I ever loved. I don't know if I ever want to love again because I don't know if I can love again. Maybe I don't like love. Maybe I don't want love.

"What if love is not what I desire?"

My father eyes me. "I saw what you wrote in your journal, Skye. I think you do want it."

"It was just scribblings," I say nonchalantly, and hold out the journal to show him. My handwriting covers the pages in cursive with black ink from Zion's oils. Sacred oils.

"Great thinkers pen their thoughts." The King smiles at me tenderly and lifts my chin to meet His gaze. "You need to let go now. Regain your strength."

I look away and stand to my feet. "How could you let him have her!?"

The King's voice rises. "You know why!" He roars. Once again, His blue eyes flame with fierce sapphire and He looks at me resolutely.

"I don't know how I can forgive you for this!" I pick up my journal, tuck it in my wings and prepare to fly away where I don't have to talk about this any further with Him.

"I am The King and I need not be forgiven nor do I make a mistake! Lilly will marry Leafe! And you need to accept that now!"

26

Leafe

"Have you ever danced with the stars?"

Lilly shakes her head with that sweet smile. "There's a first for everything!" she exclaims enthusiastically.

"I'm going to be sharing a lot of firsts with you, my queen."

"I want you to show me everything," she exclaims wide-eyed.

I kiss her forehead and scan my periphery for an incoming star. Once its light beams are close enough to catch, I will take Lilly on a dance. The stars are perfect for gliding.

My wings hold her tightly as the shooting stars light up the cosmos like fireworks. Sounds of popping and lightning strikes fill our ears, with the tranquility of outer space's presence.

Although the stars whiz by us at high-speed, safety encompasses us here. King Worthy knows how to tame the stars whenever angels are present. Undoubtedly, He brought us here so I could show Lilly. He will bend and curl them around us, so Lilly has no reason to fear.

"Have you ever seen a shooting star?" I ask her and kiss her cheek. Her face feels soft and supple, warmed by the light.

"In Texas, Jenna and I used to go stargazing. But we had to be outside the city to see them," she says.

I swivel us up and around to see from the best vantage point as we hover in the cosmos. "Across the Milky Way Galaxy, stars burst, ready to give off the last of their radiance, and with every star death there is a trail of light falling behind it. Humans call them *shooting stars*, hence the name," I say.

"King Worthy listened."

"What do you mean?"

"He listened," she repeats. "We call them shooting stars and he named it accordingly... because of us."

I realize her observation, and I revel in her ability to connect the dots. "You're right. He always takes humans into consideration with everything He does. That's why you are in good hands with King Worthy. And with me. I will always be your angel." Her perception is always fascinating. Coming from Earth, she sees life from a different perspective.

"I want you to be my angel forever," Lilly says flirtatiously.

A ray of light catches my eye. An incoming star is headed for us, perfect for gliding. "Your angel has a trick up his sleeve," I wink and clutch her tightly. "Hold on, my love!"

Slide!

I lift Lilly above my chest and catch the tail of the shooting star, with my feet gliding on its trail. It carries us away speedily. The light from its tail shoots fast, in an up-and-over curve, like an ocean wave breaking for a surfer.

"Leafe!" Lilly gasps with excitement. "The star is carrying us!"

"Yes, my love," I assure her with firm arms. "Now we're dancing with the stars," I say and kiss her on the cheek with her delicate frame in my arms.

Her ballerina stature fits perfectly in my embrace. Her eyes take in the panorama of the stars bursting all around us as we move fast. The shooting star carries us swiftly through the Milky Way Galaxy amongst the other bursting stars. Then, its trail comes to an end, as the star fizzles.

I soar with her back up to the place where we saw its inception, like we are surfers paddling back out to sea. I wait for more another star. Then I do it all over again.

"Hold on, my love!"

Lilly giggles and laughs like she is on cloud-nine. Even better, she is on cloud-trillion, here in the Shooting Star Galaxy. And I love making her feel that kind of elation.

Lilly breathes as we come to the end of the second star's wave. "That's the most fun I've ever had!" Lilly kisses me on the cheek and laughs contagiously, as I twirl her around in the climax of our dancing with the stars.

"The stars are making big waves for us tonight!" I exclaim tongue-in-cheek, smiling alongside her.

Lilly gasps, letting out the adrenaline. I can feel her heart racing as I hold her tight. "How did you do that?"

"I used to come out here and glide on the stars when I was a young angel. Skye did too."

"It felt like star surfing," she exclaims whimsically.

"Yes," I concur with her, pleased at her delight. "It's a lot like riding the waves. The first time I tried it, I was hooked."

"It's the perfect kind of ecstasy," I surmise.

"The universe knows how to make you soar."

"Now I can say I've swam in outer space and surfed in outer space." Lilly laughs with childlike pleasure. My heart races when she gets excited. I love her awe of everything the universe displays.

"Yes, my love." I kiss her forehead. "I have so many firsts to share with you."

"You said you used to come out here with Skye?"

"Yes," I answer her, realizing I said his name. Perhaps I shouldn't have. I don't want to give her reasons to think about him, especially when it's just me and her. But here we are. And the reality is Skye will always be around.

I take a deep breath and kiss Lilly again on the forehead. Words evade me in the moment. Does she want to talk about him? Or do I pretend like she didn't ask me?

I can't pretend. I love Lilly. And if Skye is a part of her past, I cannot ignore her feelings when they arise. I need her to know she can rely on me to handle the weight of it all.

"Lilly, are you still thinking about him?"

"No."

"Be honest," I tell her.

"I wasn't thinking about him until you said his name."

I won't fault her for that. I know what she means. I did bring him up, without thinking. Be cautious, Leafe. Don't bring up names that rattle your peace. Let her have the present and stop bringing up the past.

Lilly calms me and touches my cheek. "I want you to share your memories with me. Don't ever feel like you have to hold back to protect my peace. I can handle it," she persuades me.

"I just…"

"What is it?"

I hesitate, and then decide I need to tell her my honest feelings. "I don't want you to be thinking of Skye when you are alone with me."

She turns to look at me with eyes of sweet love. "You are the only one on my mind when your wings are holding me. So don't let go of me," she assures me gracefully.

"I don't want to ever let go of you."

"Good," she says with blushing cheeks and lips ready for kissing.

"Let's return to my bungalow." All I can think about is the shower I promised her, where meteors are far away and bubbles are sure to lather her skin like lavender silkiness. "If you're ready, that is?"

She nods with tranquility illuminating her face. My goodness, she is beautiful. "Yes, General," she replies readily. "I am."

General. I'm still getting used to the title itself, but to have Lilly call me General is a completely different feeling of shock. Still, I'm reminded she knew me before I revealed my true identity. She loves me for me. She chose me for me. It's what makes her love more real than all others.

The Milky Way Galaxy is far closer to Zion than the Brachian Galaxy. We arrived here via King Worthy's transportable intervention where he opened a portal from the galactic river to the Shooting Star Circle. I could fly us back to Zion from here, or I could locate the portal that returns back to my bungalow, as is my routine anytime I travel for battle. Lilly remains my highest priority. I want her experience to outweigh my personal preference.

"Do you want me to find a portal to return us home or fly back the long way?"

Lilly thinks to herself and then asks me. "What do you choose, my love?"

My love, she called me.

I love it when she calls me that.

"It's your call, Lilly. I have travelled both ways. I want to go whatever way makes you happiest."

I can already hear her thoughts leaning towards the longer flight. "Let's fly from here. I want to see more of outer space!"

Her patience intrigues me. Most humans would choose the shorter way. The instant way. But she surprises me once again with her desire to see everything the universe has to offer.

"I'd love nothing more than to show you everything, my love," I tell her with delight. "To Zion, it is!"

I kiss her sweet lips and soar away.

❧

We fly through the starry, neon cosmos back to Zion. Lilly soaks in the euphoria of outer space's beauty as my wings soar at a favorable pace. More stars trail around us with scintillation as cosmic lights spark around us like fireworks.

Lilly keeps her eyes open, watching every moment. I keep my arms wrapped around her tightly like a blanket.

Her heart rate steadies when we fly. She trusts me. Her pulse is proof.

Feeling her tucked inside my arms is more peaceful than any flight I've flown. I never had a human in my arms before when I used to fly back and forth in the cosmos from galaxy to galaxy.

It's always been me.

Just me.

I like the change of having her. Needing her. Wanting her. I don't ever want to let her sweet presence leave me.

As Zion's gates approach the south side, the golden lights flicker. I make my way for The Eagle's Pad where angels take-off and return from battle. Jewel stands guard and waves her hand with glowing, bright wings and pearly white hair. The gates open. We soar in.

I meander around The Rose Garden where fresh blooms waft in the air with floral aromas. Lilly gasps from the roses. Flowers are her favorite, I can tell. Her namesake crowns her well. I can't wait for her to bear my name alongside hers. Lilly Worthy.

"Lilly was mine, all mine!" A voice echoes in my periphery. "Lilly Worthy. I vowed to give her my name! Now she will bear it from another's hand. I can't bear the thought of it!" The voice echoes again from the bank of red roses lining down the rose garden and into the meadows. An all too familiar voice.

It's Skye.

"Did you hear that? I think I just heard Skye," Lilly whispers and sighs.

"Yes, my love," I whisper back. "Don't worry, my perfect rose. I won't let him hurt you."

"He knows we're close. I just want to get home. I don't want him to trouble us," Lilly whispers again as she holds on to me.

"I got you, my love."

My wings redirect back towards the top of The Rose Garden by The Eagle's Pad, instead of veering in his direction. It would have been faster to go that way and soar across the meadows, but I can easily circle around the outer edge of Zion's south side and take the mountain pass if it will please Lilly to evade him. It will please me, honestly. I am not in a mood for Skye's jealousy either.

Zoom!

Wings soar by me hastily.

Too late.

Skye sees us.

Skye soars up to us visibly agitated. "Leafe, you should have kept your conniving hands off of her!" he protests angrily.

"Leave us alone, Skye," Lilly says. "You had your chance to fight for me and you didn't!" Lilly protests before I can say a word.

Skye shouts. "I told my father about what Leafe did!"

"Why didn't you come to *me* and fight for *me*!? Leafe touched me when you wouldn't. He loved me more. You saw me in the Throne Room and you didn't even try to win me over him."

"He doesn't love you, Lilly," Skye asserts. "He just wants sex!"

"I wanted him too!" Lilly exclaims with heart-felt emotion.

Skye exhales. "What do you mean?"

"You always made me feel things that you never finished. My body was always miserable. Leafe doesn't leave me wanting."

"Like I said, he only wants sex," Skye exclaims.

"I can read his thoughts, Skye. He loves me. More than you do."

Skye pauses. "You can read his thoughts?"

Lilly nods.

"But my father doesn't let you read anyone's thoughts but mine," Skye says, visibly hurt.

I interject. "King Worthy gave her access, General."

"But he only lets true lovers read each other's thoughts…" Skye sighs and wipes his brow. He nods and shakes his head, like he has just seen a ghost. He knows now. Lilly loves me and I love her. Our love is true.

"I told you he loves me. And I love him," Lilly says ardently.

"Lilly flower…" Skye soars up to Lilly and reaches out to touch her hair. "You know I am your first love and you will never have another."

"Technically Leafe is my first lover. He made love to me first."

"Leafe is your first lover! What a crock! He will never measure up to me and you will find yourself wanting me back!"

"No! My mind is made up," Lilly says and pulls my arms around her waist. I embrace her lovingly. "How many galaxies have you traveled to, Skye?"

"How many galaxies?" Skye repeats the question.

"How many galaxies have you traveled to?" Lilly asks again.

Skye sighs. "I don't understand how that can be relevant."

"Answer the question," she says.

Skye speaks. "5,387."

"And how many galaxies are there in the universe?" Lilly inquires.

"Trillions," Skye says.

"Guess how many galaxies Leafe has travelled to?" Lilly asks.

"Couldn't tell you. I don't preside over his whereabouts like my father does," Skye responds.

"All of them," Lilly says.

"Impossible," Skye shrieks. "He hasn't existed that many eons."

"Tell him, Leafe," Lilly speaks up.

"It's true. I've seen every galaxy."

"While you were sleeping, Leafe was saving the universe."

"I saved you, my Lilly flower…" Skye tears up and looks away distraught. His wings lower and he sets his feet on the grass and wipes his brow again.

"Don't call me Lilly flower anymore. I don't belong to you." Lilly unfastens the necklace around her neck, in the shape of a diamond key. She holds it out for Skye to take. "This is yours. I want you to have it back," Lilly says sensitively and wipes her eyes. Then she grabs Skye's engagement ring from her dress pocket that she had taken off at the Throne Room when I proposed. "This is yours too."

Skye looks at Lilly sternly, and then directs his question at me. "Do you have anything to say for yourself, Leafe?"

I don't like his eyes on her.

Lilly is not the one to blame here, he is. If he wanted her, he could have claimed her. He let her go. He stopped fighting for her. And he is not going to look at her with anything other than respect if he knows what is good for him.

I keep my composure but make my sentiments known. "If you ever eye Lilly like that again, you will be sorry!"

Skye rises and flares his eyes at me. "Do you have any idea what I could do to you!?" Skye yells, and then stops himself and sighs.

"Let's go home now," Lilly says calmly.

"You know *exactly* what I can do, General!" I raise my voice. "Circling the galaxies and destroying evil spirits is my job. Annihilating immortality is my power, not yours. The Raven's still alive because you don't have the power to kill him."

"Forget it, let's go, Leafe!" Lilly turns to look at me with sweet eyes that soften my frustration.

I nod to agree with her. "I didn't want to leave it like this, Skye, but I knew you were not going to be cordial," I exclaim respectfully.

"Cordial with a betrayer?" Skye huffs and puffs.

"The only one you betrayed was yourself." I breathe in. "I never wanted to hurt you, Skye. I have flown with you for eternities. But Lilly is in love with me, and I am in love with her. We want to get married. And we will."

Skye inhales and exhales. He looks away to trace the outline of the rose bank trailing up to The Rose Garden. "They say roses never die in Zion," he says. "They live forever." Then he looks at Lilly again, and I ready my fists to pummel him into the earth if he makes one glare at her. "You will have to live forever with your decision."

"I've never seen Skye so worked up like this before. I don't know this side of him at all. His flagrant shots at me. At Leafe. I don't want any part of this any longer. King Worthy must have seen it in my future. This is what it would have been like to be with someone who won't let me make my own choices. I thought I loved him, but he clearly does not love me selflessly. Leafe does. I want to marry Leafe." I hear Lilly's thoughts. Her heart is raw from the epiphany of his inability to truly love her.

Lilly responds to Skye clearly. "I'd rather die a mortal life than live forever with you."

Skye stands speechless and flustered.

I think Lilly said it all.

My wings incline for flight. I prepare to soar away to my bungalow with the love of my life.

My Lilly.

My one true love.

27

Lilly

My heart pounds like a racehorse as Leafe soars away with me in his arms.

"Are you okay, Lilly?" Leafe asks me patiently. "I promise I won't let him hurt you. You're safe with me," Leafe assures me tenderly.

I nestle my head into his chest. "Yes, I am okay, I promise," I manage a whisper. But Leafe knows better. He knows it hurt me. Skye's rage really startled me and made me not want to see him ever again.

"Maybe it's what you needed to move on," Leafe exclaims.

In many ways, he is right. How could I possibly linger in the past if Skye blames me for his neglect? I don't want anything bad to happen to him, though. I wouldn't wish that. But I must make peace with the reality Skye cannot love my whole heart.

I take a deep breath, and revel in the wonder of the arms holding me now. It's still a phenomenon that Leafe is mine. I never would have thought it. But I fall more in love with him every second.

Like lightning, Leafe flies through the meadows of lilies and wheat fruitfully growing for harvest.

I nestle my head into his chest as he holds me. His aura feels peaceful in flight, despite the ordeal of Skye getting angry. I like that about Leafe.

He does not let things get to him the way humans often do. I guess that is why he is an angel.

"Tell me you'll always be my angel," I say wanting.

"Lilly, you never have to worry if I will be yours. I'll always be your angel."

"Thank you for sticking up for me back there."

"King Worthy commands me to watch over you," he kisses my head as we fly. "But I want you to know I'd do it even if He never asked. I love you, Lilly Rose."

"I love you General Leafe Worthy."

"There they go again. The fireflies. They swirl inside my body when I'm with Lilly. The way she can take a hinlor slayer and make him melt is the kind of enchantment only The King could create. She is my weakness, and ever more my strength. When I fly all I want to do is hold her tight and never let go. She has captivated me, heart, mind, body, soul, and spirit." I hear his thoughts.

"You are the one," I tell him with my thoughts.

"I love you, Lilly Jane Rose. Are you ready to be Lilly Worthy?"

"I am," I say without a doubt.

My heart is ready.

Leafe soars up to the front entrance of the bungalow and sets me down gently as he reaches for the door and opens it. Cinnamon and spice waft in from the inside. "Serenity must have lit the fireplace," he says.

"It smells delicious, like a Christmas hearth with gingerbread and cinnamon apple." I breathe in the lovely scent as I envision snowflakes falling.

"Are you ready for a shower, my queen. I did promise, after all." His eyes gaze into me with love and passion.

I lick my lips and blush at the thought of it.

I nod.

"Lilly, your body is beautiful."

"When I caress her cheek, she blushes in shades of light pink. Her green eyes gaze into me like auras. Royalty will always be her identity." I hear his thoughts.

"When I look at you, I see a queen. A perfect queen. So, I am going to make love to you right now."

Leafe scoops me up into his arms with the scent of cinnamon still lingering in our midst. The first time he kissed me, he tasted like caramel cinnamon. I have a feeling every time I smell the scent, I am going to remember. I want to remember every moment with him, even the first time he came on to me and I pushed him away. I had to, of course. I am not used to being engaged and having another lover pursue me.

But his love is stronger than any love I've ever known.

Leafe carries me down the golden hallway with gemstone-laid floors beneath his feet. I can hear Serenity singing in the distance. Everywhere I go in Zion, haloed beauties sing gracefully like I am in an eternal symphony. I could get used to it.

"What's your favorite scent?" Leafe asks me.

"Rose petals," I answer whimsically.

"As is fitting for a rose," he kisses my forehead and reaches for body wash in a hidden oak cabinet covered with pearls. He closes the cabinet and the wall transforms back into its original state of pearl and rainbow hues. Everything in his house has layers and dimensions, with sparkling light cascading from the walls, ceilings, floors, and doors. I feel like I am in a giant diamond, with endless gamma rays reflecting supernatural radiance.

I giggle at the wonderful sight. "Is everything in Zion magic?"

"Yes. King Worthy makes everything supernaturally," Leafe smiles and turns on the shower. Water drips from the chrome ceiling like a rainforest. Leafe continues, "And storage is much more manageable when it does not protrude from the wall."

"The King thinks of everything," I say fascinated. I run my hands under the water to feel the trickling goodness.

"The King thinks of everything," Leafe answers softly. "Lilly…" he says.

I turn to meet his gaze, and his body is disrobed and ready for more than just a shower. I scan my eyes over his form and my body pulsates from seeing his hardness.

"Are you ready?" he asks.

I nod my head.

Leafe smiles, picks me up, and steps over the shower edge.

Then he pulls the white silk dress over my head. His hands meander down my waist, and kisses my neck, consistently massaging my skin in circles with his lips. I reach for his head and grab his hair.

"Leafe!" I sigh.

Before I can say more, his mouth plunges into mine with wet kisses, navigating every part of my mouth like he is on a quest for hidden treasure. I reward the determination and swirl my tongue with his passionately.

Then his hands move up my body to my breasts.

"Your body is heavenly, Lilly Rose. No one touches this body but me. I am the only one who gets to touch you."

"Yes, Leafe," I sigh and nod simultaneously to affirm the command. "Only you."

Then he picks me up and wraps my legs around him. "Tell me if it's too much, Lilly," he tells me, ready to enter me.

I nod again. "Okay," I say. My body rises to euphoria as I anticipate him going inside me. An "okay" is all I can manage. Being a conversationalist right now feels out of reach when his touch sends me into the clouds, speechless. I want to soak up every touch, every feeling, every sensation of his pleasure given to me.

"Her body has my body on fire. I don't know how I can go slow, but I will restrain myself from going into her too hard at this angle. All in good time. I have Lilly for eternity, and eternal showers to take it fast. Right now, I am going to make love to her slowly and gently, getting her body used to me." In the middle of euphoria, I hear his thoughts.

You can make love to me, Leafe. I'm ready.

Leafe plunges into me, gently, and begins to make love to me. I feel the rush of nerve endings piqued with sensations of pleasure. Mmm, Leafe, you feel amazing inside me.

"My Lilly, your body is perfect." His thoughts echo in my head as I feel the pleasure increasing ever more.

Leafe thrusts into me faster now, and the intensity surges like Waimea waves in winter. My body rides the high of the fusion of his body and soul meshing with me like the moon and stars. Then I feel it coming. My body plateaus like the highest peak of Zion's mountains and Leafe feels my body inviting the climax.

"Say my name, Lilly."

"Leafe!"

"Again."

"Leafe!" I scream as I feel my body peaking.

I look up at his green eyes. His retinas flame with fire like a blazing furnace of desire.

Green eyes find me in euphoria.

Leafe breathes and surges into me a final time. "I love you, Lilly Rose."

My body releases every ounce of need, giving into every ounce of want.

Ecstasy finds us.

I brush my hair in the divine, opal vanity table with an angelic cotton towel secured around me. I hug my shoulders, feeling the warmth, and continue brushing my hair. The mirrors glow brightly and I look at the ring on my left ring finger. I pause, as I think about the destiny awaiting me and I smile into the mirrors adorned with gems.

Mrs. General Leafe Worthy. I can't wait to be his.

"Lilly, my love, you don't have to wear a towel around me," Leafe says and kisses me on the forehead as he walks in from the bathroom.

"I'm not used to being openly naked."

"Your nakedness is safe with me, my love," he bends down and looks at me eye to eye with tenderness. "But I have something better."

"What is it?"

"Open it." He exclaims excitedly.

I blush as I hold the bright red box wrapped in a silver bow. This is the first present he has given me, besides the ring of course. But this gesture feels special to me, like he thought of me just because.

I open the box and inside lays a light red gown of silk. I pick it up and press it to my chest, feeling the rich fabric against my skin. I've never felt anything more luxurious.

"This is truly divine!" I gasp. What a lovely surprise.

"Let me put it on you," Leafe stands and clutches the silk gown in his strong hands. I lift my arms, and he gently sets the silk gown over my head, shoulders, and arms, letting the silk trail down my frame like butter. "There," he says angelically and strokes my cheek. "A gown fit for a queen."

"Thank you!" I giggle, turn around, and kiss his sultry lips, tasting caramel and cinnamon once again. My favorite flavor.

I can't wait for him to see me on our wedding day.

"I can't wait to see Lilly in her wedding gown. And every gown. Lilly stuns me in everything she puts on. From angel feathers to shredded threads to fine silk to nothing at all, she captivates me. I cannot imagine how I am going to feel seeing her on our wedding day." I hear Leafe's thoughts again.

Oh, how his thoughts make my heart flutter! I love how you think of me, Leafe. I melt with every word from your heart.

"I can tell Lilly loves me. She isn't as sassy with me as she used to be. Her emotions are eclipsing her need to overpower me. And my love for her is overriding my need to hide how I feel. We are becoming one. With every breath she takes, I breathe in. I feel in sync with her."

I can hear his thoughts again. If he wants me to be sassy again, I can be. Just say the word, Leafe. I smile, knowing he understands me.

"My heart throbs knowing she gets me. Lilly is melting for me just as much as I am falling for her. Let's be honest, I am way passed falling. I am completely in love with this woman. And it feels surreal to know she knows it."

I can read your mind, Leafe. I know you love me... tell me you love me.

"I love you, Lilly," I say out loud and dive into her lips with ardor. My eyes flame passionately as I stare into her doe eyes of perfect bliss. Her cheeks blush, and I stroke the rose gold beauty of her face once again. "My feelings remain the same. I want to marry you as soon as possible."

Green eyes find me in love.

"I'm ready," I reply with assurance.

Without a doubt in mind, I know General Leafe is the one who can love me like no one else can.

I am ready to say *I do.*

"Oh, General Leafe!" A singsong greeting heralds into the room from a tiny, glittering dove. It lands on Leafe's shoulder with a wave of gold dust in her wake. "King Worthy has a message for you."

"I'm listening," Leafe responds patiently.

The glittery dove speaks. "Armageddon is now."

28

Leafe

"Take me with you!"

Lilly's words ring in my ears like fragrant rain.

I need her with me. I have no reason to hold her back from battle. I have seen what she can do. The hinlors disintegrate from her light. But the battle of Armageddon is going to be fiercer than any hinlor she has seen. More degenerate than The Raven.

"Lilly, this battle is dangerous. Are you ready?" I need to hear it from her own lips. Her perfect lips of enchantment.

"If I can defeat a few hinlors in a palace villa, I can battle this monster. I have Zion on my side." Lilly beams with eagerness to fly. She caresses my wings and touches my cheek. "More importantly, I have you."

I inhale and exhale, determining she is right. I trust her. I love you, Lilly Rose.

"You will need eyes to see. And eyes to detonate light," I answer quickly while arming myself. "I'd give you my wings if I could," I touch her cheek. "But I need you to fly with me. You will detonate light when hinlors approach. Flare your eyes at my command. The light will be enough to defeat them."

"What about The Raven?" Lilly inquires.

"He will soon meet his fate. The Black Hole will not hold him forever."

Lilly hesitates and breathes in deeply like she has had an epiphany. "You told Skye only you have the power to destroy immortality," Lilly adds inquisitively.

She knows.

"Yes."

Under Lilly's soft and feminine nature is quick discernment. She knows I will be the one to destroy him for good. And that will put her in danger as well… if she chooses to fly with me. I cannot lie to her, but I don't want her to worry over what-ifs. This is King Worthy's plan and it will not fail.

I kiss her forehead. "I don't want you to worry about that now. King Worthy will tell me when it's time."

She nods and gives in to me.

"Trust him, Lilly. He would tell you if you needed to know." I can hear Lilly's thoughts. She is worried about me, and struggling to believe I will make it out alive. I promise you, Lilly. I will live forever.

"King Worthy won't let him die… not now. He gave you Skye, and now he has given you Leafe. You don't have to fear. Love will win this battle for good."

I take a deep breath.

Just when I was preparing to marry Lilly… Armageddon strikes?

All I want to do is watch her walk down the aisle and kiss my bride. The adrenaline of battle does not allure me now as much as Lilly does. If only we could steal away and forego every crisis. I'd never need to fight another day with her by my side.

"Leafe." Lilly lifts my chin and looks at me with green eyes of angelic ecstasy. Her aura surpasses every human limitation. I look back at her finding all I need in her peaceful oasis. "You are General Leafe Worthy! Trusted by The King and commissioned to war for Zion! You are going to fight this battle and slay every giant in your path!" Her eyes brighten with intensity and soften into tranquility that seeps into me. "Don't forget who you are, my love."

I take a deep breath and find new strength coursing through me like wildfire.

"Tell The King I'll be ready in three!" I say to Purity, the holy dove. "We have history to make."

⁓

"General Leafe Worthy!" The King echoes my name in the Throne Room where angels gather to depart. Tension broods in the air. We all know the seriousness of this battle and what it means for the dawning of New Zion. "Armageddon is at hand."

"Yes, my King."

"No hinlor is to be spared. And every human life is to be kept. Understood?"

"Yes, my King."

King Worthy's eyes flame with blazing sapphires and emeralds of fire. Smoke rises from the organs where angels play sounds of exhilarated fortes. All angels stand in reverence at the echo of His voice. His Word will be the final Word. And now everyone waits for His command.

Lilly stands beside me, now adorned in white and turquoise ribbons. The turquoise is to keep her body temperature regulated in all the heat of battle. The gold is to protect her heart.

"Lilly, my dear," King Worthy says lovingly. He eyes her with kindness and intrigue.

The tension lightens as he focuses on her.

His smile seeps through.

All angels take a deep breath.

"Hello, Your Majesty." Lilly bows in her white dress, looking like a divine flower of perfection. Who wouldn't love her?

"You are loved, My dear one," He replies with a loud, bass tone voice. "You are the reason why we fight. You represent humanity. The ones created to dwell with us forever."

"Lilly will fly with me," I add and look over at Lilly with a nod of approval. It is my job to advocate for her and stand behind her.

King Worthy walks towards us.

The sapphire, glassy floor shakes from his footprints. The organs strike minor chords. Angels begin to bow like dominos all around the

251

Throne Room. He looks at her bare feet anchored on the sapphire floor and smiles with affirmation. "If she can stand on holy ground, she can fly with angel's wings."

King Worthy raises His staff and holds it over Lilly. Silver smoke detonates. Glitter twirls as He waves the staff in circular motions like an infinity loop. I cannot see what He is concocting as the smoke blurs all vision, but He is up to something.

"Wings!" Lilly gasps in shock. "I have real wings now?" I hear her inquire with excitement through the haze of smoke.

I wait for it to clear, anticipating what I am about to witness.

Smoke clears and glittering white wings rest on Lilly's shoulders, flapping peacefully like a butterfly. Lilly turns to look at me and her eyes glow with rose gold sparkles of fire.

"Lilly!" I lose my breath in awe of her pristine beauty. Rose gold gems line her white, glowing wings. My eyes enflame as I look upon the love of my life in angel wings of wonder. I always saw her as my angel. This vision is a picture I will never get out of my mind. "You look like an angel," I say almost speechless. I wipe my eyes.

"It's only for this battle," King Worthy exclaims pleased. "When New Zion dawns, all humans will be one with Zion and Lilly will take her place as future queen of Zion."

"Future queen?"

"Yes, my love."

"But that would make you future–"

"King," I answer with love in my eyes. "Yes."

❧

"How can I be queen? I thought Skye was destined for that role," Lilly exclaims perplexed as we fly for the outer edge of Zion, where legions of hinlors await our arrival.

"He was going to be King because of you, Lilly. Whoever marries you becomes King. That was The King's plan. We all thought it would be Skye too."

"I didn't know," Lilly says as she adjusts her wings.

"I assumed these wings would be heavy on my small frame, but it's quite the opposite. My wings feel strong and steady and my body, light as feather. I could get used to these. Still, the fast-paced capability of its ingenuity is making me have to adapt and adapt fast." I hear her thoughts.

Lilly's thoughts thrill me as I watch her soar on angel wings. She does not realize how well she is flying given the circumstances.

"How are the wings, my future queen?" I look over at her lovingly and soar up closer to her to check her wings.

"I'm getting to used to them," she says excitedly.

"You look like a natural," I say as I soar next to her. "Trust me, you look even better than I did when I first got mine. I couldn't get up in the air for days. You will be a pro by the time we reach the edge of Zion."

Lilly gazes at me with those beautiful rose gold eyes. "I love you," she says smiling.

"My eyes glow as I look at Leafe. My General Leafe. All of the sudden I feel my face getting hotter, and hotter. Are my eyes about to burst? What is going on?!" I hear her thoughts.

Flash!

Light rays shoot in my direction. I swerve.

Her eyes definitely work for detonation.

"Oh no!" she gasps.

I smile enthralled at her. Then, I circle around to my left side and soar closer.

"You just got excited is all. Passion makes your retinas flare, and when you flare for too long without holding back the detonation, it shoots. You'll know next time. Trust me. That's the irony of fire. It burns in passion and in destruction. Bear down on your aim, using your forehead when you need to divert your eyes' direction, in case of emergency. The aim will cause the fire to shoot just underneath your target of sight."

"You know what you're doing, my love." Lilly eyes me again with rose gold eyes and I smile knowing what is about to take place.

Flash!

Her eyes detonate in my direction.

I swerve out of the way.

"I'm sorry," she giggles from the chaos. "I just can't take my eyes of you."

"That makes two of us." I smile enchanted by my angelic fiancé, and soar for Zion's edge. We're almost there. "If there is anyone who understands the power of the eyes, it's me." I lean in to kiss her mid-flight. "Zion's edge is almost here. When we breach the atmosphere and enter outer space, stay near me, and detonate your eyes at any hinlor that approaches us."

Lilly nods her head and takes a deep breath. "I'm ready now," she tells me confidently and squeezes my hand. I squeeze it back, holding on to her as we fly, in sync, towards the horizon where Zion's edge is just ahead.

"Ok, let's practice again," I say. "Target to the left of my head, above my wing into the airspace and detonate your light."

Lilly nods and flares her eyes.

Flash!

Perfect aim.

Lilly's eyes blaze with rose gold fire, harnessed and resilient, just above my left wing. Exactly how I instructed her. I knew she would get it.

"Now we're ready to cross into the cosmos!" Lilly nods and keeps flying. "On the count of three!" I command. "1-2-3!"

We burst through Zion's edge into the cosmos where Armageddon begins.

I remind myself of the battle at hand. Hinlors are our target. Destroying The Raven is my objective. Humans coming to Zion is our end goal.

Starry, velvet skies embrace us in the womb of outer space as we enter the war to end the evil of the universe's conditions. Lilly soars by me, bright, elegant, and perfect. Her wings look steady and effortless, delicately crafted by Heaven. The King knew what He was doing when He gave her wings. I told her she was a natural, but it's clear she is supernatural. I could linger here in space forever just flying with her.

"Leafe! Look out!" Lilly asserts.

Red eyes zoom near me. "Lilly, you're mine!" the hinlor shouts.

Detonate!

The hinlor disintegrates on the spot.

"This way!" I signal to Lilly with my left hand, and we soar fast towards a supernova in the distance.

Boom!

The supernova sparks again. King Worthy always makes supernovas where evil lurks, to illuminate the darkness. Zion's Angels are already there wiping out the infestation before going to Earth to rescue all humans.

"General Worthy!" Captain Strength soars up beside me and Lilly. "Looks like you made it out of the cosmic ocean swell alive," he chuckles and we three zoom ahead towards the supernova. "Hello, beautiful Lilly."

Lilly nods and keeps flying next to me. "Hello, Captain."

Something is eerie in his eyes. I can sense it. Too many of Zion's Angels have fallen for Lilly already. Too many have left to fall into The Raven's clutches. I must keep my intuition when he is near.

"We surfed the stars," I nod and pat him on the back. "Now, I'm ready to bring the heat. What are you packing?"

"Gamma ray forte," he answers.

"Very good," I reply clearly. "Let's finish this, Captain."

Captain Strength nods. "After you, General."

I reach for Lilly's hand.

Captain Strength chops into my wrist with his bare hands.

I flare my fiery eyes at him, seeing the naked truth. "You thought you had me fooled, Strength! I see what you are now," I exclaim brazenly.

"Lilly is mine!" Captain Strength grabs onto Lilly and pulls her with him to soar away.

"Oh, no you don't!" I yell at the top of my larynx.

My wings flap rapidly towards Captain Strength. Lilly flaps her wings to break free but his arms hold her captive with brute force. When I get my hands on him, I am going to rip his muscles to shreds for touching even one hair on her head.

"Let me go!" Lilly yells, agitated. "Get off of me!"

Captain Strength leans in to kiss her and Lilly twists her head away and right hooks him to dodge his come-on.

"You need a real angel who knows how to carry you on top of the waves," Captain Strength yells creepily.

"Leafe carries me higher than you could ever carry me!" Lilly retorts.
Spit!

Did I just see what I think I saw? Lilly hurls spit straight into his blood-shot eyes. They are about to get even bloodier. I speed up to catch him.

"You show some respect, woman!" Captain Strength head-buts Lilly, and flashes of light in shapes of lips spark all around her. Captain Strength loses consciousness. Blood flows and lingers in the vacuum of outer space.

I rush to her side.

Lilly floats with her wings flapping.

"Are you okay?" I ask urgently.

"I don't feel a thing," Lilly says surprised. She presses her hand to her head and lip prints are on her hand and all around us like glitter.

"It's orange glitter." Lilly says and smiles like she has had another epiphany.

"Glitter?"

"The first time you kissed me, it left orange glitter on my lips," Lilly gasps excitedly as she shows me her hand. "See! It's all over my hand now that I touched my forehead. And that's where Captain Strength attempted to nail me in the head. Your kisses protected my head."

I lose my breath at the most beautiful realization I've ever heard. I inhale with all my might and kiss her deeply. "I love you so much, my perfect rose."

"You saved me!"

Boom!

"The supernova!" I gasp. "We need to get to the Shooting Star Circle. That's where the stars will fall from the sky onto earth. We must rid out every hinlor in sight."

"I'm ready!" Lilly nods her head with bright, glowing wings hovering until my command. I smile knowing she is invincible in my care.

"Follow me!" I say eagerly.

We soar at lightning speed towards the Shooting Star Circle. The closer we get, the brighter the glow. Zion's Angels fire off light in every direction, destroying the hinlors of evil's invention. Blast after blast, the dark creatures fall.

"We're getting closer, my love. Remember, shoot any hinlor you see. It doesn't matter the appearance. It's their eyes that give it away."

"Red eyes," Lilly affirms. "I remember."

"Yes, my love," I look at her, with arduous devotion, trusting that King Worthy wouldn't give her wings unless He knew what she could handle. I relinquish the power over full protection, knowing Lilly is more powerful than I think. And I will be by her side in case anything goes wrong.

Caw! Caw!

Red eyes come at me fast.

Boom!

Disintegrate.

"Lilly!" An unfamiliar voice calls out to Lilly.

I turn to decipher the voice. Red eyes peer at Lilly with deception.

Boom!

Lilly detonates into the hinlor and it disintegrates.

I nod at Lilly with a pleased smile. "You are breathtaking in battle, my love."

"I have a good partner!" She winks at me and keeps flying. Red eyes come at us fast and we handle the threat.

Flash! Flash! Flash!

More hinlors shoot arrows of fire like dragons in the sky.

Boom! Boom! Boom!

They fall like ash into the vacuum of outer space. I look over at Lilly whose wings outstretch with rose gold gems and fiery eyes.

Boom! Boom! Boom!

Lilly detonates rose gold light at a flock of hinlors swarming with silvery wings.

Disintegrate!

They're gone.

Lilly inhales and exhales. "I saw the red eyes. I knew they weren't angels," she alerts me.

I nod with a grin. "You got it, my love."

Spark! Flash! Boom!

All around our periphery, Zion's Angels detonate angelic light and hinlor ash falls into the atmosphere.

"I've never seen all the angels gathered at once!" Lilly gasps as she beholds the sight of the battle's climax.

"Within minutes, the hinlors will be defeated," I alert her.

"I'm with you," Lilly says with resilience in her wings. "Until the battle is finished."

My eyes flare with passionate green light as I look at the love of my eternal life in heavenly angel wings. I soar closer to kiss her.

"I'm not done yet!" Captain Strength rises out of the abyss, grabs onto my wings, and pulls hard to shred it. I hold onto my wings and knock him off.

"You could have killed Lilly!" I push him with all my might and he flies back seven thousand lightmiles. He zooms back towards me like a boomerang and rages his fists with a right hook. I dodge him. "I never wanted to fight you, Strength," I exclaim. "But you're making it hard for me to ignore your intentions."

"I had good intentions!"

"You intended to kill Lilly and I will not allow you anywhere near her."

"We both know you won't kill me! You don't have it in you, Leafe! Always the good angel. Always pragmatic."

"The only one who doesn't know how to use their head is you," I exclaim ready to exterminate.

Blast!

I detonate light rays of emerald fire into him.

Boom!

Disintegrate.

"He left me no choice," I resolve, as Lilly flies up closer to my side. I squeeze her hand and kiss her forehead. "An angel who harms a woman will not live forever in New Zion!" I tell her. "I will never let anyone hurt you," I declare with a sigh of relief he's gone.

"I know how it hurts to have to do that to someone you love."

"Love?"

"He was a brother to you, wasn't he?"

I nod.

"Take my hand," Lilly says. "Do you see this hand?"

"Yes."

"My hand fits in yours perfectly because you will always hold me in your hands." Lilly hums peacefully. I interlock my hand with hers.

"I love you, Lilly Rose," I breathe deeply with her in my embrace.

"I think you know what happens next," Lilly keenly advises.

The Black Hole. She knows my next move will be to destroy The Raven for good.

"General Worthy!" The King's voice echoes into my periphery. "The time for The Raven is now."

Lilly looks at me with rose gold fiery eyes.

I gaze into her like a tiger ready to pounce. "Are you ready, my love?" I ask and extend my hand to her in the battle-air.

She smiles at me with bright, rose-gold eyes. "Let's go get him, tiger."

29

Lilly

We fly swiftly towards The Raven. We. Lilly and me.

Flying feels exhilarating next to Lilly. I watch her wings flap effortlessly with finesse and smoothness that some of the finest flyers in Zion still have not mastered. As I observed before, King Worthy gave her wings for a reason. He knew what He was doing.

Her body flows like a lily pad on streams of the River of Life. Her wings float like feathers in the sky. Rose gold accents her perfectly. Pink blush highlights everything I love about her. Sweetness, loveliness, flowers, peace.

Still, I wait patiently for the moment when I will glimpse her donning white. Then, I will make her my wife for all eternity.

"Leafe, I can hear you, my strong General," Lilly says playfully with a wink.

I love how she hears my thoughts. I want her to know everything I am thinking about.

"The Raven will be surprised to see us," I alert her. "If he tries anything on you, flash your eyes with all your might."

"Okay, my love," Lilly says with ease. The battle doesn't scare her. This is one of the things I love most about her. She can be so innocent and pure, naïve, if you will, to the dangers of the universe. But it doesn't scare her when she sees it. I wonder what does scare her.

"Losing you," she answers as she flaps her wings gracefully. "I fear having to live without you."

"You are safe with me, my love," I promise her. "We are going to make it out of this battle, and back to New Zion." With The Black Hole looming in the distance, I know what I need to do. Lilly cannot be harmed. "If anything goes wrong, I want you to fly back to Zion without me."

"Leafe, I can't leave you. Don't make me leave you!" she answers with love.

I continue, knowing I must prioritize her safety above mine. "Search for the sun, and then the north star, and it will lead you back to Zion's gates. Your wings will take you past the threshold and into our atmosphere," I instruct her.

"But Leafe, I can't!"

"You can," I plead with her. "Baby, you can," I kiss her forehead. "I give you strength, remember?"

She nods, and we soar onward, as I halt near the entrance of The Black Hole.

"Be strong for me. I won't let The Raven hurt you."

Screech!

I pause outside the entrance to The Black Hole. "We're here," I tell her with a whisper.

Lilly waits with bright wings.

I wave my hand over the entrance and red lava enlarges from the abyss.

"The Raven is going to surface once he hears my voice," I tell Lilly. "One detonation is all it will take."

I know, however, that it could be trickier than that. The Raven is elusive, and hard to pin down. So, King Worthy bound him in chains. Once he rises from the abyss, he will break the chains and only The King knows where he will fly next. I have to detonate quickly and accurately.

"Raven!" The name echoes as I shout into the red fiery hell that is the black hole.

I wait. No Raven.

"Raven!" I echo again, waiting for his fiery eyes to show.

"Nothing is coming out," Lilly whispers pensively. "I think he knows. That is why he stays in hiding."

"It wouldn't surprise me." Lilly is right, the more I think about it. King Worthy told him his time would be coming to an end eventually. Any voice from Zion would not be a welcome one.

"What if I try to go closer?" Lilly proposes.

"To call to him?"

"Yes," she says bravely. "He may not answer to one from Zion, but he may answer to me. A woman of earth."

It's worth a shot. My goodness, I love her wits. Then again, I cannot put her in that position. If what she says is correct, he would not only put his hands on her like Captain Strength, and Zeal, for that matter, but he would ravage her completely.

"I can't let you do that, Lilly." The Raven is not worth it. I would gladly wait a trillion light years for him to come out of hiding if it would save Lilly from one ounce of pain. "He would rip you apart. You see?"

"Yes," she answers me fearlessly. "You also told me to be strong for you. This is me being strong."

"Not this strong, my love." I rush to her and curl my wings around her. I adore her courage but it stings to know that the same courage that would give her power to defeat the enemy is the same courage that has the potential to put her in the most dangerous spot of all. "I would never forgive myself if something happened to you because of that monster!"

"Who are you calling monster!?" The Raven's scowling voice emerges. I turn my head and see his red eyes peering back at us. "Boo!" he adds.

I don't flinch.

Instead, I prepare my eyes for detonation and look to Lilly for her to do the same. I motion for her to fly behind me at a safe distance away from him. Then, I hover near The Raven at the edge of The Black Hole.

The Raven's whole being blazes with fiery flames consuming his mass. The glowing angel I once knew is no more. To think we used to fly together. I wish he could have turned to the light. But he has ravaged the universe for too long with evil and suffering. New Zion cannot birth until his spirit is gone. I will not relent in executing my objective.

"Your power is over!" I shout plainly.

"Oooh, is that the pretty girl I once saw flying with Skye Worthy?" The Raven cackles.

"Her name is Lilly," I say to correct him.

"Where is your angel? Did he fly away already?" He looks at Lilly.

"I fell in love with Leafe, actually," Lilly retorts.

I can't help but blush, even if it is in front of a giant flaming monster. I love it when she says she loves me.

"Oh, well, well! So, you stole Skye's girl, eh? I thought I was the only one who stole Skye's personal belongings!" The Raven screams.

I stay calm. "Your words don't shake me, Raven. I have no shock about your taunts. It's always expected. And now, no more talking! Eternity will exist peacefully without your contagions poisoning the universe."

"We'll see about that!"

Jump!

The Raven leaps from the abyss. I detonate Zion's light. His chains break, as expected. Fire rages. Heat intensifies. I hover up and over his plunge into space, with Lilly beside me keeping her wings steady.

And now for the final blow.

"You should've known better than to let me out of the cage!" The Raven billows ferociously. "Now you're dead!"

I wait for the opportune moment.

Blast!

My eyes detonate emerald fire into his being and he goes up into wild electric flames. His immortality will be no more. He is done for.

I look over at Lilly to make sure she is safe.

"Leafe!" Lilly shrieks and points towards The Raven.

A flaming ball of fire lunges my way from his dying heart.

"No!" Lilly cries.

In an instant, she leaps in front of me. The flaming ball consumes her.

"Lilly!" I scream with terror and dive for her.

Faster and faster, she spins in the cosmos away from my protection, as The Raven dives for her enraged with fire. He shoots more rays at her and sweeps her into his writhing clutch.

Lilly's rose gold eyes look into me with flaming, passionate love, as her hands reach for me. "Finish him off!" she yells. "Let me go," she says with love in her eyes. "Let me go, my love."

Then he pulls her into the black hole of his dark chambers.

"Lilly!!!!!!!" I yell at the top of my lungs. Tears rage and my heart pounds. I breathe in and out. "No!!!" I pound the sky. "I never should have brought her here!"

I look towards The Black Hole sealing up at the entrance. I'm not letting her go! I can't! I fly towards the entrance and prepare to enter with all my strength. I don't care how much fire The Black Hole possesses. I will not hover here while that monster carries her away from me!

I fly to the edge and ready my eyes for immortality-obliterating light.

Blast!

Flashing light sparks brighter than Zion.

My eyes close and open again. Where did that come from? Smoke clears. Heat evaporates and coldness sets in. Red lava disappears.

Then I see Him.

The King.

His crown shines with golden glory and His eyes flame with sapphire light. Golden wings of highest glory shine from His being, and I can barely make out His full appearance. I bow in reverence, with a hole in my heart. Lilly is gone. And she is never coming back.

"General Worthy," King Worthy resounds with a voice like rushing waters. I keep my head bowed in reverence, unable to move from my position in the cosmos. My wings stay steady, as all of my wishes for the future crumble into a trillion pieces.

Why did Lilly have to say, "let me go?" She knows I will never be able to. Maybe she surmised it would help me move on. I'll never move on from this. I lost her forever because of my own brazenness to let her fly with me. I could have told her no. I could have protected her from the dangers of Armageddon, but she wouldn't have been satisfied with that. She wanted to be here. I needed her here.

Lilly, I cannot possibly go on without you.

Words fail me now, and tears stream from my eyes like Mount Saint Helens.

I knew the first time I saw her, I loved her. I could never ignore the feeling of being alive and happy. Elation consumed me when she was around. Zion held purpose for me because I knew she'd be there. She was bound to belong to us. All I thought about was her, alone in my own thoughts, knowing she belonged to Skye, hoping she belonged to me.

"General Worthy," King Worthy's voice echoes again.

I stay humbled before him, unable to look up, "I'm so sorry, my King!" I burst into tears. "I'm sorry!"

Tears gush out of my face with emeralds.

The green gemstones hover now in the air around me. I reach out and touch one and collide with a familiar hand. A soft hand. A ballerina's hand.

"Excuse me, but I think this belongs to you," the peaceful voice says.

I look up and Lilly stands in front of The King with rose gold eyes and bright white light all over her porcelain skin.

"Lilly!?"

"Yes, my love," her sweet voice echoes.

"Lilly!" I gasp.

The King speaks. "Lilly gave her life. Her light detonated and destroyed The Raven. She is rewarded with immortality."

I reach out and touch Lilly's cheeks. "My Lilly." Her face is warm and rosy, perfectly soft, and indomitably strong. "I love you my royal queen."

"You told me to be strong, remember?"

I kiss her lips and shower her face with more kisses. I can't stop kissing her seeing my Lilly is alive! My fiancé is alive. "Yes, I remember," I exclaim overwhelmed and blissfully happy.

"I knew The King wouldn't let me die," Lilly says with perfect peace as she gazes into my eyes with love.

Kiss!

I dive into her perfect lips of immortal essence and find my heartbeat steadied with elation.

King Worthy raises His hands with serenity. "New Zion has come."

30

Leafe

Wedding bells fill the air in Zion. My wedding. General Leafe Gold Worthy and Lilly Jane Rose. The invitations are now in my hand. It feels even more real as I look over the fine print.

Celebrating our wedding is going to be the highlight of my eternal life. And yet, to think I have the rest of my eternal life to spend with Lilly makes the future that much more exhilarating. We have infinity to look forward to.

Lilly has been picking out flowers and table settings for the celebration. I've been staying up all night watching her sleep. I love glimpsing her humanity. Angels don't need sleep, so I keep my eyes on her. I will never fall asleep on her as long as eternity persists.

Right now, all I want to look at is Lilly Rose right in front of me. Watercolors cover her knees and legs as she paints on white canvas the size of a ballroom floor. King Worthy has given me a key to the new house He was going to give Skye and Lilly. This is our house. And I can't wait to make more angels with her.

Lilly looks up at me with stunning green eyes. "It's Monet's Waterlilies!" she tells me, excitedly, for this piece. She loves painting. And I love letting her cover me in every color of her painting wheel.

"What mood are you in today, General Leafe?" She bats her eyelashes.

"Hmmm," I play along. "I must say, elated, my love… as usual."

She grabs her paint brush and dollops my wings and face. Then, my arms and chest. "Pomegranate is the perfect color for elation, my love. It gives off feelings of passion and ecstasy."

"You couldn't have colored me more accurately," I tell her with my thoughts.

"I love to bring color to our world," she thinks to me. *"Green eyes find me in bliss."*

"Your eyes always send me into bliss, my love," I think back to her.

Lilly smiles and dips her paintbrush in the water once more, and then the paint. She resumes her fresco of the waterlilies for the exhibit where paintings will float in the gardens by our reception.

Her ideas of what she wants please me. She always asks me, "What do you envision for our wedding?" I tell her the same response every time. "You. I just want you, my love."

Ring! Ring!

"Come in!" I echo from the grand room.

Honor enters through the front door with a garment bag in hand. "Lilly! Your dress is ready!"

"Honor, the paint is wet!" Lilly and I exclaim simultaneously.

"Jinx!" We both exclaim, again, at the same time. She laughs and I laugh in tandem. I find myself laughing more than I have in many ages now that I am with Lilly. She keeps me feeling joyful.

Honor hovers over the painting palette, gracefully, with glowing wings and sets the garment bag down over the forest green, velvet chair. "I am dying to see you try it on! And you know angels cannot die, my lady, so you must do it at once."

"We know," Leafe and I answer at the same time.

Leafe laughs. "Lilly knows what it's like to die and come back to life," I exclaim proudly and give her a kiss.

"I heard about that!" Honor replies and winks at Lilly. Then she bends down and strokes Lilly's brow. "You are one of the bravest humans I've ever known."

Lilly blushes and nods with gratitude.

"I echo that truth!" I speak up for her. Lilly doesn't like to talk about what happened. But I love to sing her praises. "She saved me in more ways than one," I exclaim as Lilly stands to look into my eyes. She wraps her arms around my neck and wipes the paint off my lips, with a sweet smile.

"You save me every day, my love," she affirms.

I peer into her green eyes and lean in to kiss her with my paint-smeared face. Lilly kisses me back passionately, as our tongues meander the oases of our mouths.

"Oh, I just love *love*!" Honor exclaims whimsically.

"I love that I am going to be yours," Lilly says to me with enchantment. "The moment is nearly here."

"Yes, my love. The moment is nearly here."

"King Worthy is arranging for all of Zion to be there. From guardian angels to the hallelujah chorus, every set of wings will be in attendance!" Honor expresses with her cheerful voice.

"I'd marry you even if it were just you and I and the stars to witness it." Lilly says lovingly.

"I'd marry you even if we had to run away to the Brachian Galaxy," I reply passionately.

"Aren't you glad it's all paid for?" Honor chimes in lightheartedly.

I laugh and Lilly follows suit. I hadn't had a budget in mind. There are no limits to what I'd give Lilly because King Worthy gives us access to every luxury in the universe. What I have is hers.

"Lilly can have anything she wishes!" I exclaim confidently and look back at Lilly. "If you want your dress studded in rose canary diamonds you can have it. If you want the rarest gold brought in from galaxies far away, you can have it."

"I just want you, my love." She answers with another kiss.

I give in to her, as I know I always will. "I love you, Lilly. This day is going to be the best day of my eternal life."

"That makes two of us," she replies with blushing cheeks and glowing eyes. "I love you, General Worthy."

Lilly leaves me speechless. I stare at her beautiful complexity like it's the first day I laid eyes on her. I never get over looking at her. I wipe her cheek that has my paint smeared all over her lips from our kiss. I pick her up with a plan in mind.

"Thank you, Honor, for the dress! We will see you at the wedding," I say farewell and wrap Lilly's legs around my waist.

Honor rises from the floor and hovers angelically, realizing it's her cue to give us some alone time. "Farewell, Zion's lovers!" she says merrily. "I am excited to see you in that dress, Lilly Rose!" Honor soars away, singing peacefully.

I set Lilly down on the island in the kitchen and move the cake display away. Lilly is my dessert. My wings perk up.

"Where were we?" I ask and lean in to kiss her supple lips.

Lilly opens for me, and my tongue slides into her mouth. She swirls her tongue with mine like a cyclone, and I suck on her lips gently like a tootsie roll pop.

"Leafe!" she sighs and rubs my hair. I love it when she does that. Both the rubbing and the sighing. Every part of her turns me on, and I already know where I want to take her next. I pick her up and walk her down the hallway towards the bedroom where she rests. I turn on the lights. I lay Lilly on the bed like a ballerina. Her coral dress holds her body like a glove. I run my hands over her waist, hips, and thighs. Then, I plunge into her mouth with passionate kisses.

Lilly returns the kiss with deep desire. I begin to take Lilly's dress off as I rub my hands up her thighs.

Then, I take a deep breath.

"I think we should wait. Until after the wedding," I exclaim.

Lilly sits up. "Our wedding is in a few hours, my love."

"Yes."

She smiles at me with pure innocence and waits on me to tell her what I think.

I stroke my hair. "I want to feel what it feels like to want you and wait for you all over again. I want us to wait until after the wedding to have sex again."

"We can do that, my love," she says gently.

I kiss her gently and pull away to meet her gaze of rose gold. Ever since The King gave her wings, her green eyes flare with that beautiful pink fire when she is aroused. I could gaze into her eyes for eternity.

"Are you sure?" I ask her and kiss her hand, where her engagement ring shines like the sun.

"Yes. I want to wait for you all night long, my angel."

"I am going to make love to you like you've never been loved before," I lean in again and kiss her softly.

Lilly whispers lovingly. "I'm ready to marry you, General."

31

Lilly

"Dearly Beloved, we are gathered here today to witness to matrimony of Leafe Gold Worthy and Lilly Jane Rose," King Worthy echoes with a voice like rushing waters.

Anytime He speaks, all eyes are on Him. I hope all eyes are on Him. It feels vulnerable thinking all eyes are on me, waiting on my every move.

I squeeze Leafe's hands as he stands opposite me with dreamy green eyes, glowing like fiery flames. His hands feel perfect in my grasp. So does his name next to mine. Soon, I will vow my life to him forever. He will vow his life to me.

My heart beats like a drum as I wait for the denouement of our beloved union where The King says "kiss the bride" and our promise will be forever established.

I take a deep breath as we begin the ceremony. Leafe keeps his green eyes steady on me. He calms me.

"If there is anyone who believes this couple should not be wed, speak now or forever hold your peace," King Worthy echoes regally.

All I can hear is the word, "peace" reverberating in the air as roses surround us like faithful witnesses in The Rose Garden.

Peace. If there is anywhere for peace to endure, it's here in Zion.

I gaze into the audience and everyone is silent. No protestors. No agitators. Once King Worthy moves on from this disclosure, Skye cannot win me back.

Surely, Skye isn't going to speak up, is he? He might. If he felt the nerve to.

I hold my breath, waiting for the moment to pass.

"Breathe, Lilly. It's going to be okay. It's just you and me now. You and me, my beautiful rose," Leafe tells me through telekinesis.

"I'm worried Skye is going to make a scene," I tell him with my thoughts.

"He won't," Leafe assures me through his thoughts. *"King Worthy is his father. His father has the final word. Remember?"*

He's right. Somewhere in the middle of my worry and nerves, I forgot that the one in charge is the only one who can keep him at bay. Skye won't rebel against his father.

I turn to look out into the audience, searching for his wings, to see if he attended. Why are you looking, Lilly? It doesn't matter. Even if he did make a scene, it's not going to stop you from marrying Leafe, the one you love. Look at him.

I turn back to Leafe. I don't need to take another look into the audience. Leafe is the only one I want filling my vision now. This is our moment. And no one is going to take it from us.

"I object," a voice echoes.

Gasps spew from the audience and chatter ensues.

"Stand and show yourself!" King Worthy commands.

Footsteps hasten down the aisle and stop in front of the platform raised above the roses. "My name is Grant Rose and I don't approve of this marriage."

Angels shriek and clamor in the audience.

"Please explain." King Worthy asks calmly.

"I won't let you marry my daughter until you let me give you this." My father holds out his hands with a gold ring, waiting for Leafe's answer.

Leafe remains calm.

My heart beats anxiously. Why didn't he take care of this before the ceremony?

Leafe signals for Purity. She flies closer to gather the ring, and she takes it to Leafe for him to inspect it. Leafe's eyes scan the ring with fascination. King Worthy waits patiently, presiding over the moment.

My dad speaks up again. "It's a family heirloom. I promised Lilly she would give it to her husband on her wedding day," he announces. Then my dad looks at me nervously. "Sorry, I hadn't had the moment to give it to you, Lilly."

Leafe's seriousness softens into a smile when he realizes the gesture. "I would be honored, Mr. Rose."

Purity swivels around the stage in regal fashion with golden glitter flittering in her wake. The audience oohs and ahs from her light. My eyes brighten as I watch her soar closer to me to give me the ring.

My hands feel sweaty and my heart races.

Whatever you do, Lilly, don't drop it.

"A ring fit for a royal couple," Purity says and winks. She turns to Leafe. "You're a lucky angel."

Leafe smiles and looks down, and then up at me with bright green eyes. "Yes, the most blessed of all."

"I love you," I whisper.

"Are we all ready to proceed?" King Worthy echoes into the crowd.

My dad smiles and takes a seat, with tears in his eyes.

No other protestors stand.

I take another deep breath, and King Worthy proceeds with the vows. Serenity sings my favorite song with the hallelujah chorus and Leafe reads me a love poem he wrote himself. I hadn't known he wrote poetry. My eyes tear up as I listen to his lines...

"To my beautiful rose...
my heart flies
like starry heights
when I think of you
as mine

my soul shines
like moonlit night

273

when I see your hand
in mine

now your name
will be my name
and your heart
will be my heart

thus I vow to you in love
to kiss you
to hold you
to love you
like endless light rays
from above"

Leafe folds the paper and tucks it in his pocket.

"Your words were so beautiful and thoughtful," I exclaim, deeply moved.

"I wanted to share my heart," Leafe exclaims with a bright smile.

Leafe squeezes my hands and reaches for the ring as King Worthy leads him in the final vows. "With this ring, I thee wed."

I do the same and place the ring on his finger that my father gave me. "With this ring, I thee wed."

King Worthy smiles and chuckles like He does when He is divinely happy.

"I now pronounce you husband and wife!" He declares loudly. So loudly, the universe will hear that reverberation. "General Worthy, you may now kiss the bride!"

"I have been waiting for this moment," Leafe says with pure delight. Kiss!

Cheers erupt in The Rose Garden and angels sing symphonies.

"Woohoo! Leafe and Lilly!" Angels chant.

Rose petals fall from the pink-gold sky as we walk down the aisle, hand in hand. Leafe twirls me around on the runway under Zion's stars with another kiss.

Green eyes find me on my wedding day.

"I love you, Mrs. Worthy," Leafe says with elated eyes and emerald glistening wings.

"I'm all yours, General Worthy," I reply with rose gold eyes, captivated. Kiss!

Leafe's lips collide with mine and he sweeps me up into his embrace.

"Are you ready for the party?"

"I thought you'd never ask," I exclaim.

⁓

"To the window! To the wall!" Music blares from the speakers hovering in the air around the dance floor. Everything floats in Zion, which makes it so much easier to plan a wedding. You don't have to worry about losing table space.

Serenity shrieks as she hears the hip-hop track Earth toted in with Jenna's playlist suggestions. "I don't think I've ever heard that heavenly melody," she says puzzled and slightly on edge.

"It's Lil Jon," Leafe answers her with a grin and spins me around in my ballgown.

"I'll have to add it to my repertoire!" Serenity puts her hands to her chest and makes her way to the bar.

"What's your favorite song, my lovely wife?"

"Anything with your voice in it."

"But I don't sing–" he pauses, and then touches his head. "Wait… you heard me sing, didn't you?"

"A pleasant baritone voice," I say delightfully and wink at him.

Leafe blushes and pulls me in tighter with a kiss. "I thought you were in the dressing room, my love."

"I was," I explain, enchanted with my green-eyed angel. "Then I got anxious, so I was pacing in the hallway of the palace. You should sing more often. I love your voice."

"Really?" he asks me, honestly.

"Yes," I reply dreamily.

Leafe clears his throat and prepares to sing. "I said I loved you but I lied… 'cause this is more than love I feel inside…" Leafe serenades me romantically.

My heart flutters and my cheeks blush. I return the lyrics. "I said I loved you but I was wrong… 'cause love could never ever feel so strong…" I sing back to him.

Leafe laughs and spins me around the dancefloor with strong arms and healing hands. "I love you more than words can express, my bride," Leafe says with green eyes glowing.

"I love you so much," I say deeply and lean into his kiss of fragrant desire.

Ding! Ding! Ding!

My eyes turn to the signaling toaster and the music softens. It's my dad. In one hand he holds a champagne glass and in the other he holds a piece of paper.

"Hello, everyone, I'm Grant Rose, Lilly's dad. Yes, the one who protested the happy couple at the beginning of the ceremony. In all seriousness, I knew you were the one for Lilly the moment I heard you singing in the dressing room."

"He heard me too?" Leafe whispers, mortified.

"Apparently everyone has," I say amused and altogether delighted in my sweet angel.

My dad continues. "Then I saw Lilly and you together," my dad pauses and wipes his tearing eyes. "Love was all over her face. Love was all over yours. She glows differently when she's with you than I've ever seen. She looks sincerely happy and has transformed from my little girl into a woman. You make her strong. And you see her heart, her beauty. You love her with all your heart, soul, and spirit. And that's all a father wants for his daughter. So, here's to Leafe and Lilly! May you live all your days, eternally in love and forever enchanted," he raises his glass. "To Leafe and Lilly!"

"To Leafe and Lilly!" Everyone echoes and tosses back their glasses, with the scent of bubbling champagne wafting in the air.

My father walks towards me and Leafe.

"I'm sorry I missed the first dance, honey! I was so moved by the ceremony. I needed to take a moment," he exclaims still teary eyed.

"It's okay, dad," I exclaim. "We can have that dance now if you'd like?"

My dad speaks to Leafe. "General Worthy, would you be so kind to let me have a dance with the bride?"

"Absolutely, Mr. Rose." Leafe nods and extends my hand to my father and lets go of me. I look back at Leafe mouthing the words, "I love you," and he does the same.

My father takes my hand and dances me around the dance floor, twirling in a waltz for our father-daughter dance.

"You look beautiful, Lilly!" My father tells me.

"Thank you, dad. I'm so glad you and mom could be here."

"Your mom is so proud of you, honey," my dad whispers gleefully.

We dance until the slow ballad ends. Then, a fast-paced beat begins to play with the sound of Def Leppard.

"I think your groom wants you," my dad says and points behind me, ready to give me back to my angel.

Leafe spins me around to meet his eyes.

"I still have more dances to show you, my lovely dance partner," Leafe takes my hand and spins me around. I wait for his next move, and he picks me up over his shoulders and twirls me around like a ballerina.

"Lilly!" Jenna runs up to us and plays with my hair. "You look gorgeous, my rose of Sharon."

"So do you, Jen!" I smile and hug my best friend in her exquisite toffee caramel dress.

"Where are you going on your honeymoon? Word has gotten out that all humans are all coming to New Zion. Talk about losing my Hawaiian tan! I could use a palm tree right now and a pineapple smoothie if you know what I mean," Jenna says with a laugh.

I laugh with her. "The finest Rosé you will ever taste is over at the bar, my beautiful best friend." I wink at her. "And we found an ocean in the universe even more thrilling than Hawaii."

"Really?" Jenna beams. "Where?"

"Let's just say you can surf in outer space," Leafe adds and holds me tightly, kissing my forehead.

Jenna hugs me and whispers, "Don't ever let him go." Then she waves and moves into the dance floor to join the party.

"What did she say?" Leafe inquires, suspiciously.

"She told me to never let you go." I smile agreeing with her. Leafe is a keeper.

"Smart girl," Leafe smirks.

"She knows a thing or two about losing the right one."

"And I know a thing or two about making sure I keep you forever," Leafe says candidly. "You're stuck with me Lilly Worthy," Leafe says flirtatiously. "How do you feel about it?"

His green eyes gaze into me romantically.

Green eyes find me married.

"Perfectly loved," I say from the depths of my soul.

Kiss!

Leafe's lips collide with mine in blissful union. I kiss him back like there is no one in the room but us.

"General Worthy!"

Leafe pulls away to welcome the guest.

"Skye." Leafe greets him and eyes him with caution, waiting for him to speak.

Leafe tightens his embrace around me as we stand on the dance floor under the twinkling lights.

Skye speaks. "I owe you an apology for what I said," he explains. My ears can hardly believe it. But he is making peace with me and Leafe. "And to Lilly. I'm sorry. You chose Leafe in the end and I have made peace with that."

"I appreciate that, General." Leafe grunts and then exudes green light from his eyes. Oh no. I think he's got more to say. "But with all due respect, you hurt Lilly and then blamed her for it. Tried to kill me. Tried to turn it all on us. I will make peace with you but I will not allow you around her or our future family. Do I make myself clear?"

Skye lifts from the ground with sapphire light in his eyes, and then sets his feet down and stretches his shoulders. "If you'll excuse me."

Flash!

Skye soars away into the sky, away from the party, like lightning.

Leafe looks up and closes his eyes. Then sighs. "I didn't want to have to do that to him," Leafe says and shakes his head. "But it had to be said."

"General Worthy!" The King walks towards us and everyone on the dance floor splits, making a walkway like the Red Sea. "I love you, My son."

"I am forever loyal to you, my King," Leafe bows his head and looks up at The King.

"I want everyone to hear!" The King announces. "This day, Commanding General of Zion's cosmos has married the love of his eternal life. This is no easy discovery, finding one's true love. Many years and ions pass by. But true love lasts forever," The King pronounces in royal pageantry. Seraphim fly overhead even here, and angels stand guard. He looks at Leafe, "I looked into your future and I saw eternity with you and Lilly. That's why I gave you to her. You are the one."

Leafe tears up at the words from The King.

"Hoorah to General Leafe Worthy!" All the angels cheer.

"Your eternal life will be blessed by Me in every way, my dear ones." King Worthy's eyes flame with blue sapphire and emerald light. He laughs as He scans the crowds of the joyful party. "Let the after party begin!"

Leafe spins me once again onto the dance floor. We dance into the twilight of Zion's golden hues as angels pirouette in glitter under the stars.

"We can go somewhere more private when you're ready, my bride." Leafe kisses me on the forehead, like he always does. I love it when he kisses me there.

"I'm ready when you are," I say perfectly in love.

"I've been waiting for you," he says as he kisses my neck and trails up to my mouth.

I sigh with euphoria. "Do you want to take me to the stars, my angel?"

Leafe peers into me with green eyes of ecstasy. "I'm ready for what you have in mind, my queen."

My soul gazes into his green eyes of passion. "Make love to me, General."

32

Skye

Boom!

My eyes open.

Bright light funnels into my vision like a widening tunnel of heavenly roads, ever expanding. The light is blinding. I move my head and blink my eyes to adjust to the light and new state of wokeness. Where am I? Was I dreaming?

I move my hands to touch my surroundings and I feel the velvety texture of rose petals intermingled with grapes signaling my location in Zion's Vineyards.

Ouch! A thorn. Blood rushes out of the palm of my hand at the incision. I press the wound.

"Skye," an angelic voice serenades in the blinding light. Her face remains hidden.

My wings outstretch as I try to lean in to hear the voice in the celestial aura of blinding light. "Lilly, is it you?"

Whoosh!

Gusting wind blows in and orbits around me. I feel the presence of the angel growing stronger. I should recognize the voice. I know all of the angel voices in Zion, but this voice remains a mystery. With eyes still open, straining to see clearly, I hear her voice again, echoing with power and serenity.

"Lilly loves you," the angel says euphorically. "Do not fear. You must come with me at once."

"Lilly is married!" I exhale painfully. "Why would you say she loves me? I just left her wedding and she is now Mrs. General Leafe Worthy. Leafe doesn't want me anywhere near her! I can't possibly go to her now. My heart is quaking with agony like the supernovas of my father's universe." I sigh with sweaty palms, reluctant to move.

But the light remains. So, I know the angel has not left me. Why is she still here?

"Come with me." Again, she speaks powerfully and serenely.

My eyes strain once more. Open, eyes! They won't budge. Detonate! They still won't budge.

"Only the truth can open your eyes." Her voice echoes in my ears like a gong. "Go back to the beginning. Before you brought Lilly to Zion."

Flash!

Bright light sparkles.

In an instant, rushing winds swirl around wings, and toss me up into the air. I land on the sand of what must be a beach. A warm breeze drafts in from the sea that churns in my ears.

Then my eyes open.

I'm on an island.

Palm trees and turquoise waters nestle adjacent to a harbor that looks just like Ala Moana Beach where I was with Lilly before we ever travelled to Zion to meet The King.

I peer into the ocean rolling in with turquoise waves like frothy cappuccinos. I see her.

Lilly is there.

My beautiful Lilly.

My one and only love.

Her divine essence basks in the teal blue ocean like a prima ballerina dancing on the water. I watch her as she swims to and fro with the ocean tide, cupping the salt water in her hands. She still has me in her hands.

She will always have my heart. Yet my heart pangs inside me. To think she belongs to anyone other than me crushes my very soul.

I keep watching. Her eyes twinkle as she swims. My heart melts from the glimmer in her eyes, always joyfully happy and captivated by the beauty of my father's universe.

I sigh as the reality of Leafe being her husband sets in. I can't do this. I look away and close my eyes. Why are you watching her, Skye? I can't watch her when I know she is taken. I lost her forever.

Inhale, Skye.

Exhale.

Breathe.

My father said He knows what He is doing. I have to trust His ways above my own.

I open my eyes and look towards the palm trees swaying in the wind. Then a football flies through the air.

That's ironic.

The last time me and Lilly were here, I had been throwing a pigskin football to a boy named Sam when he challenged me to a duel. Who could pass up a little boy's wish? I feared Lilly was lost because I woke up to her absence. Soon enough, she returned.

"Go long!" I hear a voice shouting.

That's also ironic. Those are the same words I said to Sam when I passed him the football.

Wait...

I look closer at the thrower and see angel wings and blue eyes. I swallow.

Is that me?

Father, what is happening?

The angel swirls around to land beside me on the sand with a commanding presence and glittery wings.

"It was all a dream, Skye," she pronounces serenely. Then she smiles at me with an intuitive disposition, the kind of eyes that would know the end of Armageddon before it happens.

"What do you mean *all a dream*?" I ask hastily.

If this was all a dream and I am still technically sleeping on Ala Moana Beach, does this mean Lilly is not married? Is she still mine?

My heart leaps inside my chest at the thought of it but I cannot get my hopes up. The King would know.

Father, is this true? Surely you hear me!

The angel with glittery wings and fierce eyes turns to face me. "Lilly never married Leafe. It was all a figment of your fears and of Lilly's fears. Your father gave you the dream to prepare you for your arrival in Zion. You need to understand that Leafe is in love with Lilly and he wants her. The King sees all things. But if your love for Lilly is strong, she will never leave you."

"Lilly's not married to Leafe!?"

"Lilly is still engaged to you, Skye. Right now, you are still in between dreaming and waking. Soon, I will send you back to wake up. When you do, Lilly will be next to you just as she was when you fell asleep at Ala Moana Beach."

"But I thought I fell asleep in Zion's vineyards with the grapes and roses where Lilly's dress unraveled?"

"That was a part of your dream. Dreams shift in and out of time and place. And there are dreams within dreams. There are many layers to the subconscious and many layers to the fears of what could be. The King wants you to overcome these fears. He compelled you to sleep at Ala Moana Beach and sent these dreams to show you what will happen if you take your eyes off Lilly. Don't let her out of your sight."

"I thought I lost her forever!" I gasp as sapphire light pores from my eyes at the release of every pent-up feeling I've been holding inside. Ever since the wedding, I lost my purpose for flying.

"You don't have to lose her. If you keep her forever."

"Of course I want Lilly forever. If she will have me."

The angel smiles with fiery eyes of white light. "When you wake up, you will see the engagement ring on her finger and the key-shaped necklace around her neck."

"She still has the key to my heart." I exhale and breathe in with strength.

"The only key." The angel eyes me with affirmative resolve.

Lilly is the only one who can unlock my heart.

"There's one more thing, Skye," the angel continues her pronouncement. "Lilly had the same dream. Your father gave it to both of you and she will wake up from her sleep understanding what will take place if she allows Leafe to tempt her. And you, Skye… now understand how Lilly needs to be loved. Do not withhold passionate love from her. Love her like a Worthy. And she will never want anyone else."

"I want to love her like a Worthy."

"Worthy is who you are. Remember who you are, General Skye Worthy."

"General?" I ask.

"Yes."

"But If all this was a dream, then I haven't been given a star yet by my father nor have I been given the title of General?"

"The King is giving you a star upon arrival in Zion's Throne Room, General Worthy." The angel announces pleased. "Walk into His Throne Room with your head held high," she eyes me with maternal affirmation. "You are, in fact, who He says you are. *General Skye Worthy.*"

I nod and breathe in with overwhelming relief. "I understand," I say.

"When you wake up, you must do one thing."

"I'm listening."

"Kiss Lilly as soon as possible. Then she will wake from her dream."

"The pleasure will be all mine, I assure you."

Tasting the savory strawberry of Lilly's lips is a pleasure I would never relinquish. I can taste the sweet aroma of her skin now. All I want is to be intimate with her.

"Don't be afraid to love her, General. Love requires sacrifice. Love her like you would love your own body. You will be one, after all. You both know what you want in your deepest desires now. Dreams have a way of revealing that. Let your kisses take you where passion meets the heavens."

Lilly wants to be loved more, and I saw that in the dream. When Leafe came onto her aggressively, she ended up giving into him. Her deepest desires wish for persistent pursuit and passionate, zealous love. This is a realization I needed. I want to give her that forever.

Thank you, Father, for showing me what my bride needs.

"What is your name?" I ask the glittering angel.

"Epiphany." She smiles with glowing skin and bright light.

"You have definitely given me an epiphany," I repeat, affirmatively.

Epiphany smiles with blissful satisfaction at her mission achieved. "That's my job, General."

I exhale with relief. All I can think about is the way Lilly will feel in my arms when I hold her once more, as mine. All mine. Lilly and I will be stronger than ever. And for all my days, I will vow to love her. Nothing will come between us. Neither angel nor Zion nor Earth nor cosmic galaxies of light could interfere with our love. I want to see her now.

"I'm ready to wake up now."

The angel nods and extends her hands for miracle working. "Your father loves you, Skye. If only you could see the vast greatness of His love for you. Only a perfect father would go through all this trouble to ensure you have everything for a successful marriage with Lilly. You are His son, and He gives His own more than they can imagine. Perfect love is His heart. Perfect love is His remedy for the universe."

Poof!

In an instant, Epiphany glides away into the teal blue sky of piercing sunlight. Lightning flashes. Thunder rolls. Light sparkles in my periphery.

I wake up.

Lilly is right beside my nestled in the sandy beach of Ala Moana just as we were.

"Lilly!!!" I gasp as I behold my divine fiancé sleeping serenely by my side on the blissful beach.

I dive in to kiss her.

Her eyes open.

"Skye!" She touches my face and squeezes every spot of my skin to make sure I am not an apparition. "Is it you? I thought I'd lost you!"

"Yes, it's me, Lilly." My heart leaps with joyful relief at her excitement to see me. She still loves me. "It's me, my love. We're at Ala Moana Beach."

Lilly touches her head with a look of bewilderment. "I just had the strangest dream and another angel was in the middle of us and you fell asleep and he carried me away and I married him because I fell in love with him." She pauses to catch her breath.

I squeeze her tightly and kiss her sweet lips. "It's okay, Lilly." I stroke her hair softly and peacefully. My fears are silenced looking into the truth of her eyes. "You had a dream. I'm here now and it's just you and me, my Lilly flower. Just you and me. Do you love me?"

"Of course, I love you!" Lilly cups my cheek and strokes my hair. I love it when she rubs her fingers through my locks. "You know I love you, Skye! You're the one who saved me."

My eyes intensify hearing her words. Lilly still loves me. She loves me. And no one else can take away our love.

"I love you too." I kiss her hands passionately. "Tell me how you want to be loved, and I will always be your angel." She nods and smiles with a giddy smile and falls into my chest. My wings embrace her. "We both had the same dream, Lilly, and we both know what that dream was."

"I'm woken up now. I want to marry you, Skye." Lilly takes my hand and presses it to her chest to feel the key-shaped necklace. "Do you hear my heartbeat?"

I nod and look into the eternity I find in her eyes looking back at me. "Yes," I say. "I feel your heart."

Lilly smiles with overwhelmed relief. "Only you can unlock my heart. And only I can unlock yours."

"I thought I lost you, Lilly," I say with a deep breath. "It's the worst feeling I've ever felt in the universe and I know I can't live without you... I promise I'll spend the rest of eternity learning how to love you more, my queen."

"Blue eyes find me in love," she thinks.

"Green eyes find me in love," I think back to her. *"You are my forever love, my Lilly flower."*

I take a deep breath and speak my heart with her, just as I have come to know from this epiphany. "Lilly, my father gave us this dream to prepare us for the temptation that we will face in Zion. There is an angel there and his name is Captain Leafe. He loves you. You need to know that there will be other angels who try to make advances on you and that our love can withstand this threat if I love you more. And I want to. I realize I did not know what you truly wanted. I thought that our kisses and touches were enough. But I know now that you need more than that. You need intimacy. Passionate intimacy. Love. Devotion. I'm so glad my father showed me what I was not seeing."

Lilly kisses my lips and looks into my eyes with strength. "I need all of you, Skye. Don't hold back from me."

"I needed to know what you need. The King showed me."

"You father is a good King."

"The most perfect King."

Seeing Lilly's love for me is a healing solvent. That dream ripped my heart out. Seeing Lilly marry Leafe. The one who would give her deeper intimacy. And now, holding Lilly, I know more than ever that I can love her the way she desires to be loved. My heart is whole. All it takes is Lilly's love to put it back together. I need her. I will always need her love.

I pick Lilly up out of the cinnamon sand and take her into the pinkish orange sky where Zion awaits us. Lilly smiles at me with the purest eyes of bliss and serenity.

"Take me to Zion, Skye. I'm ready to meet The King."

With the love of my eternal life in my arms, I fly to the stars.

33

Lilly

"Welcome to Zion, dear Lilly!" Zeal greets me at the door politely.

Zeal is here! I dreamt of him bolting towards me in the Throne Room. The King destroyed him for good when he tried to take me for himself. But here he stands, peacefully.

"Hello Zeal." Skye greets him with a chivalrous smile and perceptive eyes. I can tell Skye is looking Zeal up and down based on what happened in the dream. Skye squeezes my hand to comfort me.

"The King will filter out all souls that are not aligned with Him when Armageddon comes," Skye tells me through his thoughts. *"Don't fear, my love. We don't have to worry about that now. My father knows all things. The dream was only to warn me of what would happen if I let you out of my sight. And I will never let that happen again. Zeal won't touch you."*

"I trust you, my blue angel," I tell him with my thoughts.

Our telekinesis is still strong. I know it always will be.

"I kiss her forehead, just like Leafe would do in the dream. She said it gave her strength. But I am the only one who can be her strength. So, I will kiss her every day to remind her I am the one who protects her." I can hear his thoughts flooding me like living water. He soothes me so deeply.

Zeal interjects. "King Worthy is waiting for you. I hear a star is in your future, Skye."

Skye nods humbly. "I'm grateful," he says firmly. "Zion will continue to shine the light of The King. We will continue to defend and protect our Kingdom from every threat. Zion's Angels are strong."

"Indeed, we are, General." Zeal nods with purple eyes flaming strongly and bows his head respectfully. "Congratulations. And to your lovely fiancé, I speak for all of Zion when I say we are honored to have you in our midst." He turns to open the golden doors of the pearl-studded gates of Zion.

Zion's gates stand tall and golden, with pearls covering the gold in every dimension. Light shines from its entrance like an all-encompassing glow of surreal radiance that never goes out.

"Zion is beautiful, just as I dreamt it would be!" I say euphorically. My eyes scan the gemstones lining the walls in diamonds, garnets, opals, and every gem under the sun. The multicolored vivacity shines like a crown of royal splendor.

"It is the gem of the Heavens, my love," Skye whispers tenderly.

"The King is waiting for you," Zeal says happily.

"Thank you, Zeal!" Skye kisses my head. "My father can't wait to meet you, Lilly." Then he picks me up and we soar through the gates.

Angels sing and flutter all around us from the skies to the gardens in the distance to the rivers. Skye soars fast as I take it all in. Then we enter the towering palace with ivory doors and Skye sets me down on the sapphire glassy floor of the Throne Room. *The* Throne Room. The one from my dream. The place where The King dwells. The place where He speaks life into being.

"Skye!" The King echoes with a booming voice. His feet move towards us, shaking the floor majestically. "I have waited for this moment." He stops in front of us and looks into Skye's eyes, pleased, like a good father. "I trust you met Epiphany, My son."

"Yes, Father." Skye looks over at me, and smiles into me endlessly. His blue eyes flame just like they always do when he looks at me. Luscious, sapphire blue eyes of love.

"I know you gave us the same dream. I was terrified that she could belong to anyone else but me. To be honest, I'm shocked by Your ways… but I'm humbled by Your love. I don't know what I would have done if I had lost Lilly forever." Skye looks back at his father with a heart-felt need for his affirmation. I can see it in his eyes. He cares about what his father thinks. Looking into The King's eyes, I can see how much He loves Skye.

The King speaks. "Perfect love is the standard of My Kingdom, and I want nothing less for My son and beautiful Lilly... The future King and Queen of Zion. I knew your love would be tested once you both were here in Zion. Hinlors lurk and evil still tempts and taunts in the cosmic sphere. It will until New Zion is here. But once New Zion has come, there will never be temptation again."

Gazing at the King of Zion, I see Skye's eyes just as I did in my dream. His eyes pour love. I want Him to know my heart is devoted. "King Worthy," I say without thinking if I should speak or not. I know Skye loves me. And so does The King. I will speak freely face to face. "I love Your son, Skye."

"Lilly!" The King says my name with serenity and power. "You beautify the Throne Room, my dear." He bends down and looks at me eye-level with a crown of many jewels on His head. "I know you love My son. It's why I showed him how you want to be loved. Captain Leafe brought out a different side of you that Skye needed to see. I promise you Skye will love you passionately for all eternity."

Skye wraps his arms around me as I face The King.

I smile at the warmth of his embrace. "And I will love Skye passionately for all eternity," I say with certainty.

I turn and look up at Skye's blue eyes emitting rays of sapphire light. Firey light. Passionate light. He is mine and I am his.

⚜

The dream came true for Skye's star. King Worthy named Skye as *General*. The King said Skye and I will fly together when Armageddon dawns. Skye will lead the angel armies into battle. Then New Zion will come.

Captain Leafe was there too.

"Hello, Miss Rose," he said to greet me when I saw him. "You look beautiful." I swallowed and prepared myself for what I thought might be coming. A touch. An advance. But he congratulated Skye respectfully and didn't make a move on me. He greeted me with kindness, and assured Skye we would stand united for The King for all eternity. Skye was relieved and deeply moved to know his friendship with Captain Leafe was still as strong. General Leafe, in fact. That part of the dream was true also. General Leafe's identity was revealed while we were in the Throne Room. King Worthy continued to communicate His vision for New Zion. It was clear the unity of Zion would be upheld.

"Skye Worthy!" The King announced in front of all the angels as we stood before Him in the Throne Room. "I hereby grant you My glorious star. You are now General Skye Worthy. This title reminds you, armies of Zion, that his word is the final word and his leadership is the decree of the Heavens. He goes where I send. He does what I command. My own right arm, you are, Skye."

King Worthy placed the star on Skye's wings just as in the dream, and Serenity cloaked me in white silk. The dress feels like butter as we fly through the cosmos.

"I want to show you the stars," Skye said. Then we lifted off from the Throne Room en route to the Shooting Star Circle in outer space.

Now we bask in the scintillation of the glorious, celestial cosmos.

I breathe in Skye's oxygen as his face glows in the light.

"You shine so brightly, my royal shining star!" I look up at him as he holds me in his wings while we fly powerfully through the Shooting Star Circle. The star on his wings shines like a golden diamond. Every star in the cosmos looks upon him with triumphant satisfaction, finding their light reflecting in him.

Skye will always be my light. My angel. My love.

The dream of Leafe made me realize how easy it is to let another in if my heart is unguarded. Never again will I allow another angel to allure me. I only want Skye to be my one true captivation.

"Lilly, you are my one true love. My heartbeat and soul. My strength and my freedom. I want you with me everywhere I go, my love," he says.

"And I want to be everywhere you are, General Worthy."

"I'm still getting used to her calling me General. My father just pinned the star on my wings and blessed Lilly with anointing oil, just as in the dream. He said dreams that are 'meant to be' always come to pass. Lilly will always be my dream come true."

I can hear his thoughts. Tell me what you think, Skye. I love you with all my heart. You will always have me. Forever.

"I love you, my Lilly flower. Your beauty surpasses gardens of endless roses. My heart anticipates the moment when you will walk down the aisle in your white dress. We will both say I do. And we will never stop saying I love you."

His thoughts endear me like whispering winds on the sun-kissed oceans. It's here we are intertwined again, soul to soul, heart to heart. He reads me and I read him, like lovers in perfect synchronicity.

Spark!

A shooting star soars over the cluster of star twinkles and my eyes trace the glittering trail of its arch.

"Skye, a star!" I gasp, wide-eyed and captivated.

"They are beautiful, aren't they, my love?" Skye kisses me on the cheek.

"Almost as glorious as you, my blue angel," I say looking into his eyes, as he holds me in the cosmos of the Shooting Star Circle. "I love seeing shooting stars up close. You are my star. My royal shining star," I say euphorically in love.

Skye picks me up and zooms into the bursting star trail and it swivels around us glittering. "Stars, I command you to glisten for my love!"

At once, the trail of glitter soars around us and touches my skin softly with kisses like cosmic magic. Only I know it isn't magic. It's angelic. Miraculous. Supernatural.

"All the stars are kissing me, Skye!" I giggle from the twinkles lavishing me like rain drops.

"I want to make you feel loved in every way, my Lilly flower. The universe is under my command, and I will make it light up to please you." He smiles with desire like blazing fire.

I look into his eyes where the eternal oasis of sapphire blue beckons me into euphoria. I lean into his face with patient love, waiting for him to kiss me.

Kiss!

Skye dives in to kiss me and his lips interlock with mine in sync. His tongue twirls inside my mouth finding every spot in need of his salvation. He tastes like strawberry and white chocolate, satisfying my appetite for more of his divine essence.

With every kiss, I feel his soul melding with mine like we are candles of wax melting in a sacred cosmos. The wax drips and meanders wherever it wishes, fluttering in space without gravity. Our love finds it and reels it back in to fashion divine art.

"Tell me I'm the only one," he says. "Tell me I'm the only one you love. I want to hear you say it."

His eyes meet me in the thoroughfare of passion and climactic grandeur. I look back at him with the need for him ravish me completely, fully, wholly. A holy union of lovers in Heaven.

"You are the only one, General Worthy. I love you forever, my blue angel."

"I love you, Lilly. I want to be your only love."

Blue eyes find me in love.

"I love to see your eyes looking back at me again, my lovely flower. My future bride. My future queen," he says through his thoughts.

"I love to see all of you, my love. Deeply, transparently, powerfully. You are the Commander of Zion's Angel Armies. And you are going to defeat the hinlors once and for all when Armageddon is here. I see The King's glory in you and His wisdom to do what is right. You are strong in His power," I tell him through telekinesis. *"Wedding bells will be playing over us soon."*

"I love you, my perfect rose. You are the strength in my wings, and I won't fly without you." He tells me through his thoughts. *"I want to make love to you like you want me to. I want us to be one. I'm ready to marry you, my beautiful fiancé. My perfect lover."*

"I'm ready to marry you, Skye. I want to be yours forever," I say through telekinesis.

"Her brunette hair smells like fragrant rain in the oceans of Bali. I could get tangled in her locks forever, perusing the softness of her scalp, and kissing the tenderness of her porcelain neck. I want to touch every part of her and please her like she craves. I know she wants to make love."

I want him to make love to me. There is no doubt in my mind Skye is my lover for all eternity. He will always be mine and I will always be his. Our love was a divine collision. Destiny wants us to be intertwined.

Skye begins to kiss my neck softly and trail over my jaw and ears. "I want you to know, my love, I too have travelled to every galaxy in the universe. I was there at the beginning, with My father. The universe is known by me."

"I have no doubt, my powerful angel," I say and smile as he still trails my neck with kisses. In my dream, me and Skye got in a fight. I told him Leafe had seen more of the universe than he had. I don't know what would have prompted those words, other than the dream being orchestrated by The King to show us our fears. Maybe Skye wondered if Leafe would cause rivalry over who claimed my heart and who was the best in my eyes. Skye wants to be the best.

"I know it was just a dream, but I don't want us to fight like that. I want to fight for you every moment and hear your thoughts in every way. You can tell me anything. I will always be forthcoming about my thoughts and needs. Our love has always been heavenly and perfect, as it should be in Zion. I will never leave you, my love. I want to please you in every way you desire as a woman."

"And I want to please you in every way, Skye." I smile with peace at the revelation of his desires aligning with mine. "King Worthy gave us that dream so we would fight for love for the rest of eternity. I will never let go of you."

Skye leaps in the shooting stars and turns me around in his arms to face him as we prepare to fly back to Zion. Soon, wedding bells will be ringing, and endless adventures await us.

"Tell me what to do, my love. I love it when you tell me what to do," he says.

With eyes of love and a heart full of passion, I look up at the one I choose forever.

"Make love to me, General."

Milton Keynes UK
Ingram Content Group UK Ltd.
UKHW040909191024
449793UK00009B/95/J